DEFENDER

ABOUT THE AUTHOR

Janet Edwards lives in England and writes science fiction. As a child, she read everything she could get her hands on, including a huge amount of science fiction and fantasy. She studied Maths at Oxford, and went on to suffer years of writing unbearably complicated technical documents before deciding to write something that was fun for a change. She has a husband, a son, a lot of books, and an aversion to housework.

Visit Janet online at her website www.janetedwards.com to see the current list of her books. You can also make sure you don't miss future books by signing up to get an email alert when there's a new release.

ALSO BY JANET EDWARDS

Set in the Hive Future

PERILOUS: Hive Mind A Prequel Novella

TELEPATH

DEFENDER

Set in the Game Future

REAPER

Set in the 25th century Portal Future

SCAVENGER ALLIANCE

Set in the 28th century Portal Future

The Earth Girl trilogy:-

EARTH GIRL

EARTH STAR

EARTH FLIGHT

Related stories :-

EARTH AND FIRE: An Earth Girl Novella

FRONTIER: An Epsilon Sector Novella

EARTH 2788: The Earth Girl Short Stories

HERA 2781: A Military Short Story

JANET EDWARDS

DEFENDER

HIVE MIND 2

Copyright © Janet Edwards 2017

www.janetedwards.com

ISBN: 1981728279
ISBN-13: 978-1981728275

Janet Edwards asserts the moral right to be identified as the author of this work.

This novel is entirely a work of fiction. Names, characters, businesses, places, events and incidents are the products of the author's imagination or used in a fictitious manner. Any resemblance to actual persons, living or dead, or actual events or localities is purely coincidental.

All rights reserved. This book or any portion thereof may not be reproduced or used in any manner whatsoever without the express written permission of Janet Edwards except for the use of brief quotations in a book review.

Cover Design by The Cover Collection
Cover Design © Janet Edwards 2017

CHAPTER ONE

Someone was already dead.

Our lift plunged downwards at ultra express speed, its level indicator rapidly flickering through numbers. Our unit was on Industry 1, at the very top of our Hive city. We'd travelled down through all the fifty industrial levels, and sixty-seven of the hundred accommodation levels, before the level indicator stopped at 68.

The lift doors opened, and we sprinted out. My Strike team leader, Adika, at the front, followed by the nineteen men of my Alpha Strike team, all clustered protectively around me. A major interchange of the belt system was directly ahead of us. Within seconds, we'd stepped onto the slow belt, moved across to the medium, and then the express. We were speeding along corridors now, but however fast we were, we would arrive too late. Someone was already dead.

Adika spoke impatiently. "Lucas, you've only told us this is a strength six incident and its location. What are you sending us into?"

Lucas's voice came from the audio circuit of the crystal unit in my ear. "Current indications are that our target is either at or near the incident scene, but my Tactical team is still collating information. Nicole will give you details on the destination area now."

Lucas was speaking in the Tactical Commander voice he used during emergency runs. The tones deliberately calm and relaxed to build his listeners' confidence in our ability to handle whatever crisis we were facing. It wasn't working on me today. This incident was strength six, an impersonal code to mask the brutal fact someone had died.

I was only eighteen, I'd been doing this job for a bare few months, and I hadn't been in this situation before. Yes, I'd set out on emergency runs where someone had been injured or kidnapped, but never with the knowledge that some man, woman, or child was a lifeless corpse.

Our Hive city was a teeming mass of a hundred million people, but now there was one less, and I felt that was my fault. The anonymous victim was already dead before we entered the lift, before the alarm woke me, before our unit even got the emergency call, but I still felt personally responsible. It was my job to prevent this sort of thing from happening. To catch criminals before they committed a crime. To hunt down those who were a threat to others, so they could be helped, or at least prevented from doing harm.

I bit my lip. I'd failed to keep someone safe, but I couldn't allow myself to brood about their death any longer. I had to concentrate on stopping their murderer from killing again.

Other people were joining the express belt now. It was well after midnight, so most of the Hive would be asleep, but these were workers travelling to and from shift work. They gave curious looks at our tightly packed group. We wore casual civilian clothes over our body armour, our guns were hidden under jackets and tops, and the crystal units in our ears were transparent and virtually invisible, but we were still an odd sight. Everyone would realize we were on our way to perform some task for the Hive, and be wondering what job needed so many heavily muscled men and a single, slightly built girl.

They'd never work out the right answer. They couldn't guess we were hunting a killer because they believed the Hive was perfectly safe. All crimes were carefully covered up. Today's murder would be explained away as a freak accident. People would be kept in ignorance so they wouldn't have their lives overshadowed by fear or be tempted to commit crimes themselves. I wasn't entirely happy about that system, but...

Nicole, my Liaison team leader, started speaking. "Incident location is a storage complex. There's a housing warren to the north, a school to the east, a community centre to the south, and a sports facility to the west."

There was an anxious edge to her voice. Nicole was nineteen. Her mind was imprinted with all the information she needed to be a Liaison team leader, but she'd normally have had at least three years of practical experience to reinforce it. Instead, she'd been thrust into the role after barely a year as a team member and a scant few weeks as deputy.

I could understand why Nicole felt nervous and uncertain, but it was even worse for me. Only months ago, I'd been one of over a million eighteen-year-olds going into our Hive's Lottery of 2532. I'd been worried about the barrage of tests I'd face, frightened of what the automated process would decide was my profession and level in the Hive, and scared stiff of having my mind imprinted.

I'd pictured so many possibilities in the years before Lottery, from being a stunning success to an utter failure. I'd dreamed of doing highly skilled work and living on the elite top ten accommodation levels of the Hive. I'd had nightmares about ending up a sewage technician and living in a hovel down on Level 99. I'd never thought for one second I could be thrust into something like this, never imagined I wouldn't be imprinted at all because my Hive deemed it far too risky to imprint someone as rare and valuable as me.

Lottery had sent me into this wild new existence without either experience or imprinted knowledge to help me, and the pressure on me was far greater than on Nicole. I had my Tactical team to guide me, my Strike teams to guard me, my Liaison team to handle the logistics, but the difference between success and failure, life and death, depended on me. Someone was already dead, and if I messed this up then others might die as well.

"We've got teams of uniformed hasties blocking all corridors leading to the storage complex, and we've shut down its dedicated freight lifts," continued Nicole. "The community centre, school, and sports facility are all closed and empty at this time of night. We're making area announcements about flooding from a burst water pipe and…"

She broke off for a second. "Ah, we've got floor plans of the storage complex now. Sending them to your dataviews."

I fumbled for my dataview, tapped it to make it unfurl, glanced at the plans, and pulled a face. The place was huge. At least forty vast storage rooms.

There was a moment or two of silence after that before Adika spoke. "Lucas, we'll be approaching scene soon. We need your briefing now."

"Agreed," said Lucas. "The overwhelming majority of Hive citizens are well-adjusted and cooperative. What Amber often describes as tame bees working for the good of the community. Uncontrollable, violent tendencies in an individual normally develop due to a lethal combination of several factors including social catalysts and genetic predisposition. These tendencies manifest in distinctive behaviour patterns, so there are warning signs of a wild bee in an area before the individual progresses to actual violence. This case is extremely unusual because there were no warning signs."

"None at all?" I frowned. In theory, my Tactical team watched for areas with warning signs, and we went in and checked them, tracking down who was responsible before anyone got hurt. In practice, too many areas needed checking, and some targets progressed to violence unpredictably quickly, so we didn't always get there in time. That meant an emergency run like this one, with someone already hurt, but we'd never had an emergency run to an area with no warning signs at all.

"Absolutely none," said Lucas. "The delay in giving my briefing was because I had my team triple-checking this and neighbouring areas. The only information we have is that a patrolling hasty noticed the storage complex lights were on when it should have been empty for the night. He went inside and saw a man stooping over a woman's bloodstained body. The man ran deeper into the complex, and the hasty left and called in the emergency. He was incoherent from shock, so we're working from extremely limited details."

Lucas paused. "Our target is male and in his thirties. We believe he's still in the storage complex. Each room in there has dozens of rows of floor to ceiling shelving and container racks. Be aware that the target may hide behind shelves, or even take refuge inside one of the larger containers. You can expect him to be armed with a knife. He may also have collected other items from within the complex to use as weapons. The lack of any warning signs before escalating to violence on this scale indicates an incredibly strong triggering event. You should regard our target as highly unstable and dangerous in the extreme."

Adika groaned. "A combination of the worst possible target and the worst possible location. Everyone will need to be fully alert for this one. Guns initially on stun but be prepared to change to kill setting on my order. Time to jump belt now."

We all left the express belt and changed to a slow belt going down a side corridor. I heard something ahead of us, a rhythmic chanting, and cringed. Not that. Not now. Please, not now!

I instinctively closed my eyes and covered my ears with my hands. I tried to concentrate on my own breathing and shut out the world, but I couldn't block the sound of angry voices.

"Two threes are six. Two fours are eight. Two fives are ten."

"Nicole, there's a nosy squad ahead of us," said Adika. "Get them out of our way!"

"We've been trying to do that," said Nicole, "but closing all the corridors around the storage complex has blocked a major belt route."

"I don't care what you do with the nosy squad, make them jump down a waste chute for all I care, just get them out of our way!" Adika sounded as if he was about to explode from frustration. "You know the presence of nosies has a terrible effect on Amber."

The chanting was getting louder. "Two sixes are twelve. Two sevens are fourteen."

Closing my eyes had been a mistake. It just made me more aware of the voices shouting numbers. I opened my eyes again, and saw a defensive cluster of people further down the corridor.

"Two eights are sixteen. Two nines are eighteen."

At the focal point of the crowd, I caught a glimpse of the grey figure of the nosy surrounded by four blue-clad hasty guards. A moment later, they hurried off down a side turning. By the time we rode by on the belt, the chanting had already stopped. I heaved a sigh of relief.

"Amber, how are you?" Lucas's voice asked. "Will you need recovery time before we start this chase?"

"No," I said. "I'm all right."

"You're sure?" asked Adika. "We've got an especially dangerous target, so we'll need you focused."

"I'm certain," I said. "Sorry to make such a fuss about going near a nosy, but people hate them so much and..."

"Your feelings about nosies are totally understandable," said Lucas, in soothing tones.

They might be understandable, but I also felt they were pretty hypocritical. All through my childhood, I'd hated the telepaths dressed in their shapeless grey outfits, their faces hidden behind matching grey masks, who walked the corridors of the Hive seeking the guilty thoughts of criminals. I knew I had nothing to hide from the nosies. I knew their hasty escorts wouldn't arrest me. I knew I should be grateful to them for keeping the Hive safe. I'd still joined in with the hostile crowds, desperately chanting tables to try to stop the nosies from reading my mind.

After Lottery, I'd learned the truth. The nosies weren't telepaths at all, just ordinary hasties dressed up in grey outfits to encourage people to be dutiful and law abiding. I still dreaded seeing them though. I couldn't work when a crowd was screaming numbers and...

Red signs were flashing ahead of us. "Belt system closed for emergency maintenance. Follow diversion at next belt interchange."

Other people were transferring to another belt, but we stayed where we were, gliding on past a group of hasties in blue uniforms.

"Strike team is approaching scene," said Adika. "Jump belt. Crystal units to visual."

We left the belt, adjusted our ear crystals, and the camera extensions unfolded at the side of our faces. I tapped the fine tube by my cheek to make sure it was correctly positioned.

"Visual links green," said Nicole.

"Amber, you're now in the corridor running past the northern end of the storage complex," said Lucas. "You should be able to see the double doors of the main entrance ahead of you."

The large, yellow doors were impossible to miss. "Yes, I see them."

"The target was spotted stooping over the body just inside those doors," said Lucas. "He then ran further into the complex. The body is still where he left it, because we couldn't risk sending hasties or a medical team so close to a cornered killer."

I winced at the thought of the poor woman lying on the floor, all her hopes and dreams brought to a brutal end. Despite everything I'd seen and done since I came out of Lottery, I was still adjusting to the reality that such levels of violence existed in our Hive, so I couldn't help selfishly hoping that I wouldn't see her body.

"Our target hasn't attempted to pass any of the hasties' blockades," continued Lucas. "We expect our target is still in the complex, though there's a possibility he's found a way into the vent system. Over to you, Amber."

I sat down on the floor, leaned my back against a wall, and closed my eyes. The grey-masked nosies weren't telepaths, just fakes, but the bluff worked because there was a grain of truth behind the lies. The Hive did have five precious genuine telepaths. I was one of them, and it was time for me to do my job.

I reached out with my mind, seeking the thoughts of a killer.

CHAPTER TWO

I always struggled to find words to describe the sight, sound, touch, taste, scent of the telepathic view of the world. It was like an endless dark void with occasional small pools of light that were the minds of the people around me. It was like sitting in silence and hearing fragments of conversation. It was like touching objects that varied from cold, hard metal to warm and fluffy. It was like tasting an assortment of foods, or being in the park and catching the mingled scents of flowers on the breeze.

I took a moment to orient myself by drifting through the thoughts of my Strike team, and found them sharp with tension. They'd come out of this year's Lottery with me, carefully chosen by the testing sequence to be physically and mentally perfect for this job. They'd been imprinted with vast amounts of information. They'd had intensive training. All those things helped them, but they were still as aware as me that this was their first emergency run where someone had already died. Adika's mood was disturbing them too.

As I thought of Adika, I automatically linked to his mind. Hard-edged, like newly forged steel, and currently white hot with anger. He'd had ten years of experience as a Strike team member, and seven years more as a deputy, before getting his chance at a team leader position with me. He'd experienced a thousand emergency runs, and all his instincts told him this one could go badly wrong. He was worried that some of his men might get hurt, and even more paranoid about something happening to his irreplaceable telepath.

There was more to Adika's anger than that though. He'd spent the evening with Megan, my Senior Administrator, and they'd had a blazing row. Below the thoughts about this emergency run were deeper levels that churned with emotion.

... thought everything was going so well, but then she started shouting at me. I understand she loved her husband, but he's dead. We're alive and...

... Waste it! If Megan insists on living her life in the past, then I'll find someone who'll live for the future and...

I was frustrated and fuming at myself. Why was I so obsessed with Megan anyway? I'd had plenty of women who were better looking than her and had just as good legs. Was my age getting to me? I was thirty-five now, and...

I realized I'd drifted from reading Adika's thoughts to experiencing them as my own, shook my head, and hastily disentangled myself from his mind. I wasn't thirty-five, but eighteen. I wasn't Adika, but Amber.

Waste it! I kept making the same mistake over and over again. The other four telepaths in our Hive struggled to get more than a couple of levels below pre-vocalization, the highest level of the mind where sentences were formed before being spoken aloud. I was different, naturally operating on deeper, more emotional levels, and it was usually more of a liability than an advantage. I kept getting sucked into other people's emotions, trapped in their feelings as if they were my own.

I tried to shake off the remnants of both Adika's burning frustration and my own annoyance at myself, and reached out further into the darkness. There was a bright blur of minds that must be the nearby housing warren, and more minds both above and below me, but I should concentrate on this level of the Hive for the moment.

I tried sweeping methodically across the area ahead of me, moving from right to left, and found a nervous huddle of four minds. Hasties lurking behind a temporary barrier.

... never been caught up in anything like this before, and never want to be caught up in anything like it again. It...

... knew in theory that these things happened, but couldn't believe I'd...

... Waste it, my job is making sure people follow health and safety rules, keeping small children from...

I pulled out of their minds and moved on. Nothing. Nothing. Nothing. Then a single mind glowed, alone in the emptiness.

... Saw me. Saw me. Figure in blue saw me. Saw me. Saw me. Figure in blue saw me. Saw me. Saw...

... wiping away the dried, crusted blood from her throat. My fingers running down her arm, taking her hand, tracing the line of the delicately coloured nails and...

... was so cold. So beautiful. My ideal partner that...

"Target located," I said. "He's at the south end of the storage complex, sitting down, and leaning his back against something hard and rough. I can't judge the physical position well enough to say which room he's in, and it's too dark for me to get any clues from his surroundings."

"Is he hiding inside a container, Amber?" asked Adika.

"No, he's in a room but it's extremely dark."

"The rooms have motion activated lighting," said Nicole. "If there's no movement for five minutes it automatically dims to the minimum setting."

"I think the target has been sitting still for a while," I said. "There's nothing to give me a clue about his identity. The top level of his mind is frozen in terror, looping round and round the fact the hasty saw him. Underneath, he's thinking about the dead woman, not himself. He's wiping away the blood from her throat. No, he's *remembering* wiping away the blood, stroking her arm, and taking her hand."

"Nicole, can you override the motion activation controls and turn the lighting on in there?" asked Lucas.

"Getting my team to work on that now," said Nicole.

Most of my mind was with my target, but part of me was vaguely aware of Adika's voice giving instructions. The Strike team were dividing into two groups. Those on chase duties were moving towards the storage complex doors. Those on bodyguard duties were staying with me. One of them was picking me up, transporting the luggage of my body to a better defensive position in case the target made a break in our direction.

"Amber, is the target still sitting there?" asked Lucas.

"Yes. Still sitting there. Still thinking about the woman. She's my ideal... She's *his* ideal partner. I'm not sure she was really in a relationship with him though. It seems more as if he's fantasizing." I felt the grief in the target mind. "He didn't like the blood. The cut in her throat spoiled her. He wanted to find a scarf to cover it, but he couldn't make himself leave her side."

Overhead lights suddenly blazed at full brightness. The target was dazzled, rubbing his eyes with both hands, and then staring around in alarm. If the lights had come on, it meant someone was here! The hasties were here!

"The lights came on," I reported. "The target has been to this place several times before. He knows the lights are motion activated, so he thinks the hasties are in there looking for him."

"Amber, what weapons does the target have?" asked Adika.

"Both his hands are empty. He's standing up now. I can see part of the number on a crate to his left. It starts with S771-57. The rest is out of his view."

"We've got a location from the storage facility inventory system," said Nicole eagerly. "That code is for shop fittings, all held in the south-west corner of room 7."

Adika started rattling out a series of instructions. Chase team were moving now, closing in on their prey, but I caught a fleeting thought in the target mind.

"Wait! He didn't kill her. The woman was dead when he found the body."

"Hold positions, everyone!" snapped Adika. "You're sure, Amber?"

"I'm certain," I said. "The target was thinking about how cold she was. He'd been with her body for hours before the hasty disturbed him, so I thought that was why she was cold, but it wasn't. She was already cold when the target went into the storage complex and stumbled across the body."

"That makes no sense," said Adika. "Why would he discover a body and sit next to it for hours? Why would he even go into a closed storage complex? Was he planning to steal something?"

"Highly unlikely," said Lucas. "There's virtually no theft anywhere in the Hive, because people are afraid a nosy would read their minds and arrest them if they stole things."

He paused for a second. "I suspect the real answer is this man has some... unusual preferences in a partner. Amber said he'd been to the storage complex several times before. He instinctively ran to hide where the shop fittings are stored, because that's where he goes. He visits the mannequins, the shop dummies, and fantasizes about them. On this visit, he stumbled across his true ideal partner, not a mannequin but a genuine dead body, and couldn't tear himself away from it."

There was a stunned silence.

"Would that be consistent with your impressions, Amber?" asked Lucas.

"Yes, that would explain the..." I broke off, and rubbed my forehead. As a child and teenager, I'd suffered from occasional headaches. I hadn't been troubled by them much since Lottery, but I could feel one starting now. "I don't understand why anyone would want a partner that's..."

I'd lost count of the number of target minds I'd read in the last few months, and many of them had had deeply unsettling ideas, but I was finding this run especially hard. I wasn't sure if the sound of my voice gave away my distress, or Lucas saw my face on the images arriving from one of my bodyguards' cameras. Either way, he responded by abandoning his official emergency run voice, to use his own distinctively casual tones.

"Speaking as your current partner, I'm highly relieved to hear that, Amber. This man's preferences are probably due to an unfortunate past relationship experience. He now finds the idea of a non-rejecting partner deeply appealing."

"Nobody enjoys being rejected," said Adika dryly, "but I'd still rather have a living partner. If this man isn't our target, what do we do now?"

Lucas went back to his emergency run voice. "There's no

reason to assume the man currently in the storage complex is a threat to anyone, but he would benefit from some therapy. Is he moving at all, Amber?"

"No, he's sitting down again."

"Then the Strike team can collect him and hand him over to appropriate medical staff for assessment," said Lucas. "You'd better retrieve the body first though, so he doesn't see it again."

"Dispatching medical support to your location now," said Nicole.

"But what about our genuine target?" asked Adika.

"Our genuine target must have left the storage complex before this man arrived," said Lucas, "and that was several hours ago. Amber can run checks on the surrounding area, but she's unlikely to find him or her. The lack of warning signs in this area indicates our target doesn't spend much time here. We'll have to take the alternative approach of identifying the victim, working out all the people closely connected to her, and scheduling check runs for Amber to read their minds and find out which of them is guilty."

"So we tidy up here, and if Amber doesn't find us a new target then we can head home," said Adika. "All right. Rothan, Eli, Caleb, come with me to collect the body."

I stayed with the mind that was too frightened and bewildered to run, until I heard Adika speak again in a shocked voice. "Waste that!"

I instantly linked to Adika's mind to check if he was in danger, and saw the view from his eyes as he looked down at the body of a woman. Neck gory with blood, but face clearly visible.

Adika knew this woman. I knew this woman. It was Fran.

CHAPTER THREE

Fran's face was exactly as precise, as controlled, as elegantly made up as when I'd known her. Only the startled expression in those lifeless, open eyes was different from her usual rigid professionalism.

My forehead throbbed with pain as I remembered my last confrontation with Fran. She'd been my Liaison team leader, causing one problem after another for my unit, until the situation ended in an explosive team leader meeting. Fran had shouted abuse at me, I'd fired her, and Nicole had been promoted to replace her.

I'd thought about Fran a lot since then, but solely about how she'd affected me. I'd never asked what happened to her after she left my unit, and now she was dead.

I watched through Adika's eyes, felt through Adika's hands, as he and Rothan gently lifted Fran onto a stretcher and took her out to the waiting medical team. Fran was a Level 1 Liaison team leader, or she had been before I fired her. Why had she died in a storage complex on Level 68? Was this my fault? Had the Hive sent her to work here as a punishment for daring to distress one of its five treasured telepaths?

"Amber? Are you all right? Amber?"

I'd been aware of voices speaking from my ear crystal but been too occupied with my thoughts to listen to what they were saying. Now I realized Lucas was calling my name.

"Yes," I said, hastily. "Sorry, I was distracted for a moment. Did I miss something?"

"The Strike team are going to collect the man from inside the storage complex now, so we need your assistance," said Lucas.

I tried to drag my thoughts away from the past, ignore the pain of my headache, and concentrate on doing my job. I had to watch over my team to keep them safe. Run circuits to make sure that anyone hurt or in trouble got help quickly. "Who's going in? Everyone on Chase team?"

"Just Adika, Rothan, Eli, and Caleb," said Lucas.

I opened my eyes, reached for my dataview, stabbed the circuit button with a finger, and focused on the list of four names scrolling up the right side of the display. I could remember four names myself, but following the proper routine would help me calm down.

"Adika, Rothan, Eli, Caleb." I chanted each name aloud as I checked the man's mind, and made sure he was uninjured and in no danger. Then I tapped the display to send that name back down to the bottom of the list and moved on to the next. I'd just reached Adika again, when Lucas interrupted me.

"Umm, no need to run circuits for this, Amber. We're dealing with an innocent man, unarmed, and frozen in fear. We'd rather not add to his stress by using force or stunning him, so can you watch his mind and tell us his reactions as we try to coax him out?"

Judging from the careful way Lucas said that, he'd already said it at least once before. I was making a complete mess of this. "Sorry," I said again. "Finding the man now."

I left Adika's head and reached out to the isolated, frightened mind in the depths of the storage complex. I hesitated before speaking, making sure what I said was right. "The man is huddled in a ball now, clutching his knees with both hands. He definitely has no weapons."

"Good," said Lucas. "Adika, take your group to room 7 now. Stop when you're just inside the door."

There was a pause before Adika spoke, his voice barely a whisper. "We're in position now. There's shelving blocking the view of the south-western corner, so we can't see the man."

"He doesn't know you're in the room," I said.

"Amber, any clue at all about his name?" asked Lucas.

"No. People don't often think of their own name, and this man's thoughts are stuck in a terrified loop."

"Adika, can you please approach him alone and try not to appear too threatening?" said Lucas.

I was seeing the view from the man's eyes and hearing through his ears. The view was just his own hands hugging his knees. Even when he heard the sound of heavy footsteps on the bare floor, he didn't look up.

"Hello," said Adika.

Now the man lifted his head. I saw Adika kneeling, trying to minimize his intimidating bulk, a surprisingly open and compassionate look on his usually harsh face.

"The man's scared," I reported. "Not of Adika particularly. The man's just scared of everything at the moment. He's even scared of himself."

"You aren't in any trouble," said Adika gently. "You've done nothing wrong. What's your name?"

The man didn't speak. The top of his mind was still looping terrified thoughts about the hasty who'd seen him, but I saw the answer to Adika's question on the deeper levels. "He's Logan."

"You aren't in any trouble, Logan," repeated Adika, "but you can't stay here. You're feeling overwhelmed by the situation, and very afraid. I'll take you to some people who'll help you feel better."

The looping thoughts faltered, and then started again.

"Logan's scared of hasties, of being arrested," I said. "Tell him it won't be hasties."

"You aren't in any trouble," Adika said the words for the third time. "There are some doctors here who'll help you feel better."

The repeating thoughts faltered again before stopping. Logan studied Adika's dark-skinned face, the black hair that clustered tightly round his scalp, the sympathy in his eyes, and suddenly relaxed.

"Adika, slowly reach out your hand now," I said. "Don't touch him, just reach out."

Adika held out his hand, and Logan took it. Together we, they, stood up.

"Rothan, Eli, Caleb, stay out of view," said Lucas urgently.

Adika led Logan out of the storage complex, to where a medical team was waiting. A woman stepped forward and started talking to Logan in a soft, soothing voice.

"Amber, you can leave Logan's mind now, and do a quick check of the surrounding area," said Lucas.

As I left Logan's mind, the pain in my head eased. I linked briefly to Adika's thoughts, curious about the sympathy I'd seen on his face. Yes, it was genuine. Adika had encountered vast numbers of people with unbelievably varied problems. He was long past the stage of being shocked by them, and had nothing but compassion for anyone who wasn't a danger to others.

I left Adika and moved on to scan minds in the housing warren. Most of them were still asleep, but a few were awake, their thoughts occupied with the trivia of getting dressed or thinking ahead to the working day. One mind lit up, burning with fury, and I tensed until I saw it was just a toddler having a tantrum about not being allowed to wear his favourite clothes.

I moved on to the west, skimming through yet more minds. People travelling to work on a busy express belt. A man singing discordantly in the shower. A couple arguing about…

Lucas snapped out an order. "Potential isolation perimeter breach. Evacuate north to Orange Zone!"

"Go one corridor length north, then another cor west, and you'll reach the nearest northbound express belt." Nicole's voice was often anxious, but now she sounded close to panic.

I'd never heard anyone use the words isolation perimeter breach before. What was happening? I hastily pulled back into my own mind. I still had my eyes closed, but I could feel hands grabbing me. I was cradled against the warmth of a man's chest, and whoever was carrying me started running at full speed.

Everyone in my Strike team would know what an isolation perimeter breach was. I linked to Adika's mind, and found the same thought repeated on multiple levels.

Telepaths must never meet!

CHAPTER FOUR

An isolation perimeter breach meant that two telepaths were in danger of meeting! I was swept up by Adika's taut emotions, felt my heart start racing in response, and my headache flared up again. It was a strict rule that telepaths must never meet, included in the imprinted knowledge of all my specialist staff.

There'd been a hundred times when I'd rebelliously wished that rule didn't exist. Wished that I could meet other telepaths, see what their minds were like, and learn from their experiences. However much Lucas loved me, however hard he and everyone else in my unit tried to help support me, I was going through experiences that they could never truly understand, and there were moments when I felt dreadfully alone.

The most frustrating thing was that I didn't even know the reason behind the rule that kept me isolated from the other telepaths. I'd discussed this issue with Lucas months ago. His theory was that if all my staff were just imprinted with the stark rule that telepaths mustn't meet, without any background justification at all, then the reason behind it must be so horrifying that merely seeing it in someone's mind could leave me traumatized.

Lucas thought it would be safer for me to forget about the mystery, but it kept nagging away at me. I could believe that physically meeting a telepath was dangerous because their minds were somehow brighter, more dazzling than those of other people, but that didn't explain why telepaths weren't allowed to use dataviews to call each other. Was it because other telepaths might tell me things that the Hive didn't want me to know?

Now I could be about to learn the reason why telepaths must not meet by meeting one myself. Infected by Adika's fears, and my forehead throbbing with pain, I was no longer curious but terrified.

"Situation status report?" asked Adika, in a breathless voice.

"Sapphire and her Strike team are in area 520/4030 in Green Zone, heading north to the bulkhead doors at express belt speed," said Lucas. "Separation is currently 21 levels, 190 east to west, 560 north to south."

Adika was imprinted with the formula for calculating total three-dimensional telepath separation, but he wasn't bothering to even estimate the answer. A horizontal separation of half a zone, 500 in either direction, was the recommended minimum. We were in area 710/3470 in Yellow Zone, and currently had a separation of 560 north to south, but that would shrink hideously quickly when Sapphire was incoming at express belt speed. Lucas was doing the right thing by sending us fleeing north to maintain our distance from her.

Whoever was carrying me abruptly slackened his pace. I felt the distinctive series of movements that meant we'd joined the belt system, and were moving across from the slow belt to the medium and then the express.

"Crystal units to audio only now," said Adika. "Lucas, we're heading north on the express belt but it's crowded with other travellers. Liaison will have to get them out of our way if you want us to run along the belt."

"That shouldn't be necessary," Lucas's voice was reassuringly calm again. "Sapphire and her team just jumped belt and entered a lift. You're rapidly gaining north to south separation now. There's still a chance that Sapphire's team may need to head north again though, so you should continue to Orange Zone and hold position there awaiting further developments."

My Strike team were carefully chosen to have the right personalities for their work. Adika had reacted with instant tension to Lucas's warning of a potential isolation perimeter breach. Now the crisis was over, he relaxed just as quickly.

I felt his moment of niggling doubt, when he wondered exactly why telepaths had to be kept apart, but that was instantly swept aside. There had to be a good reason for the rule. For one thing, it would obviously be dangerous for two armed Strike teams to be working too near each other. Strike team members could be killed by friendly fire. The unthinkable could happen, and a telepath could be killed.

The Hive knew best. Separation was important. Adika dismissed that issue, moved on to thinking about another point, and became irritated.

"Why were we the ones evacuating?" he asked. "It sounds as if Sapphire and her team were on an emergency run, but so were we, and our unit has home zone priority in Yellow and Orange Zones."

"I relinquished home zone priority to Sapphire's unit," said Lucas. "Sapphire and her Strike team were actively in pursuit of a target, while we weren't."

Adika gave a grunt of grudging acceptance. He was perfectly calm now, but I was suffering from shaken nerves. I pulled back into the shelter of my own mind, and told myself there was no need for me to worry. Whatever horror would result from two telepaths meeting didn't matter. The Tactical Commanders of the five Telepath Units had a system to keep their telepaths apart. I could trust them to keep us safe. I could trust Lucas to keep me safe.

I felt a hand brush against the side of my face and adjust the setting on my ear crystal. There was the familiar clicking sound that meant the camera extension was folding itself back into the crystal unit. I belatedly remembered that Adika had given the order to set crystal units to audio. I should have adjusted the setting myself when he said that, but I'd been too distracted by fear and pain.

The fear had retreated a little, but the throbbing pain of my headache was still beating at me. Having my eyes closed, brooding on what had just happened, probably wasn't helping.

I opened my eyes, and found myself looking up at the face of Rothan, Adika's deputy team leader in charge of the Alpha Strike team. He smiled at me, and I forced a smile in return. I'd normally stand on my own feet when we were travelling on the belt system, to avoid attracting the stares of curious onlookers. It was a little late to start worrying about that though, and I was feeling oddly shaky, so I let Rothan keep carrying me.

We rode on in silence until a voice boomed from overhead speakers. "Warning, zone bulkhead approaching!"

I felt a jolt as Rothan jumped from the Yellow Zone express belt to the Orange Zone express belt. A minute or two later, our group left the belt system, moved into a side corridor and stopped.

"Strike team are now in Orange Zone and awaiting further instructions," said Adika.

"Sapphire's Strike team just secured their target," said Lucas. "They should be out of Yellow Zone within ten minutes, and then you can come back to our unit."

I looked up at Rothan's face again, and had a weird feeling that there was something wrong about him. My thoughts clouded by my headache, it took me a minute to pin down what was bothering me. All of my Strike team members were heavily muscled with black hair. I'd thought that they all had dark eyes as well, but now I could see that Rothan's eyes were a distinctive blue. How could I have made such a basic mistake?

Rothan's expression was anxious. "Is something wrong, Amber?"

"No. Yes." I brushed my hand across my eyes. "My head hurts."

"Start back to our unit now." Lucas's voice had to be coming from my ear crystal, but it sounded strangely distant.

"You want us to come back right away, Lucas?" Adika's voice sounded distant too. "I thought we were going to wait here until Sapphire was out of Yellow Zone."

"If necessary, we'll divert Sapphire's team out of your way," said Lucas. "Amber clearly has a problem, so we need to get her back to our unit as fast as possible."

I tried to say that I was fine, and they didn't need to divert Sapphire's team, but I was lost in a clouded world of pain and my lips didn't respond.

CHAPTER FIVE

Eight hours later, I was lying on a heap of cushions in the bookette room of the apartment I shared with Lucas. The room wasn't playing a proper bookette, but the holos were showing a background scene from one of the Hive beaches. The sand around me was dotted with seashells. The sea was calm, set for swimming rather than surfing. The suns were bright in the painted ceiling, and the cries of the gulls flying overhead were mixed with the sound of wind and waves.

The illusion was so convincing that I unthinkingly reached out to touch a delicate spiralling shell. My fingers went straight through it, touching the thick pile of the room's genuine carpet flooring, and I laughed at my own foolishness.

"How is your headache now?" asked Lucas.

"It's almost gone."

I rolled onto my right side, and looked at where Lucas was stretched out next to me. He was twenty-one and had been working on Telepath Unit Tactical teams for three years. For the first year, he'd just been a team member in Keith's unit, but then he'd been promoted to deputy, and finally joined my unit to carry the huge burden of being Tactical Commander. In relaxed moments like this though, he still looked and acted like a teen.

It was only Lucas's eyes that gave away the truth. They were surprisingly dark compared to his unruly light-brown hair, and you could tell they'd seen things he'd like to forget. At least, I could tell that. Perhaps that was just because I was a telepath and knew Lucas's mind so well. Did other people look at his eyes without noticing the shadows in their depths?

Thinking of Lucas's eyes reminded me of my bewilderment seeing Rothan's eyes earlier. "Something peculiar happened at the end of the last emergency run. I looked at Rothan's eyes and had a weird illusion they were blue."

"Rothan's eyes *are* blue," said Lucas. "You were confused because he was wearing brown contact lenses until yesterday."

"Rothan was wearing contact lenses to change the colour of his eyes? Why would he do that?" Lucas didn't have time to reply before I groaned and answered my own question. "This is because Lottery chose my Strike team members to be potential partners for me, and it decided I was attracted to men with black hair and dark eyes. It was only when I caught Rafael thinking about dyeing his hair that I realized he didn't have naturally black hair. I'd no idea that Rothan had been wearing contact lenses. Are any more of the Strike team doing that?"

"There aren't any more wearing contact lenses. Lottery chose most of the Strike team candidates to match the physical appearance criteria exactly. A few especially able candidates were allowed through with the wrong colour hair because that's easily fixed with a little hair dye. Rothan's test scores were so high that he was selected despite having both lighter coloured hair and totally the wrong eye colour."

Lucas smiled. "When you told Rafael that he didn't need to keep dyeing his hair, he told Adika about it, and Adika discussed it with me. Given we'd already discovered that Lottery had made an error in your physical appearance preferences, we decided to let the relevant few Strike team members revert to their natural selves. You may notice some gradual changes in hair colour over the next few weeks. Rothan's eyes going from brown to blue was inevitably an abrupt change. You don't find a blue-eyed Rothan too repugnant?"

"Of course not."

I cautiously reached out my left hand to smooth a rebellious strand of Lucas's hair back into place. The warmth of him felt reassuring, so I let the palm of my hand run down the side of his face, feeling how the smoothness of his skin changed to stubble near his jawline. Lucas had stayed by my side since I got back to the unit, so he hadn't had a chance to use shaving cream yet today.

"You're comfortable touching me again?" he asked.

I pulled a face at him, before snuggling against him and resting my head on his chest. "Yes. That was deeply unnerving. I wasn't aware until I got back here and hugged you that…"

I broke off, wincing as I remembered being revolted by the warmth of a living, breathing Lucas.

"You were suffering residual effects of your mental contact with Logan." Lucas finished my sentence for me.

"Yes. When I read the mind of a wild bee, I'm seeing the world through their eyes, sharing their thoughts, and feeling their emotions. That's often disturbing, but I've never had the effects last this long. I suppose it was harder to shake them off when I was suffering from a headache."

Lucas was silent for a moment before speaking. "Did you have a headache when the run started?"

"No." I tried to think through the events of the run. "I first noticed it when I was reading Logan's mind."

"Was that before or after we found out the body was Fran?"

"Before."

Lucas frowned. "You're sure about that?"

"Yes. I definitely had a headache when we were discussing Logan's attitudes."

"After we'd identified the body, you were struggling to follow instructions," said Lucas. "I mistakenly assumed you were just suffering from the shock of discovering Fran was dead. I didn't realize you were having problems before that. Are you recovered enough to read me yet?"

I reached out to his shining mind. The thought levels flew past at staggering speed, constantly multiplying and merging, cascading down in glorious splendour into the subconscious and beyond. I couldn't keep up with the words, but there were a host of camera images from this morning's run, most of them of my own face. Lucas was analyzing exactly what had happened to me.

"Yes," I said.

Lucas dropped into the abbreviated speed speech he often used to save time when talking to me. "Essential telepath recover contact target."

I focused on the top level of his mind, where I could see the full sentences of pre-vocalized words. Lucas was saying that it was essential to allow a telepath sufficient time to recover after contact with difficult target minds.

"Telepath Units have a mandatory twenty-four hour shutdown after emergency runs," continued Lucas. "I'm choosing to start counting that twenty-four hours from now rather than from the end of the last run. If you have any further problems, either now or after future runs, I believe we should extend your recovery time to two or three days."

I wrinkled my nose. "That would be unfair to the other telepaths. If I take more recovery time than them, it means they have to work harder to compensate."

"You read targets on deeper levels than other telepaths, Amber. You feel more of their emotions. That can be incredibly useful sometimes, but it also makes you far more vulnerable to stress."

I could tell Lucas didn't like saying that. I didn't like hearing it either.

"Occasionally taking extended recovery time won't be unfair to the other telepaths," said Lucas. "They have their weaknesses too, and all the Telepath Units constantly make adjustments and trade cases to work around them."

He paused, and I saw the glittering levels of his mind abruptly darken, as if a shadow was passing over them. "Amber, it's absolutely vital that you take the time you need to recover properly after emergency runs. Studying you near the end of that run, seeing your pain and disorientation, frightened me. Thirty years ago, our Hive lost York. Seven years ago, our Hive lost Olivia. We mustn't lose you."

I was stunned by Lucas mentioning York and Olivia. Everyone on my operational teams knew about the two recent telepaths who had broken under the strain of reading minds. My unit members needed that knowledge, to help them stop the same thing happening to me, and I'd inevitably seen some of them thinking about the details.

York had killed himself. Olivia was still alive, but could barely use her telepathy at all, so no one ever talked about her or included her in the number of current telepaths. In fact, the only time anyone had ever said the names of York and Olivia to me before was in my early days of training. I'd forced Lucas to talk about them back then. If he was voluntarily mentioning their names now, then he was truly terrified about my wellbeing.

"All right. If you decide I need extended recovery time at any point, then I'll accept the decision." I sat up. "I'm not arguing with you about keeping our unit in mandatory shutdown until this time tomorrow, but can we talk about Fran for a while? There are a few questions worrying me."

"I understand it would be less stressful for you to have answers." Lucas sat up as well, and turned to face me. "Go!"

"What happened to Fran after I fired her? Did the Hive assign her to live down on Level 68 and work in that storage complex as a punishment?"

Lucas was obviously startled by my question. "No. Assigning a highly skilled worker to basic tasks would be wasteful in the extreme. Fran's record would have been flagged as unsuitable for assignments involving contact with Telepath Units, and a new position found for her."

He took out his dataview, and spoke into it. "Nicole, my apologies for interrupting your break. Can you send me Fran's records?"

I leaned across to speak into the dataview myself. "My fault. Sorry."

"You don't need to apologize," said Nicole. "I've been looking through those records myself. I was feeling guilty about taking her job, and... Well, sending them to you now."

Lucas had made it a sound-only call, so I couldn't see Nicole's face, but her voice sounded strained. I tried to reassure her.

"There's no reason for you to feel guilty, Nicole. Fran had already left our unit before you even knew there was a problem."

"Amber's right," said Lucas. "The Liaison team members

were left leaderless and bewildered just as our unit was going fully operational. You stepped in to take over the team. You pulled things together so well that Liaison gave the Strike team perfect support on crucial emergency runs. You've done a wonderful job and helped save a lot of lives."

"Thank you." Nicole sounded much happier now.

Lucas ended the call and skimmed through the records on his dataview. "No suitable team leader post was available when Fran left us, so she was temporarily assigned as deputy team leader in a Security Unit in Navy Zone."

"That's half the length of the Hive away from us."

Lucas nodded. "Given the circumstances of her leaving our unit, Fran would be assigned to work somewhere a long distance from us."

I frowned. The people working for Law Enforcement knew a host of important Hive secrets such as the truth about nosies and telepaths. To guard against accidental betrayal of those secrets, the Hive minimized the contact they had with ordinary citizens by giving them their own level of the Hive. Level 20 was very different from the other accommodation levels, having apartments in a whole range of living standards, as well as Law Enforcement office complexes.

"Both Fran's apartment and this Security Unit were on Level 20 in Navy Zone?" I asked.

"Yes."

"So if Fran was living and working on Level 20 in Navy Zone, what was she doing in a storage complex on Level 68 in Yellow Zone?"

"My Tactical team will be investigating that tomorrow." Lucas gave me a thoughtful look. "Unless you decide to take the alternative option of handing this case over to another Telepath Unit."

"I don't want to do that."

"Speaking as your Tactical Commander, I strongly advise you to consider handing over this case, Amber. The other telepaths didn't know Fran. It would be far less stressful for one of them to hunt her murderer."

I was the notional head of my Telepath Unit, with two deputies that did the actual work. Megan was in charge of the general administration of the unit. Lucas was in charge of unit operations. I didn't get involved in the details of their work, because I didn't understand half the things they did, but I made occasional major decisions and I was determined to make this one.

"Fran belonged to our unit, Lucas. We should be the ones to find out who killed her."

"It's highly probable that a second emergency call relating to the same target arrives within the next few hours, in which case another unit will take it anyway."

"Well, if that happens, and they catch him or her, then that's fine. If not... Telepath Units are always too busy, Lucas. If we hand Fran's case to another unit, they'll follow standard procedure and make a couple of check runs. If those achieve nothing, then they'll suspend the case until there are new signs of the target."

I paused. "Once a case is suspended, it's often never solved. I don't want Fran's case left suspended forever. I need to know what happened to her."

Lucas sighed. "Agreed. Handing Fran's case to another unit won't stop you worrying about it, so we have to ensure it's properly resolved ourselves. Now I must make a quick call to Megan."

He made a second sound-only call. "Megan, Nicole's suffering a guilt reaction to the news of Fran's death. The rest of the Liaison team may be having difficulties too. Can you arrange counselling for them?"

"Yes, but Amber is the real priority," said Megan brusquely. "She was clearly deep in shock after discovering Fran was dead. Amber's counselling is my responsibility. I should be helping her work through her reaction to Fran's death, but she always resists talking to me. You must insist on her having a counselling session with me right away."

Lucas turned to me and raised a questioning eyebrow. I pictured Megan interrogating me about my feelings on Fran's death, shuddered, and urgently shook my head.

"Amber isn't ready to have a counselling session yet," said Lucas. "She needs more recovery time after the last run."

"I must have heard variations on that excuse a hundred times. Amber doesn't want a counselling session because it's too soon after a run. Amber doesn't want a counselling session because she'll be going on a run soon. Amber doesn't want a counselling session because she's going to visit her parents." Megan made a disgusted noise. "The truth is that Amber resists counselling because she's too defensive of her privacy. I suspect this problem was triggered by conflicts with her parents in infancy. It's one of the issues I keep trying and failing to raise with her."

I glared at the dataview. Megan had insisted on talking about this during our last counselling session. I'd told her that if anything had triggered my need for privacy, then it was having a younger brother constantly trying to mess with my belongings. She'd refused to accept that explanation though, and kept asking prying questions about my relationship with my parents until I walked out in anger.

I felt that same anger again now. Megan shouldn't be discussing this with Lucas. The dull ache of my headache started building again, so I rubbed my forehead. Lucas seemed to notice that, because he threw an anxious look at me before speaking into his dataview in a pointed voice.

"This isn't a good time, Megan."

"I tried to discuss Amber's counselling with you yesterday and you said you were too busy."

"That's because I *was* too busy yesterday. Keith's Tactical Commander called an emergency Joint Tactical Meeting about an incident in Burgundy Zone."

"You can't keep evading this discussion, Lucas," Megan's voice was openly angry now. "You've effectively taken over my work of counselling Amber. That was tolerable as an interim measure when you were merely her Tactical Commander, but it's completely unacceptable now that you're her established partner as well. You have to force Amber to talk to me."

My forehead was throbbing so painfully now that I'd lost my link to Lucas's mind, but his expression showed he was getting annoyed too. "I couldn't and wouldn't force Amber to have counselling from anyone against her will. Whether she talks to you or not has to be her own decision."

"Things have gone past the stage where we can let Amber avoid proper counselling. You saw the state she was in after this morning's run. We have to relieve the stress on her or she'll..."

Lucas firmly interrupted the tirade. "Megan, when I told you this wasn't a good time, I meant that Amber is sitting right next to me and can hear every word that you're saying."

There was a single, appalled, monosyllable from Megan. "Oh."

I was furious with Megan, not just because of the things she'd just said, but because I was remembering Adika's hurt and frustration during the last emergency run as well. I grabbed the dataview from Lucas and spoke into it myself.

"Megan, you've no right to tell Lucas details of my private counselling sessions. You've *absolutely* no right to tell him to force me to talk to you."

"I would never have said those things if I wasn't so worried about you, Amber. You were under severe stress during the last run. You have to discuss it with me, because I'm imprinted with all the counselling techniques needed to help you deal with it."

I groaned. "You keep pushing me to discuss things with you, but how can I do that given the things I see in your mind? You aren't just trying to mother me, but to control me. You keep secrets from me. You want to stop me talking to Lucas about my problems. You're jealous that I'm in a loving relationship while you're lost in a maelstrom of emotions, trying and failing to move on from the death of your husband."

I paused for a microsecond to breathe. "Yes, I was under severe stress during the last run, but part of that was your fault. Emergency runs are hard enough for me, having to read the thoughts of a target mind that's deep in an emotional crisis. I don't need the extra burden of my Strike team leader having an emotional crisis as well, especially when the entire Strike team have picked up the fact that something is wrong with their leader and are getting distracted and upset by it."

Megan tried to speak again. "The situation between Adika and me is difficult because..."

I raised my voice and swept on. "I don't need you to tell me why the situation is difficult. Your mind keeps screaming it at me. You're attracted to Adika, but he's moving too quickly for you. You're torn between the past and future, unsure whether to linger in mourning for your dead husband or start a new relationship. For the sake of this unit, you need to forget about counselling me on my problems, and concentrate on sorting out your own personal life. Tell Adika yes, or tell him no. He can cope with either. What he can't cope with is you changing your mind every five minutes."

I stabbed Lucas's dataview with my forefinger, ending the call.

CHAPTER SIX

I sat there seething with anger for the next couple of minutes. When I finally calmed down, I gave Lucas an anxious look. "Did I go a bit far?"

Lucas cowered in mock fear. "I don't dare to comment."

The pain in my head was easing now, and I was feeling dreadfully guilty. "It was unfair of me to say those things to Megan. I'm a telepath, I can't help seeing her deepest, most intimate thoughts, but I shouldn't throw that knowledge at her in front of you, and I've no right to interfere in her private life."

Lucas abandoned his clown act. "I'm an expert in behavioural analysis and reading body language. I already knew everything you said to Megan, except the key detail that Adika was having an emotional crisis during the last run, and that was upsetting the Strike team."

He pulled a face. "I couldn't understand why you were disintegrating so badly during that run. Now it makes sense. You weren't just under extreme emotional strain from your target, but from your own Strike team as well."

"That wasn't Adika's fault. It wasn't Megan's fault either. They're human beings, not robots, and the emergency call came at exactly the wrong time."

"I know they didn't do it intentionally, but the fact remains that their relationship issues put you under pressure before you read Logan's mind. He may not have been a murderer, but his thoughts would have been deeply disturbing, and then you discovered the murdered woman was Fran. You're obviously suffering from the cumulative strain of those things even now, which is why you just lost your temper with Megan."

My pocket started vibrating. I took out my dataview, looked at it, made a whimpering noise of despair, and buried my face in my hands. "That's a message from Megan. She's resigned."

"Query. Are you accepting her resignation?" asked Lucas.

I lifted my head again. "Of course not."

"If the situation between Adika and Megan has reached the point where it's distracting the Strike team during emergency runs, then someone could get injured or killed. We should replace either Adika or Megan before that happens, and I think the choice is simple. Adika is doing his job perfectly. Megan isn't."

"The Senior Administrator is responsible for the everyday running of the unit. Megan does that flawlessly."

"I agree," said Lucas, "but the Senior Administrator is also responsible for safeguarding the telepath's physical and mental wellbeing, acting as both their personal doctor and counsellor. It's clear that you've irretrievably lost faith in Megan as your counsellor at a time when you're in urgent need of psychological support. The simplest solution would be to accept her resignation and find a more compatible replacement."

I whimpered again. "I can't do that, Lucas. After what I said to Megan, I'd feel as if I'd fired her. Given we've just found the dead body of the last person I fired..."

"I appreciate the difficulty. Hopefully Adika will solve the relationship issues by breaking off his pursuit of Megan. We still need to find a solution to the counselling problem though. Am I right in thinking you'd be willing to continue having Megan as your personal doctor but not as your counsellor?"

I stared down at my hands. "Yes. I'm happy with Megan as my doctor, but I can't bear any more counselling sessions with her. I don't see any reason for me to have a counsellor anyway. Your imprint includes some psychology, so you can keep doing my counselling."

"No, I can't. Megan was right when she said that it was unacceptable for me to keep counselling you on a long-term basis. No one should ever receive counselling about problems from their partner."

"I don't see why."

"Because the partner often *is* the problem. I hope we'll keep discussing our problems with each other, but it's essential that you have independent counselling as well. I suggest we keep Megan as Senior Administrator, but recruit a specialist psychologist to do your counselling."

I blinked. "Can we do that?"

"We can and will do anything necessary to help you cope with the pressure of your work." Lucas paused. "If we're going to recruit a new counsellor for you, then we need to find suitable candidates as fast as possible. What sort of characteristics should we be looking for?"

I was bewildered by the speed of this. "I don't know. I haven't thought about it. I've never met any psychologists other than Megan, unless you count Buzz."

"Who was Buzz?"

"She treated me when I lived on Teen Level."

Lucas grabbed his dataview, and started tapping at it. "You had a psychologist treating you on Teen Level? How could I have missed that? I went through every detail of your medical records a dozen times when we were trying to work out why..."

"Buzz wasn't treating me on a regular basis," I interrupted him. "When I was seventeen, I tried cliff climbing on Teen Level beach to try to overcome my fear of heights, and panicked. My friend, Forge, climbed up and rescued me, but I'd hurt my head so I was sent to a medical facility."

Lucas abandoned his dataview and nodded. "I know all about that. When Lottery discovered you were a telepath, there was naturally huge concern about you having had a head injury, but multiple experts went over the scans and confirmed you'd suffered no lasting damage."

"They did?" I shook my head. "I didn't know that. Well, my injury was treated by a doctor, and then Buzz checked me for signs of memory loss or confusion before I was discharged from the medical facility."

"So that was how you met Buzz. You liked her?"

I smiled. "Yes. She was just a year or two older than me, very informal, and it was amazingly easy to talk to her. It would help if you could find someone like Buzz to do my counselling."

"We may be able to get Buzz herself. Whatever her specialist area of psychology, her imprint will cover basic counselling techniques. The only difficulty is one of security. We'd need to get her personality profile checked to see if she's discreet enough to be trusted with the truth about telepaths and transferred to Law Enforcement."

Lucas worked on his dataview for a moment. "I can't find any record of a psychologist called Buzz. Are you sure that's the right name?"

"Buzz was just a nickname," I explained. "I'm afraid I can't remember her real name."

"I'm sure we'll be able to track her down. It would help narrow the search if you know Buzz's specialist area of psychology."

"I don't."

"The different specialist areas have different level ratings," said Lucas. "Do you know Buzz's level?"

"Buzz is Level 1."

"What?" Lucas stared at me. "Are you sure about that?"

"Yes." I frowned anxiously at Lucas. "Is that a problem? Does it make Buzz too important to join our unit?"

"It's unexpected, but it isn't a problem. In fact, it means there wouldn't be any security issues at all in recruiting Buzz. The only psychologists rated Level 1 are specialists working for Law Enforcement."

"Buzz already works for Law Enforcement?" I thought rapidly through my encounters with Buzz. "When I was on Teen Level, I discovered Buzz worked for Health and Safety, but I didn't realize she belonged to the Law Enforcement division."

"I'm just surprised that a psychologist with Buzz's specialism was working at an ordinary medical facility."

"Buzz wasn't working at the medical facility permanently. I remember her saying she was only there for a day because their regular psychologist was ill." I paused. "So, what is Buzz's specialism?"

Lucas hesitated before answering. "The only psychologists rated Level 1 are specialists in victim trauma treatment and forensic psychology."

I'd heard Lucas talking about those specialists before. A Telepath Unit's job finished when a target was apprehended. After that, the experts in victim trauma treatment and forensic psychology took over, treating any victims and attempting to salvage the target as a productive member of the Hive. One key fact about these psychologists had stuck in my mind. Lottery selected them for their work because they had a very special talent.

"But that means Buzz is..."

I let my sentence trail off and Lucas said the words for me. "Yes, it means that Buzz is a borderline telepath."

CHAPTER SEVEN

Later that day, Lucas and I went to our unit swimming pool. We swam slow and lazy lengths for hours until I was exhausted, but I still had trouble sleeping that night. My body floated peacefully on the warm air cushion of the sleep field I shared with Lucas, but my mind alternated conjuring up the image of Fran's dead face, with trying to adjust to the fact that Buzz was a borderline telepath.

There were only five true telepaths in our Hive, six if you counted the broken Olivia, but Lottery discovered almost a thousand people a year with borderline telepathic abilities. These people didn't have the conscious control of their talent that I had, just getting random glimpses into the minds of others, but that was still enough to make them valuable psychologists and counsellors.

When I first met Buzz, I'd been an ordinary seventeen-year-old, who believed the grey-masked nosies were genuine telepaths. I'd learnt a vast amount since going through Lottery. If I'd had any reason to think about Buzz in the last few months, if I'd worked logically through my memories of her, then I might have guessed she was a borderline telepath.

Buzz was Level 1. She was a psychologist. It was weirdly easy to talk to her. When some hasties caught my friend, Forge, crawling through the vent system, it was Buzz who assessed him and ordered him to wear a child's tracking bracelet to stop him from taking risks. A decision like that would surely be made by a member of Law Enforcement rather than any other division of Health and Safety.

I remembered how abruptly Buzz had reached that decision on Forge. Was the suddenness of that because she'd had one of her flashes of telepathic vision? Had Buzz managed to look into my own mind as well? If she had, then what had she seen?

"Shall we get up now and have an early breakfast?" asked Lucas.

I turned guiltily towards him. "Did I wake you up? I'm sorry."

Lucas rolled out of his side of the sleep field, stood up, and stretched his arms. "I wasn't sleeping well either. I was too busy thinking. Working out the best way to handle the Megan situation. Considering scenarios that would explain how Fran ended up in that warehouse. Wondering whether bringing Buzz in to counsel you could be a dreadful mistake."

I frowned. "You told me it was safe for me to meet borderline telepaths."

"It's perfectly safe," said Lucas. "Which is deeply fortunate. Keeping true telepaths apart isn't a problem, because our Hive has never had more than a dozen at any one time. Keeping true telepaths away from the many tens of thousands of borderline telepaths in the Hive would be a logistical nightmare."

"If it's safe for me to meet Buzz, why do you think it could be a mistake to have her counselling me?"

Lucas pulled a face. "Because the news Buzz was a borderline telepath clearly stunned you. Because they are notoriously unconventional in their approach to therapy. Because I'm worried how you'll react if Buzz glimpses your thoughts."

"Even as an ignorant seventeen-year-old, I got the impression Buzz was a very unconventional psychologist, but that was exactly what I liked about her. I was stunned, I'm *still* stunned by the fact she's a borderline telepath, but that's just because she seemed as ordinary as me."

Lucas laughed. "Respectfully point out that you're one of only five true telepaths in our Hive, Amber. That makes you far from ordinary."

I gave a reluctant laugh myself. "Sometimes I can accept that, but most of the time I still feel very ordinary."

Lucas waited expectantly for a moment before speaking again. "I notice you aren't commenting on the possibility of Buzz getting glimpses into your mind."

"I honestly don't know what to say about that. I admit I'm defensive of my privacy. I've reacted badly to people gossiping about me in the past. I completely lost my temper with Adika once when he was being nosy about my relationship with you. Most of my problems with Megan were because she kept pushing me to tell her personal things."

I sighed. "If I find I'm uncomfortable with Buzz now that I know she's a borderline telepath, then I promise I'll say so immediately."

Lucas nodded. "I've tracked down Buzz's identity, and asked for her to be put on standby to visit our unit today."

"Today?" I was startled. "Won't we be busy with Fran's case today? The mandatory twenty-four hour shutdown is almost over, so we can start doing check runs."

"My Tactical team are still analyzing the situation. Besides, your problems during the last run were sufficiently worrying that finding you adequate psychological support has to be our unit's highest priority."

I didn't like Lucas's grim tone of voice when he said that. I considered checking his mind to see what he was thinking, but decided I didn't want to know. "I agree that I should see Buzz today then."

"I suggest you limit the meeting to doing the standard initial check of Buzz's mind that you do on all new unit members. If you're still feeling positive about her after that, we'll arrange for you to have a proper counselling session with her."

He paused. "You wanted me to talk to Megan for you, so I called in at her apartment yesterday evening. I'm afraid the conversation didn't go according to plan."

"What happened?" I asked anxiously.

"I told her you wanted her to stay, but she was in the same noble, self-sacrificing mood as when she left Keith's unit after her husband's death. Whatever I said, she kept insisting that her leaving would be in the best interests of both you and the unit."

"Oh." I frowned.

"In the end, I had to change from arguing against her leaving to delaying her departure. I asked Megan to put the good of the Hive above her own feelings, keep her resignation secret, and continue working while we recruited suitable replacement personnel."

Lucas shrugged. "That worked. Megan agreed to stay on as long as necessary for the transition process."

"I thought you'd stand a better chance of persuading Megan to stay than I would, but I think I'll have to talk to her myself after all."

"I agree, but I suggest you allow her a few days to calm down first."

"I suppose that's best."

"There are actually some advantages in leaving Megan's status in doubt for a little longer," said Lucas. "Technically, the Senior Administrator is responsible for recruiting new unit members. Imagine the potential complications of Megan recruiting a new counsellor for you."

I imagined them and winced.

"We currently have the opportunity to recruit your new counsellor without involving Megan, and also to establish that counsellor's position in our unit organizational structure."

"Is that important?"

"It's very important. If we persuade Megan to stay on as Senior Administrator, she'll expect your new counsellor to report to her."

I shuddered. "We can't allow that. We'd end up with Megan telling my counsellor what to discuss with me, and there'd be precisely the same problems as before. My counsellor will have to report to you instead."

"Megan shouldn't be giving orders to your counsellor, but neither should I. Your counsellor has to have the status of an independent specialist, with the sole responsibility of ensuring your mental wellbeing. It would avoid arguments if we establish that before confirming Megan in her new role."

"You're right. I'd better see Buzz this morning then."

Lucas nodded, picked up his dataview from a side table, and headed off into the shower room. I went across to the bedroom storage wall, opened it, and studied my clothes. On the left, was an array of untouched, prestigious clothes that my mother had suggested I should wear now I was Level 1 and head of my own unit. On the right, were my battered and faded clothes from Teen Level, which I no longer wore these days but somehow didn't want to throw away. In the middle, were the clothes I really did wear, which were a more respectable, higher level version of my old ones from Teen Level.

I was still staring at the clothes when Lucas returned to the bedroom, his wet hair dripping water onto the equally wet dataview he was holding. I'd spent my years on Teen Level taking paranoid care of a basic model dataview that could suffer terminal damage from water. Intellectually, I knew Lucas and I had the same models of dataview that the Strike team used, designed to survive their owner crawling through the revolting liquids of the waste system, falling off ladders, or being thrown around in combat. On some deeper level of my mind, I still found it disconcerting that Lucas would casually work on his dataview in the shower or even when swimming.

Lucas gave a last tap at his dataview, tossed it on a side table, and started getting dressed. "Why are you staring at your clothes as if you're afraid that they'll bite you?"

"I'm not sure what to wear to meet Buzz," I said. "Whether to dress formally or not."

Lucas shook his head, sending water droplets flying in all directions. "You're a telepath. You've no need to use clothes to proclaim your status, especially not to your own counsellor."

"The clothes issue isn't about status. It's... It's a game."

"I don't understand," said Lucas.

"Buzz has a system of dressing appropriately for the people she's treating. When I was a teen, she wore cheap, colourful, basic clothes. I'm trying to work out what she'll wear to meet a true telepath, so I can dress to match it."

"You mean this is a psychological game like playing rock, paper, scissors?"

I'd no idea what Lucas was talking about, cheated by checking his mind, and discovered him thinking about an archaic game where two people made hand gestures to indicate one of three choices, each of which would defeat one of the others.

"It's a bit like that," I said.

"What do you want for breakfast?"

After my restless night, my stomach was desperate for food. "Everything."

Lucas laughed and wandered off. I went to have a shower myself, and then stared at my clothes again. How would Buzz think of true telepaths? Would she see them as rare, valuable or useful? Would she wear an outfit that was ornate or just formal?

I heard a distant bing that meant the kitchen unit had finished preparing breakfast. I groaned, grabbed an official-looking onesuit, and rapidly dressed.

I found Lucas sitting at the table, eating his breakfast, and inevitably staring at his dataview. I picked up my own heavily laden plate from the kitchen unit dispensing tray, and sat next to him.

He put his dataview aside and smiled at me. "I see you decided to dress formally."

I didn't reply. I'd just taken a bite of over-hot potato slices, and was urgently gulping down a glass of melon juice.

Lucas's dataview made a chiming noise. He glanced at the screen. "Buzz is on her way to the unit."

I instinctively tensed. Yesterday, my Strike team had gone into full flight mode to avoid me meeting another true telepath. This morning, I was going to meet a borderline telepath. I reminded myself that not only was everyone sure this was safe for me, but I'd actually met Buzz before without having any problems.

"I've asked Adika to meet Buzz and take her to one of the community rooms," continued Lucas.

I was confused. "Why a community room? I usually do initial telepathic checks in a meeting room."

"The community rooms we use for social events are a more relaxed setting than a formal meeting room. They're also closer to the lifts if we want Buzz to leave quickly."

I frowned. "You seem to expect Buzz's visit to be a disaster."

"I'm not expecting it to be a disaster, but any attempt to bring in a new counsellor at this stage has a high failure risk. The fact you already know Buzz increases the chance this will work, but I have to be prepared for all eventualities."

We'd nearly finished eating breakfast, and I was wondering what Adika would think of Buzz, when I caught his annoyed thoughts nearby. For security reasons, Adika's apartment was directly opposite mine, and he'd just come out of his front door.

... unnecessary for Lucas to bring a stranger into our unit. If he needs to consult with someone, he could...

... not even answering my messages now. If Megan doesn't feel I'm worth five minutes of her time, then there's absolutely no reason for me to...

Adika strode down the corridor to the row of lifts. As he reached them, his dataview chimed with a message saying the visitor had been scanned to check her identity and ensure she was clean of weapons. She was now heading up in lift 3.

Adika tapped his foot impatiently as he waited outside lift 3. The lift doors finally opened, and I felt his startled reaction to the sight of the visitor. Adika had checked her identity record earlier, and had an image in his mind of an elegantly dressed young woman, with a professional expression on the face that was nearly as dark as her neatly ordered black hair. The girl facing him now was obviously the same person, but her hair was curling in wild disorder, and she was wearing a red top and skirt in one of the basic styles worn by girls on Teen Level.

Ungroomed and unprofessional to the point of being deliberately insulting. Lucas is really scraping the bottom of a slime vat consulting someone so...

... contrast with Megan's immaculate clothes and...

I burst out laughing.

"What is the joke?" asked Lucas's voice.

"My idea was totally wrong. Buzz isn't dressed to meet a telepath. She's dressed to meet me. She's wearing the same outfit as when I first met her."

I closed my eyes to concentrate on Adika's thoughts. He took a scanner from his pocket, waved it at Buzz, and spoke in tones of rigid disapproval. "Identity confirmed as Simone 2512-1004-106."

"That's right, but everyone calls me Buzz."

As Buzz spoke, I left the familiar territory of Adika's mind and reached out towards her instead. Her thoughts had a strange colour, taste, texture to them and were hard to read at first, but then they abruptly came into focus.

... has to be Amber's Strike team leader with that dominant stance and...

... man has the muscles of a structural pillar...

... body language screaming anger. What's been happening in this unit to...?

"Your official identity is Simone 2512-1004-106." Adika's voice was even harsher now. "Should you be required to visit here again, I suggest you wear more formal clothes."

The part of me that was Amber was worried by his rudeness, but Buzz's thought levels were rippling with amusement. "How would you react if I advised you on what weapons you should carry?"

... while he's working out what to say to that, and deciding it's safest to say nothing at all, I should drive home the attack. Best bewitching smile and hold out my right hand, pressuring him to shake it.

He's trying to ignore it, but getting uncomfortable. One second, two seconds, three seconds, and the man of granite is starting to feel foolish. I keep pushing him, and... Yes, I've got him! He reaches out to shake my hand and... I don't get an insight from him. Well, it was worth a try. Physical contact sometimes helps, but in this case...

"This way please." Adika turned to lead the way down a corridor, and...

** Insight **

Ah, the human structural pillar is suffering from sexual frustration not anger. If the man was just a little younger, I'd be tempted to help him with that problem. Imagine what it would be like to...

Buzz's thoughts blurred into graphic images that would have shocked me before I went through Lottery. Now my Alpha and Beta Strike teams were both composed of eighteen-year-old young men, so I'd seen stray fantasies covering most things that were physically possible, as well as several that weren't.

I wasn't bothered by the images in Buzz's mind, but I'd learnt what I needed to know, so I pulled out of her thoughts. When I opened my eyes, I was startled to find Lucas had moved his chair closer to me, and was staring intently at my face.

"You were reading Buzz then?" he asked.

"Yes. I don't think her borderline telepathy will worry me. I saw the moment when she had what she calls an insight. It wasn't really like reading thoughts. More like seeing a flicker of light in the corner of your eye, hearing a few bars of music, or…"

I stood up. "I have to change out of this hideously uncomfortable onesuit and go and see Buzz."

I dashed into the bedroom, yanked off the onesuit, dressed in a random set of my ordinary clothes, and sprinted for the apartment door. As I went out into the corridor, I heard the sound of Lucas's laughter from behind me.

CHAPTER EIGHT

When I entered the community room, I found Buzz sitting in one of several comfortable chairs, while Adika glowered at her from another. Adika stood up, and gave me a puzzled look.

"I thought our visitor was here to talk to Lucas."

"Slight change of plan," I said happily. "She's talking to me instead."

"I'd better stay until you've checked…"

"No, I've already done that. Everything is fine."

Adika seemed even more puzzled now, but he went out of the door and closed it behind him.

Buzz gave me one of the infectious grins I remembered from when I'd known her on Teen Level. "I'm afraid I've been teasing your Strike team leader, but I've a suspicion you were… watching that."

"Yes." I sat down in Adika's chair. "You look exactly the same as when I first met you."

"I did my best to look the same." Buzz studied me for a moment. "You look different. Not just a year or so older but more experienced. Of course you've been through a lot recently."

"Yes, I have." I rushed into asking the question that had been nagging at me. "When we first met at that medical facility, did you notice anything… unusual… about me? Did your insights tell you that I was a true telepath?"

"I noticed something when we first met," said Buzz, "but that first meeting wasn't in the medical facility. It was in a lift."

"What? When did we meet in a lift?"

Buzz gave me a wary look. "It was when you were on a wheeled stretcher being taken down in a lift to the medical facility. Do you remember a telepath squad came into the lift with you?"

"I could never forget that. The nosy arrested the paramedic who was..." I let the words trail off. "Are you saying that...?"

She nodded guiltily. "I was the nosy. When telepath squads are doing standard patrols of the Hive, an ordinary hasty with a talent for acting will dress up to play the part of the nosy, but on special occasions a borderline telepath does it. This was one of those special occasions. Sapphire's Tactical team had been investigating a case of a girl being harassed. Anonymous threatening calls. Notes being pushed under her apartment door."

Buzz shrugged. "Tracking the calls proved the girl's ex-boyfriend was behind it, so the Tactical team didn't bother Sapphire with the case, just referred it to me to be dealt with as a nosy publicity exercise. That's when a borderline telepath goes out dressed as a nosy, intercepts the suspect person, and pretends they were walking past by chance and saw something incriminating in their thoughts. Once the borderline telepath has used their insights to confirm the person's guilt, they get their hasty squad to arrest them."

With only five true telepaths in the Hive, there was always a huge queue of areas with warning signs that were waiting for a check run. I'd known that Tactical teams reduced the burden by referring straightforward cases to be dealt with by hasties or borderline telepaths, but not what happened after that. I muttered a single, stunned syllable. "Oh."

"Anyone could dress up as a nosy, and go through the pretence," continued Buzz, "but it's done by a borderline telepath as a safeguard that no mistake has been made. The idea is to help build up the myth that the nosies are telepaths, not destroy it by arresting the wrong person."

"I see."

"What happened back then was that I went into the lift with my hasty squad and went through the standard, scary routine with your paramedic. Heightened emotions in a subject probably make no difference to a true telepath, but they help a borderline telepath like me get a clear insight."

Buzz paused. "You aren't saying very much. I felt I should explain the truth about how we met right away. If it's going to be a problem, then we'd better discover that now rather than later."

"Before I went through Lottery, I believed the nosies were real," I said, speaking slowly because I was still working out my own feelings. "I was terrified of them. I hated the idea of them reading my mind. Being stuck in that lift with a nosy squad was traumatic. I was strapped to a stretcher, with an inhuman nosy looking down at me, snooping through my thoughts. Discovering that nosy was you... Well, it's a shock."

"When I was a child, I believed the nosies were real too," said Buzz. "For me, they were just creepy creatures that made me feel uncomfortable, but some of my friends had a deep-seated revulsion of them. If you think this is a terminal issue for you, then just say so."

"I don't know if it's a terminal issue or not. I've got two separate reactions going on in my head. Part of me is reliving the terror I felt back then. Another part of me is looking at it with the knowledge I have now. The truth is that you were only doing your job, arresting someone who was likely to be a danger to his ex-girlfriend, while promoting the myths that deter criminals and keep the Hive a safe place."

I shook my head. "Nosies are a very complicated problem for me. It's not just that I was terrified of them as a child, but the difficulties I have if I'm near a nosy squad now. People around them react with a range of powerful emotions. Anger. Horror. Guilt. Loathing."

"You mean that you feel all those massed emotions?" asked Buzz.

"Yes. I try to block them out, but it's hard to keep up my defences against the emotions of a whole crowd of people. Their mouths are screaming numbers. Their minds are screaming hate. It's like being trapped in one of my childhood nightmares."

I pulled a face. "The worst thing is that the crowd is aiming their hatred at the nosy, but I know it should really be aimed at me. A nosy is an ordinary person hiding behind a strangely shaped mask to make people think they're a fearsome telepath. Every time that I go out of my unit, I walk among people who don't know that I'm a telepath, and I feel like I'm hiding behind a mask too. In my case though, the mask is to make me look human."

Buzz frowned and looked as if she was about to say something. I wasn't sure that I wanted to hear it, so I hurried on. "I'll need to let my thoughts settle down before I know how I feel about this. Please carry on explaining what truly happened back then."

"If you're certain that's what you want?" Buzz gave me a doubtful look.

I nodded.

"I got a strong insight from the paramedic that established his guilt, so I arrested him, but I had the complicating factor of him being in charge of a patient. I'd never been in that situation before. My imprint includes basic medical knowledge as well as all the psychological information, but I wasn't qualified to take responsibility for a patient with a head injury. I decided we'd better all go along to your medical facility."

She paused. "Once I'd finished dealing with the paramedic, I was able to pay more attention to you, and became aware of something odd. Your body language was that of someone on the edge of complete panic, but I wasn't getting any insights from you. That was unusual. By the time we'd reached the medical facility, and I still hadn't had even a whisper of an insight from you, I had a theory about what was going on."

Curiosity was warring with my churning emotions about Buzz being the nosy who'd terrified me. Curiosity won. "You suspected I was a true telepath?"

"I never considered the possibility of you being a true telepath. They're so vanishingly rare. My theory was that you were a borderline telepath. Lottery finds nearly a thousand of us a year, so it seemed credible I'd stumbled across one."

"You thought that because you weren't getting an insight

from me? Does that mean borderline telepaths never get insights from each other?"

"We do get insights from each other, but much less frequently than we get them from ordinary people. I don't know why that is. Well, we delivered you to the medical facility, and then took your paramedic to a specialist unit for assessment. I was still curious about you though, and worried at the thought of a potential borderline telepath having a head injury. I gave in to temptation, called your medical facility, and said…"

I interrupted her. "Wait a minute. I remember you telling me you were helping out at the medical facility because their regular therapist was ill that day. I thought we met by random chance. That wasn't true?"

"It was random chance that I was the nosy who arrested your paramedic, but there was nothing random about me doing your psychological check. I shamelessly abused my position, calling the medical facility and insisting on checking your treatment and evaluating you myself."

Buzz hesitated. "I can't remember telling you that the regular therapist was ill. You must have asked me why I'd been working at that medical facility, and I made up an excuse. The truth is that he wasn't ill. In fact, he was extremely annoyed about me wading in and stealing one of his patients."

"Oh."

"So I changed out of the nosy outfit into more suitable clothes." Buzz laughed and gestured at her top and skirt. "These clothes. Then I went back to the medical facility and talked to you, but I got no insight at all. Actually, I still haven't had an insight from you. I'm beginning to wonder if it's impossible for borderline telepaths to get an insight into a true telepath's mind."

I blinked. "Don't you know whether it's possible or not?"

Buzz waved both hands. "It's supposed to be possible but very rare. I don't know if that's right or not. You're the only true telepath that I've ever met. I know plenty of other borderline telepaths who've met true telepaths when collecting a target for treatment. Some of them say they've had an insight, but…"

She waved her hands again. "They could be making that up

to show off, or they could genuinely believe they've had an insight when they haven't. It's easy to misinterpret your own feelings as an insight from someone else. Anyway, the lack of insights convinced me that I was right about you being a borderline telepath, but I realized that any well-meaning attempt to warn you could do far more harm than good. I'd have to wait, contact you again after you'd gone through Lottery, and ask if I could be any help with the major shock and adjustment phase."

"But you never did that. Why not?"

Buzz gave me a blank look of incomprehension. "For the obvious reason. We spoke in a call or two, and had another brief meeting, and then there was a wait of a year until you came out of Lottery. When I looked up your result, I saw you were listed as a Level 1 Researcher."

She sucked in her breath sharply, as if echoing her reaction back then. "I knew a person was only listed as a Level 1 Researcher for two reasons. Either you had an innate, genius-level talent for science, which I found hard to believe, or you were a true telepath. That was even harder to believe, but then I discovered rumours were flying round Law Enforcement about Lottery imprinting staff for a new Telepath Unit."

"I was a true telepath rather than a borderline telepath, but you could still have contacted me," I said.

"Really? Contacting another borderline telepath, offering the help of someone who'd been through exactly the same experience just two years earlier, would have been perfectly reasonable behaviour, but contacting a true telepath..."

She shook her head. "I knew there'd be a list of approved callers for you, such as members of your family. I wouldn't be on that list, so my call would be intercepted, and I'd have a suspicious Strike team leader questioning my reasons for calling you. They wouldn't be impressed by me saying I'd had a couple of encounters with you a year earlier. Even if I was allowed to speak to you, what help could I offer a true telepath?"

"I see the problem," I admitted.

"It's still a problem now, Amber. My experiences as a borderline telepath are nothing like yours. I see fleeting glimmers where you walk in the brightest of lights. I can only guess at how disturbing and stressful it is to read the minds of your targets."

She looked me in the eyes. "I'm an expert in taking the people you catch, assessing and treating them, but my imprint covers very little about how Telepath Units work. My understanding is that a Telepath Unit's Senior Administrator is imprinted with the appropriate knowledge to counsel the telepath. What help can I offer you that the accredited experts can't?"

"You just see fleeting glimmers where I walk in the brightest of lights, but you do see something. Everyone tells me that I need counselling, and they're probably right, but my counselling sessions with Megan were a disaster. The truth is that I don't want to discuss my inner feelings with an accredited expert. I want to talk to someone like me. True telepaths mustn't meet, so..."

"So a borderline telepath is the next best thing," said Buzz. "The question now is whether I'm the right choice of borderline telepath. I was the nosy who terrified you in that lift. Have you worked out how you feel about that yet?"

I answered her question with a question of my own. "What's it like wearing the nosy mask? What do you think when you look out of those inhuman purple eyes?"

"Do you want the absolute truth?" asked Buzz.

"Yes."

"Well, the nosy mask covers my whole head, and I'm wearing the grey outfit on top of my usual clothes. That means I'm usually thinking that I'm far too hot."

My laughter mingled with the sound of my dataview chiming. I took it out of my pocket, and read the message on the screen. "My Tactical Commander says there's been an important development in our current case. He's calling a team leader meeting to discuss it, so I'd better go."

I stood up. Buzz had once worn the mask of a nosy and frightened me. I could run away from her because of that, or I could start facing up to the whole tangled web of emotions that I had about nosies.

"I'd like to try to make this work," I said. "I'll let you know a suitable time for our first proper counselling session, but my schedule is a bit unpredictable."

"I appreciate you have unexpected calls on your time for things like emergency runs."

"Do you need me to show you the way back to the lifts?"

"I think I can find my own way along half the length of a corridor." Buzz waved her hands in a shooing gesture. "Go and save the Hive, Amber."

I laughed again, went out of the room, and hurried towards the operational section of the unit. I found Lucas standing just inside the security doors. He frowned at me.

"I messaged you to say we'd have a team leader meeting after you'd finished talking to Buzz, but I specifically said that you mustn't hurry your conversation."

"We'd finished talking," I said. "I want to carry on and have a proper counselling session with Buzz. Now what's the development in Fran's case?"

"The medical report has arrived. It says that Fran died twenty-two hours before we retrieved her body, and that changes everything."

CHAPTER NINE

As Lucas and I walked down the corridor, we saw Nicole speeding towards us in her powered chair. The three of us met by the door to meeting room 4. When we went inside, we found Adika and Megan were already sitting at opposite sides of the table, carefully avoiding looking at each other.

Nicole gave them a wary glance that showed she'd heard the rumours that were flying round our unit, and positioned her powered chair in the gap between them. Lucas and I sat down in the two remaining ordinary chairs, and Adika burst into angry speech.

"Lucas, would you like to explain what that luridly dressed girl was doing in our unit?"

Lucas smiled at him. "Of course. She was here for Amber to carry out the usual initial telepathic check on new unit members."

"She's joining our unit?" Adika scowled at Megan. "I wasn't informed that we had a recruitment in progress. What post is being filled?"

Megan flushed but faced him defiantly. "Mine."

Adika gave a stunned shake of his head. "I don't understand."

"The situation is quite simple," said Megan, in glacial tones. "I have resigned. The recruitment of my replacement is being kept strictly confidential to avoid creating uncertainty in the unit."

Adika turned to Lucas. "What's going on here?"

"Exactly what Megan just told you," said Lucas. "Buzz is being recruited to replace Megan."

Lucas had an oddly intent look on his face. I linked to his mind, and found him studying Adika's shocked reaction to his words.

… right that Megan hadn't told him about…

… since Strike team are selected to respond instantly to…

… Adika's controlling his face, but the muscles in his hands…

"To explain the situation more fully," Lucas added smoothly, "Buzz is a psychologist who will be replacing Megan as Amber's counsellor."

I pulled out of Lucas's mind, glanced round the table, and saw Nicole was looking anxiously at Megan. "I'm sorry to hear you're going," she said.

"I emphasize the need to keep Megan's departure confidential until we've completed recruiting replacement personnel," said Lucas. "For the time being, we should just say that Buzz has been recruited as a counsellor for Amber."

Everyone nodded.

"Now we need to move on to the real purpose of this meeting, which is our current case. Fran's body was found lying on the floor of the area 710/3470 storage complex on Level 68. However, the medical report states that Fran died twenty-two hours before we retrieved her body. Clearly people would have noticed the body if it was in that position during the previous day, so it must have been moved there after the storage complex closed for the night."

Adika had been frowning at Megan, but now he turned to face Lucas again. "Why would a murderer risk moving a body around? Even if it was disguised in some way, the murderer would be conspicuous carrying something that large, and terrified of running into a nosy patrol who would read his or her guilty thoughts. No one could expect to stop themselves thinking about a body when they were actually carrying it!"

"Presumably the body was moved because the original murder spot would have given away the identity of the killer," said Lucas. "It's unusual for a target to plan that logically and cold-bloodedly, but we're usually chasing them either before they first break out into violence or immediately afterwards. This target had twenty-two hours to calm down and plan how to dispose of the body."

He shrugged. "My Tactical team agree with you about the problems of moving a body using corridors, the passenger belt system, or the lifts. We believe the target used the freight transport system instead."

I felt my usual frustration at my lack of imprinted knowledge. "I remember the Hive freight transport system being mentioned in school lessons, but we weren't told any details about it."

Lucas tapped at his dataview, and a standard three-dimensional holo diagram of the Hive flashed into existence, hovering above the table. The hundred accommodation levels were highlighted in green, with the fifty working levels above them marked in blue.

"There are two networks of freight transport belts to move freight containers horizontally around the Hive," said Lucas. "One on Level Zero, the giant interlevel that divides the industrial levels of the Hive from the accommodation levels. The other on Level 100, right at the bottom of the Hive."

Grids of red lines appeared on the holo diagram. "Every level of the Hive has storage complexes at regular intervals," Lucas continued. "These are constructed at identical points on each level, so dedicated freight lifts can run up and down each column, moving freight vertically around the Hive."

The red lines were joined by a host of red columns. I saw a white flashing dot on one of them.

"The white dot marks the position where Fran's body was found," said Lucas. "As you can see, it could have been moved from any storage complex in the Hive by using the freight transport system. However, the simplest possibility is that it was just moved from one of the storage complexes either directly above or below the one where it was found. All the storage complexes in a column have matching working hours, so they'd all have been closed at night."

Adika leaned forward in his chair, examining the holo diagram. "That's believable. The target kills Fran in one of the storage complexes in that column. It's the middle of the night, so there's plenty of time to find a good hiding place for the body before people arrive for work. The target then returns late the next evening, puts the body in the lift, takes it up or down a random number of levels, and abandons it. No risk of anyone seeing anything suspicious. No danger of meeting a nosy patrol who'd spot a mind that was screaming guilt."

"Exactly," said Lucas. "This explains why we had no previous warning signs in that storage complex. Our target just picked it as a random place to dispose of the body. My Tactical team has been checking the corresponding areas on all the other levels of the Hive, looking for ones that do have warning signs. We have one major suspect area."

Lucas tapped at his dataview again, the holo diagram zoomed in on the red column that ran through the white flashing dot, and then a second flashing dot appeared higher up the column.

"The area 710/3470 storage complex on Level 31 has made a series of damage reports that are steadily increasing in severity. Petty vandalism doesn't necessarily progress to even the mildest violence, let alone murder, but in our current circumstances it's highly suspicious. This area was on the waiting list of areas to be checked by one of the other Telepath Units, but I've arranged for it to be handed to us."

I frowned. Two questions were bothering me. "So Fran was probably killed in the storage complex on Level 31 rather than Level 68, but I still don't understand what she was doing in a storage complex, especially one that was closed for the night."

"She may have gone there for a reason connected to the damage reports," said Lucas.

"Fran was very fussy about details," said Nicole, with a bitter edge to her voice. "If she suspected someone wasn't following her orders precisely, she'd go to tremendous lengths to prove it."

I moved on to my other question. "Why was a problem area in Yellow Zone owned by another Telepath Unit? Orange and Yellow Zones are our home zones, so it should have been ours.

Does that mean this area has been having problems since before our unit was active but no telepath has had time to check it?"

"There are areas that have been waiting far longer than that to be checked, but this isn't one of them," said Lucas. "In theory, Telepath Units automatically own the problem areas in their home zones. In reality, things are much more complicated."

He changed the holo diagram to show the coloured zones of the Hive running from Burgundy at the north end to Violet at the south. "Since our Hive is one zone wide by ten zones long, and we're currently working with only five Telepath Units, the units are each assigned two home zones."

"Are all the Telepath Units on Industry 1 like ours?" I asked.

"Yes. All the Telepath Units are in isolated areas right at the top of the Hive. That's more peaceful for the telepath and also minimizes the distance from priority areas."

"Priority areas?" I wrinkled my nose. "You mean the top accommodation levels that house the people most vital to the Hive?"

"No," said Lucas. "I mean the key systems located in the industrial levels. A target running wild sabotaging those could paralyze entire areas of the Hive, or even cause large scale injuries and deaths."

I'd never thought of that. "I see what you mean. When I was a seventeen-year-old living on Teen Level in Blue Zone, we had a power failure that lasted for two days. It was terrifying. Total darkness everywhere. Nothing working. People lost in corridors and trapped in lifts."

"Mira's Telepath Unit was handling that emergency run," said Lucas. "It was the classic example of what seems like a simple run turning into a nightmare. The target was heading through the vent system to a nest he'd made next to the Blue Zone power complex. The Strike team thought they had him cornered, but he'd left an inspection hatch open to give him an escape route into the power complex."

Lucas pulled a pained face. "The target wriggled through the inspection hatch, sprinted along a corridor to the power control centre, and killed himself jumping into the central core of the power supply nexus. The resultant power surge destroyed most of the nexus control systems, and took out the power to the whole of Blue Zone."

I was stunned. "I thought that was just an accidental power failure."

"Nobody could blame Mira for what happened," said Adika. "She's an excellent telepath, but anyone would have struggled to decipher complex thoughts about technical schematics and work out what the target was planning."

"Getting back to the subject of how areas are allocated, these are the positions of our current five Telepath Units." Lucas added five flashing dots to the diagram.

I leaned forward, eagerly matching the placement of the dots to the scraps of information I'd gathered on the other telepaths. "Keith has Burgundy and Red Zones, then I have Orange and Yellow, and Sapphire has Green and Turquoise. Is it Mira next or Morton?"

"I don't think it's a good idea to go into all this detail on other telepaths," said Megan. "It will encourage an unhealthy curiosity in Amber."

Lucas turned to face her. "From the beginning, you've insisted that we should protect Amber from stress by hiding certain basic information from her. I know you believe in that approach because it worked with Keith, but that was only because Keith can barely read the level of the mind below pre-vocalization. I've repeatedly argued that Amber is a far stronger telepath. It's impossible for us to hide information from her. We can only force her to spend time piecing it together from passing references she sees in our thoughts. A process that just creates extra strain and confusion."

"This is an area where the decision of the Senior Administrator overrides that of the Tactical Commander," said Megan. "I am still acting as Senior Administrator until you recruit someone to replace me."

"To be precise," said Lucas, "this is an area where the decision of Amber's counsellor overrides that of the Tactical Commander. Since we have already recruited a replacement counsellor for

Amber, and that counsellor has not yet stated her opinion on this point, I'm free to make my own decisions about providing Amber with information."

Megan gave a despairing wave of her hands and sat back in her chair. "If you insist on doing this, then I hope you're aware of the risks involved."

"I'm fully aware of them, and basing my decisions on the fact that the Hive knows best."

Adika had been watching the exchange with a frown, and now joined the conversation. "It's undeniable that the Hive knows best, but I don't see how you can claim the Hive agrees with you rather than Megan on this."

"I can claim it because the Hive has chosen to exclude some information, such as why telepaths should not meet, from the imprints of Telepath Unit staff. The Hive must have done that to avoid the danger of a telepath seeing potentially damaging knowledge in our minds. Don't you agree, Adika?"

"I suppose so," said Adika.

"Therefore you must also agree that any information covered by our imprints must have been approved by the Hive as safe knowledge for telepaths." Lucas didn't wait for Adika to think that through, but turned back to me and continued our earlier conversation. "Mira's home zones are Blue and Navy."

I glanced at Megan, worried by her attitude of depression, and found myself linking to her mind.

... hope that my replacement is more successful than me at counselling Amber. She could hardly be less successful, and perhaps that proves Lucas is right about...

... admit I've been distracted by my own issues, but my counselling approach should have worked. Amber's psychological profile results in Lottery showed that she was a perfectly obedient member of the Hive, with an ingrained trust of authority figures. When I pressured her to talk about problems, she should have given way, confided in me, and gratefully accepted my advice on...

... remember arguing with Lucas about that psychological profile. He said it was far too perfect, that a telepath could read

the correct response to questions in the minds of Lottery staff, and pointed out a couple of incidents on Teen Level where Amber exhibited anomalous behaviour. I still can't believe that her telepathic skills were advanced enough to...

... truth is that I learned more from Amber shouting at me than from any of our sessions together. She felt I was trying to control her, and she was right. I'd started by acting the maternal authority figure, but crossed the line into personal fantasy, trying to make Amber into the child that Dean and I...

Megan's mind abruptly filled with grief for the loss of her husband and the children they'd planned to have. I hastily pulled out of her mind, and tried to make sense of the reference to my psychological profile results in Lottery. I'd been desperate to do well in Lottery, and give the impression I was a dutiful member of the Hive. Had I somehow chosen test answers that misled Megan?

"Amber?" Lucas's voice interrupted my thoughts.

I realized that he'd said something and was expecting me to reply. "I'm sorry. I missed whatever you just said."

"I was explaining that Morton has Purple and Violet Zones."

I forgot about psychological profiles, and studied the sequence of dots that represented the five Telepath Units. "There's a big gap between Sapphire's unit and Mira's unit. Is that where Olivia's unit is?"

I heard gasps from all three of Megan, Adika, and Nicole at the mention of Olivia's name, but Lucas responded calmly. "Yes. Olivia's unit is not a fully operational Telepath Unit, but she still does simple check runs. Her Tactical team is included in the continuous data exchange between Telepath Units, and we naturally have to maintain the safe half a zone of horizontal separation between her and other telepaths."

Lucas paused. "I'll highlight the areas our unit owns in yellow."

All the colours vanished from the diagram, to be replaced by a scattering of yellow patches. I stared at them in bewilderment. It was true that most of the yellow was focused in Orange and Yellow Zones, but... "That's a bit of a mess."

Lucas laughed. "I know it looks that way, but allocating areas is a complicated process. Ideally, suspect areas are dealt with by relaxed check runs, so the travel time to reach them can be much less important than other factors."

He pointed at the diagram. "For example, you see we own some areas right down the far end of the Hive in Morton's home zones. Morton's Tactical Commander handed those areas to us because they're very difficult to access and move around, and you're our youngest and most physically fit telepath."

I nodded. "I see what you mean."

"For exactly the opposite reason," Lucas continued, "Morton's unit owns many easy access areas that are actually much closer to other Telepath Units. There are multiple other factors to take into consideration as well, like the KASIA issue."

Megan seemed lost in abject misery, and Adika was projecting grim disapproval, but Nicole laughed.

"What's KASIA?" I asked warily.

"It stands for Keith Already Said It's Alright," said Lucas. "If Keith checks an area once and finds nothing, he's reluctant to go there again. If his unit believes there really is a serious problem in an area, and Keith refuses to do a repeat check run, then it gets handed to another unit as a KASIA."

I was tempted to laugh, but then I wondered if the staff in other Telepath Units made jokes about me. Would they make fun of my chronic untidiness or something even more embarrassing?

"A lot of thought goes into deciding which unit owns which areas," said Lucas, "but emergency runs override those decisions. Lives are in danger, so speed is paramount. The alarm call is sent to the nearest available Telepath Unit. After the emergency run, that unit automatically takes ownership of the area in case there are any further related events."

He turned off his holo diagram, and leaned back in his chair. "So our unit now owns the area containing the suspect storage complex on Level 31. I assume you'll want us to do a check run there, Amber?"

"Yes. Can we check it now?"

"If that's what you want, then you can take the Alpha Strike team and head out in thirty minutes." Lucas turned to Adika. "Do you want to put Rothan in charge of this check run, or go out yourself?"

Adika's eyes flickered towards Megan before he replied. "Rothan is a good man, but still relatively inexperienced, and this isn't a standard check run. We're hunting a target who has already killed once and will be prepared to kill again, so I'll go myself."

CHAPTER TEN

Lucas and I headed back to our apartment. He sat in a chair watching me strip off my clothes and change into the slippery mesh of my body armour.

"I approve of you stopping the ridiculous attempts to hide things from me," I said, "but it may make it harder to persuade Megan to stay in the unit."

Lucas sighed. "My Tactical team are in favour of Megan leaving."

"They've found out about Megan resigning?"

"No, they're arguing the case for firing her. Possibly firing Adika as well."

I frowned. "What? Why?"

"Because the last run was incredibly stressful for you, and Adika and Megan's relationship problems added unnecessary extra pressure."

I stared at him. "You told your Tactical team what I said about Adika and Megan? That was private information!"

"I didn't tell them anything. When you and the Strike team arrived back, the crowd waiting at the lifts to meet you included my whole Tactical team. I took you straight to our apartment to let you recover in peace and quiet, so we missed seeing Adika and Megan having a spectacularly public second argument."

"Oh." I groaned. "That explains why Megan was in such a bad mood when you called her to ask about counselling for Nicole."

"Yes. It was obvious to everyone that Adika and Megan's

argument was a continuation of one that had happened just before the emergency run. My Tactical team members worked everything else out for themselves. When I walked into the Tactical office this morning, the whole lot of them started yelling at me."

I blinked. "Your team yelled at you?"

"When Adika barks orders at the Strike team, they obey him without question, but Tactical team members have to be free to criticize their Tactical Commander. There's no point in me having a Tactical team to help me if they aren't allowed to mention my failings and make suggestions for improvements."

Lucas pulled a face. "I told you I was frightened when I saw you at the end of that emergency run. My Tactical team members were frightened too. They could all see that you were showing classic fragmentation symptoms."

I didn't know what Lucas meant by the ominous word fragmentation, and I wasn't sure that I wanted to find out. I picked out some casual clothes to wear over my body armour.

"My Tactical team know exactly what losing you, going back to only four true telepaths, would mean for our Hive," said Lucas. "Not keeping up with check runs means more emergency runs. In turn, that means even less time for check runs and the number of emergency runs increases again. It's the death spiral that leads to bigger and bigger incidents until the Hive collapses in chaos."

He ran his fingers through his hair. "We were in that death spiral for several years before Lottery found you, getting desperately close to the disaster scenario where we couldn't hide the incidents any longer, and the nosies were revealed as fakes. In one ghastly year, we had that situation you mentioned where the power was taken out in the whole of Blue Zone, a vast fire in Burgundy Zone, and Keith was stabbed."

"Keith was stabbed," I repeated numbly. "I didn't know about that."

Lucas gave me a startled look. "I assumed you'd seen me thinking about Keith's stabbing, but didn't want to discuss it."

"No, I hadn't. I haven't seen it in anyone else's thoughts either."

"I'm the only one here who knows it happened. I was still

working in Keith's unit at the time. Megan had left barely two days earlier. Fortunately, Keith just suffered a minor arm injury, and was fully recovered in less than a week. He didn't want people told about it, because there was no possible way to describe the events without showing him in an extremely bad light, so the information was restricted to the Tactical Commanders of the other Telepath Units."

Lucas paused. "I remember having a conversation with you about how Strike team members were carefully selected to have the right personality for their work. I said that they would, if necessary, kill a target and carry on with their lives without brooding on it. They could be tortured by regrets if they felt they'd failed to protect an innocent bystander though, and they'd be utterly devastated if you were injured. I was definitely thinking of Keith's stabbing then."

I tugged a tunic over my head. "We had that conversation after my first emergency run. I was in total telepathic shutdown from shock, so I wasn't reading your mind."

"That's true. Perhaps I haven't thought about it since then because I've been fully occupied with our current problems."

I pulled on the rest of my clothes. It seemed more likely that Lucas had thought about the stabbing several times, but I'd missed seeing it. Lucas normally had at least a dozen levels of thoughts rushing by at once, and I had to struggle to keep up with the speed and complexity of even one of them.

"Anyway, we mustn't have a repeat of Adika having an emotional crisis during a run," continued Lucas, "so I'd like you to read his mind right now as a precaution. If he's reacting badly to Megan's resignation, then we need to delay this check run."

I nodded, and cautiously reached out to Adika's thoughts. I was expecting to be hit by wild emotions, but met only grim acceptance. Adika found uncertainty stressful, but could adapt to new situations at lightning speed. He'd been considering ending a relationship that had consisted of little but arguments and frustration, and now Megan had made the decision for him. She was leaving our unit, and it was unthinkable that he would leave to follow her. Adika had waited seventeen years to get a Strike team leader position. He was finally able to serve the Hive to his full potential and he wouldn't give that up for any relationship.

There was some regret mingled with the acceptance. Megan had exactly the type of polished beauty that attracted Adika, but he couldn't afford the distraction of a relationship outside the unit. He would have to find other outlets for...

I didn't want to find out what Adika meant by other outlets, so I pulled back into my own head. "Adika is perfectly calm and controlled."

"That's consistent with his response at the end of the meeting," said Lucas. "He's chosen to put his work ahead of his personal life."

I sighed, picked up my crystal unit from its shelf, and fitted it into my ear. "Yes, I suppose he has. I can't see my wristset light. Did I leave it in the pocket of the clothes I wore on the last run?"

"Probably," said Lucas, "but Hannah came in to clean the apartment while we were swimming yesterday. The clothes heap on the bedroom floor has gone, so I suspect your wristset light is being washed."

I groaned. "I've killed one wristset light by standing on it, lost another crawling through an air vent, and now I've got to confess to Adika that a third one has vanished in my laundry."

"I'm just relieved that you take better care of your gun."

"Oh yes, I nearly forgot my gun." I picked up the gun, attached it to my belt, and glanced in the mirror to check it was hidden by my clothes. "I'm ready."

Lucas and I hiked across the ludicrously large expanse of my apartment to reach the door to the corridor, and then headed for the lifts. The doors of the giant-sized lift 2 were open, and Adika and the Alpha Strike team were already inside.

"Now I think about it," I said, "it isn't surprising that my Strike team always get to the lift before me in emergencies. It's not just that they run faster than me. It takes me ages to get to my apartment door."

Lucas laughed and hugged me. "Be very careful during this run. If you find the strain becomes too much for you, or Adika's mind goes into turmoil again, then you should say that you've got another headache. I'll immediately order the Strike team back to our unit, and we can either decide to repeat the check run later or hand the case to another Telepath Unit."

"I'll do that."

Lucas hesitated before speaking again. "Amber, you may encounter the target's memories of killing Fran. Those could be deeply disturbing."

"I realize that, Lucas. I still feel I have to do this myself. If I catch Fran's killer I'll feel I've paid any debt that I owe and can move on."

"Accepted."

Lucas hugged me again, and sprinted off towards his office. I joined the Strike team in lift 2. "I'm afraid I've lost another wristset light."

Nobody said a word, but I could see several of the Strike team were struggling not to laugh. Both Adika and Rothan reached into their pockets, they each held out a spare wristset light, and I looked from one to the other indecisively.

"Take both," said Adika. "Then you'll have an extra one in case of… future problems."

The Alpha Strike team comedian, Eli, lost the battle for self control, and burst out laughing as I accepted both the wristset lights. The lift doors closed, and the lift started moving downwards at the relatively sedate standard express speed since this wasn't an emergency response.

"Alpha Strike team is moving," said Adika.

"Tactical ready," Lucas's voice gasped.

As I heard Lucas's voice, my mind instinctively linked to him. He'd just run into the Tactical office to join the rest of his team. His eyes were checking a bank of screens, scanning rapidly past a holo diagram of our destination location, a scrolling information feed from Liaison, a vast blank screen that would show a mosaic of images from our crystal unit cameras when they were turned on, and a tracking screen showing green dots of team members, currently all tightly wedged together in the lift. He finally sat down at the control bank labelled "Tactical Command."

"Liaison ready. Tracking status green," Nicole said.

I reluctantly broke my mental link to Lucas and checked my dataview. Clicking the circuit button told me we had the full Alpha team with us. I had five men, including Rothan, assigned as my bodyguards for this trip. Adika must be feeling nervous if he put his deputy team leader in charge of guarding me instead of using him on chase duties.

"We are green," I said.

"This isn't a standard check run." Lucas had got his breath back now. "We're looking for a target who has already killed, so the situation may escalate into extreme violence within seconds. The target will be alert for any signs of official activity. If he catches sight of a mob of heavily muscled men, he'll guess you're after him. At that point, he'll either turn and run, or attack in an attempt to kill as many of you as possible."

"If he attacks," Adika broke in, "everyone's first priority, whether they're on bodyguard duty or not, is Amber's safety. This target has already killed one member of our unit. He mustn't get anywhere near our telepath."

"You'll be arriving by lift to avoid any risk of being seen," Lucas continued his briefing. "You'll exit the lift directly opposite the side entrance of a community centre, go straight inside, and into the meeting room on your left. You will remain in that room, protecting Amber while she does her initial checks of the area."

His tone lightened a little. "Liaison has reserved the room for a meeting of a weight-lifting club. Amber doesn't look too convincing as a weight-lifter, but if anyone asks questions she can claim to be helping the club by acting as treasurer."

There was a pause before the lift slowed to a stop and the doors opened. We headed out to join an express belt. Adika was in the lead, with Rothan and my other bodyguards gathered around me, while those on chase duties divided to go ahead and behind. We were nowhere near our destination yet, but my Strike team were already tensely protective of me.

The other passengers on the express belt seemed to pick up something from my Strike team's body language, because they all kept a respectful distance from us. We finally jumped belt, entered another lift, and went up three levels.

"Approaching scene," said Adika.

The lift doors opened, and my Strike team moved out in full defensive formation. I was surrounded by men much larger than me, so I couldn't see much until we arrived in our reserved room.

"Amber, you should begin by checking the storage complex that's south of your current position," said Lucas. "We expect that our target either works there or regularly collects goods from there."

I hadn't seen the corridor signs outside the lift, so I'd lost my sense of direction. "Which way is south?"

Twenty men helpfully pointed to the south.

"Thank you." I glanced round what was a typical community centre room, with bland, functional furniture. I chose a cushioned chair, sat down, closed my eyes, and started my orientation routine.

Rothan was standing next to me, so I entered his mind first. He was studying the room walls. Most of them were just flimsy panels, but one was a structural wall. In the event of an attack, the safest place for Amber would be...

I moved past the minds of the other Strike team members, reaching southwards, and touched the thoughts of a teacher singing one of the Hive Duty songs to his class of five-year-olds. As he reached the chorus about the zones of the Hive, the children joined in, singing in enthusiastically loud but tuneless voices. "Burgundy, Red, Orange Zones. We are united. Yellow, Green..."

"Liaison, is the school between us and the storage complex?" I asked.

"Yes," said Nicole.

I tried not to sound too negative. "Having a school full of children between us and our target seems potentially dangerous."

"The school should be empty," said Nicole. "We told them they had to close to allow urgent electrical safety checks, and they said they'd take the children to the park for their remaining classes."

"Ah. Well, something has obviously gone wrong, because there's still at least one class of children in there."

"What? We're investigating that now." There was a long pause before Nicole spoke again. "Apparently one of the teachers misread the closure time in our message. We didn't send a team of hasties to make sure the school was empty, because we were told to avoid a visible hasty presence."

"You were correct to avoid sending in hasties, Nicole," Lucas's voice interrupted her anxious explanation. "The sight of them could have alarmed our target and triggered him or her into violent action. Is the teacher taking his class to the park now?"

"Yes."

I closed my eyes again, reached out to where over-excited children were forming up in pairs to head for the park, and drifted on further south. I'd no way of knowing exactly where the boundary lines of the storage complex were, so I dipped into the thoughts of a random person. A girl worrying about thirty-six missing jars of tomato puree.

I didn't linger in her mind to find out what she planned to do about the missing jars. Her mind was that of a loyal Hive worker doing her job, a tame bee, and I was searching in the right area.

I moved on, checking other minds. A man who'd just dropped something heavy on his foot and was thinking words that would startle even Adika. Three random workers driving trucks towing containers. Then I found what I was looking for. A mind that glowed bright with anger and frustration.

CHAPTER ELEVEN

I'd often encountered the anger and frustration of people going through an emotional crisis about their personal relationships. This time the reason for the anger was different and very, very wrong. I was seeing the mind of someone who hated their work.

I was startled because no one in the Hive should feel like that. Every year, all the eighteen-year-olds of the Hive went into Lottery, to be assessed, optimized, allocated, and imprinted. They were all terrified when they entered Lottery. I'd been one of them only months ago. Scared of the assessment tests that would discover all my strengths and weaknesses. Panicking about what work I'd be allocated, whether it would be high or low level. Petrified of having my mind imprinted with data.

Everyone was frightened going into Lottery, because they knew it would decide their Hive level, their profession, their entire future life, and there was no possible appeal against the judgements it made. Everyone was frightened going in, but most of them were very happy leaving. Not because imprinting turned them into dutiful robots, or because all of them came out as high level, but because of optimization. That was the process that matched the skills of each person against the Hive's need for workers, while considering an extra factor. Which work would give this person the most happiness and fulfilment?

The Hive's requirements took precedence of course, but with over a million eighteen-year-olds in Lottery there was plenty of flexibility available. Virtually everyone was given work that was ideal for them. It could be high level or low level, there would be an element of jubilation or disappointment to colour their feelings for a time, but they'd definitely love the work they'd been given. Everyone except the rare cases like me. There was no point in sending a true telepath through optimization. Whether we loved it, or hated it, the Hive would only give us one task to do.

But I was the exception. For most people, optimization worked. I hadn't believed that at first, but I'd read enough minds in the Hive that I had to accept it now. I was familiar with the feel of the minds of the tame bees, contentedly labouring for the Hive, basking in the happiness their work gave them. Optimization was beneficial for both the people and the Hive, because contented workers were far more productive, but I still occasionally had nagging concerns about whether it would be better to have the right to choose your own future.

There was also the dark unknown issue of what happened in other Hives. There were currently one hundred and seven Hive cities in the world, each totally independent, their actions only limited by the rules of Joint Hive Treaty that stopped Hives from harming each other. I had no idea what life was like in any of the other Hives. The occasional malcontent spread rumours that there were Hives where life was far better, with riches and freedom for all, but they knew no more than I did. It could equally well be true that people had a far worse time in other Hives, living in harsh conditions, and compelled to do work they hated.

But here in our Hive, we had optimization, and it worked. So why was I looking at a mind where happiness and contentment had been replaced with anger and frustration? It made no sense. This was a man working in a storage complex. He couldn't have been forced into his role because the Hive was desperate for his rare and precious skills. What had gone wrong here? I searched the top levels of his mind for answers.

Waste him! A supervisor's badge on his overalls and he thinks he runs the Hive. Want to hold him head down over a lift shaft. Want to drop him down the lift shaft! We're on Level 31, so 68 or 69 levels for him to fall. Lots of time to enjoy hearing the screams before he dies.

The supervisor's pompous, smug voice was talking to me. Talking down to me like I'm something out of a slime vat. Why can't he leave me alone?

"You're forty minutes late, Ashton. Again!"

"So? Once I'm here, I do twice the work of anyone else, don't I?"

"I'll have to give you an official warning if you keep this up. I've no choice."

No choice. No choice. Yap, yap, yap. It used to be so good when I worked on Level 89, but I hate it here. Getting ordered around by this smug, self-important supervisor. Delivering goods to self-satisfied people living in fancy apartments. Hating coming here every morning. Counting the minutes until I can go home to Level 82 where nobody sneers at me.

I picked up the container, didn't bother using a truck, just hefted it effortlessly onto my shoulder and walked away. Once I reached the right storage rack, I put the container in place and looked round. Nobody there. I went to the shelves at the end of the room and chose a box with the warning signs for both fragile contents and hazardous chemicals.

I picked up the box and shook it hard. There was the sound of breaking glass. I put the box down, watched the black liquid oozing from the bottom of it, and walked away laughing.

Another hazard cleanup to organize, great supervisor. More accident reports for you to submit. Been having a lot of them lately, haven't you? They'll be asking questions. Giving you official warnings. Can't blame me, nothing to do with me, never allowed to touch fragile boxes.

I headed out of the door and stopped laughing because it wasn't enough.

Don't want to smash things. Want to smash him. Dropping him down a lift shaft isn't personal enough. Maybe just pick him up and drop him on his head. Over and over again. Hear him begging. See how many times it takes to...

Dutiful Supervisory Storage Administrator always the last to leave. I play scared of getting warned, and stay late to catch up the time I missed. Just the two of us alone here.

Tonight?

I'd been swept up by Ashton's burning resentment, but now the gruesome fantasy in his head reminded me that I wasn't Ashton but Amber, and I had a job to do. "Target located," I said. "He's in the storage complex now. Moving containers from the lift area into room 23. His name is Ashton. He's a very big man. He used to love his job when he worked on Level 89. He's still proud of being the strongest man in this storage complex, but hates working on Level 31. Ashton thinks the supervisor here is deliberately sneering at him and trying to make his life miserable."

I paused. "Maybe that's true, maybe it isn't, but Ashton hates being at work. This has been going on for months and he's at breaking point. He's just been smashing bottles of hazardous chemicals. He's thinking about killing the supervisor tonight."

"We don't want to trigger the target into violence when he's near other people," said Lucas. "We have to isolate him first."

"It's hard to evacuate the storage complex without evacuating the target as well," said Nicole.

"We don't move the other people," said Lucas. "We move the target. You say he's the strongest man working there, Amber?"

"Yes. At least, he thinks he is."

"Nicole, send a request to that storage complex," said Lucas. "You need a man to collect a container from an awkward place that no trucks could access. It's heavy, so they'll need to send their strongest man. Tell them the location is…"

Lucas hesitated for a moment before rattling off a string of numbers. "The quickest route to that location is through a section of housing warren currently closed for refurbishment. Adika should place men there to pick up Ashton as he goes through."

Adika gave a rapid series of instructions. The Strike team members were dividing into two groups now. Chase team were moving out, while my five bodyguards stayed with me. I was vaguely aware of my body being moved to sit on the floor and lean against something hard. That would be Rothan placing me in his carefully chosen defensive position. I didn't let it distract my mind from my target. He was shifting containers, carrying them himself whenever possible rather than using machinery to help him.

Waste that supervisor! What's he come to nag me about this time?

"Ashton, we need you to collect a container. Access is difficult. You'll need to lift it out by hand."

... mouth stretching wide in a grin. Need me now, don't you?

"Target has been asked to get the container," I said. "He's heading out of the storage complex now. Outside the doors, and walking past a corridor direction sign. He's taking the long way round to avoid the shopping area. Hates seeing the Level 31 people cooing over the fancy clothes on display."

"He's going the long way round to avoid the shopping centre," repeated Lucas sharply. "That will take him right past your community centre."

"Bodyguard!" Rothan's voice cut in with the single word order.

I felt the intimate warmth of bodies pressing against me on all sides. My bodyguards had drawn their guns and formed a human wall around me. Our target would have to kill them to reach me.

"The target doesn't know we're here," I said hastily. "He believes he's been given a genuine request to collect a container."

My bodyguards didn't move or relax. The worst nightmare of the Strike team was happening, a target getting dangerously close to their irreplaceable telepath.

I was nervous myself. I could see all the thoughts in my target's mind. I knew he had no idea I was reading him, had no idea I was here, had no idea I even existed, but he was still moving steadily closer to me. I realized he was going to walk right past the outside wall of the community centre, and I was leaning against that wall!

"Amber, keep talking to me," said Lucas. "What's the target thinking? Tell us if there's the slightest hint of a threat to you."

"There's no problem," I said. "The target doesn't suspect anything. He's thinking about which way he'll go when he's past the community centre. Trying to decide the shortest route."

I concentrated on keeping talking, babbling the trivial thoughts of the target mind as he moved closer with every step. He was only the length of a corridor away, the length of a room away, the length of a table. I'd never had a target anywhere near this close to me. Rothan had put me here so I would have my back to a solid, structural wall, but there were no walls in the telepathic view of the world. My target seemed as if he could just reach out a hand and touch me.

And then Ashton was moving further away with every step, and I could breathe again. My bodyguards were still pressed tight against me. Lottery had made some errors when it decided my physical appearance preferences for a partner, but my Strike team were attractive men by any standards, and I had to admit that was making this moment just a fraction easier. Ugly bodyguards, or the awkwardness of being pressed intimately against another woman, might be a welcome distraction from the tension, but…

"Target has reached the next junction and is heading west now," I said.

"That puts him well clear of you." The sigh as Lucas let out his breath was audible over my ear crystal.

"Stand down," said Rothan.

The warmth surrounding me vanished as my bodyguards all took a step away to give me space again. I felt a familiar surge of emotion for my Strike team, not just for the five protecting me now, but for all of them. They were my friends, they were my brothers, and I loved them. They'd save me at any cost, and they'd never take advantage of moments like this. I could trust them. Totally.

"Target is at another junction," I said, in a shaky voice. "Continuing west."

"He should turn south at the next junction," said Lucas. "That will bring him into the closed area of the housing warren."

"Chase team, set your ear crystals to visual now." Adika's voice had an odd edge to it.

"Visual links green for all Chase team," said Nicole. "Zak, can you adjust your camera extension position, please? We're mostly seeing your hair."

A brief pause, then Zak's voice. "Is that better?"

"That's good," said Nicole.

"Target is at the next junction now," I said. "Turning south as expected."

"Kaden's group stay hidden while the target goes past you," said Adika. "When you see my group intercept him, you move out and block his retreat."

"Acknowledged," said Kaden.

"Target in view now," said Adika. "My group should wait for my command. Wait. Wait. Wait. Strike time now!"

I dumped my link to the target mind, opened my eyes, grabbed for my dataview, and stabbed the circuit button. The list of Chase team members was on the right. I chanted the name at the top of the list as I linked to his mind, checked his status, tapped the name to send it back to the bottom of the list, and moved on to the next.

"Adika." I entered a mind screaming expletives. Adika had forced himself to hold his tongue as the target walked past his telepath, knowing he was much too far away, the whole Chase team were much too far away, to help. He'd had to trust Rothan to handle things, while suffering horrific visions of losing his telepath. No point in going back to the unit after that, because the unit would cease to exist without its telepath. In old traditions, warriors fell on their swords, but these days…

I dragged myself away from Adika's emotions and moved on to the next mind.

"Kaden." I was staring at the target's back in shock. Waste it, the man was huge.

"Zak." I was watching Adika move forward and speak to the target. Hearing his voice through my ear crystal and with Zak's ears as well. "Ashton, you need to come with us. There've been…"

"Tobias." The target was turning, running away from Adika, and I was sprinting after him.

"Matias." I was stepping out, blocking the target's path, firing my gun on stun, and being tossed aside like a doll. Automatically rolling on landing, going onto my hands and knees, then up again to…

"Eli." I was throwing myself on…

"Rafael." I was lying on the ground, with the target's hands round my neck. I tried grabbing at his arms but they were like iron bars. I couldn't breathe. Everything was going black and…

"Help Rafael!" I yelled. "He's getting strangled."

The pressure on my neck, no, it was on Rafael's neck, was suddenly gone. I was gasping for breath, sitting up, and looking into the anxious eyes of Zak. I gave him a reassuring smile. "I'll live."

I felt the warmth of his hand as he ruffled my hair. "You'd better."

"Dhiren." I moved minds again, and found myself staring at a heaving mass of bodies on the ground. I wanted to help restrain the target, but he was buried under my own team mates.

"Target secure," said Adika's breathless voice. "Secured with a bit of difficulty I might add. We must have shot him on stun a dozen times before it had any effect."

"Body mass is a factor in how long it takes for stun to take effect," said Lucas. "If you shot him a dozen times, you'd better check he's still breathing."

"His pulse and breathing are fine," said Adika. "We've got restraints on him now. Two sets to be on the safe side."

"Sending in hasties and medical support," said Nicole. "We've lost visual links from half the Chase team. We assume that's just cameras getting damaged in the fight."

I stopped chanting names aloud, but did another full circuit of the Chase team to check for injuries. "Rafael seems fine now, but Matias may have a dislocated shoulder, and Kaden got a nasty bump on the head."

"Rafael, Matias, Kaden, and anyone else with injuries should report to our unit medical area for checks as soon as we get back," said Adika. "What were you all playing at anyway? Fourteen of you against one man and you were still losing!"

The only response was an embarrassed cough that I thought was from Kaden.

"Everyone does extra unarmed combat training for the next few weeks," said Adika grimly.

"I think the target's coming round now," said Eli. "Yes, his eyes are opening."

"Already?" Adika's voice was pitched high with disbelief. "The man's incredible. Why didn't Lottery allocate him to a Strike team?"

"He may have been ideal for it physically, but his behaviour shows he's mentally unsuited to a role in Law Enforcement," said Lucas. "Adika, can you please show Ashton a holo of Fran? Make sure you're looking at his face when you do it, because I want your visual link to give me a clear view of his reaction."

"What?" asked Adika. "Why?"

"We have to confirm the target's guilt before we can close Fran's case as complete with target apprehended," said Lucas. "The normal way of confirming guilt would be to question him while Amber checks his mind, but I don't want Amber seeing his memories of murdering Fran."

"All right," said Adika.

I bit my lip, hesitated, and then set my dataview to show the team member location display. A simple tap on Adika's name showed me the view from his visual link. I didn't usually bother looking at the view from someone's camera, just dipped into their head to see the view through their eyes, but this time I didn't want to have to cope with any thoughts that weren't my own.

Ashton gave a dazed look at the restraints on his wrists, and then stared straight up at Adika's camera, at Adika's face.

"Do you remember this woman?" asked Adika.

Ashton glanced at the holo of Fran. "Never seen her before."

"Are you sure?" asked Adika.

Despite the fact he was lying down, with two sets of restraints on both wrists and ankles, Ashton somehow managed to shrug his shoulders. "What's she got to do with anything?"

Lucas groaned. "I'm afraid Ashton's body language suggests he genuinely doesn't recognize Fran."

"Does that mean we have to get Amber to read his mind now?" asked Adika.

"Read my mind?" Ashton's eyes widened in alarm as he heard Adika's words. "You've got a nosy hiding round here?

Look, I may have broken a few things. A box slipped out of my hands. Accidents happen."

"Yes, Amber can read Ashton's mind now," said Lucas. "Amber, you should be ready to pull out instantly if I'm wrong and Ashton did kill Fran."

I closed my eyes, checked Ashton's mind, and saw his horror that a nosy was reading his thoughts. The freak would be seeing all the things he'd done, the fragile consignments he'd broken, the paint he'd...

"He's responsible for all the vandalism," I said. "He's been thinking of hurting people too, but so far it's just been fantasy. He only fought the Strike team because he was panicking about being arrested."

"Can you do a deeper check?" asked Lucas. "Make sure this isn't an issue of memories being blocked by a mind in fugue or divided into multiple personalities?"

I worked my way down the frantic thought levels until I was deep into the subconscious. "He's never seen Fran before," I repeated.

There was a delay while Ashton was handed over to the medical staff, and then Adika gave a deep sigh. "So Ashton isn't our murderer. We've got the wrong target again."

"Not exactly the wrong target," said Lucas. "If we hadn't caught Ashton, he'd probably have lost control and attacked his supervisor within the next few days or weeks. Now he can have counselling, medication, and be assigned to new work at a storage complex lower down the Hive. Perhaps somewhere around Level 90. Working lower in the Hive than his own level will make him feel superior, bolstering his self respect instead of undermining it. He'll soon be a happy, productive member of the Hive again."

"Which is all very nice and very worthy," said Adika, "but we still have to find out who killed Fran. What do we do next, Lucas?"

"I've no idea," said Lucas. "Once you're safely back at our unit, I'm going to have a brainstorming session with my Tactical team. We need to rethink every assumption we've made so far, because one of them must have been dreadfully wrong."

CHAPTER TWELVE

Lucas and I went through the security doors into the operational section of our unit.

"Are you sure you want to come along for this?" asked Lucas. "A brainstorming session can take hours, sometimes even days, and I could sum up all the useful ideas for you afterwards in as little as five minutes."

"I'm sure," I said. "I've seen you thinking about brainstorming, and I'm curious about exactly how it works."

Lucas shrugged. "Well, you can always sneak out if you get bored or bewildered. I warn you that things may get strange. The whole point of brainstorming is to break out of the rigid, straight-line, logical thinking we usually follow. Straight-line logic works well 95 per cent of the time, but when it fails we have to challenge our ideas, question our assumptions, chase random trains of thought, and consider possibilities we would usually dismiss as ridiculous. Just about everything we say in this session will be useless, but it could throw up something interesting."

We went through a door into the vast expanse of the Tactical office. The Liaison area had individual offices for each team member, as well as an operations room where they gathered during emergency and check runs. The Tactical team preferred to work together, constantly sharing information, ideas, and progress, so they just had this one massive room. One end of it was formally laid out with desks, while the other was the brainstorming area.

Lucas clapped his hands. The other eleven members of the Tactical team looked up from their desks.

"Brainstorming time," said Lucas. "Amber is joining us for this one."

Everyone stood up. I'd checked the minds of all Lucas's Tactical team members before they were confirmed in their positions in the unit, but the only one I really knew was Emili. She was both Lucas's deputy and Rothan's girlfriend.

Seeing the Tactical team together like this, I was struck by how wildly different they all were. With the exception of Adika, all of my Strike team had come out of the last Lottery with me. Since they were uniformly young and male, Lottery had balanced the sexes in my unit by choosing my Liaison team, Admin team, and medical staff to be mostly young and female.

In contrast, the Tactical team were as random a group as possible, including men and women, every type of physical build, and aged from nineteen-year-old Emili to seventy-year-old Gideon, with his thin white hair and face etched with worry lines.

I'd seen from Lucas's thoughts that this didn't happen by chance. A Tactical team was deliberately chosen to be a varied group to contribute different viewpoints.

"Are we taking any particular angle?" asked Emili.

"We're going wild hunt on this one," said Lucas. "Look at things sideways, upside down, with no limits."

There was a general nodding of heads. They all moved down to the brainstorming area of the office, with its selection of comfortable chairs and couches. I watched in confusion as they arranged themselves, most of them choosing to lie on the couches or thick rugs, but a couple somehow managing to sit upside down in the chairs.

Lucas saw my expression and grinned at me. "We need to look at the situation with a different mental angle. Being at a different physical angle can help that process."

He stretched out on a couch. I hesitated before taking the safe option of curling up in a large chair next to him. I stared wistfully at where Emili was doing a handstand against the wall. I liked the girl. I thought we might have been friends in other circumstances, but being the priceless telepath, combined with the fact that Rothan's job could lead to him dying in my defence, made it difficult to even have a casual conversation with her.

"Everyone, close your eyes and relax," said Lucas. "Amber, it's best if you don't read minds during this. It's not just that there'll be some disturbing images floating around, but seeing what others are thinking would influence your own unconscious thought processes. We don't want your contributions echoing those of anyone else and biasing the flow in one direction."

"My contributions?" I'd obediently closed my eyes, but now I opened them. "You want me to join in with this? But I don't know how it works."

"The more random factors the better," said Lucas. "Listen for a while and join in when you've got the idea."

He paused for a moment. "Go!"

People started speaking, and I closed my eyes again. With my telepathy shut down, I'd no idea who was talking most of the time.

"What do we know?"

"We have Fran's body."

"Do we?"

"The Strike team recognized the body as Fran."

"It looked like Fran on the visual links."

Lucas's voice. "There are ways of faking appearance."

"Maybe it's a fake body."

A fake body? Lucas had warned me this might get strange, but... I shook my head and concentrated on listening to the voices.

"The medical report confirmed it was Fran's body after tissue analysis."

"The pathologist could have lied." That sounded like Emili.

"We can get Amber to check that." Lucas's voice again. "Establish base point. We have Fran's body. Go!"

"We have a time of death."

"Can we believe the time of death? The pathologist..." The voice broke off its sentence. "Sorry, I'm looping. Time of death accepted pending verifying medical report."

"Time of death indicates the murderer moved the body."

"Time of death indicates *someone* moved the body."

"Do we have more than one target?"

"Was the body moved at all?"

"The body must have been moved or the staff of the Level 68 storage complex would have seen it."

"They could have seen it and been too scared to contact Emergency Services."

"Why would innocent people be scared? They'd expect a nosy to check their minds. Know they wouldn't be blamed."

"We could have a large number of targets. Entire staff of storage complex guilty. All took part in murder."

I frowned. Some of these comments seemed totally ridiculous.

"Random staff of other storage complexes arriving with deliveries," said Lucas. "They'd step out of the lift and tread on the body."

"Entire staff of all storage complexes in Hive took part in murder." That was Emili.

Lucas laughed. "Temporarily establish base point. Body was moved."

There was a one second pause and they were off again.

"Where did Fran die?"

"Logically it should have been in one of that column of storage complexes."

I was startled by a massed shout. "Forget logic!"

"Body left in storage complex. Person leaving body had some knowledge of storage complexes. Establish base point?"

"Grudgingly and temporarily establish base point," said Lucas. "We're getting ominously close to where logic took us."

"Body was moved. How?"

"Not passenger transport system. Too many witnesses. Too many nosy squads."

Lucas groaned. "And we're back to the freight transport system. Heading down the same blind alley that we hit using logic."

"How body was moved doesn't matter. Original location does. Where?"

"Freight system covers whole Hive."

"Risk of transporting body increases with distance travelled."

"Less risk of passing nosy squad on freight transport system. Less fear of having mind read when with body."

Either I was getting used to the system of random voices making equally random contributions, or what they were saying was making more sense now. I considered joining in, but kept hesitating so someone else spoke first.

"Why risk being with body at all? Ship in container."

"Establish base point," snapped Lucas. "Body shipped in container to storage complex."

"Container arrives at storage complex. Then what?"

"Label checked. Taken to appropriate storage area."

"Someone comes at night. Gets body from container and leaves it in front of lifts."

"They left the body where it was bound to be found," said Emili. "Why? It could have been left in the container and undiscovered for weeks, or even months."

"Would be discovered eventually. Unaccompanied container must be labelled with routing information. Possibly gives starting point as well as destination. Starting point was the true murder scene. Identifying it could lead us to the murderer."

"Hold while I check the facts on routing information," said Lucas. A moment later, he spoke again. "Each freight container has a code etched into it. The central freight system has records of every journey a container makes, with routing information that includes the starting point."

"That's why the murderer didn't leave the body in the container," said Emili. "The routing information could help us find him or her. So where's the container now?"

"The murderer wouldn't leave it in the Level 68 storage complex. There would surely be bloodstains inside the container. Those could attract attention, so the murderer would send it off again on the freight system."

"We could track down all containers sent from the level 68 storage complex."

I finally spoke myself. "It wasn't sent from the level 68

storage complex. The murderer took the container up in the freight lift to the storage complex on Level 31, filled it with thirty-six jars of tomato puree, probably smashed some of the jars so the puree would cover any bloodstains, and sent it off to a new destination."

There was a stunned silence. I opened my eyes. Everyone else had their eyes open now too, and they were all staring at me.

I hurriedly explained. "When I was checking minds in the Level 31 storage complex, I saw someone worrying about thirty-six jars of tomato puree that had gone missing. I wasn't interested at the time, but now..."

Emili frowned. "Ashton could have been responsible for the missing jars."

"I read Ashton's mind when he was panicking about a nosy being nearby," I said. "He was trying not to think about his crimes, which actually made him think of them all in detail. He chose expensive or hazardous things to smash, and he never stole anything."

Lucas nodded. "So the murderer went to the effort of taking the container to the Level 31 storage complex, and filling it with tomato puree to cover up the bloodstains, before sending it off to a random destination."

"The murderer might not have sent it off from the Level 31 facility," said Emili. "If I wanted to minimize the chance of it ever being found, then I'd take it to a third storage complex and send it off from there."

"That's true." Lucas sighed. "Tracking down every container sent from all the storage complexes in that column, and checking them for signs of blood, is close to impossible. There's a storage complex on each of the accommodation and industry levels, they'll each be shipping out hundreds of containers a day, and some of those containers will already have been sent on to second or third destinations by now."

A distinctive, lazy male voice spoke from behind me. "I know I'm dragging straight-line logic into this, but you're building up a very inconsistent murderer profile here. Someone has a mental break leading to uncontrollable violent tendencies. Escalation is so sudden it skips the stage of injuring anyone and goes directly to murder. That's immediately followed by recovery to a state where our murderer can create and successfully carry out a complex plan, dumping the body and disposing of the container used to transport it."

"Two targets then," said Lucas. "One had a mental break and killed Fran. The other was perfectly stable and disposed of her body. Why would the stable second target risk covering up someone else's murder?"

"To protect someone they loved," said Gideon.

"The complex plan to dump the body indicates a logical, intelligent mind," said the lazy male voice. "However much that sort of person loved someone, they'd surely realize that the violence wouldn't stop with one random killing, and they couldn't hope to keep covering up a whole series of deaths."

"It wasn't a random killing." That was Emili's breathless voice. I saw her topple gently down from her handstand and stretch out on the rug.

There was silence for a couple of seconds before Lucas spoke. "Follow theory."

I closed my eyes again and listened to voices babbling.

"No mental break. A perfectly stable, logical murderer."

"Consistent with carefully planned disposal of body."

"Stable people don't commit murder because they're scared of the consequences if they get caught. The Hive has nosy squads patrolling everywhere. People believe their guilty thoughts will be read. That's a huge deterrent against committing any crime, but especially murder."

"If you believe the nosies are real."

At least three people spoke at once. "One of us!"

"Everyone in Law Enforcement knows that the nosies are a myth and the Hive only has five true telepaths," said Lucas. "Just about everyone Fran had contact with was in Law Enforcement."

"Lottery selects Law Enforcement staff to have a strong moral code and loyalty to the Hive," said the lazy male voice that I still couldn't identify. "Even ones like Strike team members, selected to be risk takers with a capability for violence, are also chosen to be fundamentally moral. Why would someone with a strong moral code kill Fran?"

"People can be affected by events after Lottery and change their attitudes," said Emili. "Lottery selects Telepath Unit staff to be tolerant of having their minds read, but Fran developed a hatred of telepaths."

"So our theory is the murderer dumped the body in that storage complex to make this look like a random killing by someone suffering a mental break," said Lucas. "Actually, the murder was committed by someone with links to Fran and a very good reason for killing her. The murderer may not have been troubled by moral issues, or possibly felt their reason was morally justifiable."

He paused. "Did our murderer take the goods from that Level 31 storage complex by chance, or was it deliberately chosen because it was already flagged for high levels of vandalism?"

"A deliberate choice would be consistent with a highly meticulous murderer," said Emili. "It would also imply the murderer had access to Law Enforcement systems."

"Our theory is that someone in Law Enforcement killed Fran," said Lucas. "One of us. Query. Literally one of us? Someone in this unit?"

I gasped, but the Tactical team eagerly pounced on the idea.

"Fran was unpopular."

"Unpopular enough for someone to kill her?" asked Lucas.

"Most of the Liaison team members hated her," said Emili, "but why would they kill her months after she'd left our unit?"

"Maybe there's a bigger motive than personal feelings," said Gideon. "Fran verbally attacked our telepath. Might have physically attacked her as well if Adika hadn't restrained her."

I bit my lip. The comment reminded me of Fran screaming abuse at me, and also what Lucas had said about Keith being stabbed. Keith had insisted on that being kept secret because the events showed him in an extremely bad light. I'd heard that Keith enjoyed teasing his people about their secrets. Had Keith taken his teasing too far, so one of his own unit members had lashed out and stabbed him?

"The harmful effect on Amber was clearly visible," said Emili.

It was? Waste it! I'd tried my best to keep my feelings hidden back then, but my Tactical team were all imprinted with information on behavioural analysis and body language. They were bound to see I was deeply distressed.

"And that was closely followed by our first operational run," added Gideon grimly. "One of the established critical points for a telepath. Amber struggled to cope with the combined stress. If she hadn't…"

I wished I'd been in Gideon's mind when he said that. What did he mean about the established critical points for a telepath? I knew that York had broken under the strain of being a telepath after a few months and killed himself. I had the impression that had happened after his first operational run. What were the other critical points? Olivia had lasted longer than York before breaking, but I didn't know exactly how long or what had proved too much for her. I could ask Lucas later if I really wanted to know the details. I wasn't sure that I did.

The Tactical team were still happily chasing their latest theory. "A threat to our telepath is a threat to the existence of our unit," said Emili. "Telepath Unit postings are the highest status positions in Law Enforcement. Someone could have killed Fran out of revenge for endangering both our telepath and their career."

"They could have been trying to defend the Hive itself," said Gideon. "After several years with only four Telepath Units, the Hive was growing increasingly unstable, heading towards a complete breakdown of social order. Harming Amber would have sent the Hive back into that death spiral, so the murderer could regard killing Fran as a noble and morally justifiable act in defence of the Hive."

"Other teams in our unit would be less aware of the Hive stability issue than we are," said Emili cheerfully. "That makes us the main suspects. Would we kill someone if we believed they threatened the survival of our Hive?"

"Yes," they chanted in unison.

"The chief suspect has to be Lucas," said Emili. "He's not just our Tactical Commander, but in love with Amber too. Fran threatened to destroy his career, his unit, his Hive, and the first successful relationship in his life. With all that at stake, of course he'd kill her."

I was shocked into opening my eyes again and looking at Lucas. He appeared to be deeply amused.

"You've almost convinced me with that argument," he said. "Are you suggesting that I committed the murder totally rationally, or while suffering an episode of dissociative fugue so I'm not even aware of my own guilt?"

"It wasn't Lucas," said the lazy male voice.

I twisted round in my chair, curious to see who owned that voice, and saw a man of about fifty was speaking. His dark face had distinctive high cheekbones, and his name was... was something beginning with K.

"Kareem's right," said someone else. "Amber would know if it was Lucas even if he was in dissociative fugue when he actually committed the murder."

Yes, the man's name was Kareem. I'd thought it began with a K.

"Perhaps Amber does know it was Lucas and is protecting him," said Emili. "Perhaps that's why she's insisting on our unit investigating Fran's murder. Perhaps that's why she came to our brainstorming session, so she could intervene if we worked out Lucas was guilty."

I decided the entire Tactical team were lost in fantasy land and closed my eyes again.

"It wasn't Lucas," repeated Kareem. "Our murderer is intelligent, very intelligent, but he isn't on Lucas's level. If Lucas had killed Fran, he'd have made it look like a natural death, so we wouldn't be having this discussion."

"So who did kill Fran?" asked a woman's voice.

"Amber would know if we had a murderer in the unit," said Lucas.

I didn't believe anyone in my unit had murdered Fran, but I'd got swept up into the surreal spirit of this by now. "I don't read everyone regularly," I said, "and I'm limited to seeing current thoughts. I'd notice if someone had committed murder though. There's a change in the... texture of a mind that's under great stress. It would attract my attention."

"It might be someone who wouldn't be stressed by killing to defend Amber, or worry about it afterwards," said Gideon.

"Adika!" Several voices chorused the name.

"Adika had to restrain Fran to prevent her from physically attacking Amber," said Lucas. "He might see Fran as a continuing threat."

"We could take the easy option, you know," said Gideon. "Check the security system to see who was in our unit at the times when Fran was murdered and when the body was dumped."

"But that would spoil our fun," said Lucas.

"And it still wouldn't rule out Adika," said Emili. "He controls our unit security system, so he could alter the records."

After Emili's suggestion that Lucas had killed Fran, I couldn't resist teasing her in return. "Adika wouldn't have to kill Fran himself. He could have sent one of the Strike team to do it. He'd probably have chosen Rothan."

"Rothan was with me at the relevant times so he's innocent," said Emili calmly.

"You'd say that even if Rothan was guilty," said Kareem.

"Definitely," said Emili. "If both Adika and Rothan felt it was necessary to kill Fran to safeguard the Hive, then I'd do anything I could to help them."

"We now have a conspiracy involving Adika, Rothan, and Emili," said Lucas. "Amber must surely have read the details in at least one of their minds, but is presumably protecting all three of them."

"Amber, did you kill Fran yourself?" asked Gideon.

"Me?" Startled, I struggled up into a proper sitting position and opened my eyes. "No, of course not."

"Because if you did, you can just tell us." Gideon laughed. "We've just pointed out that we'll go to any lengths necessary to protect you. If you murdered Fran, then we just have to work out a good story to explain how she died and we can close the case."

"It would be very easy to blame it on Ashton, but hardly fair on the poor man," said Emili. "Can anyone think of a way Fran could have accidentally cut her own throat?"

"Far easier to claim it was suicide," said Lucas.

"A suicide who moved her own body twenty-two hours after she died?" Kareem shook his head. "You must be able to do better than that, Lucas."

"Fran didn't move her own body," said Lucas. "Someone in the storage complex found it, panicked, and hid it. By the following night, he'd calmed down and realized there was no need for an innocent man to be afraid of anything, so he went and put it back."

"So we do another check run there, and Amber reads his mind and discovers what happened," said Gideon. "Which unfortunate person do we blame for panicking and hiding the body?"

"We don't blame anyone," said Emili. "Amber feels sorry for the person involved, so she won't give us their name."

I really couldn't work out if they were serious about this or not. I didn't want to read their minds just in case they were. "Don't be ridiculous. I didn't kill Fran, and I'm not protecting the real murderer either."

"Then we seem to have reached our conclusion," said Lucas. "Someone in Law Enforcement killed Fran. If it wasn't one of us, then the obvious suspects are the people in the Security Unit where she's been working for the last few months."

He paused. "We'll schedule a check run for the day after tomorrow. I'm not sure a telepath's Strike team have ever gone out to do a check run in a Hive Security Unit before, so we'll have to work out a discreet approach."

Everyone nodded.

"Are you hungry yet, Amber?" asked Lucas.

"I'm starving."

"Then let's go back to our apartment now and eat."

We stood up, walked back to our apartment, and into the living room. "Can't we do the check run tomorrow morning?" I asked. "I understand you're worried after what happened during the emergency run, but I'm not suffering any problems or headaches this time."

Lucas turned to face me. "I know you aren't, and I'm deeply relieved about that, but we should still be careful. The check run today didn't find the target we were looking for, but Ashton's mind was in a highly unstable state, so you need the full twenty-four hour recovery time."

I sighed. "Very well, we'll wait the full twenty-four hours, but that still means we could do the next check run tomorrow evening."

"In theory we could, but it would be a sensible idea for you to have your first proper counselling session with Buzz tomorrow and leave the check run until the following morning. We can't afford to take risks with you, Amber. You're irreplaceable."

Lucas leaned forward to kiss me. At the touch of his lips, my mind automatically linked to his, and I shared the moment when his anxiety at the thought of losing me changed to a different kind of tension.

With the second kiss, the boundaries between us blurred. I was Amber pressing my body against the warmth of Lucas. I was Lucas gasping in response. Lost in the feedback loop, his reaction building mine and mine building his, we forgot about Fran and check runs and everything except the two of us.

CHAPTER THIRTEEN

The next day, Lucas and I were waiting at the lifts to meet Buzz. The doors of lift 3 opened precisely on time, and I saw she was wearing the red skirt and top again, and her black hair was rioting as wildly as yesterday. She stepped out of the lift, grinned at me, and then raised her eyebrows at Lucas.

"Buzz, this is Lucas," I said. "He's my partner, and also my Tactical Commander."

"I'm pleased to meet you." Buzz held her hand out towards Lucas.

Lucas looked at the offered hand but didn't shake it. "I'm pleased to meet you too. I've heard a lot about you."

Buzz kept her hand held out. I watched with amusement. Her tactic had worked on Adika, but I had a feeling it would fail on Lucas.

"One word of advice," said Lucas. "Don't try basic pressure techniques on a Tactical Commander."

I couldn't help laughing. Buzz threw a rapid glance in my direction, and then gave Lucas a wounded look.

"You live with a true telepath. How can you be scared of shaking hands with a simple borderline telepath like me?"

Lucas sighed. "That type of blatant manipulation wouldn't even work on a member of our Strike team."

"It might," said Buzz. "It's surprisingly easy to manipulate the action types if you use one of their trigger words like fear or cowardice."

"In general that's true," said Lucas, "but this is a Telepath Unit. Our Strike team members are of the highest calibre, selected not just for physical strength and fast reflexes, but intelligence as well."

Buzz frowned down at her hand for a second then looked up at Lucas again. "Can I have one more try?"

"This is your third and final attempt." Lucas gave her the annoying smile that he usually saved for teasing Adika. "If that fails, would you like us to play rock, paper, scissors next?"

I laughed again.

"Amber came out of Lottery almost eight months ago," said Buzz. "If I've been brought in to counsel her now, it means that at least one previous counsellor has failed. There are several possible reasons for that. I'm trying to assess your character so I can eliminate one of them. As a borderline telepath, mental insights are a key part of my assessment process, and physical contact often helps me get an insight. Would you please shake my hand?"

"Actually, the one word 'please' would have worked just as well as that speech." Lucas shook Buzz's hand. "Can I let go now?"

"It would be helpful if you could hold my hand just a little longer." Buzz looked embarrassed. "Insights are a bit random."

"Since I'm in a committed relationship, and my girlfriend is watching us, I'm putting a five minute limit on this hand holding," said Lucas. "Perhaps we can use the time productively by covering some basic details. We've allocated you an apartment in the unit, so you can move in as soon as you wish. I've also arranged for you to have access to our Telepath Unit case records."

Buzz shook her head. "I don't need access to your records. Previous attempts at counselling Amber have failed, and I haven't had an insight from you yet, but Amber has made it... Ah!"

"Insight?" asked Lucas.

"Insight." Buzz let go of Lucas's hand. "I was right. Whatever went wrong with the counselling before, it wasn't your fault. Underneath your comedy act, you're desperately keen for this to work."

"So we can stop playing mind games now?"

Buzz nodded. "As I was saying, Amber has made it clear that she doesn't want our relationship to be one of an expert professional counselling a patient, but that of two friends discussing problems. That means I won't be reading your unit records on Amber's past cases, or asking other people about them. I will only know what Amber chooses to tell me. I won't be recording information she tells me either. Anything she says to me will remain strictly private between the two of us."

She turned to face me. "Are you happy with me working like that, Amber?"

"Yes."

"If we want to discuss things like two friends, then it's best if you avoid reading my mind during our sessions. I work by instinct rather than rigidly following any standard method of psychological counselling, but I do sometimes think about them, and you might find those thoughts disconcerting."

"I agree," I said. "I'll try not to read your mind, but using my telepathy is so automatic to me that I may do it accidentally."

"I understand that." Buzz looked at Lucas. "Are you happy with that approach too?"

"Yes. The standard professional methods failed, so I agree with you trying a different angle, but I need to warn you about Fran."

"No!" Buzz waved both hands at him. "Absolutely no interfering. If Amber wishes to talk about something, she will do so. If she doesn't, she won't."

"I was just trying to help."

"If you want to help," said Buzz sternly, "you should go away right now."

Lucas pulled a face of mock despair, turned, and walked off towards the operational section of our unit. Buzz stood watching suspiciously until he was safely on the other side of the security doors.

"What did your insight show you of Lucas's mind?" I asked eagerly.

Buzz shrugged. "Just what I already said. He's worried about you. He wants this counselling to work."

I blinked. All the glowing magnificence of Lucas's mind, all the glittering multitude of thought levels, and Buzz had just seen that he was worried about me. It seemed unfair that Buzz was so close to being a telepath, but could only glimpse fleeting shadows of the world as I saw it.

"Where should we go to talk, Amber?" asked Buzz. "It should be a place where you feel comfortable and relaxed."

"The park." I led the way along the corridor to the unit park, and paused to open the storage cupboard just inside the door and take out a small box. I gave it a shake to check it was full, then walked down the path to the picnic area. I sat at one of the tables, and gestured that Buzz should sit opposite me. "Watch this!"

I opened the box, grabbed a handful of birdseed, and threw it on the ground. There was a flurry of wings as multicoloured birds flew down from the surrounding trees to feast. I threw another handful of seed, turned to smile at Buzz, and was startled to see she was watching me rather than the birds.

"You love it here," she said.

"Yes. I find the park a restful place. Do your insights let you hear the Hive mind?"

"I'm not sure what you mean by the Hive mind."

"The Hive mind is the thoughts of the hundred million people in the Hive," I said. "I hear it all the time. It's like I'm sitting next to a giant fountain, and hearing the sound of all the falling droplets merge together into one roaring noise of water. Our unit is in an isolated area, so the Hive mind is quieter here, but it's still there day and night. Mostly it's comforting, but there are times when it gets louder and has a rough edge to it."

"You find that rough edge disturbing?"

"Sometimes. When I'm tired or stressed. I'm less aware of it here in the park though. When I had a headache as a child, I found that sitting somewhere quiet in the park would help ease it. I think the minds of the birds and animals, possibly the insects too, soften the impact of the mass of human minds. The effect is even stronger when I'm Outside. The sound of the Hive mind is still there like background thunder, but there's a whole host of animal and bird minds too."

"Outside?" Buzz's eyebrows shot up in alarm. "You mean you've been outside the Hive?"

"Yes. Even the mention of Outside used to terrify me until a couple of months ago, but then I had to beat my fear of it to go out there to solve a case."

The birds were giving me hopeful looks, so I threw them more seed.

"Tell me more about your headaches," said Buzz.

"There isn't much to tell. I had occasional headaches when I was a child and when I was on Teen Level. My telepathic abilities were blocked back then, but maybe the headaches were something to do with the pressure of the Hive mind. I certainly had dreadful headaches when the special Lottery techniques were bringing my telepathic abilities to the surface, but then they stopped."

"You don't have headaches at all now?"

"I've had a few slight headaches since Lottery. The only really bad one was on our last emergency run. Things got a bit difficult." I wasn't sure whether I wanted to talk about that or not, so I changed the subject. "Did the Lottery processes trigger your borderline telepathy too, or did you have it as a child?"

"I used to have intuitions as a child," said Buzz. "There were people I didn't want to be near, and people I instinctively liked. The triggering processes in Lottery made that... Well, it was as if a blurred image suddenly came into focus, and I could see the insights that gave me those feelings."

Buzz's eyes widened, and she pointed at something behind me. "Are we under attack?"

I turned and saw a mob of men running along the path towards us. "No, that's my Beta Strike team doing laps of the park for training."

"The deliciously handsome young man in the lead looks strangely familiar."

I laughed. "That's one of my two deputy Strike team leaders. Forge is in charge of the Beta Strike team. You met him on Teen Level."

"I did? When?"

"Forge lived on the same corridor as me on Teen Level. Some

hasties caught him exploring the vent system, and you made him wear a child's tracking bracelet for weeks."

"Oh yes." Buzz gurgled with laughter. "I remember his look of outrage. I was trying to teach the boy not to take risks, but I wouldn't have bothered if I'd known Lottery would give him a Strike team position. Forge must love chasing criminals through every hidden place in the Hive."

"He does."

The Beta Strike team were running past us now. Forge turned his head to look at us, his face changed to a ludicrous expression of dismay, and he accelerated to full sprinting speed. His team were taken by surprise, but hastily chased after him.

Buzz gave another gurgle of laughter. "I think Forge recognized me."

"He's got very vivid memories of you and that tracking bracelet." I frowned at Buzz. "Forge, Adika, Lucas, and I are the only people in the unit who know what happened back then. You mustn't mention it to anyone else. Adika had the whole tracking bracelet incident removed from Forge's record when he was promoted to deputy Strike team leader. If the Beta team members found out the story, it could undermine Forge's leadership authority."

"I would never do anything to undermine Forge's ability to do his vital work for the Hive," said Buzz solemnly.

"Good."

"I remember you talking about how Forge had a weird effect on you on Teen Level. Did you ever find out why?"

"Yes, I did." I grimaced. "I'll tell you the whole story one day. The short version is that Forge doesn't have a weird effect on me any longer."

"You started dating another boy back on Teen Level. I forget his name."

"That was Atticus. We only went on one or two dates in the end. We decided it would be a mistake to get involved with each other when we'd have to split up before going into Lottery."

"So you're living with Lucas now. Does Forge have a partner as well?"

I was avoiding reading Buzz's thoughts, but I couldn't miss the way her mind had changed its colour and brightness. "Forge is still getting over breaking up with Shanna. She was his girlfriend all through his years on Teen Level, it ended disastrously, and I don't think he's ready for another relationship yet."

Buzz grinned. "I used my most casual voice and disinterested body language when I asked if Forge had a partner. Silly of me to waste effort on that when you're a true telepath."

I put the lid back on the seed box and sighed. "I should talk to you about Fran."

"Lucas mentioned Fran. I stopped him talking about whoever she is, because I don't want him pressuring you into telling me anything."

"I read minds, but Lucas reads faces. He knows I want to talk to someone about Fran. I haven't been able to do that because everyone in our unit, especially Lucas, has such strong feelings about her. You've never met Fran though, so you won't suffer from anger or guilt at the mention of her name."

Buzz gave a nod of acceptance. "It sounds as if something very serious has happened."

"It couldn't be more serious. Fran used to be my Liaison team leader. I fired her months ago, just before our unit went to operational status. A few days ago, we went on an emergency run and found Fran's dead body. She'd been murdered."

Buzz gave me a blank, appalled look. "Murdered? Did you catch the person who killed her?"

"No. We're still hunting that target."

"Finding Fran's body must have been a huge shock for you."

I pulled a face. "Yes. It churned up a lot of old emotions. Hiring Fran as the unit Liaison team leader was a total disaster."

I stared down at the table for a moment before speaking again. "That disaster was entirely my fault. Most of my staff came out of Lottery with me, but some key roles required existing experienced staff. Megan, my Senior Administrator, was in charge of my training, so hers was the first mind I ever read. Fran was the second. She'd come out of Lottery twenty-five years ago, been considered for a Liaison team post in Sapphire's

Telepath Unit, but been rejected by Sapphire. That had given Fran a hatred of Sapphire and telepaths in general."

Buzz frowned. "If Fran had learned to hate telepaths, why would she want to be your Liaison team leader?"

"Fran was very ambitious, and Telepath Unit positions are the most prestigious in Law Enforcement."

"But why did you accept her?"

"Because I was a well-intentioned, naive fool," I said bitterly. "I was stunned when I was hit by all the anger and resentment in Fran's head. I knew I should reject her, but I'd always loathed nosies myself. Every time I saw one of the nosy patrols roaming the Hive, I'd hated the idea of them rummaging round in my thoughts. It seemed incredibly hypocritical to reject Fran for feeling exactly the same way about me."

"I see," murmured Buzz.

"I had this ridiculous idea that there wouldn't be a problem if I avoided reading Fran's mind, so I accepted her as my Liaison team leader. She kept her feelings in check until it became clear to everyone that Lucas was interested in me as a potential partner. Fran couldn't control her revulsion after that. She couldn't bear the thought that he'd want to kiss, to hug, to love something like me. The cracks began to show, and..."

I winced. "We were here in the park, having a team leader meeting, when Fran started arguing with Lucas. Adika joined in on Lucas's side, and then the whole situation exploded."

I remembered the way Fran had looked at me in open disgust, her normally professional voice changing into something viciously discordant, as she spat hatred at Lucas and me. "Fran said that she didn't know how Lucas could bear to touch me, I told her she was fired, and she started screaming about me being an ugly, mutant freak."

I shook my head, trying to banish that memory, and fought to keep my voice steady as I finished the story. "Adika grabbed Fran, dragged her away, and I never saw her again. Nicole took over as Liaison team leader the next day, and everyone carried on as if Fran had never existed."

I sighed. "That must sound really peculiar to you, but the

staff of Telepath Units will go to tremendous lengths to avoid distressing their precious telepaths. Nobody mentioned Fran's name. They barely even thought about her once our unit was at operational status, because they were so busy with other things."

"But you couldn't forget what Fran had said?"

"No. All through my childhood, I thought of the nosies as unnatural, frightening, mutant freaks. My parents and brother hated them too. In fact, they still hate them, so they must never find out I'm a telepath."

"They still think that you're a Level 1 Researcher?" asked Buzz.

"No. My parents and brother have found out that I run some sort of Hive Security Unit, but they don't know that telepathy is involved. I work hard to avoid reading their minds, but I'm scared I'll do it by accident one day."

I dismissed that issue with an angry wave of my hand. "When I came out of Lottery, and Megan told me I was a telepath, I realized the real truth. The nosies are just ordinary people, and I'm the mutant freak."

"So Fran's words hurt you deeply because they echoed something in your own mind? Do they still hurt you now?"

I'd tried to forget Fran's words, but they were carved, like never-healing scars, on my brain. I couldn't say that aloud, even to Buzz, so I settled for a single word answer. "Yes."

"Most people have five senses," said Buzz. "Does losing one of those senses make them more or less human?"

"No."

"I sometimes have an instant of telepathic insight into the minds of others. Does that make me a mutant freak? Do you look at me and see a thing out of nightmare to be regarded with horror and revulsion?"

"No."

"You have a fully controlled telepathic sixth sense, Amber," said Buzz. "It makes you stronger in some ways, and far more vulnerable in others. It does not make you more or less human."

I blinked away the moisture from my eyes, and we sat there in silence. I didn't know why I'd told Buzz the stuff about me thinking of myself as a mutant freak. Now I felt strangely empty.

It must have been at least five minutes before Buzz spoke again. "Will you continue dealing with Fran's case yourself, or will you hand it to another Telepath Unit?"

"Fran hated me, and I didn't like her much either, but she was one of my unit, one of my people. I feel I should deal with her case myself. If I catch her killer, then it will mean I'm free to move on without looking back. Does that make any sense?"

"It makes sense to me. This is about getting closure." Buzz paused. "I don't want to read the records of your past cases, but I would like your permission to monitor the comms during your future emergency and check runs. Do you have any problem with that?"

"No. There's nothing private about what happens during a run. Half my unit will either be actively involved or monitoring the comms in case they're needed to help."

"Good." Buzz groaned. "Now I must go and apologize to Lucas. In general, I don't want him forcing information on me or dictating what we talk about, but he was correct to try to warn me about something as extreme as you finding the body of someone you knew."

CHAPTER FOURTEEN

The next morning, Adika, the Alpha Strike team, and I set off on the check run to Fran's Security Unit. We had an unexpected addition to our party, because Lucas had decided to come with us.

Occasionally one of the Tactical team, usually Lucas, came with us on routine check runs to talk us through the situation. I was nervous about it this time though. We weren't going out to hunt down a budding vandal, or someone behind a series of threats that could soon turn to violence, but an established killer.

"Tactical ready." Emili's voice spoke from the crystal unit in my ear.

She was using the same calm, relaxed tones that Lucas used during emergency runs, but it wasn't quite as reassuring coming from her. Lucas was a brilliant Tactical Commander and had successfully guided us through some horrific runs. I knew that Emili and the rest of the Tactical team would have been sitting with Lucas during those runs, feeding ideas and suggestions to him, but he was the one who'd filtered through those ideas and chosen which orders to give us.

"Liaison ready. Tracking status green," said Nicole's voice.

It felt wrong to be going through the ritual checklist with Lucas standing beside me. I wanted Lucas safe in my unit rather than in the middle of whatever unknown dangers lay ahead.

I checked my dataview. "Status green here too."

Lucas started briefing us on what lay ahead. "This is a virtually unique situation. We're going out to check a suspect area that's a Hive Security Unit located on Level 20. There's an instinctive reaction that this will be a safe place. Level 20 is the home territory of Law Enforcement. Security Units are full of dedicated people working to protect the Hive."

He shook his head. "That instinctive reaction is entirely wrong. If we're right, and Fran's killer is working at that Security Unit, it makes them doubly dangerous. Our target knows the nosy squads are fakes, there are over one hundred million people in the Hive, and just five genuine telepaths to check minds for guilt. We must assume our target knows what those five telepaths look like. Amber must not go near that unit."

Adika and my whole Alpha Strike team were in the lift. None of them moved or said a word, but I could sense the tension in the air. I wasn't sure whether I was picking that up telepathically or just from their body language.

"Be aware that we may be dealing with multiple targets," said Lucas. "If so, we can expect at least one of those targets to be in the Security Unit, but possibly not all of them. We can't risk Amber setting foot on Level 20, but there's the point that people who don't work closely with telepaths always forget. Walls, floors, and ceilings are no barrier to telepathy. You may not be able to see a telepath, but they can still read your mind."

He paused. "We have a choice between positioning Amber directly above or below the Security Unit. Below the Security Unit is a very busy Level 21 shopping area, and above it is a Level 18 park. Like any park, that extends to take up the space of two levels above and one level below it. The area on the levels above is taken up to give the park its extra height, and the area on the level below is taken up by soil."

"The park is a much better location than a crowded shopping area," said Adika. "I don't want my men scattered among what may or may not be innocent shoppers. I want them close around Amber."

Lucas nodded. "I totally agree. We couldn't risk closing the shopping area because our target may be monitoring Law Enforcement systems. Whatever excuse we used, the target would be suspicious of a closure so close to the Security Unit. We can keep people at a distance in the park by simply getting the park keeper to mark an area off as closed for new planting. Being a level further away from the Security Unit won't make any difference to Amber when there are no minds on the intervening level, just soil."

"Ah," said Adika, "so that's why my team are all carrying spades. We're supposed to be gardeners working on the planting. I'm glad there's a good reason for issuing us with the spades. I was worried you were about to make a sarcastic comment on the problems we had apprehending the last target, and tell us you'd armed us with spades so we could hit people over the head."

Lucas grinned. "I leave the sarcasm to you, Adika. You're far better at it than I am."

"Shouldn't we have plants as well?" asked Eli.

Adika groaned. "Why did you ask that question, Eli? You know what Liaison are like about details. They'll want to load us up with seed trays now."

"Liaison did suggest we brought plants," said Lucas, "but I overruled them. You are gardeners digging a new flowerbed. In the unlikely event that anyone asks why you haven't got any plants, they're being delivered tomorrow."

"Has the area of the park already been closed for planting?" asked Adika.

"We're calling the park keeper now," said Nicole's voice over the crystal comms. "We decided it was best to leave it to the last minute."

Our lift doors opened on Level 18 and we transferred to the belt system. Lucas stood next to me, his arm round me, and started explaining the bit of the plan that was troubling me. Bystanders would believe he was just quietly talking to me, not that the scattered groups of muscled men were all hearing his words too.

"Normally a target mind is very distinctive because they are in extreme emotional crisis. This target probably isn't, so will be harder for Amber to identify. We also have the problem that Amber can't directly access someone's memories herself, she can only see their current thoughts. Fran was killed nearly a week ago. For the following day or two, the memories of that would have constantly been in the target's mind. By now, there will be long periods of time when they are thinking of completely innocent things. We need to make sure the target is thinking about Fran when Amber checks that unit, so once you're in position in the park I'm going to pay them a visit."

I wrinkled my nose. I really didn't like the idea of Lucas going into that Security Unit.

"Turning up unannounced might trigger the target into a panic reaction," said Lucas, "so I called the unit at nine o'clock this morning. I said we'd failed to find Fran's killer, and unfortunately our heavy workload meant we now had to follow standard procedure and suspend the case until there were further signs from the target responsible."

He shrugged. "I said that I realized this was a small Security Unit, with less than fifty people, so everyone would know Fran well and be disappointed by this news. Since they're my fellow workers in Law Enforcement, I felt obliged to visit and address a meeting of the entire staff, to give them my deepest apologies and assure them we'd done everything possible."

"A personal apology is a little unusual, Lucas," said Adika.

"Very true, but I made the point that Fran had worked with us too. Anyway, the meeting has been arranged for eleven o'clock. Everyone in the unit has been messaged to tell them to attend. Our target will now be torn between two responses. Fear that I'm coming because we suspect something. Hope that I'm telling the truth and we're abandoning the case. The target has to make a decision. Whether to give in to fear and make an excuse to leave the unit, or stay hopeful and go to today's meeting."

Lucas laughed. "Our target has had an hour to think through their options. That's enough time to work out that if we're truly suspicious of people in that unit, then doing something like claiming to be ill and going home would attract attention to them. Our target's only real chance of escape would be to leave the unit and immediately go into hiding, but they'll know how hard it is to hide for long periods in the Hive."

He paused. "Even if we're dealing with multiple targets, and the one inside the unit can call on someone outside to hide them, they'll be unwilling to abandon everything to spend the rest of their life cowering in someone's spare bedroom. Their other option is to gamble that I'm telling the truth, in which case they'll just have to sit through that meeting and they'll be safe. That's a far more attractive thought for them, so I'm expecting hope will win over fear and they'll come to the meeting."

"You aren't going into that unit alone, Lucas," said Adika.

"Everything I say and do in the meeting will be aimed at reassuring the target or targets that we've given up the hunt and they are safe," said Lucas. "They will sit there and quietly listen to me. If something unexpected happens that makes them turn violent, I have my ear crystal, gun, and body armour. No one will see the gun or body armour under my clothes, and if anyone spots my ear crystal then that's easily explained by me needing to keep in touch with my Telepath Unit in case we have an emergency run."

"You aren't going into that unit alone," repeated Adika. "You need someone to protect you."

"Should the extremely unlikely scenario unfold where multiple targets attack me at once, there will be over forty other Security Unit staff at that meeting to help me subdue them. We may be dealing with two targets, conceivably three, but I really can't believe an entire Security Unit has gone rogue."

"You aren't going into that unit alone," said Adika, for the third time. "Rothan's going with you."

Lucas sighed. "I'm Tactical Commander in charge of unit operations. That makes me your boss, Adika."

"Of course you are," said Adika, "but your safety is my responsibility. Rothan's going with you, *sir*."

"But…"

"Rothan is going with you, Lucas," I cut in. "You're Tactical Commander, but the telepath is in overall charge of the unit, and I'm giving you a direct order."

Lucas laughed. "All right. I'll tell people that I've brought Rothan with me because he was on the emergency run. He personally retrieved Fran's body, so can answer any questions they have."

We had a long ride south on the express belt after that. I held Lucas's hand tightly. He was usually the one staying somewhere safe while I went into danger, but this time the roles were reversed. I told myself that Rothan was Adika's best man. He'd take good care of Lucas.

"Approaching scene." Adika's voice alerted me to the fact we'd finally arrived at the park.

We went in through the park entrance, followed the main path for a while, and then took a side turning past a small notice saying "Closed for new planting". The path led into an area of trees. We kept walking for a couple more minutes until Lucas checked his dataview and stopped.

"We're now directly above the Security Unit," he said. "I'll leave you to enjoy your digging."

"You and Rothan will leave us to enjoy our digging," said Adika pointedly.

"This isn't a good place for a flowerbed," said Eli. "There's too much shade from the trees."

"I'll make sure we send shade loving plants to go there," said Nicole.

"And the soil will be terribly dry with all these trees around," added Eli. "The plants will need watering for weeks. We'd be much better digging the flowerbed over to our left."

"We're digging the flowerbed here because it's right above the Security Unit's largest meeting room," said Adika. "Why are you such an expert on flowerbeds, Eli?"

"My uncle is a park keeper," said Eli. "I used to help him out sometimes as a child. When I was on Teen Level, I used to think that maybe Lottery would make me a park keeper too."

"It's not too late, Eli," said Adika. "I'm sure our unit park keeper would welcome an assistant. Just say the word and the job's yours."

"No, no," said Eli hastily. "Being on the Strike team is much more fun."

There was laughter from the rest of the Strike team. I didn't join in because I was hugging Lucas.

"Be careful," I said.

"This check run is far more hazardous for you than me, Amber. When you're reading minds, be ready to pull out the second you see any images of Fran's death."

"I promise I will."

I reluctantly let Lucas go, and watched him and Rothan walk off through the park. When they were out of view, I sighed, and sat down by a tree. Eli was quite right about this being a bad place for a flowerbed. The dry ground was rock hard.

I leaned my back against the rough bark of the tree, closed my eyes, and reached out with my mind. Adika was disconcerted by how difficult it was to thrust a spade into the ground here. Eli was happily enjoying a reminder of his childhood. Kaden was trying to pull up a tree root and losing. He hacked it in two using the edge of his spade instead.

I moved on past the thoughts of my Strike team, down through the blankness of the earth-filled area of Level 19, and on to the minds scattered around on Level 20. I was searching for one with the colour, scent, taste of stress and tension, and there were several. I picked one at random. A man was staring at the contents of a box, and thinking about Fran.

… visitor from the Telepath Unit can take Fran's things to her family for us. Avoid the whole issue of…

… barely anything in this box. Just a few efficiency awards. The woman was…

So glad I won't have to talk to her family and pretend I liked her.

I moved on to the next stress-filled mind. A woman was sitting at a desk, her fingers drumming on the top of it, her eyes focused on the clock. Another couple of minutes and she'd have to go to that meeting. She could cope with listening to the man talk about Fran, but…

Please don't let him ask me to speak! Please don't let him ask me to speak! I was Fran's team leader, it would be perfectly natural for him to ask me to say something, but please don't let that happen.

The words were on the level of pre-vocalization. I was confused, because it looked as if the woman was forming the words in her mind just before saying them aloud. There wasn't anyone in the room with her, she wasn't making a call, and she wasn't working on a document, so... I suddenly realized she was desperately, fervently praying.

I was startled. I'd never stumbled across a mind this deep in prayer before. Religion was accepted by the Hive as necessary for the happiness of some people, but only Hiveism – worship of the Hive itself as a collective gestalt – was ever mentioned in public. This woman couldn't be a Hiveist, because its followers disapproved of prayer. A true believer should have no need for it, because they were content in the absolute acceptance that the Hive knew best.

If this woman was praying, then she must believe in one of the older religions that were forbidden by the Hive. Well, not actually forbidden. The older religions were among those organizations the Hive labelled as non-conformist, but tolerated so long as they operated discreetly.

The Hive Ramblers Association was another example. That had fifty thousand members, who went walking and camping in the countryside, but few other people knew the organization existed. The Hive wanted its citizens to think of it as their entire universe. The myths about the fearsome Truesun and the horrors of Outside were encouraged to make people afraid of the world beyond its walls, in exactly the same way the myths about the nosies were encouraged to make people law abiding.

I'd gone into Lottery as a typically ignorant eighteen-year-old, expecting to be imprinted with all the knowledge I'd ever need. I'd come out of it as one of only a handful of people in the Hive who would never be imprinted, because tampering with the mind of a telepath might damage their priceless ability.

I would never be imprinted, but I'd picked up a host of interesting facts from the random minds I'd read, and one thing had become clear to me. The Hive controlled information as a way to control people. It wasn't true that imprints included everything people needed to know. Imprints included everything the Hive *wanted* them to know.

The woman's prayer had ended now. She stood up and

reluctantly headed for the meeting room. The upper levels of her conscious mind were filled with flickering images of the last few months. She'd been promoted from deputy team leader to team leader, and was just settling into her new role when Fran arrived to fill the vacant deputy position. Fran had made it clear from the first day that she thought she was far more experienced, far more qualified, and far more skilled than the person giving her orders.

Constantly telling me I was wrong, telling everyone else I was wrong, telling them how they should really do things. Making my life unbearable.

This was the reverse of Ashton's situation, where a supervisor had made his underling suffer. Fran had been relegated from Liaison team leader in a Telepath Unit to just a deputy position in a small Security Unit, and had turned her bitter resentment against her new team leader. Lottery used optimization to assign people to work they loved, but a determined bully could still make them miserable.

I wondered if Fran's team leader had reached breaking point. Ashton had believed in the nosy myth, and limited himself to smashing bottles, but this woman knew there were only five true telepaths in the Hive. Had she risked murder to free herself of Fran?

Further down in her mind, the thoughts were heavily tinged with guilt. Was that guilt because she was lying to herself about being sorry, or because she'd killed Fran? I went deeper again, to the level where conscious and unconscious thoughts mingled. Here was pure, honest, blissful relief.

Wish she'd just left, not been murdered, but my life is worth living again. Wonder who killed her? Wonder if she was wrecking their life just the same way that she was wrecking mine?

This was no murderer, just someone feeling the same sort of guilt I felt myself, guilt that Fran was dead and I hadn't liked her. I'd wasted enough time unravelling the levels of emotion here. The woman was in the meeting room now. It was crowded with people, nearly fifty minds jostling close together, and I needed to check all of them.

I dipped into a mind that was making no pretence to itself at all.

Bored, bored, bored. Never even spoke to the woman, and I have to sit here and listen to people yap about her. I have deadlines to meet!

I moved on to a man who was only interested in the legs of the woman next to him.

On again to the woman, who knew the man was looking at her legs, and was getting annoyed about it.

... thinks he's irresistible. I'd rather go swimming in a slime vat than...

The next man had worked closely with Fran, and had loathed her.

Not surprised that someone killed her.

Lucas arrived, his mind flaring like a beacon. I couldn't resist dipping into his thoughts, and saw them racing by on a bewildering number of different levels. Nobody had left the unit since he sent his message. Every member of staff had come to this meeting. If the Tactical team's theory was right, then our target was in this room.

Lucas looked round at the faces, analyzing expressions and body language, looking for anyone displaying signs of guilt. He'd probably find at least a dozen. From what I'd seen so far, most people who'd worked with Fran had hated her, and were feeling guilty about that now she was dead.

Lucas was talking now. I forced myself away from his glittering thoughts, and started searching for my target again. I could hear Lucas's speech through my ear crystal as well as through a succession of different ears in the meeting room, but I was too busy checking thoughts to listen to his words.

I usually skimmed over minds when searching for a target, looking for one that had a glaringly wrong shape, colour, or texture. This time our target was rational and logical, so I had to study the thoughts of each person in depth. It was depressing to see how much everyone had disliked Fran. I finally found an exception. One person with a distinctively orderly mind, and thoughts that were tinged with a soft hint of regret.

... couldn't help admiring her meticulous attention to detail, and when we talked about music she seemed to come alive. We had the same taste in...

I was distracted by a weird feeling, like an itch deep inside my head. I recognized that feeling. I'd had it several times in the past, always at moments of crisis, and by now I knew exactly what it meant. Someone was in danger.

"Lucas! Rothan!" I cried. "Get out of there!"

Lucas broke off his measured speech. "What's wrong?"

"I itch! Get out of there right now! Move!"

I dumped the mind I'd been reading and linked to Lucas. He and Rothan had both drawn their guns and were heading for the meeting room door. The audience was staring at them, open-mouthed with shock.

"Sorry," shouted Lucas. "Got to go. Emergency call from..."

His words were drowned out by a shrilling noise. There was a standard set of alarm sounds that were used everywhere in the Hive. I'd been taught them all in school before I went to Teen Level. That was the sound of a fire alarm.

Emili's voice was gabbling orders from my ear crystal. "Lucas, head north. The Security Unit exits are north and south, and the northern one is closest. Alpha Strike team, stand ready to evacuate Amber. Beta Strike team, emergency alert, grab full fire equipment and cutters and head to lift 2. I repeat: Beta Strike team, emergency alert, grab full fire equipment and cutters."

"Beta Strike team acknowledging full fire equipment and cutters," said Forge's voice.

"Nicole, is that a genuine fire?" asked Emili.

"It's a genuine fire alarm. Emergency fire containment teams are responding. We can't tell if it's a genuine fire."

I was in Lucas's head, looking through Lucas's eyes, as he opened the meeting room door.

"It's definitely a genuine fire," he said. "There's smoke coming up from under the floor."

CHAPTER FIFTEEN

My body was curled in a ball, my hands holding my legs to stop them from shaking. My mind was with Lucas, as he looked down at the thick smoke coming up from the floor level air vent, up at the corridor direction sign flashing emergency red, and then over his shoulder at the people spilling out of the meeting room door behind him.

Rothan grabbed his arm and started towing him towards the northern exit. Lucas hurried along with him but his thoughts were busy analyzing the situation.

"An accidental fire at this time is unlikely in the extreme," he said. "We walked into a trap. We're up against something bigger than we thought. Much bigger. Be alert for a possible synchronized attack on Amber too."

"Strike team, drop those spades, draw guns, and form a perimeter," snapped Adika.

I didn't care what was happening around me, I only cared about what was happening around Lucas. He and Rothan had reached a junction and stopped.

"Waste it!" Rothan's voice gasped. "Northern exit is an inferno. Turning back and heading south."

Rothan and Lucas turned round to run the opposite way. There was a whole mob of panicking people ahead of them now, and smoke was filling the air. The main lights flickered and died, so just the emergency lighting was left.

"Northern exit is on fire," shouted Lucas. "Head south."

Everyone was turning and running for the southern exit. Rothan still had his hand on Lucas's arm, but Lucas shook him off and darted into a side room.

"Lucas!" Rothan yelled. "Where the waste are you going?"

"Need to check something." Lucas put his hand on the wall, and he and I cried aloud in unison as I shared his pain. Lucas pulled his hand away, and blew on it. "The outer wall's red hot. Those flames at the northern exit were clearly fuelled by accelerant. There must be a ring of inflammable liquid around the whole unit."

He went out of the room to rejoin Rothan, just as the mob came running back along the corridor. People were screaming about the southern exit being on fire too. Lucas had to shout above the din.

"Rothan, we need to find a different way out. Down is no use, there's fire under the floor already, so we have to go up through the ceiling. Not into the vent system, it'll fill with smoke too fast. We need to get into an interlevel maintenance crawl way." He was staring up at the ceiling, looking for the telltale markings that would show a crawl way running overhead.

"Lucas, that's a Security Unit," said Adika. "They're built with defensive shields round them. Reinforced outer wall, and reinforced layers above and below. Those block every way in or out, including the maintenance routes. If you go up into one, you'll be trapped. You have to get to an outer wall and wait for the emergency response teams to cut you out."

"We're going up into the crawl way," repeated Lucas. "We've no choice. The smoke is already building up in here, we won't be able to breathe soon, and the floor will catch fire under us in a few minutes' time. There shouldn't be a reinforced layer above this Security Unit. There's no need for it because we're directly below the soil level for a park."

"But how will you get through the soil? It..." Adika broke off and answered his own question. "We have spades."

"Exactly," said Lucas. "You dig down to get us."

"Where are they now, Amber?" asked Adika. "Where do we start digging?"

I stood up, eyes closed, my mind still with Lucas, groping my way forward as I moved to stand directly above him. From the telepathic view, there was nothing between him and me but empty space. In reality, there was a whole level's depth of soil.

Lucas and Rothan had moved into a large office now. Rothan climbed onto a desk, took tools from his pocket, and started removing a ceiling plate. The Strike team were experts on the hidden arteries of the Hive, the vents, the crawl ways, the waste system, and all the other places where their targets might try to hide.

Everyone else was crowding into the office now. The screaming had stopped because people were covering their mouths with bits of clothing, struggling to breathe with the poisonous black smoke filling the air. I wasn't going to leave Lucas's mind to read their thoughts, but they were obvious from the desperate way they were watching him and Rothan. They were trapped, surrounded by flames, but these two strangers seemed to have an escape plan.

"Beta Strike team is moving," said Forge's voice. "We have full fire equipment and cutting gear."

"We're sending advanced digging equipment to the park," said Nicole. "Medical support is incoming too. Fire containment reports the fire is breaking downwards to Level 21. They've ordered the evacuation of the area around the Security Unit on Hive Levels 19 through 22. The next…"

Eli's voice interrupted her. "Lucas, this spot is full of tree roots. We'll never dig down through them in time. You need to move either south or west, clear of the park trees."

Rothan had the ceiling plate loose now. "Lucas, Amber is reading your mind. Get up into the crawl way and find a point where the Strike team can reach us. I'll stay and help everyone else up."

Lucas climbed up onto the desk. People were crowding round it. They understood what was happening now. One of the telepaths, Amber, was nearby. Her Strike team was coming to save them. They still had a chance to live.

Everything suddenly went dark. The emergency lights had failed, and there was a new outbreak of screaming. Lucas tugged his wristset light down from under his sleeve, and turned it on. Rothan's light was on too. Twin white beacons of hope.

Rothan grabbed Lucas, lifting him bodily upwards, and Lucas scrabbled his way into the crawl way. "Don't lose the ceiling plate, Rothan. When everyone's inside, you'll need to block the hole to keep the smoke out."

The crawl way was a claustrophobically small tunnel, and of course the usual motion-activated lighting was dead. Lucas shone his wristset light around, looking for a direction sign, and I felt the first touch of panic in his mind.

There has to be a direction sign. Everywhere has direction signs. Ridiculous to burn to death just because you can't find... There's one!

"Heading west," he said. "Get people moving after me, Rothan."

I heard Rothan yelling. "Small people first, because I can lift them up quickly. Only one person standing with me on the desk, or it'll fall over. As I lift that person up, the next one climbs on the desk."

A woman started speaking, in a loud but calm voice. "Everyone form a line! When I call your name, join the queue. Mell, Rogar, Jet…"

That had to be the Security Unit leader. Between them, she and Rothan seemed to be getting things under control. Lucas was aware of the laboured breathing of people following behind him.

I was moving too, walking above where Lucas was crawling. I felt someone take my arm, and gently guide me round some obstacle before letting me go again. The ground under my feet felt softer now, then very soft.

"Lucas, stop!" ordered Eli. "This is perfect. Dig, everyone! Dig!"

Someone grabbed me, carried me aside, and put me down in a sitting position on what felt like thick grass. I opened my eyes for a second, and saw the entire Strike team madly digging down into what must have been a beautiful ornamental flowerbed just a minute earlier.

"This is very soft soil," said Eli. "We'll make fast progress but we'll need a wide hole because the sides will collapse inwards. Caleb, Zak, Tobias, shovel the spare soil out of the way onto the grass. The rest of you..." He hesitated. "Sorry, I know I shouldn't be giving orders."

"Tell us what to do, Eli," said Adika. "You know more about this than the rest of us."

I focused on Lucas again. He was sitting still in the crawl way now. A line of people were next to him, sobbing and gasping for air. It was very hot and very hard to breathe.

Too much smoke getting in, far too much smoke, but we can't shut people out to die.

"Rothan, how many more people out there?" he asked.

"About a dozen," said Rothan. "The floor's smouldering now, so we've got them on chairs round the desk. It'll just be another..."

Nicole interrupted him. "Fire containment reports fire still spreading. Evacuation extended to Hive Levels 18 through 23."

Emili spoke in a voice of utter despair. "Alpha Strike team, evacuate with Amber."

"No!" I screamed. "We can't leave!"

"I'll keep half the team here digging," said Adika, "but I have to send the rest to protect you, Amber. Lucas warned us there might be an attempt to ambush you on the way back to our unit."

"I'm not going back to our unit," I said flatly.

"Be reasonable, Amber," said Emili. "Fire containment has ordered your area to be evacuated. We have to get you to safety."

Lucas joined in the argument, struggling to keep his voice calm and measured when he could barely breathe. "Amber, you must go. We can't risk you. Telepaths appear very rarely, and the Hive has been especially unlucky in the last few decades. Ideally, we need eight telepaths. We'd be in deep trouble if we went back to just having four, but it's worse than that. Morton has increasing health issues. He won't live forever, and the projections are clear. With only three telepaths, the Hive would go into social meltdown within a year."

Lucas knew I was reading his mind, so he was arguing with his thoughts as well as his words.

Please, Amber. Let them evacuate you so I know you're safe.

Usually Lucas's thoughts raced on a multitude of glittering levels, but now there were barely three and they were down to normal human speed. Lucas was short of oxygen and suffering from heatstroke. His mind had calculated the probabilities, and accepted he was going to die.

An automated voice spoke from overhead. "This area is being evacuated for safety reasons. Please leave immediately."

I opened my eyes and saw the park lighting had changed colour. The suns were red instead of white now, and had altered shape from round to flashing arrows pointing to the nearest exit. I closed my eyes again.

"I'm not leaving," I repeated.

"Amber, please go," said Lucas. "The rest of the Alpha Strike team will still be digging, and the Beta Strike team will be here soon."

"No!"

"Alpha Strike team should now evacuate Amber using minimal necessary force," said Emili.

"It's not just Lucas down there," I said. "It's fifty other people as well. Your boyfriend, Rothan, is down there, Emili!"

"You think I don't know that?" Emili snapped.

"Amber, you have to evacuate," Rothan choked out the words. "We've got everyone into the crawl way now. We can hold on a while."

I knew that every second I kept arguing was an extra second that twenty men instead of ten were digging. Someone was picking me up, so it was time to use the ultimate threat.

"If you drag me out of here, and Lucas dies, then I will invoke my right under Hive treaty to transfer Hive. There are one hundred and six other Hive cities, and every one of them would welcome a telepath."

The hands put me down again and there was dead silence for a minute.

"You can't do that, Amber," said Lucas.

"I mean it."

An unexpected voice spoke over our crystal units. Megan

always listened in to our runs, but didn't usually say a word. This time she had plenty to say.

"Amber means it. I believed Keith could have saved my husband from dying if he'd tried harder, so I had to leave his unit. If you force Amber to evacuate, and Lucas dies, she will feel the same way about this Hive. If there's the slightest possibility that she could have saved him by staying, or the men who left with her could have saved him by staying, then this Hive will lose her."

"Compromise," gasped Lucas. "Four exits from park. Four escape routes. When down to two safe escape routes, Amber leaves."

Please, Amber, I'm begging you. Don't let me die knowing my death destroys my Hive!

I was in Lucas's head, so I answered the way he would have done. "Compromise accepted."

"Nicole, we need people on all four park exits, checking the escape routes are clear," Emili said, in a deeply relieved voice. "Alpha Strike team, keep digging."

I listened to the heavy breathing of the Strike team and the thuds of their spades. The sound of men digging, working to exhaustion point to save their team mates and friends. There was one brief interruption, when the digging equipment arrived, and spades were cast aside in favour of roaring, powerful machinery. All the time, Lucas's conscious thoughts kept fading, until they were down to a single pale thread.

"Lucas," said Emili, "what's your situation down there?"

"Coping," Lucas breathed the single word.

"Rothan?" asked Emili.

There was no response.

"Rothan?" she asked again.

Still nothing.

"Amber, I know you won't want to leave Lucas's mind, but..." Emili let the sentence trail off.

We all knew Rothan had been the last into the crawl way, the longest breathing the lethal smoke. I didn't want to leave Lucas's mind, was afraid of what I'd find if I did, but I owed Emili this.

I reached out along the minds in the crawl way. Most of them were unconscious. I couldn't tell if anyone had died, because a dead person had no thoughts left to read. At the end of the line, I found Rothan.

"Rothan's alive," I said. "Unconscious. He's dreaming about you, Emili."

"Good," she said shakily. "That's good."

As I went back to Lucas's thoughts, Nicole spoke in a grim voice. "There's smoke coming up through the floor at the southern park exit."

"Are the other three exits still clear?" asked Emili.

"Still clear," said Nicole.

"Turn on the rain at the south end of the park," said Emili.

"Working on that," said Nicole.

One escape route had gone. If another went, then I'd have to leave. I'd given my word to Lucas. Waste it, I should have argued, held out for staying until one escape route was left.

A few seconds later, I heard a rush of feet and a babble of voices as Forge and the Beta Strike team arrived. "You need to let my Beta team take over as soon as you reach the crawl way," said Forge. "We've got the protective gear and the cutters."

"I think we're getting close now," said Eli.

Lucas was unconscious now, his mind still troubled by fears, not for himself but for our Hive. That was my fault for refusing to leave. If making people stay hadn't helped, if we didn't save him, then it would be my fault that Lucas died worrying about our Hive.

"Have the cutters ready," ordered Forge. "I think I can see the crawl way. Yes! Cutters now!"

I opened my eyes, and saw the men crowding round the hole, a couple of them holding evil looking blades. A group of people in medical uniforms were standing nearby.

"If anyone can hear me down there," shouted Forge, "keep your heads down."

"Their heads are already down," I said. "They're all unconscious."

A painfully loud, squealing sound started, that made me

want to thrust my fingers into my ears. It lasted for fifteen seconds, I counted every one of them, and then it stopped. There was smoke coming out of the hole now.

"I see Lucas," said Forge. "I've got Lucas!"

A limp body was passed out of the hole.

"Retrieval squad, get in there and start passing out the rest of them!" said Forge. "Be careful where we've cut our way into the crawl way. The edges are razor sharp."

More of the Beta Strike team moved in, looking like unfamiliar strangers in their orange protective suits and breathing masks. They were crawling into the hole and retrieving more bodies, but my attention was still on Lucas. He was stretched out on the grass now, with a doctor working on him, putting an oxygen mask over his face and giving him an injection in the chest. More doctors were arriving and taking charge of the other casualties.

"Fire containment reports that the fire is now contained on Level 20," said Nicole.

I saw Lucas's body jerk, and he suffered a massive coughing fit. He was awake again! I closed my eyes and reached out with my mind. Not looking into Lucas's thoughts, but those of the doctor leaning over him.

... monitor the effects of the smoke inhalation, but we've given him injections in both lungs and he's responding. This one should make a perfect recovery.

I was jubilant for a second, but then saw what else he was thinking.

By the time they reach the ones deeper in that crawl way...

The park suns changed from ominous red to their normal colour. I went across to sit by Lucas's side, hold his hand, and made myself smile reassuringly into his dazed eyes despite the thought dominating my mind. My Beta Strike team were working their hardest to pull out the rest of the people trapped in the crawl way, but Rothan would be the last one to be saved.

CHAPTER SIXTEEN

Lucas drifted in and out of consciousness for the next couple of minutes, and then started trying to ask questions despite the oxygen mask covering his nose and mouth. The doctor made two attempts to persuade him to stop talking, before giving him another injection that sent him into instant, blissfully peaceful sleep.

The doctor gave me an apologetic look. "I'm sorry I couldn't let him talk to you, but it's very important to keep a patient quiet and still while the treatment works on their lungs. We'll be transferring him to a medical facility or hospital after that, and..."

This man was part of a random emergency response team. He had no idea this wasn't an accidental fire, and he didn't know he was talking to a telepath. I was just the girl who was holding the hand of his patient, and obviously cared deeply about him. I could see the rest of his explanation on the pre-vocalization level of his mind, so I interrupted him to save time.

"You were quite right to sedate Lucas. It's the only possible way to stop him asking questions. He's stable now, and it's better to keep him here than move him when his lungs are in the vital first stage of treatment."

The doctor's worried face cleared. "I didn't realize you were imprinted with medical information."

"Go now," I said. "Other patients need you."

He hurried away. I stayed sitting on the grass, holding Lucas's hand, watching the scenes of frantic activity going on around me. I'd have found this situation far easier if there was something, anything, that I could do to help, but there wasn't.

I rubbed the moisture from my eyes with my free hand, set my ear crystal to receive only, and listened to the others talking. There were breathless comments from Adika, Forge, and the Beta team members working round the hole and in the crawl way, and the occasional announcement from Nicole. Emili had gone very quiet, but the Tactical team would have little to say now this was a straightforward rescue situation.

"Fire containment reports the fire is out on Level 20," said Nicole. "Their teams are directly beneath the crawl way now, dampening down lingering hot spots."

The Beta team and people in medical uniforms were crowding round the hole in the ground, so it was hard to see what was going on in there. The Alpha team had moved out of the way to give them space, and were gathered under a nearby tree. Most of them were stretched out in exhaustion on the grass, but the five on bodyguard duties were standing up and alertly watching me.

I saw another limp body being passed out of the hole, and a little knot of doctors taking charge of it. After a combination of observing people and reading their minds, I understood the routine now. The patient was given injections and an oxygen mask, and a triage specialist assessed their condition. If the patient just had mild smoke inhalation problems, they'd join the groups of people waiting on stretchers while the healing fluids injected into their lungs did their work. If they were in a more serious condition, they'd be rushed off to the Navy Zone Fire Casualty Centre that specialized in treating patients suffering from burns and smoke inhalation.

This time the activity around the body was totally different. The doctors worked with desperate urgency before their shoulders sagged and they stepped backwards. A minute later, the patient was quietly shrouded in a white sheet and carried away.

I bit my lip. The Beta team were keeping a head count of the people rescued. That was number twenty-five, and the first death. Law Enforcement systems kept a record of everyone going in and out of Security Units, so we knew that Lucas, Rothan, and forty-nine staff members had entered that Security Unit this morning. No one had left before the fire started, so there were twenty-six people still in there.

"Are you all right, Amber?" asked a familiar voice. "Do you need me to explain why Lucas hasn't been transferred to a medical facility yet?"

I looked up, startled that Megan was at an incident scene, and then realized why she was here. This area was officially safe now, and our own people were among the injured, so our unit's medical staff had come to help. Megan's Senior Administrator imprint included medical expertise, so she'd come with them.

"I don't need any explanations," I said. "There are about thirty minds around here that are thinking it's best to limit any disturbance to the patient while the lung injections work."

"It will be about another hour before we can move Lucas," said Megan. "By then, he should be well enough for us to take him back to the unit and let him finish recovering in our own medical area. I'm assuming you'll want to stay here until then, but the Alpha Strike team can escort you home if you prefer."

"I want to stay here with Lucas. I couldn't leave anyway. Not when Rothan's still in that crawl way."

"How is he now?"

I closed my eyes, and reached out with my mind. I hadn't checked Rothan since they brought out Lucas. Not because I didn't care, but because I cared far too much. Rothan had been in such a bad state the last time I checked him that I was terrified there'd be nothing there for my mind to read. I touched the pale threads of unfamiliar thoughts. Waste it, was…? No, Rothan was there!

"Rothan's mind is very, very faint, but there's better air in the crawl way now, and I think that's helping him." I remembered I'd set my ear crystal to receive, so only Megan was hearing me. "I'd better tell Emili."

"I'll tell her." Megan adjusted her ear crystal. "Emili, Amber says Rothan's still holding on. Where are you now?"

"I've just arrived at the park entrance," said Emili's breathless voice in my ear crystal.

I'd noticed Emili hadn't said much lately, and assumed that was because Tactical didn't have much they needed to say. That was probably true, but it was also because Emili was on her way here. She must have said she was leaving the unit, but I'd been too distracted to pay proper attention.

Strictly speaking, Emili was acting Tactical Commander and should have stayed in the unit, but once the situation turned into a simple rescue she could follow events on her ear crystal. I couldn't blame her for giving way to her emotions and coming to the park herself.

"I saw a team from Hive channel 1 arriving," said Emili. "What are they doing here?"

"We couldn't hide a fire on this scale," said Nicole, "so we put it on the Hive status updates as a freak electrical fire that had spread startlingly fast. When Hive channel 1 heard a heroic rescue was in progress, they rushed a team over here to take images of the scene to use in this evening's 'All Hive Update' programme."

The deep groan I heard on my ear crystal had to be Adika.

"They're hoping to interview some of the heroic rescuers as well," added Nicole.

I knew from reading his mind that Adika had a wide vocabulary of obscene words, but he didn't usually use them where I could hear him, limiting himself to such mild comments as "waste it" instead. Now he said a startlingly crude phrase.

There was a second of awed silence before Nicole bravely spoke. "I'll take that as meaning you aren't keen on the idea, Adika."

"Strike teams are supposed to deal with trouble without attracting attention to themselves. Of course I'm not…" Adika broke off for a moment, clearly battling against using that phrase again. "Not very keen on my men being interviewed. Nicole, you can tell Hive channel 1 that the heroic rescuers are too busy doing the heroic rescuing to be interviewed. You can also suggest that Hive channel 1 should go and… waste themselves!"

I could understand why Adika was in such a foul mood. The people around the hole were handing out another limp body.

This was casualty number forty-four, and the second person to be shrouded with a white sheet. There'd be another six people before we reached Rothan. A man who was Adika's deputy, his brother in arms, and his friend.

The moisture was back in my eyes again as I turned to Megan. "Thank you for saying what you did. It stopped them dragging me away from here."

"I knew how you felt," said Megan.

"I know you…" I couldn't finish the sentence because I was crying too much. Ever since I came out of Lottery, I'd resented Megan's attempts to mother me. I'd fiercely told Lucas that I didn't want or need someone replacing my own mother. He'd said that I should think of Megan as a safety net. A substitute parent who'd be there if needed.

I'd admitted that having to hide the fact I was a telepath meant I couldn't discuss a lot of things about my new life with my own mother, but never believed I'd want to call on the safety net of Megan. The Hive Duty songs that I'd been taught in school constantly repeated that the Hive knew best, and the Hive had known far better than me when it selected my Senior Administrator. You didn't need safety nets until you were falling, and I was falling now.

I found myself hugging Megan. She wrapped her arms round me, and whispered comforting words in my ear. I was aware of another person being handed out of the hole in the ground. The medical staff were hard at work, so this one was alive. Only five more to go before Rothan.

Emili's voice spoke from beside me. "Amber, what's happening? How is Rothan?"

I made myself close my eyes and check the minds underground again. The familiar ones of Forge and two of the Beta team. A stranger, an emergency medical response worker, giving a sad, brief shake of his head in acknowledgement that his current patient was beyond human help. The unconscious minds were faint flickers in comparison. I tried not to count them, but I couldn't fail to when there were only three.

I couldn't face telling Emili that Rothan was dead. I did the cowardly thing, pulling away without checking if one of those three remaining minds was his, so I could truthfully plead ignorance.

I opened my eyes and turned to Emili. "I can't tell. The casualties still left down there are unconscious, and their minds are very faint compared to the rescuers."

I broke off. Emili was staring at another body being lifted out of the hole and shrouded in white. Megan kept one arm around me, but freed the other to hold it out in invitation. Emili moved closer, and leant gratefully against her.

"Emili, I'm sorry I made things difficult for you by insisting on staying here," I said.

"Don't apologize for that, Amber. I can work out the numbers. You stayed, and that meant the whole of the Alpha team stayed here digging instead of only half of them. Five minutes quicker getting into the crawl way. Five minutes quicker to start pumping out smoke and pumping in air. Lucas would probably have lived anyway, but Rothan wouldn't. Those five minutes have given him a chance."

Emili paused. "I've often worried that Rothan would get himself killed protecting you. Foolish of me. The statistics say that Strike team members are ten times more likely to have their lives saved by their telepath than to die in their defence."

She gave a bitter strangled sob of a laugh. "I can't even blame this on Rothan's work. Whatever job the Hive had given Rothan, even if it had made him a pipe cleaner in the depths of the Hive, he'd still have ended up in a situation like this. He's the noble, self-sacrificing type, rushing into danger to help others without a thought for his own safety."

The three of us stood there, Megan in the centre, her arms round Emili and me, as two more figures were lifted out of the hole. They were worked on by medical teams, and then rushed away on stretchers. Emili was obviously cheered by the fact they were alive. I wasn't. I knew there were three more people down there, and only one was alive. If the next person brought out was living, it meant that...

"We've reached Rothan," said Forge's voice through my ear crystal. "His condition is critical, but he's getting emergency treatment right here in the crawl way, and then he'll be rushed to the Navy Zone Fire Casualty Centre."

Emili gave a gasp of relief. I was relieved too, but I was also confused. How could they have reached Rothan already?

"We seem to be missing two people," said Forge.

CHAPTER SEVENTEEN

By the time the still sleeping Lucas had recovered enough for us to take him back to our unit on a wheeled stretcher, the fire containment crews had found one of the missing people. He must have either got lost in the chaos, or decided he stood a better chance waiting for an emergency response team, because his body was in a room next to the reinforced wall of the Security Unit. Megan said he'd have died of smoke inhalation before the flames reached him. I hoped she was right.

There was no sign of a second body, so it must be buried under wreckage. That left the death count at four, with one person missing, and seven people in a critical condition.

As soon as we arrived back at our unit, Emili put Gideon in charge of the Tactical team in her absence, and left for the Navy Zone Fire Casualty Centre.

I followed Lucas's stretcher to a white-walled room in our medical area, watched him being carefully lifted onto a bed, and then sat down in a chair next to him. Megan positioned some metal blobs on Lucas's forehead and chest, studied a display on the wall where multicoloured lines were zigzagging up and down, and gave a smile of satisfaction.

"Lucas needs to stay quietly resting," she said. "There's no hope of him doing that when he's conscious, so I've decided to keep him sedated until tomorrow morning."

I nodded. Lucas was lying unnaturally still, his mind was a grey shadow of its normal glowing splendour, but he was going to recover. I dragged my gaze away from him and looked at Megan.

"Does Rothan have any chance of surviving?"

She hesitated.

"I know you got an update on his condition while we were coming back to the unit. I also know that you didn't pass that information on to Emili, which means it was very bad news. I think it will be easier for me to hear this in words, rather than see the images in your mind, so please don't make me read your thoughts."

Megan sighed. "It was a long time before the rescuers reached Rothan. He was given treatment for carbon monoxide poisoning when he was still in the crawl way, but he also suffered severe hot smoke inhalation. That has caused pulmonary damage that's far beyond the level treatable by medical knowledge in our Hive."

"You're saying that Rothan is going to die?" My voice sounded like that of a cold and distant stranger.

"I'm saying that he's in a critical condition and needs help from a Hive that specializes in advanced medical treatments."

"Then get him that help and get it quickly! Get it for the other patients who need it as well. Whatever influence a telepath has, use it. If you need me to shout at anyone, threaten anyone, just tell me and I'll do it."

"I've already flagged this with Telepath Unit priority, and added a covering statement in your name," said Megan. "The treatments have been ordered, but the problem is that they have to be grown from each patient's own cells. An aircraft should already be taking tissue samples to the other Hive. Those samples will be used in an accelerated growth process, and the resulting genetically tailored treatments will be flown back to us."

"How long will that take, and what are the chances of the genetically tailored treatments working?"

"The treatments should arrive about forty-eight hours from now. Our Hive used this type of treatment for fifty patients after the big fire in Burgundy Zone last year, and our experience confirms the selling Hive's claims on the trade system. Nine out of ten patients will respond to the treatment and rapidly progress to make a full recovery."

I checked my understanding. "So if Rothan and the others can manage to stay alive for the forty-eight hours until this treatment arrives, then they have a nine out of ten chance of surviving and making a full recovery?"

"Yes. They'll be given every available help to hold on until the treatment arrives. You should go back to your apartment now, Amber. Have something to eat and try to rest. I'll let you know at once if there's any change in Rothan's condition."

"I'd prefer to stay here with Lucas."

I was braced for an argument, but Megan just left the room. I heard strange noises in the distance, which were explained when two of the medical staff entered the room with a bed on wheels. They positioned it neatly against the wall.

"Thank you," I said.

They hurried off. A couple of minutes later, Megan returned, pushing a trolley holding jugs of drink, glasses, and a covered dish.

"We'll be making hourly checks on Lucas, but other than that we'll leave you in peace."

She moved towards the door, but I called her back. "Megan, can we discuss some things?"

"Yes." Megan went to sit on the edge of the wheeled bed, and I turned my chair round to face her.

"I shouldn't have ranted at you about your personal relationship with Adika."

Megan shook her head. "I was upset after arguing with Adika. You were suffering from stress after that emergency run. We both phrased things in a way we wouldn't have done in other circumstances, but what you said was true. My personal problems had reached the level where they were endangering the Strike team and had made you lose confidence in me as your counsellor. That's why I'm leaving."

"There has to be a better solution than you leaving us, Megan. You've been doing a wonderful job running the unit. Would you be willing to continue as Senior Administrator, with just the slight change that you don't do my regular counselling?"

I wasn't reading Megan's mind – I was afraid of what I might see there – but her frown seemed to mean she was considering my suggestion.

"I knew Buzz when I was on Teen Level," I added. "I find her easy to talk to, and the fact she's a borderline telepath is very helpful, but there are times when you can support me in a way that she can't. Today was one of those times."

I paused. "I'd hate to lose your support, Megan. I'd hate to lose you."

There was a minute of silence before Megan spoke, her voice uncertain as if she was still thinking this through. "That arrangement might be possible, but for medical reasons I'd have to delegate rather more work to team members."

"Medical reasons?" I repeated anxiously. "You're ill?"

"I'm going to have a baby," said Megan.

I was totally bewildered. I'd read Adika's mind several times in the last few days. I was certain that his relationship with Megan hadn't progressed to the physical stage where a baby was possible.

"My husband, Dean, and I always wanted children," said Megan. "We'd just decided it was the right time to try for our first baby, when Dean was killed. I'd left Keith's unit, and was in a temporary position trying to work out what I should do with my life, when the last Lottery discovered you were a telepath."

I'd seen all this in Megan's mind before, the details so closely intertwined with intimate memories and emotional pain that I'd hurried past them. Now she spoke about them in a voice that showed she'd finally passed through her grief to find a new way forward.

"I was offered the post of your Senior Administrator, which appeared to solve the problem of my future," Megan continued. "I'd lost Dean, we wouldn't be raising our children together the way we'd planned, and I couldn't imagine rebuilding my life with anyone else. I thought I could make a fresh start as your Senior Administrator, and live a new life coldly focused on my career and serving the Hive."

She pulled a face. "It was ridiculous of me to think I could simply blot out emotion from my life. I found myself doing the opposite, smothering you rather than supporting you, as I tried to turn you into my substitute child. Then there was the complicating factor of Adika. He looks very like Dean, and I kept seeing similarities between their characters too."

I made a sympathetic noise. Megan would be bound to see similarities between her late husband and Adika. Lottery had selected them both as having the right physical and mental characteristics for the Strike team.

"Every time I looked at Adika, it was like seeing Dean again," said Megan. "I couldn't help giving into that sometimes, letting myself get lost in the fantasy that I was with Dean again, and then something would remind me of the truth and I'd feel horribly guilty."

She paused. "I've been making Adika unhappy. I've been making myself unhappy too. After I resigned my post as Senior Administrator, I started thinking about my future again. Suddenly everything was much clearer, and I knew what I truly wanted."

She was smiling now. "I've lost Dean, but I can still have his baby. It won't be exactly the way we planned, there'll be a gap in my life and that of the baby where Dean should have been, but I'll do my best to give the child all the love and guidance it needs. I put in the request to Fertility Support yesterday, and they replied within the hour. I have to wait for my request to go through the standard approval processing, but they say that's just a formality in my case. Dean was a Strike team member who died performing his duties, so the Hive will automatically provide unlimited medical support for his recognized partner to have his child."

Megan was looking at me, waiting for me to say something. I was still stunned by this but I managed to scrape some words together. "I hadn't realized this was possible. It's wonderful news, Megan, really wonderful. I'm sure the unit can work round whatever arrangements you need."

"It would be perfect if I could have my baby and keep my position here." Megan laughed joyfully. "I set up the phased opening plan for our unit nursery months ago. I never thought it would be needed for my own baby."

"We'll have our own unit nursery?"

"Yes. When there's an emergency alert, there's no time for parents to take babies to an external nursery."

I had a surreal image of my Strike team arriving at lift 2, and throwing babies to waiting nursery workers. Did that mean the unit would have its own school as well? I opened my mouth to ask the question, but Megan was eagerly talking again.

"There's no problem if multiple fertilization attempts are needed, because the doctors have plenty of Dean's tissue samples in storage, but I'd still prefer to opt for double embryo implantation to maximize my chance of first attempt success."

I tried to make sense of that, failed, and took a look at the top levels of Megan's mind. She was excited. She was happy. She was imprinted with medical expertise, so all that excitement and happiness was being expressed in highly technical words that I didn't understand.

"If I opt for double embryo implantation," Megan continued, "that means there's a high probability of a twin pregnancy where I might need extra rest, but I could recruit a second deputy team leader to help me."

Double embryo implantation meant Megan might have not one baby but twins. I blinked. "I'll explain everything to Lucas once he's properly recovered, and I'm sure he'll agree with me that you should recruit any additional staff you need to help you. Would you like me to tell Adika as well?"

"No. I've disrupted Adika's life and made him unhappy. I should talk to him myself and explain exactly..."

Megan was interrupted by a chime from her dataview. She took it out, tapped it to make it unfurl, and frowned at the screen. "I've got an update from the Fire Casualty Centre."

"Rothan?" I asked anxiously.

"Rothan's condition is still critical. The Security Unit leader has died." Megan stood up. "That news will distress and frighten Emili. I should call her myself rather than let her hear the information from a stranger."

I nodded. "Go ahead."

Megan hurried out of the room, and I leant back in my chair feeling sick. The Security Unit leader had helped Rothan organize the escape into the crawl way. She'd calmed her terrified people, and waited patiently on a chair with her lungs burning from the smoke and the floor smouldering under her, insisting on being the last one that Rothan lifted to safety before pulling himself up and putting the ceiling plate back.

I pictured myself in that woman's place, and didn't believe I could show the same determined courage. I would never be in a situation like that though, because no one would let the precious telepath sacrifice herself to save others. That thought didn't make me feel any better.

I poured out a glass of water, drank it, then stretched out on the spare bed and lay there watching Lucas, reassuring myself that he was safe.

CHAPTER EIGHTEEN

When Lucas woke up the next morning, he was physically much better, lungs almost recovered from the smoke inhalation, and with only a few minor burns on his hands. His mental state was a very different matter. The first thing he asked was whether everyone had made it out alive.

Lucas was an expert in body language, so he'd know if I lied to him. "There are five dead and one missing."

Lucas winced. "Rothan?"

"Six more people, including Rothan, are in a critical condition waiting for another Hive to create a genetically tailored treatment for them."

"Five dead." Lucas lay on the bed, glaring up at the ceiling as if it was a personal enemy. "With one person missing, and another six in a critical condition, the death count will probably get even higher."

He wasn't talking in his speed speech. He was using every single word, hammering the facts home in an accusing voice that wasn't aimed at me but at himself. "Almost all Strike team members will end up with a death count on their record. They don't worry about it, because that death count is the number of targets they had to kill to save innocent people's lives."

He grimaced. "Every Tactical Commander ends up with a death count too. Not on their official record, but in their head. They do worry about it, because that death count is the number of innocent people killed by their wrong decisions."

He was lost in distress and I didn't know how to help him. "Lucas, you shouldn't be talking this much. Megan said you mustn't strain your throat and lungs."

"I expected to have a death count eventually, I'm only human after all, but I didn't expect it to be five in a single day."

"What happened wasn't your fault, and if you don't shut up I'll get Megan to sedate you again."

He studied my face, and decided I meant it. "If you don't want me to talk, you'll have to read the words in my head."

I groaned and dipped into his mind. The normally glittering thought levels were dark and turbulent. Lucas was tortured by guilt, wanting to punish himself for being alive when others were dead. I daren't plunge into that emotional maelstrom, so I focused on his pre-vocalized words.

"You think this wasn't my fault? You think that fire was accidental?" Lucas's thoughts asked aggressively.

"Of course the fire wasn't accidental," I said. "We've only had the preliminary report from the fire experts analyzing the scene, but they've confirmed a highly inflammable liquid accelerant was used to make the fire spread so fast. The fact the fire wasn't accidental doesn't make it your fault though."

"That fire was started deliberately," thought Lucas, "and it was started because I marched into that unit to talk to people about Fran. I thought I'd stir up the guilty thoughts of the target or targets, you'd identify them, we'd send the Strike team in to arrest them, and the case could be closed and forgotten."

His face twisted in pain. "I made a dreadful mistake that's killed five people."

"That's not true, Lucas!" I shouted the words at him, trying to break through the fog of guilt and make him listen to me.

"Yes, it is." His thoughts were full of bitter self-accusation. "I was so smugly sure of my own brilliance, so blindly confident, that I didn't think through all the scenarios. I was aware that we could have multiple targets, and they might not all work in that Security Unit. I should have considered the possibility that a target inside the unit might call a target outside and tell them about my planned visit."

"You think that's what happened?"

"I can't trust my own logic any longer, but it seems the most likely explanation. Once a target outside the unit heard about my visit, they'd realize there was a risk that the one inside would be caught. If a telepath saw even a single stray thought about accomplices, they'd have a Strike team chasing them next."

I frowned. "So the target or targets outside the unit decided to safeguard themselves by starting that fire?"

"Yes. They poured a circle of accelerant all the way around the unit, and started a blaze that would kill their accomplice, the interfering Tactical Commander, and everyone else unfortunate enough to be inside."

"Even if that's what happened, the deaths weren't your fault, Lucas. You weren't the one who started the fire."

"I should have known this would happen," said Lucas aloud. "My mistake. My responsibility. What are the names of the people I killed?"

"I don't know. The incident coordinator is still trying to work that out."

"Why is that taking so long? Everyone needed identity cards to get in or out of the Security Unit. The incident coordinator just has to scan those cards to get their names."

I sighed. "It was hot enough in the crawl way to trigger the anti-tampering protection on the identity cards and scramble their information. The priority during the rescue was to treat people, not to find out who they were. The more serious cases went to the Navy Zone Fire Casualty Centre for intense specialist treatment, while the rest ended up scattered across twenty different medical facilities and hospitals. The incident coordinator has a list of all fifty-one people who entered the Security Unit before the fire, but is still working out where each of them is being treated."

"You mean where those I didn't kill are being treated."

"You didn't kill them. You and Rothan saved almost all their lives. The accelerant made the fire spread so fast, that the man who waited for rescue by the reinforced wall died before the fire containment teams could reach him. Everyone in that unit would have died the same way if you hadn't led them into the crawl way."

"Oh yes," said Lucas, in a harsh voice. "I led them into the crawl way. Saving myself first, while Rothan stayed to help the others and was the last to escape."

"Now you're being ridiculous," I snapped at him. "One of you had to lead the way so I could tell the Strike team exactly where to start digging. One had to stay and help the others. Lottery selected Rothan for the Strike team because of his physical strength and fitness. He could lift all those people up into the crawl way. You couldn't. You might have managed a few of them, but not all fifty people. Rothan knew that, you knew that, everyone knew that. It's a fact, Lucas. Admit it."

"Yes, it's a fact. That's why I didn't argue at the time, but it didn't make me feel any better then and it doesn't make me feel any better now."

I groaned. "You can't keep lying there and blaming yourself like this. You need to focus on deciding our next move."

"I'm not deciding anything," said Lucas. "Not now and not ever again. I've proved myself totally incompetent so I'm putting Emili in charge."

He was intent on self-destruction. I reminded myself he was still a sick man, and counted to ten to avoid yelling at him. "You can't put Emili in charge. She's at the Fire Casualty Centre where Rothan's being treated. It would be cruel to drag her back here when she doesn't know if he'll live or die."

Lucas shrugged. "Then the case will have to wait until she gets back."

"The case can't wait. First our targets killed Fran. Then they tried to murder fifty-one people. What will they do next?"

Lucas just shrugged again.

I'd been sitting in a chair at his bedside. Now I stood up. "You said we should hand this case to another Telepath Unit. I talked you into keeping it, which was a big mistake. I'll contact the other units and ask their Tactical Commanders if one of them can take it."

"You can't give this case to another unit. Neither Keith nor

Mira could handle something on this scale, and Morton's unit is unavailable while he has some medical treatment for his health issues."

"Sapphire then."

"Sapphire won't touch a case that involves fire. She's terrified of it."

"What?" I was startled. I'd thought Sapphire was the flawless telepath with no weaknesses at all.

"Haven't you noticed we do more than the normal number of runs involving firebugs?"

"Yes. No." I shook my head. "I've no idea what would be a normal number of runs involving firebugs, and stop talking aloud!"

Lucas went back to just thinking the words. "We get our own firebug check runs, and a lot of the ones that should be going to Sapphire as well. Most of her Beta Strike team were caught in last year's vast fire in Burgundy Zone. Now she won't touch anything involving arson, not even the simplest check run for a child playing with fire."

I moistened my lips. "What happened to Sapphire's Beta team?"

"Everyone on Chase team duties was trapped, encircled by flames. Sapphire managed to guide all but two of them out. She was still linked to the minds of the last two, still trying to find them a route to safety, when the flames reached them."

I winced. I'd been with the unconscious Rothan and Lucas as their minds were slowly fading, but being in the minds of people you cared about when they were fully conscious and burning alive in agony... "No, we can't hand this to Sapphire, and that means you can't give up this case, Lucas."

There were no words in his head in response to that, just pure, amorphous denial.

"Lucas, you're blaming yourself for the deaths in yesterday's fire, but you said yourself that every Tactical Commander ends up with a death count sooner or later. You have to learn to cope with it."

"Maybe I can't."

"Yes, you can," I said fiercely. "Lottery imprinted you as a Telepath Unit Tactical Commander. That means you have the qualities in you to cope with this. Lottery doesn't make mistakes."

"Lottery doesn't make mistakes, but there are random factors. Subsequent experiences change people. Remember what happened with Fran."

"Fran is irrelevant. That was a totally different situation."

"Kareem then."

"What do you mean?" I checked the images in Lucas's mind, saw the stray thought chains attached to them, and pieced together my own answer. "Twenty-five years ago, Kareem was a Tactical Commander. He was in charge of an emergency run that ended badly."

"He was in charge of an emergency run that ended catastrophically. Now he's only able to criticize other people's theories. He can't trust himself to form his own. I didn't understand his reaction before, but now I do."

I frowned. "So Kareem dropped down to just being a member of a Tactical team. For the last twenty-five years, he's…"

I broke off. It was twenty-five years too late to change things for Kareem. What mattered here and now wasn't Kareem's past, but Lucas's future. "You aren't taking that option, Lucas. You're a brilliant Tactical Commander. You're human, so you'll sometimes make mistakes, and no one else will blame you for them nearly as much as you blame yourself. You're beating yourself over the head with your guilt, but I'm not convinced you made a mistake this time."

Lucas was still thinking about Kareem. There were critical points for telepaths where they could break under the strain of their work. There were critical points for Tactical Commanders too.

Lucas knew he'd reached a critical point, and one of two things was going to happen. The first was that he would break under the harsh reality that his decisions could kill people, run from the responsibility, and hand his position to Emili or anyone else who would take it. The second was that he would shoulder the burden and move on; accepting he was good at his job but nobody could ever be perfect.

He'd known this moment would come eventually. He'd been imprinted with the information to prepare him for it, but knowing about something in advance didn't always make it easier to cope when it happened. Lucas's mind was torn by conflicting emotions, but one thing was clear. Whichever path he chose now, there would be no turning back.

I would keep on loving Lucas whether he was a Tactical Commander calling instructions in my ear crystal, or just quietly sitting in a corner of the Tactical office and listening to events, but I didn't know how Lucas would feel about himself. If he turned away from the job he loved, chose to imprison the glowing light of his mind within self-imposed boundaries, how would that affect him?

I was a telepath, so things on the mental level were as important to me as the physical. I felt that Lucas was in as much danger right now as when he'd been trapped in the crawl way. He'd worked so hard to help me, and now I had to find a way to help him in return. I wasn't imprinted with knowledge of psychology, I wasn't imprinted at all, but I had to find words that would reach him.

"You can only work with the information you have, Lucas, and this time it wasn't enough. The target or targets had cut one woman's throat. There was no reason for you to expect that to escalate to an attempt at mass murder using a complicated arson attack."

"That's true," said Lucas aloud. "Total change in both method and scale. Definitely two targets. Quite possibly more."

His mind was suddenly racing away, thoughts analyzing the situation on multiple levels. Lucas could never stop himself thinking. There were times when I found that maddening, but now I was hugely grateful for it. If I could keep Lucas thinking about the case rather than brooding on his own guilt, he might work his way through this.

My pocket started vibrating. I took out my dataview, tapped it to make it unfurl, and saw a message from the incident coordinator with the final casualty list. A set of fifty-one names, each one tagged as dead, critical, recovering, or missing.

If I told Lucas I had the list, he'd go back into guilt mode and start demanding names again, so I lifted a finger to close my dataview. At the last second, I saw the name that was tagged as missing. I blinked at it in disbelief.

"Lucas, you know that Law Enforcement systems recorded fifty-one people entering the Security Unit before the fire started?"

"Yes?"

"Well, according to Law Enforcement systems, one of those fifty-one people was Fran. She's supposed to have entered the Security Unit at four o'clock yesterday morning. That was several days after she was murdered, and five hours before you called the unit to warn them about your visit."

CHAPTER NINETEEN

"Stop right there!" ordered Megan, looking regally intimidating and speaking in a voice of thunder.

The members of the Tactical team froze, turning into a line of statues, still guiltily clutching the chairs they were carrying. I was awed. I'd never seen Megan act like this before.

"This is a medical area," continued Megan. "A sanctuary where sick people have the peace and quiet they need to recover. You don't traipse through it dragging furniture. You don't…"

She finally noticed me at the back of the group, and broke off her sentence. I didn't need to read her mind, because her thoughts were plain to see in her disconcerted face. You never lecture telepaths. Her voice instantly changed to be sweet and coaxing.

"Amber, you know Lucas needs to rest to complete his recovery. We can't allow a mob of people into his room, worrying him about work."

I waved the Tactical team on towards Lucas's room. They hesitated, unsure which authority they should be obeying, but my second wave sent them scurrying on down the corridor with their chairs, reminding me of a line of ants carrying eggs.

I turned to Megan and lowered my voice. "We have to allow the Tactical team into Lucas's room, Megan. He's having a crisis of confidence. If we let him stop working on this case now, if we let him lie there brooding about the people who died in that fire, then he'll insist on resigning as Tactical Commander and giving his post to Emili."

"He can't do that," said Megan.

"I know. Emili's frantic with fear about Rothan, in no state to take over Lucas's responsibilities, and I don't think she's had enough experience to be promoted to Tactical Commander yet anyway."

Megan shook her head. "No, I mean it's impossible for Lucas to give the Tactical Commander position to Emili. She's only imprinted for the deputy position. She can take over for a few days if Lucas is out of action, but her psychological profile in Lottery showed she wouldn't handle the strain on a long-term basis."

"Lucas must have been even closer to breaking point than I'd realized to forget Emili wasn't imprinted for Tactical Commander. That proves we have to keep Lucas working on this case, because if he stops, he stops forever. Believe me about this, because I'm a telepath, and I can see what's happening in his head. Lucas is in deep water, Megan, and if we don't make him keep swimming then he'll drown."

I dipped into the highest level of Megan's mind, saw her absorb that, accept it, and start panicking about the difficulty of finding a replacement Tactical Commander. Lottery found very few people with the necessary combination of intellectual ability and intense sensitivity, who also had the emotional toughness to survive the pressure.

"If Lucas is brooding," she said, "I could keep him sedated for the next couple of days until he's physically ready for work again."

"That wouldn't help. I've seen the way Lucas's mind keeps analyzing things in his sleep. Even if he was sedated, Lucas's subconscious would still be going over and over what happened, hammering home his guilt. We need to throw as much information as possible at him, and get his mind thinking about the case constructively again."

Megan gave a sigh of agreement, and walked away. I hurried on down the corridor to Lucas's room. The Tactical team had wedged their illegally imported chairs in a semi-circle around Lucas's bed, and he was briefing them. I went to sit in the single, legitimate chair by his bedside.

"... difference in methodology indicates we have at least two targets," said Lucas, "the one who cut Fran's throat and a firebug, but there could be three or even more. Since we're certain Fran died days ago, we have to assume one of our targets used Fran's identity card to enter the Security Unit at four o'clock yesterday morning."

"That person must have been the firebug, making preparations to set fire to the unit," said Kareem. "The firebug couldn't have been triggered into action by your visit, Lucas, because that wasn't arranged until five hours later."

I'd said this to Lucas several times already. I'd told the Tactical team to keep saying it as well. I gave Kareem an approving smile.

"It's true that the firebug must have had an unrelated reason for entering the unit," said Lucas. "However, he or she then learned about my visit, and that discovery triggered them into starting the fire. It's an undeniable fact that my meeting was timed for eleven o'clock and the fire started precisely ten minutes later. That can't have been coincidence."

"No, it can't have been coincidence," said a female voice.

I looked round to see who'd said that, saw it was a woman with closely clipped hair in an unlikely shade of purple, and glowered my displeasure at her. She ignored me and kept talking.

"I don't believe your visit was the reason for the unit being burned, Lucas, but I do believe it was the reason it was burned at exactly ten minutes past eleven."

Gideon pointed a finger at her. "Justify that with a logic sequence, Hallie."

"Logic sequence part one," said Hallie. "Law Enforcement systems show the firebug used Fran's identity card to enter the unit at four o'clock in the morning. The cards of the other forty-eight staff members were used to enter the unit between eight o'clock and nine o'clock. There's no record of anyone leaving the unit at all. Therefore the firebug must have hidden somewhere in the unit before the members of staff began arriving, and the obvious hiding place was Fran's office. The firebug knew it would be empty, and they had Fran's identity card to unlock the door."

"That's plausible," said Gideon.

"Logic sequence part two," said Hallie. "Once inside the office, the firebug could use Fran's identity card to activate her desk's link to Law Enforcement systems. That would automatically display any incoming messages, including the one sent out to every unit member instructing them to attend Lucas's meeting at eleven o'clock. That would be the ideal opportunity to start a fire."

Gideon nodded. "You might as well complete the sequence before we challenge."

"Logic sequence part three. Once the firebug had started the fire inside the unit, the alarm sounded, sending the exit doors into emergency evacuation mode. Nobody needed to use their identity cards to leave, so the firebug could just walk out and start the additional fire outside the unit. Amber wouldn't notice anyone by the exit, because she was focused on reading the minds in the meeting room."

Gideon looked round at the team members. "Any challenges?"

"Are we justified in assuming it was the firebug that entered the unit rather than a different target?" asked Kareem. "Did the unit internal or external fire alarms sound first?"

"The internal fire alarms sounded first," said Lucas. "They detected the smoke coming up from under the floor. I recognized the smell of accelerant in the smoke from attending previous cases involving firebugs, and knew the floor itself would catch fire soon, which is why…"

Lucas started coughing. He had to gulp down water from the glass at his bedside before he could speak again. "Which is why I took everyone up into the crawl way."

I bit my lip. I was worried about Lucas's physical condition, but I had to let him keep talking. It would be easier to heal damage to his throat than to his mind. I refilled his glass with more water, and he took another sip.

"Since the fire inside the unit was started first, I agree it was the firebug that entered the unit at four o'clock," he said. "A firebug would never delegate the pleasure of starting the fire to anyone else. However, that's still consistent with the firebug entering the unit for a different purpose and being triggered into starting the fire by my visit."

"No, it isn't," said Kareem. "Stop trying to prove yourself guilty, Lucas, and examine the facts. The firebug used a large amount of accelerant to start the fire inside the unit. Nobody carries round accelerant unless they're already planning to start a fire."

"The firebug could have found the accelerant inside the unit," said Lucas.

Kareem sighed. "I concede the firebug could have found some flammable liquids inside the unit. Now explain the time factors to me. The firebug started the fire at ten minutes past eleven. That set off the fire alarm. It was less than two minutes before people found there was a wall of fire encircling the whole unit. How could the firebug have spread accelerant along every outside wall of the unit in less than two minutes?"

Lucas frowned.

"You can't give me an answer because there is no possible answer," said Kareem.

"Exactly," said Hallie. "The firebug must have placed accelerant outside the unit before entering. The decision to burn the unit had already been made before four o'clock. Therefore the reason for burning the unit was unrelated to Lucas's visit."

"If the firebug had already decided to burn the unit, why didn't they start the fire at night when there would be far less risk of being caught?" asked Kareem.

"Presumably because the purpose of the fire wasn't just to destroy the unit but to kill everyone who worked there," said Gideon grimly. "The firebug probably intended to start the fire soon after everyone had arrived at work, but delayed a little because of Lucas's meeting. Having all the staff gathered in one room made it easier to start the fire, and the firebug may also have been tempted by the chance to kill a Tactical Commander."

"That's right," I said eagerly. "Lucas, I hope you accept now that your decision to go to that Security Unit didn't kill anyone. It actually saved dozens of lives. If you and Rothan hadn't been there to help, nobody would have survived the fire."

There was a long pause before Lucas spoke. "I suppose that could be true."

I reached out to his mind. The thought levels that had been dark with guilt and self-accusation were brighter now, cautiously considering the possibility that he hadn't caused those deaths.

"It *is* true," I said firmly. "The only…"

I was interrupted by several dataviews chiming in a medley of different notes. "The detailed fire analysis just arrived," said Hallie.

Lucas looked round urgently. "Where's my dataview?"

"Megan took it away to stop you working," I said.

Lucas groaned. "Show me the report."

I took out my dataview and displayed the report on the ceiling. There was silence while Lucas studied the ceiling and the rest of us studied our dataviews.

"Lengths of hose, filled with inflammable liquid, and sealed at both ends," said Gideon finally. "Long lengths placed at intervals around the outside of the unit. Shorter lengths left inside under the floor. That's a very distinctive and methodical approach. Rather than spreading accelerant, lighting it, and running, this firebug was setting traps to be lit at a time of their choosing."

"This firebug is highly experienced," said Lucas, "and not solely driven by the joy of the fire itself. The extra pleasures of anticipation, planning, power, and control are important as well. Everything has to be precisely done."

He stared up at the ceiling again. "So the firebug placed the long lengths of hose outside the unit first, then went inside and placed the short lengths of hose under the floor. That would involve taking up and replacing sections of flooring, but he or she would have a clear window of four hours to do the work."

"When staff started arriving at the unit, they'd see a few lengths of hose lying around outside," said Gideon, "but they'd just assume there was maintenance work going on. They wouldn't see the lengths of hose hidden under the floor of the unit at all."

"The firebug turned the unit into a death trap," said Kareem. "Why was he or she so determined to kill everyone?"

Lucas tugged at his hair. "This started with Fran being murdered. This is all about Fran. It must be. We've been thinking of Fran as being a victim. What if we were wrong about that? What if she was originally one of our targets? In fact, what if she was originally their leader? She could have recruited the other targets to work for her, but they turned against her and killed her."

I blinked. I'd never liked Fran, but she'd served the Hive dutifully for decades, and been a member of my own unit. It was hard for me to make the mental leap from thinking of her as a murder victim to imagining her as the leader of a dark conspiracy.

"Our brainstorming session came up with the theory that we had at least one target who belonged to Law Enforcement," said Gideon. "You're suggesting that particular target was Fran herself?"

Hallie glanced nervously in my direction. "Fran was very angry about being fired."

"She might have been tempted to take revenge on our unit," said Gideon.

I remembered the fury on Fran's face when she called me an ugly mutant freak. Would that anger fade over time, or harden into a bitter grievance? I remembered that Fran's hatred of telepaths had begun when Sapphire rejected her as a candidate for her unit. That was twenty-five years ago, and Fran's anger hadn't faded. Yes, it was credible that Fran would want revenge. It wouldn't be my unit she wanted to hurt though. She'd want revenge on me personally.

"Fran was only left free to roam the Hive because she wasn't capable of harming our unit by herself," said Lucas. "Fran knew she'd never talk any members of Law Enforcement into helping her, so she decided to go through the records of old targets and recruit some of them."

I sighed. "Please stop dodging the issue by talking about harming our unit and say what you really mean. We all know that Fran thought I was a mutant abomination. You're suggesting that she recruited some past targets to help her kill me."

Everyone else in the room winced. "In fact, we were avoiding saying that to protect ourselves, not you, Amber," said Gideon. "It's not easy for us to picture someone murdering our telepath. It would be utter disaster for our unit and the whole Hive."

"It's an especially painful thought for me," said Lucas. "I get hit by both the disaster for our Hive, and the personal disaster for me."

"Sorry," I said, "but that's related to the point I was about to make. Fran hated telepaths but she was loyal to the Hive. Would she really try to kill me when she knew how much my death would harm the Hive?"

There was a moment of silence while everyone thought that through. "Tactical teams track down a large number of potential criminals by examining the evidence and using behavioural analysis techniques," said Gideon. "Perhaps Fran convinced herself that we could catch all potential criminals that way if we tried harder, so we didn't need telepaths."

"If we tried harder," repeated Hallie. "We try as hard as humanly possible already, we refer every case we can to be dealt with by borderline telepaths and hasties, but the fact is that the most lethal targets are often the hardest to catch using conventional approaches. A hundred million people packed tightly together are dreadfully vulnerable to attack. Without telepaths to help us, events like yesterday's fire would be happening on a daily basis."

Gideon shrugged. "You know that, and I know that. The question is whether Fran was angry enough to persuade herself it wasn't true."

"I suppose she might have reached that level of anger," I said doubtfully, "but why would past targets agree to help her? Surely they'd have been successfully treated so they wouldn't want to reoffend."

Lucas pulled a face. "Ideally, successful treatment totally removes the target's desire to reoffend, but in some cases it just reduces it to the extent where a target doesn't reoffend out of fear of the consequences. If Fran explained to those people that the nosy squads were fake, and there were only five genuine telepaths in the Hive, it would change the balance between temptation and fear."

"Fran could have been threatening them too," said Hallie. "She had access to Law Enforcement systems. She could add something to their records that got them sent back for further treatment or even meant they were securely confined."

"Let's assume for a moment that this theory is right," said Lucas. "Fran recruited several dangerous past targets, took away their fear of nosy squads by telling them the truth about telepaths, and threatened them to make them obey her. For some reason, she went to meet her recruits. They grabbed their chance to free themselves of her threats by killing her."

"The really interesting question is why Fran would risk going to meet her recruits," said Kareem.

"There's an even more interesting question than that." Gideon turned to look at me. "Amber, imagine that you're Fran. You've recruited some lethal people. There's a compelling reason forcing you to go and meet them. What arrangements would you make to safeguard yourself?"

I gave him a bewildered look. "Why are you asking me? You're all tactical experts."

"Exactly," said Gideon. "You aren't a tactical expert. Neither was Fran. What arrangements would you make?"

"If I was in that situation, then I'd take Adika and the Strike team, but Fran didn't have that option." I gnawed at my bottom lip. "It would be safest to have the meeting in a public place with lots of people around, but Fran couldn't risk being seen with a group of past targets. Given the circumstances of her leaving our unit, it would lead to her being questioned, and probably having her mind read by a telepath."

I shrugged. "I'd have to meet my recruits somewhere deserted, but I'd take precautions. Either tell someone what I was doing, or record some information to leave behind. That way I could tell my recruits that they'd get caught if they harmed me."

Gideon smiled. "And that's why the Security Unit was burned. Fran tried to protect herself by telling her recruits that she'd left information about them at her workplace. They killed her despite that, and then burned the unit to destroy the evidence."

"That's plausible," said Kareem, "but if you're right then Fran's evidence is now a sad heap of charred ash."

"Not necessarily," said Lucas. "Fran's recruits tried to kill everyone who worked in the unit. That could mean Fran mentioned a co-worker to them. She might have confided in someone, but it seems more in character for her to record the evidence. She could lie about what it was, and ask someone to take care of it for her."

He sighed. "Well, it's just a theory, but it fits the facts, so it's worth investigating. We now have two possible ways to make progress. Firstly, we check the records for firebugs with a history of using similar methods. Secondly, we question the unit survivors to see if Fran had either told them some information, or more likely given them something to keep for her."

"When I was reading the minds of people in the meeting room, I found most of them disliked Fran," I said. "There was only one person who'd been friendly with her. They shared a love of music."

"Do you know this person's name?" asked Lucas.

"No. I don't even know if they were male or female. I'd only just started reading their mind when the fire started."

"Then we especially need to find that person." Lucas's voice took on a decisive note. "I'll lead the firebug record analysis. Kareem can lead the questioning of the survivors. Hallie, you carried out a standard check of Fran's apartment soon after her body was found, looking for anything that could explain why she'd gone to that storage complex. You'd better go back and do an in-depth search for anything that's been deliberately hidden."

Hallie nodded.

"Gideon, you're our defence specialist," said Lucas. "The firebug tried to kill everyone in the Security Unit. There could be further attacks on the survivors. You need to arrange immediate protection for them."

"We can guard them most effectively if they're all gathered in one place," said Gideon. "Since we can't move the patients who are in a critical condition, that place has to be the Navy Zone Fire Casualty Centre. Their other patients can be transferred to the Fire Casualty Centres in Blue and Purple Zones for treatment."

"Just remember that gathering the survivors together gives our target the chance to kill them all at once," said Lucas.

Gideon laughed. "I'm a defence specialist with fifty years of experience, Lucas. There's no need to treat me like a child on his first day at school."

"I realize that you're well aware of the risk factors," said Lucas, "but I can't help being nervous after that fire."

"I'll specifically guard against arson attacks, Lucas," said Gideon, in a soothing voice.

I'd achieved what I needed to do – Lucas was planning tactics rather than blaming himself – so I stood up. "It sounds as if you'll all be very busy for the next few hours, so I'll leave you to carry on with your work."

CHAPTER TWENTY

Eight hours later, I was with Adika and the Alpha Strike team in lift 2. "Alpha Strike team is moving," said Adika.

"Tactical ready." Lucas's voice was far less husky now. Megan had grudgingly allowed him to take charge of this evening's check run, though she'd made him promise to stay lying down on a couch in the Tactical office, and go back to the medical area as soon as the run was over.

"Liaison ready." Nicole's voice started as a whisper in my ear crystal, but rose to normal volume as she adjusted her sound level. "Tracking status green."

I checked the Strike team display on my dataview, and felt a pang of pain that Rothan's name was missing from the list.

"Amber?" Adika prompted me.

"We are green." It felt wrong to be saying my standard words, implying all was well, when Rothan was in the Navy Zone Fire Casualty Centre, hovering between life and death. He only had to hold on until tomorrow afternoon, and the vital medicine would arrive to help him, but somehow I was getting more rather than less anxious with each hour that went by. It would be so cruelly unfair if Rothan lost his fragile grip on life just minutes before the genetically tailored treatment came, or he was among the one in ten patients who didn't respond to it.

I told myself that I had to stop worrying about Rothan, and concentrate on catching the firebug before he or she started another killer blaze. I reached out with my telepathic sense to do some blatant snooping in Adika's mind. I knew that Megan had talked to him about her planned baby. If his thoughts were filled with chaotic emotions about the news, I needed to find it out now rather than at a key moment during the run.

Images of Megan flickered in the depths of Adika's mind, but the higher levels were fighting against thinking about her. Our last check run had turned into a nightmare. Adika was tensely aware there was a high risk of this one doing the same, and he couldn't allow himself to be distracted.

Lucas's voice was speaking from my ear crystal now, so I drew back into my own mind and listened to his words.

"My Tactical team has been working on two approaches to solving our case. The first is talking to all the survivors. We're particularly looking for one person who shared a love of music with Fran. So far we haven't identified that person or learned anything useful from anyone else."

He sighed. "Our research into firebugs has been progressing better. It's obvious if an area has a firebug developing, so most of them are caught and treated early in their careers. The fire in the Security Unit was started by an unusually experienced firebug. Someone who'd carried out a significant number of arson attacks in the past before finally being caught and successfully treated."

"Given the scale of that fire, I'd argue the firebug's treatment was far from successful," interjected Adika.

"The firebug's treatment was successful until another target triggered him or her back into action," said Lucas calmly. "We believe the firebug is now working in combination with that target and possibly others as well."

Lucas stopped speaking because the lift doors were opening. I glanced at the lift level indicator, and saw we were on Level 36. Once we'd transferred to the belt system and were moving again, Lucas resumed his briefing.

"This firebug isn't just unusually experienced, but also intelligent, organized, and methodical by nature. Every detail of their arson attacks is planned in advance and precisely carried out. My Tactical team went through the old records, looking for firebugs with similar characteristics, and came up with a list of a dozen main suspects. Checks on the current behaviour of those suspects flagged one of them as especially interesting. We're heading out to check him now."

Lucas paused. "Our suspect, Martin, appeared as a firebug when he was aged sixteen. There were a series of fires of steadily increasing severity before Mira's team caught him actually lighting fire number ten. Martin completed his treatment five years ago. He's now a Level 36 Salvaging Processes Specialist, with an impeccable work record. That work does involve visits to storage facilities, and dispatching containers of materials on the freight system, but the real reason we're focusing our attention on him is that he moved to a new apartment a month ago."

"Is moving apartment suspicious behaviour?" asked Adika.

"It is in this case," said Lucas. "Martin's new apartment is in an area that's been having major problems with the waste system. A new waste shaft had to be installed, which blocked the main access route to one of the corridors. The inconvenience, combined with noise and smell issues, made all the residents move to new apartments elsewhere. The corridor was left completely empty until Martin specifically requested an apartment there."

"That does seem a little odd," admitted Adika.

"Martin has had no relationships that have lasted longer than a few days, so he lives alone," continued Lucas. "He deliberately moved to an apartment where there weren't any neighbours to notice what he does. That could mean he has something important to hide. We're hoping he'll be in his apartment this evening and Amber will be able to read his mind."

There was silence after that as we rode the belt system on through a series of corridors. The Alpha team were deeply worried about Rothan, so even Eli was too subdued to make random comments or jokes. I caught Adika wishing he would. This morbidly grim atmosphere wasn't good for his team. If Eli didn't start playing the clown soon to lighten the mood, he'd have to do it himself.

"Time for you to jump belt," said Lucas at last. "You'll be basing yourselves in a hairdressing salon just behind Martin's apartment while Amber does her checks."

Adika groaned. "Please don't tell me we're pretending to be hairdressers. The thought of Eli cutting someone's hair terrifies me. We're supposed to save people from being injured, not chop off their ears ourselves."

"You don't have to pretend to be anything," said Nicole. "The hairdressing salon closed an hour ago. You can just let yourselves in and lock the door again behind you."

We walked through a small shopping area, turned down a side corridor, and Adika spoke in a dry tone of voice. "Approaching hairdresser."

There was smothered laughter from Eli.

Adika waved an electrical object at the door of the salon. The door opened, and we all trooped inside. I picked a comfortable looking chair and sat down.

"Which way is the suspect's apartment?" I asked.

Adika pointed at the back wall.

I closed my eyes, touched Adika's mind to orientate myself, and then reached out in the direction of the apartment. It was less than a minute before I opened my eyes again.

"Either Level 36 people have apartments vastly bigger than mine, or our suspect isn't home at the moment."

I heard Lucas's sigh over the crystal comms. "Unfortunate. We'll have to settle for checking his apartment for lengths of hose or bottles of inflammable liquid. After what happened in the Security Unit, I think we should play safe and send in a robot. Which ones have you brought along?"

"The modified pipe cleaning robot we use for narrow spaces, and the new experimental robot," said Adika.

"The new robot is called Spike," said Eli.

"Have we started giving our robots names now?" asked Adika.

Eli responded to the encouraging note in Adika's voice. "Only Spike. He's different from the others. They're just remote controlled, but Spike's got autonomous onboard artificial intelligence."

Adika laughed. "Do you have the faintest idea what autonomous onboard artificial intelligence means, Eli?"

"No," said Eli, "but Spike is clever. When we tested him back at the unit, you could see the way his lights flashed when he was thinking over a problem."

"Well, we'll see how Spike copes with an operational situation," said Adika. "Eli, Zak, Tobias, and Dhiren can come along with me, while everyone else stays here on bodyguard duties. Matias, you're in charge of the bodyguards."

There was no hint of danger, but I played safe, closed my eyes, and started silently running a circuit of the five minds leaving the hairdressing unit. I had a succession of views of a boring corridor, totally featureless except for the occasional apartment door. That was followed by a second boring corridor, a third, and a fourth.

"We're getting close to Martin's apartment at last," announced Adika. "You were right about it being in an inconvenient place, Lucas. There's a very odd smell in this corridor too. I can see why all the other residents chose to move out."

He paused. "Eli, time to unpack Spike."

I swapped to Eli's mind, watching through his eyes as he took Spike out of its bag and set it on the corridor floor. It looked like a red, oval blob, a bit bigger than a man's head.

"Spike, wake up," said Eli.

Six angular, insect-like legs appeared round the blob, and then a small circular disc rose slowly up on a rod from its centre until it reached waist height. The front pair of legs stomped on the ground, followed by the middle pair, and then the back pair. At least, Eli thought Spike was stomping its front legs first, but personally I couldn't see any difference between the back and the front of the robot. Finally, lights rippled round the disc.

"Hello, Spike," said Eli.

"Hello, Eli," said Spike, in a surprisingly human voice.

There was a ripple of laughter over the crystal comms, and Adika gave a theatrical sigh. "I thought I put Tobias in charge of the new robot."

"I kept telling Eli that," said Tobias, "but he wouldn't listen."

"Tobias isn't a good person to take care of Spike," said Eli. "He doesn't appreciate Spike has true personality."

I moved to Adika's head, felt his relief that Eli's comedy routine was breaking through the grim mood of the Strike team, and shared his laughter.

"All right," said Adika, "Eli can be in charge of Spike. Can you get it to unlock the apartment door for us?"

"Spike isn't an 'it'," said Eli. "Spike is a 'him'."

"You see what I was up against," grumbled Tobias.

Adika laughed again. "I don't see how you can tell what sex Spike is, Eli, but since you insist... Can you get him to unlock the apartment door?"

"Spike, unlock apartment door," said Eli.

Spike's lights flashed. "Eli, I see three apartment doors."

"Spike, unlock *that* apartment door." Eli pointed a finger.

Spike's three pairs of legs rippled as it, as he, advanced towards the door.

"Amber," said Eli, "I was wondering if you could read Spike's mind, and tell us what he's thinking about when his lights flash."

I was startled into losing my mental link with Adika and opening my eyes. I saw my bodyguards desperately trying to smother their laughter, and waved my hands at them, palms up, to express my disbelief. I considered asking if Eli thought I could read the minds of other electrical items, such as dataviews and kitchen units, but decided to go for the tactful reply instead.

"Umm, sorry Eli, telepathy doesn't seem to work on Spike."

"Pity," said Eli. "I suppose he thinks on a different wavelength or something."

I pulled a face at my bodyguards. "Possibly."

I closed my eyes again, and returned to Adika's view of the situation. There was a gadget sticking out of Spike's circular disc of a head, and it was doing something to the door lock.

"Eli, the apartment door is now unlocked," said Spike.

"Spike, go in there and take a look around," said Adika.

"You can't say it like that," said Eli. "You have to give instructions in clear, defined sequences. Spike, engage camera link mode."

The gadget withdrew back into Spike's circular disc, and was replaced by a camera extension.

"Robot visual link green," said Nicole's voice. "Sorry, I mean Spike's visual link green."

"Spike, enter the apartment," said Eli.

Adika took out his dataview, and tapped the green flashing dot labelled "robot". Amusement flashed in his mind.

It won't be long before Eli talks the Liaison team into changing that label to say Spike.

Then Adika was concentrating on the image from Spike's camera as the robot's legs rippled forward, nudged the apartment door open, and it went inside. "What the waste are we looking at?" asked Adika.

"I'm not sure," said Lucas. "Everything in the apartment seems to be black. Walls. Floor. Furniture."

"Has there been a fire in there?" I asked.

"Nothing looks damaged, just black," said Lucas. "It would help to have more light."

"Spike, engage maximum lights," said Eli.

The image got rather brighter, but I still couldn't make sense of it.

"I think those are plates and cups on the table," said Lucas. "It looks like Martin got some black liquid he works with, and sprayed it all over this apartment to destroy any evidence. We've definitely found the right firebug."

He paused. "Eli, can Spike give us any information on the black stuff?"

"Spike," said Eli, "describe the black layer on the floor."

"Eli, the layer on the floor is black," said Spike.

I felt Adika's hand go across his mouth as he heroically tried not to laugh.

"Eli, the layer on the floor is wet," said Spike. "Eli, no further details are available."

"I'm afraid that's all that Spike can tell us," said Eli.

"The substance could be hazardous," said Lucas. "We'll have to send a sample for expert analysis before anyone goes in that apartment. Bring Spike out of there now, Eli."

"Spike, return to me," said Eli.

"Do we go back to the unit now, Lucas?" asked Adika.

"Yes. It looks like Martin has abandoned his apartment and gone into hiding. He plans meticulously, so I doubt he's left anything behind that will help us find him. We're finally making progress though. My Tactical team are already collecting more information on Martin, and looking for clues to his hiding place and the identity of the other targets."

Our trip back to the unit was enlivened by people making jokes about Eli and Spike. When we arrived back, Lucas was waiting outside the lift to welcome me home, but Megan only allowed us two minutes together before sternly ordering her patient back to the medical area.

"I'm perfectly recovered," said Lucas. "You can discharge me now."

"You aren't perfectly recovered," said Megan. "You aren't even moderately recovered. If you go back to the medical area now, rest quietly, and sleep well tonight, then it's possible that you'll be recovered enough for me to discharge you tomorrow morning. I'll still want to run checks on you twice daily for the next week though."

Lucas turned to me. "Amber, tell Megan that I'm perfectly recovered."

I laughed and shook my head. "I agree with Megan."

Lucas groaned. I watched him walk off as Megan's prisoner, and then headed back to our apartment to have something to eat. I'd just finished my meal when there was a chime from my dataview.

I pulled it from my pocket, tapped it to make it unfurl, and frowned. The screen was totally black except for a one-word question. "Alone?"

I hesitated, worried by the oddity of this, but any calls or messages from outside my unit would have been checked by Adika. I sent a reply. "Yes."

The screen of my dataview lit up, showing a stunningly beautiful, blonde woman of about forty. I stared at her in bewilderment. I was sure I'd never met her, but her face seemed familiar, as if I'd seen her image in someone's mind.

"Hello, Amber," she said. "My name is Sapphire."

CHAPTER TWENTY-ONE

I gaped at Sapphire. "What? How? Is it safe for telepaths to talk like this?"

"It's totally safe for us to call each other. You must have realized by now that the Hive carefully restricts access to knowledge. Telepaths inevitably stumble across minds that hold especially secret details, learning things the Hive would rather we didn't know, so there are attempts to stop us from sharing that information with each other."

"Does that mean it's safe for us to meet in person as well?" I asked eagerly.

She gave a slow shake of her elegant head. "No. We must never meet in person."

"Why? What's wrong with two telepaths meeting?"

"It's undesirable for you to be burdened with that knowledge at this point. In normal circumstances, I wouldn't even call you until you'd completed your telepathic development."

"But..."

Sapphire's cold voice interrupted me. "*Becoming* a telepath is hard, Amber. You will learn that *being* a telepath is even harder. For now, you should just accept that catastrophically bad things can happen if telepaths meet in person."

Ever since I'd been told I was a telepath, I'd been wondering why I couldn't meet the handful of others in the Hive who were like me, but Sapphire clearly wasn't going to tell me. If I kept arguing with her, she might end this call and never make another. Besides, something about her words had unnerved me.

Sapphire waved a dismissive hand. "Let's move on to the purpose of my call. According to the continuous data exchange between the Telepath Unit Tactical teams, your Tactical Commander lover is recovering from the injuries he sustained in the Security Unit fire."

"Yes. Lucas is..."

She kept talking over the top of me. "However, one of your Strike team, your Alpha deputy, is among the patients still in a critical condition at the Navy Zone Fire Casualty Centre."

I settled for the single word answer this time. "Yes."

"My sympathies and understanding." Sapphire's expression had been remote and disinterested, but now there was a brief flicker of pain before her face returned to being a rigidly controlled blank. "I'm calling you because the daughter of one of my Beta Strike team members is also among those critically ill patients. Are you aware that my Beta team was caught in a major fire last year in Burgundy Zone?"

"Yes, I was told you lost two of them." I automatically repeated the same words that Sapphire had used. "My sympathies and understanding."

"My whole Beta team were deeply affected by the news that Soren's daughter had been injured in a fire. They are concerned for the daughter of their brother in arms, while also struggling with their own old traumas being reawakened. We've received information on the continuous data exchange warning that the Security Unit fire survivors may be targeted by further attacks. Soren has asked permission to go to the Fire Casualty Centre and help guard his daughter, and the rest of my Beta team wish to accompany him."

"The rest of your Beta team? Can you spare them all?"

"My Tactical Commander, Penelope, feels my Beta team's level of distress is currently too high to risk using them in even the simplest check run. Besides, their absence should only be of a limited duration. I've been advised that Kirsten will be given her genetically tailored treatment tomorrow afternoon, and she should hopefully be well enough to be transferred to the safety of my Telepath Unit medical area within the following few days."

Sapphire paused. "I therefore wish to grant my Beta team's request. However, basic good manners mean that I need your consent before allowing my people to encroach on your case."

There was something oddly pointed about the way she said that. "Basic good manners are a set of rules for telepaths?" I asked.

"You can think of them as a set of rules if you like. We refer to them as basic good manners, because that's what they really are. It is good manners for me to ask your consent before involving my people in your case. It is bad manners for another telepath to nose around inside my people's minds. It is extremely bad manners for that telepath to call me and gloat about discovering my personal information."

It was clear that she was speaking about an actual incident, and I could guess which telepath had been guilty of extremely bad manners. Keith enjoyed teasing people about their secrets.

"Keith," I said.

"Yes. Bad manners have consequences. I no longer communicate directly with Keith."

I was getting a strong message here. Whether you referred to them as manners or rules, breaking the telepath code of behaviour would make you unpopular, and serious offences would mean other telepaths wouldn't communicate with you again. I definitely didn't want that to happen. There were so many things that I could learn from other telepaths.

Logically, displaying good manners would count in your favour, and agreeing to Soren and his friends helping guard his daughter was probably good manners. I wanted to agree to the poor man's request anyway.

"I can imagine how Soren must be feeling right now, and give my consent for your Beta Strike team to help guard the Fire Casualty Centre." I hesitated. "I assume it would be bad manners for me to tell anyone else about our conversation, so it's best if you inform my Tactical Commander of your Beta Strike team's involvement yourself."

Sapphire nodded. "It would be extremely bad manners to tell outsiders that telepaths have conversations with each other, because that would inevitably lead to attempts to break our channels of communication. Even Keith and Olivia accept that would be undesirable."

I blinked. "You're in contact with Olivia?"

"Yes. Olivia is a telepath. She may be difficult at times, but in her case bad manners must be excused as being due to reasons beyond her control." Sapphire had the unmistakable air of someone about to end a conversation. "Thank you for giving your consent. It is appreciated."

"Please wait," I said. "I need to know how to contact you."

"At this point, it is good manners for you to wait for contacts to be initiated by the rest of us."

Sapphire obviously felt that she was the experienced telepath, while I was the mere novice who should accept her authority. This seemed like a time where diplomacy would achieve more than arguments, so I phrased my reply carefully.

"I'm worried that I might need to ask the consent of another telepath for something, and not know how to do it. I wouldn't wish to be guilty of bad manners."

"I concede I've created problems by contacting you prematurely," said Sapphire. "I should not engage with you further at this stage, but it would be unreasonable to expect you to forget this conversation happened."

She was silent for a couple of seconds. "Very well, I will explain how you can contact us, but you must not do that for trivial or inappropriate reasons. You know the continuous data exchange between the Tactical teams uses a dedicated secure connection between the Telepath Units?"

"Yes."

"That also allows the staff of the different units to be linked together in conference calls for events such as the Joint Tactical Meetings. If you start a new conference call, then you can invite a person from any Telepath Unit to join it. That call is then treated as internal, so it bypasses all the security checks."

"Oh. That's really…"

I let my sentence trail off because my dataview screen had gone blank. I looked at it in frustration. Sapphire had ended the call, and there were dozens more questions that I wanted to ask. I was tempted to call her back, but I was sure that would be classed as extremely bad manners.

Ever since I came out of Lottery, I'd been burning with curiosity about the other telepaths. I'd collected snippets of information about them, built up mental pictures of their personalities, and imagined the conversations I could have with them.

Now I'd finally spoken to Sapphire, and the conversation had been nothing like I'd imagined. Sapphire had been nothing like the person I'd imagined either. In fact, she'd appeared more like an automaton than a real human being. Her voice had been coldly neutral. Her words had been unnaturally formal. Her face had been a blankly beautiful mask.

If it hadn't been for the one moment when that mask slipped, and I saw her fleeting expression of pain, I might have accepted that Sapphire was an emotionless vacuum obsessed with rules of behaviour, but that instant had been enough to show that she was hiding her true self.

Sapphire had come out of Lottery twenty-five years ago. She'd be familiar with the minds of everyone in her unit, including the behavioural analysis experts on her Tactical team. She'd have learnt how to prevent her body language and voice from betraying her emotions. She'd used that knowledge against me, to hide her own personality behind an impenetrable shield.

Why had she done that? Why did she want to avoid more contact with me? Why did telepaths have their strange rules of good manners?

I'd always wanted to talk to another true telepath. I'd expected it to give me answers, but talking to Sapphire had just added more questions.

CHAPTER TWENTY-TWO

The next day, I had lunch with Buzz in the park. We sat at a picnic table, eating hunks of bread and cheese, and sharing crumbs with the birds. It was oddly relaxing, reminding me of my days on Teen Level, when I'd often buy food at a sandwich bar and take it to the local park to eat.

I found myself talking about the first time I met Lucas. "I'd been taken to Hive Futura, our abandoned seed Hive, for my initial telepathic training. Only Megan and I were there, and I was feeling dreadfully lonely, but then Lucas arrived. His thoughts were like a host of racing express belts, filled with people in shining Carnival costumes, and I was swept away in wonder."

There was more to it than that, of course. I wasn't just drawn to Lucas because his mind was stunning, but because of his vulnerability. Lucas was both incredibly gifted and deeply human.

"You must be thinking how different I am from Lucas," I said. "He's utterly brilliant, and I'm a very ordinary girl. He's very open, while I'm private and defensive. The fact I'm a telepath bridges the gap though."

I paused. "I suppose I should be talking about the fire, but I can't. Not yet. Not when Rothan is still..." My voice shook too much to finish the sentence.

Buzz grimaced. "I appreciate how horrific the fire was for everyone involved. I was just sitting in Liaison's operations room during the run, looking at the images from your cameras and listening to your voices, but that was enough to terrify me. I'd known that Telepath Units dealt with the most dangerous incidents in the Hive, but didn't realize how bad those incidents could be."

"That was an exceptionally bad run," I said. "Especially for a check run rather than an emergency. Check runs are usually perfectly simple."

I was hit by a memory of my first check run. Lucas had gone along with me and the Strike team, and we'd ended up eating in a restaurant and then buying him some socks.

"Borderline telepaths often discuss a hypothetical question," said Buzz. "If someone offered us the chance to be true telepaths instead of nearly telepaths, to join the select group of you, Sapphire, and the others, would we accept it or not? Most of us say they'd accept. I've never been sure what I'd do, but now I know I'd refuse."

She sighed. "To be honest, I'm still processing my own feelings about the fire. I'd understand you not being ready to discuss it yet. However, I think you've already been talking to me about it."

I didn't know what she meant, automatically reached out to find an explanation in her thoughts, but stopped myself just in time. The relationship I had with Buzz was working, and I didn't want to risk spoiling it by reading her mind.

"Your greatest fear during the fire was that you'd lose Lucas," said Buzz. "That's why you've been talking about how important he is to you."

I frowned. "That does make sense."

"Some things appear unrelated at first, but then you find they're really closely connected," said Buzz. "I've been thinking about the problems you have going near nosy patrols. People react to nosies with powerful emotions, and you get hit by that horror and disgust."

"Yes."

"I was wondering if that was why you developed such an aversion to nosies as a child. You weren't just picking up your parents' attitudes, but sensing the massed emotions of hostile crowds."

I shook my head. "That can't be right. My telepathic abilities were blocked until I went through Lottery."

"Were your abilities totally blocked, or were you actually sensing emotions on a subconscious level even then? You read deeper levels of the mind than other telepaths. That could make a crucial difference."

I thought that through for a moment.

"I could be wrong about that," added Buzz. "I'm used to having the advantage of my insights when I'm counselling people, but they don't work on you."

"You could be wrong," I said, "but it's possible that you're right."

"If I am right, then it would also explain why you're defensive about your privacy. You've been fighting all your life to defend your mind from the thoughts and emotions of others."

"That's certainly a better explanation than Megan trying to blame it on my parents. My mother kept nagging me about tidying my room, but she never…"

I was interrupted by a chime from my dataview. I hastily stood up. "I'm sorry, but I have to go now. We're visiting Rothan at the Navy Zone Fire Casualty Centre this afternoon. I know I won't be able to talk to Rothan, I probably won't even be able to see him, but I want to be somewhere nearby when the genetically tailored treatment finally arrives."

I couldn't make myself say the rest of it aloud. Buzz would work it out for herself anyway. Rothan's fate would be decided this afternoon. If he was among the lucky nine in ten that responded to the treatment, then he'd show signs of improving within two hours. If he didn't, then he would die within the next few days.

Buzz waved a hand in farewell, and I hurried off towards the lifts. I'd expected to find Adika, Forge, and the Alpha Strike team waiting for me in lift 2. Adika and the Alpha team were just as eager as me to be at the Fire Casualty Centre during the critical time, and Forge had talked Adika into including him on the trip since he was Rothan's closest friend in the unit. I didn't expect to find Lucas with them.

"Amber, are you wearing your body armour and equipment?" asked Adika.

"Yes." I frowned at Lucas. "Does Megan know you're here?"

"Megan has authorized me going on this trip."

"Really? The Fire Casualty Centre is on Level 25 in Navy Zone. It's only a few hours since Megan discharged you from the medical area, and gave you a long lecture about the importance of resting. I find it hard to believe she's authorized you travelling all the way to Navy Zone."

"Well, she wasn't totally happy about it, but she accepted that she can't stop me doing this. Rothan was injured saving my life."

It was impossible to argue with that. I nodded to Adika, and he closed the lift doors. As we started heading downwards, I was startled to hear him begin the standard ritual.

"Alpha Strike team is moving."

Gideon's voice spoke in my ear crystal. "Tactical ready."

Nicole came next. "Liaison ready. Tracking status is green."

"What's going on?" I asked. "This isn't an emergency or check run. We're just going to visit Rothan."

"We're taking a telepath to an area that's under maximum defence alert," said Adika. "We either treat this as seriously as an emergency run or we don't go at all."

I sighed, gave in, and checked the displays on my dataview. "Green here too. I assume the area is under maximum defence alert because you're worried there could be another attack on the fire survivors."

"Yes," said Lucas. "They're all gathered at the Navy Zone Fire Casualty Centre now. The other patients have been evacuated to other centres, and no visitors are being allowed entry."

"How are the Liaison team explaining this situation to people, especially the staff of the Fire Casualty Centre?"

"The staff of specialist casualty centres are imprinted with limited information about some major Hive incidents being caused by deliberate sabotage," said Lucas. "Since they don't belong to Law Enforcement, their imprints imply such sabotage is always caused by enemy agents rather than members of our own Hive, but that still makes it easier to explain situations like this."

Nicole's voice joined the conversation. "We've told the staff of the Fire Casualty Centre that the fire survivors are being targeted by an enemy agent. The wider cover story is that fire containment discovered toxic materials had been released by the fire. The survivors have been brought to the Navy Zone Fire Casualty Centre for treatment, and visitors aren't being allowed to avoid the risk of cross-contamination."

"We've made an exception to that no visitor rule for Rothan's parents and brother," said Lucas. "They're at the Fire Casualty Centre with Emili, so everyone should be careful what they say in front of them."

Our lift had arrived on Level 25, but Adika kept the doors closed. "I appreciate you letting Rothan's parents and brother visit the Fire Casualty Centre, but surely there's a risk of it causing complications?"

"Rothan's parents and brother have been told the toxic materials story," said Nicole, "and been given fake tablets that they believe will neutralize any toxins. If they question you visiting the facility, then you can explain that you were all at the fire scene so you've also been given these tablets."

"As it turns out, it's telling other Telepath Units the truth that has caused the complications," said Lucas. "We assigned a number of hasty teams to guard the Fire Casualty Centre. Gideon tells me that Sapphire's Beta Strike team have arrived to assist them. I hope you don't have a problem with that, Amber."

I daren't speak or even make a sound in response, because Lucas knew me too well. Some clue in my tone of voice might tell him I'd already heard about this.

"How did Sapphire's Beta Strike team get involved in our case?" demanded Adika.

"A team member's daughter is among the critically ill survivors," said Lucas. "Soren asked to come and visit Kirsten. We allowed that as a courtesy from one Telepath Unit to another, but then he decided he wanted to help guard the Fire Casualty

Centre, and Sapphire gave permission for the rest of her Beta team to join him."

"I hope you've made sure that Sapphire won't try to visit the Fire Casualty Centre while Amber's there," said Adika.

"It's been agreed that Sapphire won't visit the Fire Casualty Centre herself," said Lucas. "We just have to deal with the awkwardness of Sapphire's Beta team being in an area that's under our jurisdiction. Please remember that you're all under stress because you're worried about Rothan, but Sapphire's Beta team will be just as worried about Kirsten. They'll also be remembering the fire they were caught in last year where two of their team died. This isn't the time to indulge in any Strike team rivalries. We should focus on our common interest in keeping the fire survivors safe."

"Agreed," said Adika. "Whatever comments, jokes, or outright insults are made about us being inexperienced greenies compared to Sapphire's Strike team, we will ignore them and remain perfectly polite. Understand, everyone?"

There was a chorus of assent from the Strike team, Adika opened the lift doors, and we joined a southbound express belt for the long ride all the way to Navy Zone. We finally arrived at a major belt interchange, where we jumped belt, and walked down a short, double-width corridor to the Fire Casualty Centre. I saw what had to be Sapphire's Beta Strike team standing outside the main doors.

I had Strike team members with the whole range of possible skin tones, but they were all male, mostly with black hair, and had something similar about the bone structure of their faces. Sapphire's Strike team members were all male too, and looked even more alike, all fair-skinned, with blond hair, blue eyes, and determined chins. I was tempted to read their minds, and find out what they thought about me, but that would be bad manners.

I watched as their leader bowed his head in acknowledgement to me, and then addressed Adika. "Our best wishes for the recovery of Rothan."

"Thank you, Murray," said Adika. "Our best wishes for the recovery of Kirsten."

The blond men moved aside, and we walked into the Fire Casualty Centre.

Adika laughed. "I'm guessing that Sapphire's Tactical Commander gave her Beta Strike team a similar lecture to the one that you gave us, Lucas. Is the gossip true, and half of Sapphire's Strike team members aren't naturally blond but dye their hair?"

"I can't comment on rumours," said Lucas.

"Rothan hasn't just been dyeing his hair, but wearing contact lenses," I said pointedly.

Adika sighed. "True. If Rothan had had a different psychological profile, he'd probably have been assigned to Sapphire's Telepath Unit rather than ours."

I was puzzled. "Why would Rothan need a different psychological profile to be assigned to Sapphire's unit?"

"Strike team members aren't just chosen to be appropriate physically for their telepath," said Lucas. "They're also selected to avoid major conflicts of attitude. If a telepath was constantly reading the minds of people with diametrically opposing views on fundamental issues, then it would create stress and generate multiple other problems."

There was something odd about Lucas's tone of voice when he said that. I checked his mind, and was surprised to find him thinking of Keith rather than Sapphire.

... happened to Keith, it could be argued that all unit members should be selected that way, but the resulting bias in attitudes of the Tactical team would...

... and everyone has limits to what they'll tolerate. Keith was bound to push someone too far eventually. Hopefully Gaius has managed to...

... so grateful that Gaius is Keith's Tactical Commander rather than me!

This seemed to be something to do with how Keith had got stabbed. I was too occupied with thoughts of Rothan to bother about that now, so I left Lucas's mind.

Adika was leading the way down a corridor. "Which waiting room do we want, Nicole?"

"Waiting room 3," said Nicole. "Turn left at the end of this corridor."

We arrived at waiting room 3, and I saw Emili was slumped into a chair, fast asleep. A man and woman were sitting next to her. They must be Rothan's parents. A boy, surely Rothan's younger brother, was lounging on the floor in the corner of the room. Those three were all awake but had the resigned air of people who'd already suffered endless hours of suspense and expected more to come. I was filled with sympathy for them, picturing how my own parents and brother would feel in a situation like this.

Somehow my concern for them made me connect to the mind of Rothan's father. He was studying the people who'd just flooded into the room. They obviously worked with his son. He'd known that Rothan's job was something important to do with the security of the Hive, and it could be dangerous at times, but still hadn't been prepared for the news that Rothan had been critically injured. He'd no idea that the lone girl who'd arrived among so many men was a telepath.

Adika went over to Rothan's parents and spoke in a low voice, saying something complimentary about Rothan and the lives he'd saved.

"We hadn't realized Rothan was involved in rescue work," said Rothan's mother.

"We aren't specialist rescue workers," said Adika, "but we happened to be close by when the fire started."

As Rothan's mother spoke, I automatically moved to touch her mind. She was vaguely proud that her son had saved lives, but most of her mind was focused on fervent hopes that the doctors could save his. I drifted on to where Rothan's younger brother was thinking how impressed he'd been when Lottery allocated Rothan a mysterious Level 1 post protecting the Hive. He'd hoped that in two years' time, Lottery would give him similar work as well. Now he was scared that it might. He…

I felt guilty seeing the boy's private fear that he was a coward, and pulled back into my own head. I'd no business reading these people, but I'd been trained to react to a Strike team member's name by instantly linking to their mind to check if they were in danger. Now using my ability had become as natural as breathing, and just thinking about anyone could make me link to their mind.

Everyone in my unit had been imprinted with the fact telepathy worked like that, and their telepath would sometimes wander through their thoughts. They'd understood it from the beginning, but I hadn't. When I first came out of Lottery, I'd had the naive, idealistic idea that I would be the telepath who was different. I'd tightly control my telepathy, respecting other people's privacy unless it was expressly part of my job to read their minds at that moment.

I was still trying to control my telepathy around a few especially significant people. My parents, my brother, and now Buzz as well. That meant being constantly on my guard when I was with them. I mustn't trespass into their thoughts for even a second, because each contact with a mind made it more familiar and harder to stop myself reading it again.

It was utterly impossible for me to be that defensive with everyone else. Since I couldn't stop myself from reading minds, I'd invented some new moral guidelines for myself, about keeping secrets confidential and only using my knowledge to help others. There was nothing I could do to help any of Rothan's family right now. Nothing anyone could do until the medicine arrived.

I turned to Lucas. "Can we see Rothan?"

"Megan said we'd be able to look through a window into his room. We won't be able to see anything of Rothan though, just the cocoon that's keeping him alive."

"I'll take you there, Amber," said Adika. "Lucas, Forge, Kaden, and Eli can come with us."

The rest of the Strike team dodged aside to let us out of the door. Once outside, Adika paused. "Forge in the lead with me. Amber and Lucas next. Kaden and Eli are rearguards."

I took my position in the formation with a resigned sigh. The Fire Casualty Centre was heavily guarded by teams of hasties, but that wasn't enough to make Adika believe I was safe here. The only place he let me walk around alone was my own Telepath Unit. I couldn't even visit my parents without Adika and a couple of bodyguards coming with me.

Adika took a left turn into another corridor, and stopped by a door with two uniformed hasties outside it. Adika established who we were, and the hasties gave me an awed look before opening the door. I went into a room that was divided into two by a glass partition. On the far side of the glass was the white medical cocoon that enclosed Rothan.

I closed my eyes and looked with the view of a telepath. The glass partition, the room walls, and the cocoon all vanished. There were the minds of Lucas, Adika, Forge, and Eli standing next to me, and the faint glimmer that was Rothan's mind ahead of me. It was shut down to the very deepest level of the unconscious, with no words or images, just something restful, like the sound of water babbling along in our park stream.

The other four telepaths in the Hive couldn't reach the subconscious levels of the mind at all. I wondered if there were levels even further down that I couldn't reach either. I stayed there for several minutes before opening my eyes again. I'd never thought much about religion or prayer, but thinking good wishes about Rothan wouldn't hurt him and made me feel a little better.

I finally turned away from the glass partition, and we went back to the waiting room. There weren't enough chairs for all the Strike team to sit down, but that didn't matter because they kept drifting in and out of the room, taking turns to go and look at Rothan's cocoon.

I'd been sitting there for about five minutes, when there was a sudden gasp from Emili. She sat up straight, and looked round in confusion at the number of people in the room.

"We wanted to visit Rothan," I said.

Emili nodded and rubbed her eyes. Her hair was a wreck, and her face had the blotchy look of someone who'd been crying. She clearly didn't care. I checked her thoughts and found she'd had endless drinks – Rothan's brother had been desperate to do something useful and kept ferrying them drinks – but she'd refused all food today.

"You can't keep starving yourself, Emili." I said the words, then realized I shouldn't know whether Emili had been eating or not. I mentally slapped myself for making such a basic mistake, but fortunately Rothan's family didn't seem to have noticed it.

Emili shook her head. "I couldn't eat anything now. Rothan's medicine should be arriving soon."

Emili had been awake all night, willing Rothan to stay alive until the medicine came, not daring to think beyond that moment to the agonizing suspense that would follow as she waited to see if his condition would improve. Eventually exhaustion had won, and she'd fallen asleep for a while.

I closed my eyes and reached out with my mind, trying to find out when the medicine would get here. I rapidly head-hopped through conscious, unconscious, and sleeping minds, frowning as I noticed one of them in particular. I paused to examine it in more detail, before moving on again to where a man was drumming his fingers on the table top.

... nearly an hour before the aircraft lands, and then the medical courier needs to...

We still had quite a while to wait then. I tapped Lucas on the shoulder, and jerked my head towards the door. He raised his eyebrows, but silently followed me out of the room.

As soon as we were outside, I turned to face him. "Lucas, I've just touched the mind of the man from the Security Unit. The one who was friends with Fran."

Lucas gave me a startled look. "My Tactical team questioned all the conscious survivors, and no one admitted to sharing a love of music with Fran. We assumed that meant the person was either dead or among the unconscious, critically ill patients."

"That's right. This man is unconscious."

"He's unconscious but thinking about Fran?"

"No, he's too deeply unconscious to be thinking about anything."

Lucas looked puzzled. "If he isn't thinking about Fran, how can you tell he's the right person?"

I waved my hands helplessly. "I don't know. Minds are a bit

like faces. When you're familiar with one, you can recognize it whatever the person is thinking."

"But you aren't familiar with this mind. You've only read it once."

"I've only read this mind once, but it's rather distinctive. There's something unusually orderly about it. Anyway, the man is in that direction."

I pointed down the corridor. Lucas glanced round, saw Adika, Forge, Kaden, and Eli had followed us out of the waiting room, and nodded. "Then we'd better go and identify him."

I led the way through the sprawling Fire Casualty Centre to a room that matched Rothan's exactly. The same glass partition. The same medical cocoon. The same flashing lights on the wall. The one difference was that a formally dressed woman was standing and staring through the glass partition. She turned round, looked stunned at the sight of so many people, and then smiled.

"You're friends of Richar?"

"No," said Lucas. "We're from the Telepath Unit investigating the fire."

I was shocked by the way the woman's face crumpled in disappointment. I hastily skimmed the top levels of her mind. Her name was Mika, and she worked for Law Enforcement as an incident coordinator. She'd contacted relatives and friends of all the critically ill survivors except Richar. There didn't seem to be anyone to contact in his case, and it was very important to her that she found someone, somewhere, who cared whether the man lived or died.

... so much like me. The same age. The same history of losing touch with relatives after coming out of Lottery. The same difficulty in making lasting friendships. The same...

... still hurts to remember how my parents suddenly grew distant and my sister blocked my calls. It's not an unusual reaction of course. Ordinary citizens are wary of hasties, so when their son or daughter comes out of Lottery as...

... met so many people, helped so many people, but I'm always associated in their mind with a loved one getting hurt or

killed. They move on. I move on. If it was me in that medical cocoon, the incident coordinator would be struggling precisely the same way I'm struggling with Richar. Fifty years old and...

She made an effort to pull herself together. "Can I be of assistance in your enquiries?"

"This patient's name is Richar?" asked Lucas.

"Yes. Richar 2482-1019-116," said Mika.

"There's a possibility that Richar may have either been told something, or been given something, which could help us find the firebug who started the Security Unit fire. Hopefully the genetically tailored treatment will help Richar, and we'll be able to speak to him in a few days' time. Did he have any personal possessions with him when he arrived for treatment?"

Mika shook her head. "I'm afraid that he only had his identity card and the clothes he was wearing."

"Thank you." Lucas turned and led our group out of the room, stopping in the corridor to adjust his ear crystal. "Liaison, Tactical, are you still listening in to us?"

"Yes," said Nicole's voice.

"No, we've all fallen asleep," said Gideon.

Lucas laughed. "Amber has identified Fran's music-loving friend as Richar, a patient who is unconscious and in a critical condition. It will be days before Richar recovers enough to be able to give us information himself, but there's a chance Fran gave him some evidence to keep for her, so we should check his apartment."

"Do you want me to take the Strike team there now, Lucas?" I asked.

"No, there shouldn't be any minds at the apartment for you to read, and I don't want the whole Strike team parading around the area. If we attract attention to the fact we're searching Richar's apartment, there's a danger we could trigger a series of arson attacks against that and the apartments of other survivors."

He paused. "Richar's apartment must be on Level 20 in Navy Zone, but what's the exact location?"

"Area 510/7580, corridor 17, apartment 3," said Nicole.

"That's quite close to the Fire Casualty Centre," said Gideon. "One of the Strike team might be able to make the trip through the vent system so no one sees him at all. I've already got all the relevant plans to help me set up the Fire Casualty Centre defences, so just give me a moment to check them."

Lucas turned to Eli. "Did you bring Spike along with you?"

"Yes," said Eli eagerly. "I left him in his bag in the waiting room."

"In that case, we can send Eli and Spike to search the apartment," said Lucas. "We've no reason to think our targets have been there, but Spike can go in first to check for hazards, and then Eli can join him. I'll watch the images from their crystal unit cameras and direct the search."

Gideon's voice spoke again. "The good news is that Eli can get from inside the Fire Casualty Centre to just outside Richar's apartment without entering any public areas at all. The bad news is there's one point where he'll have to take a shortcut through the waste system."

Eli groaned.

CHAPTER TWENTY-THREE

I sat in a spare waiting room with Lucas, Adika, Forge, and Kaden. Lucas was projecting the image from Spike's camera on the white wall in front of us. It showed an apartment door.

"Spike, enter the apartment," said Eli's voice.

The image jolted around a bit, and then we got a view of a standard apartment hallway. Eli guided Spike on into the living room, and I gasped.

"Now I understand what Amber meant when she said Richar had an unusually orderly mind," said Lucas.

There was a moment of silence while we all absorbed the view of the floor to ceiling shelves that lined every wall, and the precisely arranged row of objects on each of them.

Adika stood up for a moment to get a closer look at the objects. "Everything seems to be labelled and in alphabetical order."

"Richar is a Filing Optimization Expert," said Lucas. "Clearly Lottery chose him for that work because he loves organizing things."

"Richar admired Fran's meticulous attention to detail," I said.

"Well, this should make our search easy," said Lucas. "If Fran gave anything to Richar, then the man will have labelled and filed it. The obvious place to start looking is under 'F' for Fran. Can you turn Spike to face the wall to his left please, Eli?"

"Spike, turn ninety degrees left," said Eli.

"And there it is," said Lucas. "A small box wrapped in gift paper, and neatly labelled 'Birthday present from Fran'. When is Richar's birthday, Nicole?"

"Three days away," said Nicole.

"The ideal arrangement," said Lucas. "Fran knew that meeting her recruits would be dangerous. She tried to safeguard herself by giving Richar what she said was a birthday present but we hope actually contains information."

He pulled a face. "Fran knew someone with Richar's orderly mind would never open his present before the correct day. If all went well, she could make an excuse to retrieve the present and replace its contents before then. If things went badly, then Richar would open his present. Presumably there are instructions inside about what to do with the information."

He paused. "Things went badly for both Fran and Richar. Eli, please get Spike to retrieve that box and bring it back to us at the Fire Casualty Centre."

"Do I have to come back through the waste system?" asked Eli's voice.

"I'm afraid so," said Lucas. "Please put the box in the bag with Spike, so it doesn't come into contact with anything nasty."

Eli sighed.

It would take a while for Eli to get back to the Fire Casualty Centre. I closed my eyes, and searched for the barely perceptible thoughts of Rothan, wanting to check on his condition. I found him, but there were two minds close by that flared with urgency.

Worried that something was wrong, I dived into one of the intensely focused minds, and found myself looking down at an open cocoon containing a naked Rothan. My hands tensed as I drove a needle into his left lung. I glanced at a scanner.

"Confirm position," I said.

"Position confirmed," said a woman's voice. "Inject now."

I injected the first dose, laid that syringe aside, and reached for the second.

"Amber?" Lucas's voice spoke my name softly. "Is something wrong?"

I pulled back into my own mind, opened my eyes, and smiled

at him. "No. The medicine just arrived. They're giving Rothan his injections now."

My telepathic sense was still open, so I felt the wave of relief coming from around me. Adika's sharply chiselled thoughts dragged me in.

... boy must respond to the treatment. He's young. He's perfectly fit. He's a fighter and he's got everything to live for.

I pulled myself away from Adika's mind, and moved on to find Emili. Her mind was fervently echoing Adika's thoughts, willing Rothan to win this battle for his life.

"The doctors have told Emili and Rothan's family," I said.

I closed my eyes again, and went back to Rothan's mind. Watching. Waiting. Was his condition improving? Were his thoughts getting stronger? I still wasn't sure, when I was distracted by the creak of the waiting room door. I opened my eyes and saw Matias come in holding a gaily wrapped box.

"Where's Eli?" asked Lucas.

Matias seemed to be struggling not to laugh. "You don't want to see Eli. You definitely don't want to smell Eli. We've locked him in a shower and we aren't letting him out until he smells like a human being rather than a slime vat."

Lucas looked warily at the box. "Is that safe?"

"We put it through a whole barrage of hazard tests," said Matias. "Then we borrowed some of the Fire Casualty Centre equipment to do extra scans. There's only a standard format data cube in there."

"I was actually wondering if it had come into contact with anything in the waste system."

Matias sniffed the box. "It smells all right."

"Perhaps you'd like to unwrap it for us," said Lucas.

Matias tore off the wrapping paper to reveal a small plastic box. He opened it and held out a data cube.

Lucas frowned at it. "There's a label on this that says 'Send to Nicole 2513-0864-331'."

"Me?" Nicole's voice gasped the word in my ear crystal. "Why send it to me rather than you, Lucas?"

"Knowing Fran, I'm afraid she wanted you to see this first for malicious reasons." Lucas took the data cube and connected it to his dataview. "There's a single recording on the cube."

Lucas did a lot of tapping at his dataview. After a couple of minutes, Adika got restless.

"What's the delay, Lucas?"

"The recording is password protected."

Adika yawned and turned to me in search of entertainment. "Do you need any more wristset lights yet, Amber?"

I laughed. "No, thank you. Hannah discovered the one I left in my pocket before she put it in the laundry, and I found another in my bookette room, so I now have four. I've a bad habit of leaving things in my pockets. I accidentally put a data cube through the laundry machine when I was living on Teen Level."

"That doesn't surprise me at all," said Adika.

"If you'd seen Amber's room on Teen Level," said Forge, "you'd be amazed that the heap of clothes on her floor ever made it to a laundry machine."

"You should be more respectful to your telepath, Forge," said Adika, in tones of mock reproof. "Are you getting anywhere with the password protection yet, Lucas?"

"No. I've tried all the passwords Fran used when she belonged to our unit, and some other obvious possibilities, but no luck so far. Nicole, the data cube was intended for you, so Fran would choose a password she thought you'd guess. Any ideas what it might be?"

Nicole groaned. "A few days before Fran was fired, she was being difficult about providing research information to you, Lucas. I disobeyed orders, and sent you details about someone called Sabella. When Fran found out, she was furious, and ranted at me for hours."

Lucas tried entering that into his dataview. "Yes, Sabella is the password."

"I'm no psychologist," said Adika, "but that seems an unnecessarily nasty choice of..."

He broke off, because a holo of Fran had appeared standing in front of us. It was only being displayed by Lucas's dataview, so it was far less realistic than a bookette holo would have been, but it was still disconcerting to see a living Fran looking at me. She was dressed in a rigidly formal, blue onesuit, and I recognised her silver earrings as being the same ones she'd worn almost daily when she was in my unit.

Lucas tapped his dataview, and the holo disappeared again. He stood up. "I'll find somewhere quiet to watch this, and then come back and report what I've learned."

Adika frowned. "Why can't we all watch it?"

"Because I'm hoping there's useful information on this recording, but there will probably be some destructive comments from Fran as well. There's no need for anyone but me to hear them."

I sighed. "I know that you're trying to protect me from Fran's malice, Lucas, but you can't. Remember what you told Megan. It's impossible for you to hide information from me. If I don't watch Fran's message myself, I'll just end up seeing fragments of it in your thoughts."

Lucas pulled a pained face. "That's true. The only way to avoid that is if no one in our unit watches the message. I could get another Tactical Commander to watch it and summarize the facts for us, but crucial details can be lost when people pass on information."

"You don't need to be so worried about this, Lucas. Fran called me a mutant freak when I fired her. Buzz and I have talked about that. I expect we'll talk about whatever Fran says in this message too. After all," I said, with deliberate lightness, "Buzz is a mutant freak as well."

"That makes a significant difference." Lucas sat down again. "Amber, would you be happy if we limited the audience to the people here in this room?"

I'd barely time to nod my head before Adika spoke.

"Forge, Kaden, and Matias can be on guard duty outside during this." Adika jerked his head towards the door, and the three of them hastily left the room.

"Liaison, we're turning off our crystal units while we watch this recording," said Lucas.

We adjusted our ear crystals, and I turned to Adika. "You

didn't need to exclude Forge, Kaden, and Matias. None of them would be influenced by anything Fran says."

"When Fran was fired, I got Forge and Rothan to escort her out of the unit," said Adika. "Rothan told me she was ranting insults about you as they went down in the lift, and it really upset Forge. I don't want to subject him to Fran's poisonous remarks again, and I can't exclude Forge and not Kaden or Matias."

"That makes sense," I said.

"Are you ready to watch the recording now, Amber?" asked Lucas.

"Yes."

Fran reappeared and gave us a self-satisfied smile. "Nicole, I know you won't want to hear from me. You've successfully ingratiated yourself with the inhuman creature, Amber, and you're enjoying yourself as Liaison team leader. You won't welcome a reminder of the fact you stole your position from someone far more competent, but you can't ignore this message. I've got information for Lucas about a serious threat to the Hive."

Fran paused for breath. "I was fired from the unit, and forced to take a menial deputy team leader post in a Navy Zone Security Unit. Despite the injustice, I worked faithfully for the good of the Hive, but then a woman called me. She wore a hooded silver cloak and a Carnival mask, so I couldn't tell anything about her, not even the colour of her hair. She said she was known as Jupiter. She told me she was leading an uprising of a great army of discontented, oppressed citizens. They would purify the Hive, and all five of the mutant telepaths would die in a single day."

Adika jumped to his feet. "We need to get Amber back to the unit right now!"

"Calm down, Adika." Lucas froze Fran's image. "This is fantasy. There is no great army of discontented, oppressed citizens in this Hive. Everyone is given work they love. Even the lowest level people are well fed and have comfortable accommodation. Luxury differentials between levels are carefully limited, so people see being higher level as desirable and appropriately rewarded, but less important than being happy."

I knew that what Lucas said was true. I'd seen it in countless minds. I wasn't totally happy with the way the Hive decided everyone's level and profession for them, but the system worked. The biggest problems people had were with their personal relationships. I had the disturbing thought that some Hives might try to avoid that issue by choosing people's partners for them, and was deeply thankful that our Hive didn't take that approach.

"We were right that Fran was a member of the group that killed her," continued Lucas, "but she wasn't their leader. Jupiter recruited Fran by describing a fantasy Hive. A place full of people who shared Fran's views. Fran believed those lies because Jupiter was describing her personal dream, the way that she wanted the Hive to be. Adika, you're in danger of believing the lies too, because this is your personal nightmare. It has no reality though."

Lucas started the holo playing again.

"I was to be known as Venus," said Fran, "and my mission would be to kill Amber. There was to be a fake alarm call to bring her and her Strike team to Level 50. I would be waiting by the lift doors, stab Amber to death as she came out, and be honoured as a great heroine."

Fran shook her head. "I believed Jupiter at first, but there were some oddities. In her second call, she asked me questions about telepaths, but they weren't the right questions. Her third call was supposed to be an inspiring speech to her whole army of supporters, preparing them for a joint attack. She mentioned me as Venus, and two other heroes known as Mercury and Mars, but she just talked about general rebellion rather than the importance of exterminating the mutant telepaths."

Fran lifted a hand to smooth her already perfectly ordered hair into place. "The next time Jupiter addressed her army, talking about the joint attack, I used some special Liaison monitoring techniques. I couldn't see the identities of Jupiter or the other people she was talking to, because the call was routed through a blocking process, but her speech was only going out to three people including me."

Adika finally sat down again.

"Jupiter lied to me about purging the Hive of telepaths," said Fran. "I don't know what her true plan is, but I'm going to find out. I sent a message, routing it through the same blocking process that Jupiter used, calling the other two followers to a meeting tonight. They must be the people she spoke of as Mercury and Mars. I'll go to meet them dressed as Jupiter, learn their real identities, and find out details of the missions they've been given."

She smiled smugly. "I'll add the results of my investigation to this message, and send it to you as absolute proof that the Hive has no need to use unnatural freaks to hunt criminals. Threats can be discovered and dealt with by loyal members of the Hive using standard methods."

The holo image vanished, and Lucas sighed. "That's all there is. Fran went to the meeting and was killed."

Lucas detached the data cube from his dataview and put it in his pocket. "So the group leader was a woman who used a Carnival costume and the undoubtedly false name of Jupiter to hide her real identity. She gave Fran the name Venus, and her other two recruits were called Mercury and Mars."

He paused. "Those are a strange set of names. Venus is a girl's name, and Mercury is a metallic element with peculiar properties. I don't know Jupiter or Mars at all. I'll check for links between the names."

Lucas worked on his dataview for a moment. I was startled when it made a staccato bleeping noise. An unfamiliar male voice spoke.

"This is Information Archive. You have searched for restricted information. Please state your identity and the reason for your request."

"I'm Tactical Commander Lucas 2511-3022-498," said Lucas. "I'm requesting this information with Telepath Unit priority."

"I cannot release this information without a specific, compelling reason why it is required," said the voice.

"This information is needed to progress the search for a group of targets," said Lucas, with an angry edge to his voice.

"These people have murdered an ex-member of my Telepath Unit, killed five more people in an arson attack that totally destroyed a Hive Security Unit, and are conspiring to assassinate our telepath. Is that reason specific enough and compelling enough for you?"

"Your information request is approved," said the male voice hastily, "however this information has highly sensitive implications. It must not be repeated to people outside your unit."

"Understood. Now what's so terribly secret about these names?"

"There are one hundred and seven Hive cities in the world," said the voice. "The world has one moon orbiting it. The world is one of multiple planets orbiting the Truesun."

I blinked. There were multiple planets? There were multiple worlds?

"Mercury, Mars, Venus, and Jupiter are the names of four of the other planets orbiting the Truesun," continued the voice. "Are you in need of further related information?"

"I think that's all for now, thank you." Lucas ended the call, and there was a moment of silence before he gave a dazed shake of his head. "That was... interesting information."

"That was staggering information," said Adika. "Multiple other worlds!"

"Do you think there are Hives on these other worlds?" I asked.

"I've no idea. We've all seen the moon when we were Outside. I noticed some stars were different from the others, but..." Lucas shook his head again. "The idea of other worlds is bewildering and distracting, but we need to focus on our current case. Crystal units back on now, please."

Lucas tapped at his ear crystal. "Hello again, everyone. Forge, Kaden, and Matias can rejoin us now."

He waited for them to come back into the room before speaking again. "Amber, Adika, and I have watched Fran's message. It appears that someone calling herself Jupiter recruited Fran and two other people to carry out missions against the Hive. Interestingly, Jupiter called her three recruits Venus,

Mercury and Mars. Those names are linked for a reason that's kept highly secret by our Hive, so should be known to very few people."

He paused. "Fran was Venus. She went to meet Mercury and Mars, pretending to be Jupiter, and hoping to get details of the other conspirators' identities and missions. She must have made a mistake that gave her away. I believe she told Mercury and Mars that she'd given information to a work colleague. She hoped that would deter them from harming her, but they killed her anyway."

"One of Mercury and Mars is our firebug, Martin," said Gideon's voice. "It seems likely that the other person killed Fran in a moment of anger. Martin then moved Fran's body to the storage complex to try to make it look like a random killing, and started the fire at the Security Unit in an attempt to destroy Fran's information and kill the work colleague who had it."

"Agreed," said Lucas. "We're therefore hunting three targets, calling themselves Jupiter, Mercury, and Mars. Jupiter doesn't take action herself but manipulates others to follow her orders. One of Mercury and Mars is our meticulously planning firebug, Martin, while the other has moments of uncontrollable violence."

"So what do we do next?" asked Adika.

"Jupiter is the key to solving this," said Lucas. "She recruited the others. That means she either knew them personally or had access to their Law Enforcement records."

Adika groaned. "But we know nothing about Jupiter."

"Yes, we do," said Lucas. "We know that Jupiter has access to some highly secret information. When I'm back at the unit, my Tactical team will work out what imprints might include that information, and..."

"Sorry to interrupt," said Megan's voice, "but I've got a message from Rothan's doctors. His vital signs are climbing."

"That means he's responding to the treatment?" I asked eagerly.

"Yes."

"High up!" yelled Forge and Lucas in unison.

I closed my eyes, reached out for Rothan's mind, and smiled.

"Yes, Rothan's still unconscious, but his thought levels are definitely stronger than they were."

"Rothan will have to remain in the medical cocoon for at least another day," warned Megan, "but all the signs indicate he should make a swift recovery."

"And the other patients?" I asked.

Megan seemed to hesitate before replying. "Most of them are responding to treatment."

"Most?" I asked anxiously.

"One hasn't responded yet," said Megan. "There's still a small chance, but…"

The way Megan said that told us the chance was very small indeed. Our jubilant mood suddenly darkened.

"We'd better get back to the unit," said Lucas grimly. "Rothan is recovering and we have work to do."

I didn't need to read his mind to know what he was thinking. One of the critically ill patients was probably going to die. Lucas didn't want me here when that happened. He didn't want me seeing all the grief-filled minds. I didn't want to see them either.

We went back to waiting room 3 to collect the rest of the Alpha team. The exuberantly happy faces of Emili, Rothan's parents, and his brother showed they hadn't heard about the other critically ill patient who wasn't responding to treatment. None of us mentioned it when we said goodbye. They should be allowed to enjoy the good news that Rothan would recover, without being troubled by guilt that another patient might be dying.

When we went out of the Fire Casualty Centre, Adika paused by Sapphire's Beta Strike team to exchange polite farewells with their leader, Murray. I heard distant music coming from the major belt interchange ahead of us, and saw some of the Hive roaming entertainers had gathered in the open area next to it, putting on an impromptu performance for a crowd of arriving travellers.

As we walked on towards the belt interchange, my mind automatically reached out to the entertainers. There were two dancers in jewelled costumes, several musicians, and a man dressed as a comic monster with a lumpy back. The man and woman dancing had the same delight in their minds as my Strike team had when they rejoiced in their physical fitness. The musicians were swept up by their music. The man dressed as the comic monster was thinking...

... would have been so much simpler if Mars had kept his temper instead of lashing out and killing...

... still can't understand how anyone survived the Security Unit fire. I have to make sure they all burn to death this time, but getting into that Fire Casualty Centre is...

If whoever has that information talks...

I changed my ear crystal from the receive setting to transmit. "Target acquired!"

CHAPTER TWENTY-FOUR

Adika gave me a startled look, and tapped his ear crystal. "Alpha Strike team is moving."

"Tactical is confused but ready," Gideon's voice came over the crystal comms.

"Liaison is ready. Jade, cover hasty coordination desk, and someone find..." Nicole's voice abruptly cut out as she belatedly remembered to turn her comms transmission off.

"Who is our target?" asked Gideon.

"Nobody look his way or you'll frighten him," I said. "Our firebug, Martin, is here to burn the Fire Casualty Centre. He's among the performers entertaining the crowd, disguised in a comic monster suit."

"Strike team, gather closely round Amber, blocking Martin's view of her," said Lucas. "We have to assume that Fran gave Jupiter details about our telepaths, including images of them, and all that information was passed to our firebug. If he sees Amber, then he'll start running."

I skimmed through the levels of my target's mind, relaying relevant thoughts. "Jupiter gave the firebug the name Mercury. He likes to think of himself as that rather than Martin, because Jupiter said Mercury was a fiery name. It was Mars who lost his temper and killed Venus."

I sensed Mercury's mind change its colour, taste, brightness. He'd noticed a group of dark-haired men at the end of a wide corridor. "Mercury has seen us. He's wondering why we're standing here. Sapphire's Beta team have been guarding the Fire Casualty Centre all day, so Mercury has got used to their presence, but he's suspicious of us."

"There's a bank of lifts over to our left," said Lucas. "We'll walk towards them and get inside one."

We moved on to the lifts, and stood there waiting for thirty seconds. "Nicole, where is our lift?" asked Lucas impatiently.

"I'm working on the lift system myself," said Nicole. "All the lifts in that bank have got passengers already, so… One is empty now! Locking it to priority usage and it will be with you in three seconds."

The light above the right-hand lift flashed to show it had reached our level, and the doors opened. We went inside, and Lucas closed the doors behind us.

"I'm taking us up one level and keeping the doors closed," he said. "We need Mercury to be reassured by the lift lights changing to show we've left, and one level won't be far enough to strain Amber's mental link with him."

The lift made the brief movement upwards. Now I was out of view of other people, I could sit down, close my eyes, and focus my full attention on my target.

"Mercury thinks we've gone," I said. "He's stopped worrying about us and is thinking about how Mars killed Venus."

I saw a horrific image of Mars's knife sweeping across Venus's throat, but I was deep in Mercury's mind, with his emotions swamping my own. I felt only cold annoyance at the impulsive murder that had caused him so much inconvenience.

"Venus told them she'd given a data cube to someone," I reported. "She said that meant they wouldn't dare to harm her, and gave a triumphant laugh. That was when Mars lost his temper and killed her. If Mars had been sensible and controlled himself, they could have forced Venus to tell them who had the data cube. Instead, they only discovered who Venus was, and where she worked, when they searched her body and found her Security Unit identity card."

I saw another image, this time of Mercury's hand removing a Carnival mask from Fran's face. Mercury thought it was odd that her expression in death was one of surprise rather than fear.

"Mars is male then," said Lucas. "Is he here as well? Does Mercury know his identity?"

"Mars shouldn't be here. Mercury doesn't know who Mars is, or what he looks like. The only time they met was when they were called to that meeting with Venus, and all three of them were wearing Carnival cloaks and masks."

"Is there anything else at all about Mars and Jupiter?" asked Lucas.

"Mercury was furious with Mars for killing Venus. I told Mars to stay out of things while I reported what had happened to Jupiter and cleaned up his mess. No, *Mercury* told Mars to stay out of things while he cleaned up his mess."

"What's the plan, Lucas?" asked Adika. "Do you want to drop out and go back to the Fire Casualty Centre to call tactics for us?"

"I'd rather stick with Amber's bodyguards," said Lucas. "Mercury is here to try to burn the Fire Casualty Centre. I've already been nearly cooked alive in one of his fires, and I'm not eager to repeat the experience."

"Should we tell the Fire Casualty Centre to evacuate?" asked Nicole.

Megan's voice spoke on the comms. "They can't evacuate the critical cases like Rothan. Moving them now would disrupt the crucial recovery phase, and they wouldn't survive long enough for additional medicine to be delivered."

Adika said a much ruder version of waste it. I felt like saying it myself, but it was more important to report what I was seeing in Mercury's mind.

"The monster suit is a strange shape because Mercury is wearing a backpack underneath it. That's crammed with canisters of inflammable liquid."

There was a full minute of silence before Adika spoke. "Lucas, do we go for the strike?"

"I can't make up my mind," said Lucas. "I hate this situation. We've got a firebug carrying canisters of inflammable liquid. He's positioned next to a crowd of over a hundred people.

Amber, if we corner Mercury, is he likely to panic and set fire to himself?"

"I can't tell," I said. "He's not thinking about the possibility of getting caught."

"We can't risk it," said Lucas. "If Mercury sets fire to the liquid he's carrying, he could kill or injure dozens of people. On the other hand, I was trapped in a fire myself only days ago, so I could be letting my own fear cloud my judgement. Gideon, what's your call on this one?"

"I'm a defence expert, Lucas. I'm not qualified to call a strike."

"Kareem then."

"I haven't called a strike decision in decades, Lucas, and I'm definitely not calling this one," said Kareem's voice. "However, I'm happy to point out we must take this firebug alive. We need him to lead us to Mars and Jupiter."

"True." Lucas went silent again.

I was getting worried now. Lucas shouldn't be expressing doubt in his own judgement like this. He knew that people couldn't trust a Tactical Commander's decisions if he didn't appear confident about them himself.

I risked leaving Mercury's thoughts to check the glowing beacon of Lucas's mind. Normally it had a host of thought levels, each chasing different ideas, but now all the levels were united in working through a single problem. He'd been hit by a crisis of confidence after the fire, thinking it was his fault that people had died. When he found out that wasn't true, he'd picked himself up again, but now he was faced with making this decision and...

If I call a strike now, and it goes wrong, there could be even more deaths than last time. Deaths that truly are my fault.

If I don't call a strike, and the target gets away, he'll set more fires and kill more people. Deaths that truly are my fault.

Even if I get this call right, there'll be another, and another, and another. Eventually...

Adika's voice was openly impatient now. "Lucas? What do we do?"

I pulled myself away from Lucas's thoughts for a second,

opened my eyes, and turned to look for Adika. He was right next to me, staring at Lucas, so I grabbed his arm and shook my head urgently.

Adika frowned down at me, but I was already closing my eyes and returning to Lucas's thoughts. I didn't know what I could say to help him. I'd convinced him he hadn't made a mistake last time, but I couldn't convince him he'd never make a mistake in future. What Lucas was thinking was perfectly true. A Tactical Commander had to make endless decisions, and eventually one of those decisions would kill people.

I didn't know what to say, but someone else did. Kareem's voice spoke over the crystal comms. I was puzzled at first, because I could hear him through Lucas's ears but not my own. Then I realized that Kareem had got Liaison to set up the comms so he could talk privately to Lucas.

"Decades ago, I made two mistakes, Lucas. The first one was calling a strike at the wrong time. It killed seventeen people. The second one was quitting as a Tactical Commander. That killed hundreds of people."

Kareem paused. "I didn't fully understand that for a very long time, and by then it was far too late to change my mind. I'd been given my post as Tactical Commander because I was the best candidate available. After I quit, someone had to take over who wasn't quite as good. Every time they made a bad decision when I'd have made a better one, every time someone died as a result, it was my fault not theirs, my death count not theirs. My death count is getting larger with every year that passes, and it will keep increasing until the day I die."

He gave a heavy sigh. "The question isn't whether you'll kill people, Lucas. All Tactical Commanders make mistakes that kill people, because we are human beings and fallible. The question is whether you'll kill less people than the most capable replacement candidate for your job. You're nearly the best Tactical Commander in the Hive. With a little more experience, you'll be the very best. Don't walk away or you'll have a huge death count."

Lucas's mind seemed to have totally shut down. There were

no thoughts at all for several seconds, and I was starting to panic, then I saw a single sentence overlaid with grim resignation.

I will have my death count.

After that, the usual multi-levelled thought trains came rushing back, and Lucas started speaking in the familiar, calm voice he used on emergency runs. "We need to ambush our target in a place clear of any people or vital equipment that can be harmed by fire. Tactical team should find me potential ambush locations."

He paused. "Once we've chosen our location, Chase team will be positioned ready to pressure the target into moving into our ambush. Forge, I want you to leave the lift now and go back to the Fire Casualty Centre, entering by the rear entrance to avoid being seen by Mercury. You will then move to just inside the front entrance and wait there. When Chase team are in position, you'll head straight towards Mercury, moving at a slow, purposeful walk. Your goal is to make him nervous enough to run, without frightening him into taking any drastic measures."

There was the sound of the lift doors opening and closing.

"Mercury prepares everything meticulously in advance," continued Lucas. "He'll have planned an escape route in case of trouble. What's he thinking now, Amber? Any indication of which way he's likely to run?"

Lucas was back to his true decisive self. I shouldn't be studying his thoughts now but those of my target. I hastily searched for Mercury's mind again and started babbling random facts. "Mercury is angry and frustrated. He set up the Security Unit fire to make it impossible for anyone to escape, but somehow dozens of people survived. One of them may have Venus's data cube, and that puts the joint attack in jeopardy."

"Joint attack," Lucas repeated my words urgently. "Any more details on this joint attack?"

"Mercury's mission is to light a fire, the greatest of all fires, which will rage through Purple Zone. The only information on Mars's mission is that Mars expects to die carrying it out. That doesn't make sense to Mercury. He wants to savour the sight of his fires burning, not to die in them."

The thought train I'd been following had ended now. I skimmed through Mercury's mind looking for another that was relevant. "Mercury is worried that Law Enforcement will find out Venus's information before the joint attack. Even if the data cube was destroyed in the Security Unit fire, the person who had it could still be alive. They may know some of the information."

I shook my head and corrected myself. "No, Mercury's absolutely certain they'll know *all* of the information. If anyone gave a mysterious data cube to Mercury, he'd instantly check to see what secrets were on it."

"Fran talked about her own mission," said Lucas, "but not those of Mercury or Mars. I think she'd discovered their missions were to attack the Hive itself rather than telepaths, and that's why she turned against the group. If Fran had contacted Nicole or me back then, she'd be alive right now, but it was too shameful for her to admit she'd been involved in a plot to harm the Hive. She tried to identify the other conspirators in a desperate attempt to prove her loyalty."

He sighed. "You still can't see anything else about Mars's mission, Amber?"

"Nothing at all," I said. "Mercury's thoughts are focused on his own fire. He thinks both Mars and his mission are far more trouble than they're worth."

"The joint attack must have been planned to include simultaneous attacks by Venus, Mercury, and Mars," said Lucas. "Jupiter could attack too, but she appears to be playing the role of puppet master here rather than taking an active part herself."

"I've found something else," I said sharply. "Mercury asked Jupiter to move the joint attack to an earlier date, but Jupiter said Mars had to attack a week from today. Both the day and time were crucial. She told Mercury that all the Security Unit survivors are in the Fire Casualty Centre and they are being questioned. She ordered him to burn the place before they talk."

"Jupiter knows too much," said Lucas. "She can't be getting information from Fran any longer, so she must have access to Law Enforcement systems herself."

"Mercury is feeling pressured now," I reported. "He can't

work out how to burn the Fire Casualty Centre. He's tried every possible way to approach it, but they're all too heavily guarded. He can't get close to a wall let alone an entrance. There are hasties patrolling the levels above and below. He can't find any weak spots at all."

"Congratulations on setting up flawless defences, Gideon," said Lucas.

"Thank you," said Gideon's voice.

I was still chasing round thought levels. "Mercury found an entry point into the air vents. He tried to use it to reach the Fire Casualty Centre, but even the vents were blocked or guarded. Mercury gave up that approach, but he's left the vent cover off in case he needs to run."

"Can you tell us where that entry point is?" asked Lucas.

"No, I just got a flicker of an image. There's a ladder going up."

"Does the ladder go down as well?"

"Yes, but Mercury is only interested in going up. He seems to feel that height is an advantage."

"When we trigger Mercury into running, he'll head up," said Lucas. "His air vent entry point has to be nearby if he's seeing it as his escape route. Gideon, transmit us the details of your best ambush location above us."

"Our best ambush location is a park on Level 3," said Gideon. "Sending details to your dataviews now. Controlling a target's flight all the way from Level 25 to Level 3 won't be easy, but this is an ideal place to ambush a firebug. The park is being extended, and work on the new area has got as far as ripping out everything on Level 4 through Level 1, so there'll be virtually nothing to burn."

"We're evacuating all maintenance workers from that area now," said Nicole.

"Eli, you're in charge of Bodyguard team," said Adika. "Chase team, we're heading out now. Red group will go with me, taking another lift to the ambush area. Everyone else will head into the air vents."

The lift doors opened and shut. There'd just be my five bodyguards and Lucas with me in the lift now.

"Mercury is getting restless," I said. "He's thinking of doing another lap of the area. There has to be a way to set that Fire Casualty Centre on fire. The survivors must…"

I broke off my sentence. Mercury's mind was flaring red with alarm. I saw the view from his eyes, the single massive blond man sprinting through the crowd towards him, a fleeting glimpse of the large group of other blond men starting to move as well, and then I, Mercury, was turning to run at full speed.

"Mercury's running!" I shouted. "Sapphire's Beta team are chasing him."

CHAPTER TWENTY-FIVE

"Waste that!" said Lucas. "How did Sapphire's Beta team spot our firebug?"

There was a despairing groan from Adika. "They're worried about a possible attack on Soren's daughter. They must have noticed us stop, suspected Amber had picked up a target, and started monitoring our comms to find out what was happening. The continuous data exchange between the Tactical teams uses a dedicated secure connection. They could have…"

Nicole interrupted him. "Yes, they've linked into our comms via the secure connection. They masked their identity as one of our own Beta team. Do we cut the link?"

"They're listening to us now? No, don't cut the link." Lucas's voice changed to be harshly imperative. "Sapphire Beta team, pull back, pull back! You're risking your own lives and those of others by chasing our target."

This situation hadn't been covered in my training. "Do I keep relaying information from Mercury?" I asked in confusion.

"Amber, keep relaying information," said Lucas. "Sapphire Beta team, break off pursuit. Kareem, get Penelope on our comms."

"Mercury has entered the vent system," I said. "He's ripped off his monster costume and is heading up the ladder."

"Everyone get to your ambush positions!" Adika sounded ready to explode with anger. "Murray, Soren, someone on Sapphire's Beta team talk to us!"

There was no response.

"Forge, where are you?" asked Lucas.

"I saw Sapphire's mob start running, and chased after them. I'm right behind them now." Forge's voice was breathless. "Do I pull back?"

"Forge, stay with them," said Lucas. "Kareem, we urgently need Penelope. If you can't contact her, then get Sapphire's deputy Tactical team leader instead."

"I'm talking to Penelope now," said Kareem.

My mind was with Mercury, seeing the view from his eyes as he climbed a dimly lit, infinitely long ladder. Well, it wasn't actually infinitely long, but there'd be about seventy-five levels above Mercury, and another seventy-five below him. In my opinion, that was close enough to infinite. It was the sort of ladder that I'd never dare to climb myself because of my fear of heights, but I was feeling Mercury's emotions not my own, and he was focused on escaping his pursuers.

"Mercury's still climbing the ladder in the vent system," I reported. "He can hear people behind him. They're gaining ground on him because he's loaded down with the backpack full of canisters."

An unfamiliar female voice spoke from my ear crystal. This had to be Sapphire's Tactical Commander, Penelope.

"Beta team, what's happening out there?" she demanded, in glacial tones. "Why are you chasing Amber's target? Murray, answer me this second or you'll spend the rest of your life scrubbing slime vats!"

"We aren't chasing Amber's target, Penelope," replied a male voice. "We're chasing Soren. He suddenly ran off after Amber's target, and he's ignoring my orders to stop. We're trying to catch him up and restrain him."

Penelope made an exasperated noise. "Lucas, do you want our Beta team to disengage or continue pursuit?"

"Forge, what's your status now?" asked Lucas.

"I'm inside the vent system. Sapphire's Beta team are all climbing the ladder chasing after Soren and Mercury. I'm at the back of the line. I'm a specialist climber, so I could go a lot faster if people would get out of my way."

"Sapphire Beta team, disengage pursuit!" ordered Lucas.

My mind was with Mercury. He glanced down at the line of shadowy figures on the ladder chasing him. The leading man was getting much too close. Mercury reached into his backpack to pull out a canister and light the fuse.

"Take cover!" I screamed. "Fire bomb coming down at you!"

I saw the view through Mercury's eyes. The figures frantically wedging themselves into side passages as the sheet of flame plunged down at them. Mercury frowned and started climbing again.

"Forge, are you all right?" I yelled, and instinctively linked to his mind. I found Forge was crammed into a narrow maintenance crawl way with three other men, watching a mass of flames fall past them.

"I'm fine, but that was far too close." Forge's voice was slightly higher pitched than usual.

"Sapphire Beta team remain where you are," said Lucas. "Forge, what's Soren doing?"

Forge stuck his head warily out of the crawl way to peer upwards. I saw his glimpse of a figure above him. "Soren's climbing the ladder again. Do I follow him?"

"Yes, follow him," ordered Lucas. "Amber, can you check Soren's mind and give us some clue how to stop him."

I left Forge's thoughts, and reached up past the huddled glows of minds in side passages, to the still moving, red-hued one that had to be Soren. He was hearing Murray's voice shouting at him through the crystal unit in his ear. He was thinking...

I recoiled from the pain in Soren's mind. "No force in the Hive will stop Soren now. He was monitoring our comms, looking at the man who'd started the fire in the Security Unit, at the moment he got the message that his daughter had died. He will kill Mercury at any cost."

Lucas groaned. "Amber, go back to Mercury's mind, and warn of any more fire bombs."

I found Mercury's mind again. He was climbing upwards, thoughts seething with frustration.

... should have all been turned into human candles, but they were warned in time to get out of the way...

... one of the real telepaths must be around. Venus was right. They should all be killed. Ruining my pleasure in...

... will have my victory a week from now. The greatest fire of all...

Part of me shared Mercury's excitement as he imagined lighting his great fire, while the rest of me was still flinching from the pain in Soren's mind. He'd got the message that Kirsten had been given the treatment, he'd dared to hope that she'd survive, but then...

I was Soren, racked with pain over my daughter's death, remembering the day she was born, and how I'd held the tiny, perfect baby in my arms. I was Mercury, savouring the power of fire, and dreaming of lighting the greatest fire of all. I was Amber, troubled by a stabbing headache.

"Soren, listen to me," said Penelope, in a compelling voice. "Mercury is part of a group of conspirators. Amber's unit need him alive to help them catch the others or many more people will die. More daughters, more sons, more..."

There was an odd, echoing sound, and Mercury's foot lit up with pain. He gasped, and clung to the ladder.

"Soren shot Mercury in the foot," I shouted.

"Amber, leave Mercury and get back into your own head," ordered Lucas. "Forge, take cover. If Mercury falls..."

I was pulling out of Mercury's mind when agony hit me again, this time engulfing my left side and chest. I convulsed, lost my hold on the ladder, and started tumbling downwards helplessly. I was probably already dying of my wounds, but a fall of eighty levels meant certain death anyway. I wouldn't light the greatest of fires after all. How could fate be guilty of such unfairness, such injustice, such extremely bad manners?

I was Amber, not Mercury. I tore myself free of the thoughts that were flaring in death and screamed a warning to Forge. "Mercury's falling! He's been shot again."

My thoughts were with Forge, and instantly I *was* Forge. I was looking up at where Soren was clinging to the ladder above me with one hand, while holding his gun in the other. The tumbling figure of Mercury hit Soren hard. Now both of them were falling towards me.

There was no time to reach a side passage. Only one option then. I clipped my belt to the ladder, gripped a rung with my right hand, and flung myself to the side, plastering my back against the wall and hoping both the falling men would miss me.

One figure tumbled past without touching me, and then the flailing leg of the other hit my left shoulder like a hammer blow. I lost my grip on the ladder, but my belt held me in place long enough for me to grab hold of another rung. I looked down at where Soren and Mercury were plummeting to their deaths.

"Forge?" Lucas's voice asked urgently.

"I'm a bit battered but still hanging onto the ladder," said Forge. "Soren and Mercury are both falling faster than an express lift and… Gah! I think Mercury's backpack exploded. Liaison had better get fire containment to check what happened down there."

"Working on that," said Nicole.

"Amber?" Lucas's voice was even more urgent now. "Amber, come back to yourself!"

I retreated into my own mind, opened my eyes, and found Lucas was crouching next to me. "What were you doing?" he demanded. "You know it's dangerous to stay in the head of a target that's under attack."

My forehead was throbbing with pain. My mind was spinning with Soren's thoughts, Mercury's thoughts, Forge's thoughts. I slapped Lucas's face, sending him sprawling onto the floor, and leaned forward to spit my anger at him.

"You think it's easy to pull away from thoughts that are lost in despair or overwhelmed by agony? It isn't. They suck you in and won't let you escape."

I saw the appalled expression on Lucas's face, and became aware of my bodyguards watching us in stunned silence.

"I'm sorry," I wailed. "I didn't mean to hit you, I didn't mean to yell, but my head hurts."

The faces around me blurred and then everything went dark.

CHAPTER TWENTY-SIX

The first thing I was aware of was that my head had stopped hurting. The second was that I was lying on something hard and lumpy. The third was that I was horribly cold.

I opened my eyes and saw dizzyingly tall trees reaching up towards an impossibly high, grey-painted ceiling. No, that wasn't a ceiling, but a cloudy sky. I was stretched out on ground that was covered in coarse grass, and weirdly I was wrapped in several silver Carnival cloaks. Despite the cloaks, I was still cold, because the ground was freezing and there was an icy wind.

"I'm Outside." I sat up.

Lucas's voice spoke. "That's right. You said that your head hurt and then you passed out. We'd normally have rushed you back to our unit, but that was half the Hive away. We were considering taking you to a park, because we knew you felt comfortable in parks, when Buzz joined in the discussion. She said your headache was a symptom of telepathic overload, and getting you to a park would be good, but taking you Outside would be much better."

I turned and saw Lucas was sitting next to me. He had a cloak draped over his shoulders as well, but his was in the black and red of a Halloween costume rather than Carnival. He smiled at me and continued talking.

"Buzz hasn't been counselling you for long, but she's a borderline telepath and seemed sure of what she was saying, so we brought you up to the nearest Hive exit. The second we got you Outside, you relaxed, as if the pain in your head was easing. A little later, you moved from unconsciousness into natural sleep. I felt it was best to let you wake up in your own time."

I shivered, and tugged the cloaks tighter around me. "Why is it so much colder than the last time we were Outside?"

"That's because it was early autumn last time we were out here, but now winter is starting. There are four seasons during the year: spring, summer, autumn, and winter. You may find it helps to think of them as related to the four Hive festivals. Carnival is in spring. Valentine in summer. Halloween in autumn. New Year in winter."

My thoughts drifted for a moment. New Year was the festival for families, and had always been very important to me. I'd never paid any attention to Valentine, because that was for lovers, and I hadn't been part of an established couple when I was on Teen Level. Now I was with Lucas, next Valentine festival could be very different.

"The weather Outside changes with the seasons," continued Lucas.

I dragged my thoughts back to the present. "And the weather in winter is colder than autumn?"

"Yes."

I noticed a red mark on Lucas's left cheek, and a memory surfaced. "I'm sorry I hit you," I said guiltily.

Lucas put an arm round me, and pulled me against his warmth. "I'm not sure it was you that hit me. If it was, then I deserved it. You suffered severe problems after the run where we found Fran's body. You appeared to have no ill effects at all after the next run where we caught Ashton, but I knew that didn't necessarily indicate an improvement in your condition, since there was a key difference between the two runs."

I frowned. "What key difference?"

"On the first run, you were being hit by multiple pressures. Adika's relationship crisis. A disturbing target mind. Your own reaction to finding Fran's body. Having to avoid getting too close to Sapphire and her team was an additional stress factor. On the second run, you just had to cope with a single target mind."

Lucas pulled a pained face. "I was worried about letting you take on chasing Mercury. You were in an emotional whirlpool after waiting to see if Rothan would live or die. You'd watched that unsettling message from Fran. Adding the pressure of reading Mercury was obviously going to be a strain, but I couldn't think of any viable alternative options."

"That's because there weren't any other options. There wasn't time to get another telepath to take over our target, you couldn't order us to walk away and leave Mercury free to burn the Fire Casualty Centre, and you couldn't send our Strike team after him without my support. Just imagine what would have happened to Forge, and to Sapphire's Beta team as well, if I hadn't warned them about Mercury dropping that fire bomb on them."

Lucas winced. "Exactly. So I risked setting things up to ambush Mercury. I thought we could pull out at any moment if you seemed under too much strain. I wasn't allowing for Sapphire's Beta team spying on our comms and disrupting our chase. I've never known an emergency run descend into total chaos like that. I'm terribly sorry. You should really hit me again."

"I don't want to hit you again. What happened wasn't your fault. It wasn't Soren's fault either. You must understand why he reacted the way he did."

"Everyone understands why Soren reacted the way he did," said Lucas sadly. "Most human beings capable of emotion would have lost control in a similar situation."

I hesitated before speaking again. I had some questions bothering me. I thought I knew the answers to them but I had to be sure. "What happened at the end of the run? I've got fragments of Soren's thoughts, Mercury's thoughts, and Forge's thoughts all muddled up together. There's an image of Mercury falling. He's dead, isn't he?"

"Yes."

"Soren?"

"I'm afraid he's dead too."

"But Forge is alive, isn't he?" I asked urgently. "He must be.

There's what has to be an image from his thoughts, where he's holding onto the ladder and looking down at the other two falling."

"Forge is very much alive," said Lucas. "He'll have some dramatic bruises for the next few days, but the Strike team are used to being covered in bruises."

I sighed with relief. "Is there any more news about Rothan?"

"Rothan's condition is steadily improving. His doctors say that his youth and physical fitness should mean he makes a rapid recovery."

I gave another sigh. "That's good about Forge and Rothan. Not so good about Soren. I hope Sapphire won't blame us for his death."

"I'm sure she won't. Her own people were there and will tell her what happened."

Multiple thoughts were churning through my mind, but one was more important than the rest. "If Mercury is dead, then we've nothing to lead us to Jupiter or Mars, and the joint attack is only a week away."

"It's no longer a joint attack," said Lucas. "Venus was supposed to stab you, and Mercury was going to light a great fire, but they're both dead. Jupiter is just a puppet master, so that means only Mars will be attacking, and we have a full week to work out his plan and deal with him."

He paused. "I knew you'd be asking all these questions, Amber. I accepted I'd need to answer them to give you some peace of mind, but you must stop worrying about the case now. Buzz was right about bringing you Outside. She says you should stay here for at least another six hours to complete your recovery, and I feel we should follow her instructions exactly."

"Six hours! It looks as if the sun will be setting soon, so we'll freeze to death with just these Carnival and Halloween cloaks over our ordinary clothes. Where did these cloaks come from anyway?"

Lucas laughed. "When we came out here and discovered how cold it was, I sent a couple of the Strike team back into the Hive to scavenge extra clothing. The exit is surrounded by offices, so the only things around were some boxes of costume cloaks and masks left behind after an office party. We'll have proper clothes and tents soon though. The Beta team are on their way through the Hive, and they're bringing all the camping equipment we used on our long trip Outside."

Lucas reached up to adjust the crystal unit in his ear. "Adika, how long will it be before the tents get here? I'd like to get Amber out of this icy wind as soon as possible. I wouldn't mind getting myself out of the icy wind as well."

I heard a faint murmur that was Adika answering him. I wriggled an arm free to adjust my own ear crystal and discovered it was missing. Lucas had probably stolen it to stop me being disturbed by the sound of voices.

"I'm delighted to hear that." Lucas adjusted his ear crystal again, and turned back to me. "The Beta team should be here soon. Buzz is coming with them in case you need her support. Like most of the Hive, she's afraid of Outside, so she'll be staying just inside the exit doors. Her plan is to work on her fear so she can eventually join us Outside at times like this."

"You think we'll be taking refuge Outside on a regular basis?"

"Back in the early days of your telepathic training, we had a conversation about the Hive needing you to fill a dangerously stressful role. I said that your unit staff would do everything we could to help you relax and be happy."

"I remember. We discussed the huge apartment, the luxury food, and," I pulled a face, "Lottery choosing attractive young men for my Strike team."

"We knew you liked being in the park. I thought you found the minds of the birds and animals helpful, so the park keeper has been bringing in new species. I should have made the logical connection that being Outside would help you even more, but I didn't. You used to have such a great terror of Outside that I assumed it would keep having a negative effect on you. Foolish of me."

"It wasn't foolish at all."

"Yes, it was. A Tactical Commander shouldn't make the basic mistake of failing to re-examine his options after a situation radically changes. Buzz walked into our unit, looked at things with a fresh perspective, and told us the blindingly obvious."

Lucas paused. "Today you hit your limit, overloaded, and collapsed. If you show any signs of fragmentation on future runs then we're taking you Outside immediately. I…"

He broke off because there was the sound of voices from somewhere behind us. "That must be the Beta team arriving with the tents. Would you like us to have a tent over here where it's quiet, or shall we join the rest of them by the camp fire?"

I felt an odd pleasure at the mention of the word fire. It rekindled images of the sheet of flame falling down the air vent, and Mercury's delight at the thought of men burning like human candles. I was clearly suffering some lingering effects from sharing the firebug's thoughts. I shook my head to dismiss them.

"You want us to have a tent over here then?" Lucas reached for his dataview.

I realized he'd misinterpreted me shaking my head. "No, I'd like to join the others by the fire." I clutched my array of cloaks and scrambled to my feet. "Where is it?"

Lucas stood up, the dark Halloween cloak billowing around him in the wind. "This way."

We walked through the trees, and now I could smell smoke on the wind. I quickened my pace, eager to reach the fire, and instantly wondered if my eagerness was my own or belonged to Mercury. I could convince myself it was my own eagerness. On the long trip Outside, we'd sat round the camp fire on dry evenings, cooking food, talking, and laughing at Eli's jokes. Fires were attractively warm and friendly things, especially on a bitterly cold day like this.

I saw a crowd of men in a clearing ahead of us, busily erecting tents, and paused to watch the frantic activity. The Alpha and Beta Strike teams were working together, so I was struck by the number of them. There'd be a few more bodyguards watching me from among the trees as well.

"Forty men on my Strike team," I muttered. "More than a hundred people in my Telepath Unit. All of them fussing over the wellbeing of one telepath. Is it really worth it?"

Lucas smiled. "Respectfully point out that we all do plenty of other work as well as fussing over your wellbeing, Amber, but yes, it's well worth it. How many times have you stopped an assault or murder before it happened?"

"I didn't stop Fran's murder."

"Nobody could have stopped Fran's murder. She gave her killers information on how to avoid being caught. She arranged to meet them alone. She made them furiously angry. She did everything except hand Mars the knife he used to kill her."

"I suppose that's true."

I stood still for a moment longer, troubled by my memories of the chase after Mercury, especially the way it had ended, with me hitting Lucas and screaming... Well, I didn't know exactly what I'd screamed before I collapsed, but the whole of my Alpha Strike team would have heard it, and my bodyguards had witnessed me attacking Lucas like a wild thing.

It was going to be embarrassing facing them after that, but I had to do it sooner or later. I forced myself to walk out into the clearing, and saw all the bustle of activity stop as every man turned to stare at me. I tried to pretend to myself that their tense body language was just because they were Strike team trained and alert for danger, but failed. The truth was that my behaviour earlier had frightened them.

Adika came up to us, his face carefully neutral, and handed each of us a bulky padded jacket. I dropped my Carnival cloaks, and thankfully slid my arms into the comforting warmth.

Lucas tugged his jacket on as well. "Amber is feeling much better now. She'd like us to have one of the tents over here."

Adika waved at the nearest tent. There was an awkward moment of silence, and I felt I had to say something.

"I'm sorry I acted strangely after the run. The combination of Mercury's mind and Soren's mind was very difficult, but hopefully it won't happen again."

"We'd certainly prefer you not to collapse again, Amber," said Adika, "but I wouldn't describe it as acting strangely, and there's no need to apologize for it."

"I was actually talking about hitting Lucas."

Adika shrugged. "I wouldn't describe that as acting strangely either. I'm often tempted to hit Lucas."

I heard a ripple of laughter from the watching Strike team, and they seemed to relax. I had my telepathic abilities firmly shut down, too nervous to read even Lucas's mind, but I could guess what they were thinking. Amber had behaved oddly after that run, but she was herself again now.

Lucas sniffed suspiciously. "What's that dreadful smell? Please don't tell me that you're doing camp fire cooking again."

"Camp fire cooking?" I repeated hopefully. "Are you making any of that pastryish, breadish thing? The one with the bits of stuff inside it?"

"We are," said Dhiren. "We're making some with the usual recipe, but also trying several new experiments."

"We're all going to die," said Lucas, in apocalyptic tones. "Do you want to rest in the tent now, Amber?"

"No. I'd like to sit by the fire and watch them cooking."

Lucas sighed, but led the way towards the fire. I wanted to sit right next to it, I wanted to feed it with branches until it blazed out of control, but I forced myself to pick a spot on the fringes of its warmth instead. I sat down and leaned my back against a tree.

Lucas sat next to me. "If we stay out here until the end of the six hours, we won't be heading back to the unit until very late in the evening. You can decide whether you'd rather spend the night here in the tents."

I grunted an acknowledgement. Dhiren, Kaden, and Eli were busy cooking food. The rest of the Alpha and Beta teams were finishing putting up tents and drifting to sit near the fire, but I noticed someone was missing.

"Where's Forge?" I asked. "Were his bruises so bad that he had to go for medical treatment?"

"I don't think so. He was here a few minutes ago." Lucas called out in a louder voice. "Adika, what have you done with Forge?"

Adika was studying a tent that had a slight list to one side, but he turned his head for a moment to call back to us. "Forge is inside the Hive exit with Buzz. She wanted someone to advise her on how to adjust to being Outside, and suggested Forge, so I sent him over."

I groaned.

"Something wrong?" asked Lucas.

"I'm just worried why Buzz specifically asked for Forge to help her. I know she thinks Forge is deliciously handsome, but I warned her he was still getting over breaking up with Shanna and isn't ready for another serious relationship yet."

Lucas grinned. "I think Forge can defend himself against any unwelcome advances. He's twice Buzz's size, trained in unarmed combat, and carrying a gun."

"That's true," I said dubiously, "but Buzz can be a little unscrupulous about these things. I remember her telling me that she once trapped a boy in a lift with her so she could persuade him to kiss her."

"If she traps Forge in a lift, he can use his ear crystal to call his Beta team to rescue him."

I saw Eli coming towards us. He held out two plates of the oddly shaped pastry items that I remembered from our last trip, and I grabbed one.

"Which of these pastry things are made with the old recipe, and which are the experiments?" I asked.

"We're not sure. We got a bit muddled during the cooking process." Eli offered the other plate to Lucas.

"No, thank you." Lucas shook his head firmly. "I'm too young to die. I'll have a protein bar and a crunch cake later."

I munched my way through three of the pastries, couldn't manage the fourth one, and coaxed Lucas into eating it. Warm, contented, and full, I leant back against my tree.

"Admit it," I said. "The pastries taste good."

"That one was less bad than usual." Lucas pointed towards the camp fire. "You can stop worrying about Forge. He's over there with Eli, and the blissful expression on his face makes me think he's been enjoying Buzz's company."

I watched Forge talking to Eli, and frowned. Forge did look suspiciously happy. "You think that he's ready to move on from his relationship with Shanna then?"

Lucas laughed. "As an expert in behavioural analysis, I think that Forge has already moved on at express belt speed. Not that it takes any expertise to work out what's just happened between him and Buzz. Most of the Strike team seem to have taken one look at Forge's face and leapt to the same conclusion."

Eli was certainly looking amused about something. He handed two plates of food to Forge, and leaned forward to whisper in his ear. Forge flushed with embarrassment.

I sighed. "After years of seeing Forge with Shanna on Teen Level, it's strange to think of him being with someone else. I just hope that Buzz hasn't rushed him into anything he'll regret."

Matias sneaked up behind Forge, and tried to steal a pastry from one of the plates, but Eli slapped his hand away.

"Bad manners!" he scolded.

A memory hit me. Mercury falling down the air shaft, his body in agony, his mind raging that fate was guilty of such unfairness, such injustice, such extremely bad manners.

"Did you want to speak to Forge before he goes back to Buzz?" asked Lucas.

I was too deep in shock to answer him. I'd just worked out who Jupiter was.

CHAPTER TWENTY-SEVEN

To avoid attracting attention, we took the lift right down to Level 100, and used an express belt there to travel back through the Hive. Everyone thought of Level 100 as the lowest of the hundred accommodation levels of the Hive, but it was really just a maze of tanks and pipes. It was nearly midnight when we started our journey, so there was virtually no one working among the dusty pipes to stare at the large number of muscled men loaded down with heavy backpacks.

The members of the Strike team chattered away happily, but I barely said a word as we rode through the Hive. We went through the open bulkhead doors between Navy Zone and Blue Zone, Blue Zone and Turquoise Zone, and on through the colours. All the way, my mind was focused on the problem of Jupiter.

I was sure I was right about Jupiter's identity. I'd seen Mercury thinking the words "extremely bad manners", the exact phrase that Sapphire had repeatedly used when talking to me. By itself, that could have just been coincidence, but Lucas had made the point that Jupiter knew too much. That was very true. What profession in the Hive would have access to information on Law Enforcement cases, while also knowing highly restricted facts about other worlds that orbited the Truesun?

If Jupiter was a telepath, then it would explain everything. A telepath could have used the phrase "extremely bad manners" when talking to Mercury. A telepath could access Law

Enforcement systems. A telepath could pick up random secret information from the minds they read.

I couldn't casually throw accusations at another telepath though. I had to talk to Jupiter first to rule out any possible mistake.

"Jump belt." Adika's voice interrupted my thoughts.

I followed him off the belt and to the familiar bank of express lifts that served our unit. Lift 2 was giant size, designed to take the combined Alpha and Beta teams at once, but not when they were loaded down with camping gear as well.

"The Beta team will have to wait here for the lift to come back for them," said Adika.

Adika, Lucas, the Alpha team, and I went into the lift. I noticed that Buzz chose to stay and wait with Forge and the Beta team rather than come with us.

The lift headed up through the accommodation and industry levels of the Hive. As soon as the doors opened on Industry 1, the Strike team members hurried off with their load of camping equipment. Lucas turned to face me.

"You've been very quiet. If travelling through the Hive has been too much for you, we could take you back Outside through the closest Hive exit."

I shook my head. "We couldn't make the Strike team put all those tents back together again."

Lucas laughed. "Yes, we could. The extra training would be good for the Beta team."

"No, I don't want to go back Outside in the cold. I'll sit in the park for an hour instead. We're right at the top of the Hive here on Industry 1, so being in the park is almost like being Outside anyway."

I started walking towards the park, and Lucas fell into step beside me. "It's true that there's nothing but the Hive outer structural shield and soil above our park."

"Exactly," I said, "and those things effectively don't exist on a telepathic level. The moons and stars programme will be running in the park, so I can watch the bats and nocturnal creatures."

"I'll come and sit with you," said Lucas.

"Don't you need to have a meeting with your Tactical team?"

"It's a little late at night for meetings."

I'd been afraid Lucas would say that.

"It's unfortunate that the only other parks on Industry 1 are those in the other Telepath Units, so we can't use them as refuges for you," added Lucas.

We'd reached the park doors, and I was trying to work out a polite excuse to give me some time alone, when I heard my own voice snapping at Lucas. "Do you have to follow me round and spy on me for every minute of every day? Can't I have a single hour of privacy?"

"Of course you can," said Lucas hastily. "I'll leave you in peace if that's what you want. If you decide you'd like to talk to either Buzz or me, then you can call us."

He turned and hurried off. I stared after him for a moment. I was sure it wasn't me that had said those words. Despite the length of time we'd spent outside the Hive, I still wasn't free from Mercury's influence.

I was tempted to chase after Lucas, explain what had just happened, and ask his advice, but I needed this vital time alone to talk to Jupiter.

I followed the path along the stream to a bench under a maple tree. I'd been avoiding this spot for months, because it was where we'd held the explosive team leader meeting that ended in my firing Fran. Now I sat down on the bench where Fran had sat that day, dumped my jacket on the seat next to me, and took out my dataview.

It was easy to link into the dedicated secure connection between the Telepath Units. I hit a problem when I tried to start a new conference call, because that required security codes, but using Adika's codes worked. After that, I just had to issue the invitation to join my conference call, and add the one-word text message. "Alone?"

Given the time of night, I expected to have to wait for a response, but it came almost immediately. "Yes."

I took a deep breath, and tapped my dataview to set the call to visual. "Hello, Olivia. My name is Amber."

As I said the words, Olivia's image appeared on my dataview screen. She was standing in her bookette room. Her white dress was ankle length, and decorated with trailing lengths of silver gauze. She wore matching silver flowers in the light brown hair that straggled loose around her shoulders.

Olivia had come out of Lottery eight years ago, which meant she was twenty-six years old, but the effect was oddly like a child had dressed up in her mother's carnival dress.

I set my dataview to project her image as a life-sized hologram standing in front of me. Now I could see the faint lines of strain around her eyes, she looked much less like a child. "Why did you do it, Olivia?"

"I haven't done anything. I couldn't do anything. I'm just the useless broken doll." Olivia tipped her head on one side. "I've heard about you, Amber. You're the new telepath. Trying hard. Doing your best. Such a good girl. I was like that once."

She started singing one of the Hive Duty songs, but with some of the words changed. I was ridiculously startled by the act of disrespect.

"I used to be like you. We are united." She spread her arms and twirled round with the grace of a dancer. "You will be like me. We are united."

She stopped singing, let her arms drop in a defeated gesture, and spoke in grieving tones. "You are starting to crumble too, Amber. I can see more than one person looking out of your eyes. We will be two broken dolls together."

I'd planned this conversation during the long journey through the Hive. I'd imagined what I'd say, and what Olivia might say, but I hadn't expected anything like this. I fought to keep my voice calm and repeated my question.

"Why did you do it, Olivia?"

Olivia glanced over her shoulder as if looking for someone. "You don't understand. I shouldn't be talking to you. *They* don't want me to talk to you."

"They? You mean your unit staff? I do understand that. Telepaths learn a lot of random knowledge from the minds we read. The Hive doesn't want us sharing that knowledge with each other."

Olivia shook her head, and one of the silver flowers fell from her hair. "I didn't mean my unit staff. I meant the others. They're always watching me. Look!"

She gestured with her hand, and a crowd of hologram figures appeared behind her. They looked as if they were based on real people, but unnervingly none of them had anything but a blur for a face.

"Why did you do it, Olivia?" I asked the question for the third time. "Why did you recruit Venus to kill me? Why did you want Mercury to light the greatest of fires? What is Mars's mission?"

Olivia gave that wary glance over her shoulder again, and lowered her voice. "I don't know what you're talking about. One of the others must have done those things."

I fought to keep my anger under control. "Your recruits, Venus and Mercury, are dead. Four innocent people died in the Security Unit fire, and two more died later from their injuries. A member of Sapphire's Beta Strike team died chasing Mercury."

"Sapphire!" Olivia shouted the name. "Beautiful Sapphire. Brave Sapphire. Perfect Sapphire. We were friends once, but I wasn't as strong as her. She doesn't like talking to me now."

"You killed all those people, Olivia. It could have been far more. It could still be far more. What is Mars's mission? What will he attack?"

The childlike face had a petulant expression now. "I told you that it wasn't me."

One of the faceless hologram figures stepped forward to stand next to Olivia. It was a red-headed woman dressed in a formal onesuit, but as she reached Olivia's side I saw her clothes and hair change to match Olivia, and then the blurred face became Olivia's face too.

"I am Jupiter," the twin Olivias spoke in unison, their voices cold and emotionless. "I was the one who recruited Venus, Mercury, and Mars. I was the one who gave them their missions."

I was bewildered. "Why?"

"I did it to damage the Hive. I did it to save Olivia."

"To save Olivia from what?"

"From them." The two Olivias turned and waved their hands at the crowd behind them. "Olivia is lost in the final stages of fragmentation. We are already legion, and every time Olivia reads a dangerously strong target mind we add another to our numbers."

After the run where we found Fran's dead body, Lucas had said something about me showing classic fragmentation symptoms. I'd taken the cowardly option, avoided asking what he meant because I wasn't sure that I wanted to know. Now I was looking at the answer.

"Fragmentation," I said. "When a telepath reads an especially difficult target mind, they can be left with lingering residual effects."

"Yes," said Jupiter. "If a telepath fails to shake off those residual effects, then a portion of the target's personality can remain in their mind as a permanent alien influence. The presence of such invading personalities weakens the telepath's defence against future residual effects, so the pace of fragmentation increases. Olivia's own personality was totally overwhelmed years ago."

Only one of the Olivias was speaking now. I wasn't sure whether it was the real one or the hologram, but it didn't really matter. Either way I was having a conversation with the part of Olivia that was Jupiter.

I rubbed my forehead. I could feel a headache starting. I hadn't been reading any minds at all, not even the safely familiar ones of my unit members, since the end of that chaotic chase after Mercury. Logically, that meant I couldn't be suffering any sort of telepathic overload. The headache was probably just the result of me imagining being in Olivia's situation.

"I don't understand how harming the Hive could save Olivia."

"In my professional opinion, there is only one treatment that can help Olivia."

I blinked. "Your professional opinion? Are you, I mean *were* you some sort of doctor?"

"I was a specialist in the area of reset psychology. Are you aware of the procedure where a patient's mind is reset to a previous point in time?"

"Yes. The chain of memories is unravelled back to a point in the past, so the patient returns to being the person they'd been weeks or months earlier."

Jupiter sighed. "That's both vague and inaccurate, but the full technicalities would be beyond your comprehension level. Suffice it to say that the only hope of a cure for Olivia is to reset her to a point before she went through Lottery and her telepathic abilities were activated."

"But that was over eight years ago."

"Exactly. A reset on such a drastic scale is rarely used. I myself have performed it just nine times, but I believe it is the only option in this case. I've had several discussions with Olivia's doctors, requesting this treatment on Olivia's behalf, but I've been unsuccessful. Their argument is that a reset of such magnitude could remove Olivia's telepathic abilities entirely. She is still of limited use to the Hive, carrying out occasional simple check runs, so they refuse to take the risk."

Jupiter shrugged. "I decided the only way forward was to remove Olivia's usefulness by making her into an active threat to the Hive. I'm only too aware of the fantasies and obsessions of the rest of our ranks, so it was easy to recruit a few of their originals and give them suitable missions."

"I can't believe Olivia ever hunted Fran as a target. If she had, my Tactical team would have known about it."

Jupiter laughed. "Solely choosing my recruits from those on official records as Olivia's targets would have been a little obvious. Fortunately, or unfortunately, Olivia has reached the stage where she doesn't just add the targets she chases to our numbers. Many of us came from random telepathic contacts with obsessive minds in the grip of strong emotion. Fran was one of these. I felt her connection to you made her an ideal recruit."

I rubbed my forehead again. Whatever the reason, I was definitely getting a headache. "You set up a massive joint attack on the Hive. You're some sort of doctor. Weren't you worried by the thought of all the deaths you'd cause?"

"No. Lottery selects reset psychologists to have low empathy with others. It's essential to have a coldly detached viewpoint when your work involves removing entire swathes of another human being's life experiences."

"You made careful plans," I said, "but they went wrong when Mars killed Fran."

"Yes. I made an error of judgement over Fran. Olivia read her mind by chance when she was heading out to do a check run in Navy Zone. Fran was travelling on the same express belt, about to start work in her new position at the Security Unit, and brooding on how you'd unjustly fired her and wrecked her life."

Jupiter paused. "Our version of Fran is filled with so much anger and resentment that she would kill you even if she knew that action would result in the total destruction of the Hive. I failed to allow for the fact that the original Fran had moved on from that initial blind rage and might turn against us."

"There's just one thing that I don't understand. Why do you want to cure Olivia? Surely curing her will destroy you."

"Look at the number of people behind me," said Jupiter. "There are more of us than this, far more than the bookette room can display, and we're fighting a constant battle for dominance. I'm winning at the moment, but the mob is growing steadily larger. It's only a question of time before they destroy me, so I'm going to destroy all of us first."

She smiled. "You haven't asked me how I became one of the legion. I was one of Olivia's targets. Are you curious about why she was hunting me? Would you like to know what crime I committed?"

"No, I wouldn't. I made this call to talk to Olivia, find out what she wanted, and negotiate with her. Now it turns out that I'm negotiating with you instead."

I shrugged. "You wanted to prove Olivia was dangerous so that her doctors would agree to reset her. You've killed a lot of people, so I think you've made your point. Tell me about Mars and his mission, and I'll make sure Olivia gets reset."

Jupiter shook her head. "I don't believe you have the power to get Olivia reset. Many people in high places will need to make that decision, and it will take more than a handful of unimportant deaths to convince them to reset a telepath. Mars must complete his mission and cause a death toll so great that it cannot be ignored. I won't give you any information that helps you stop him."

She laughed. "Of course you could come and get the information yourself, Amber. Come and read Olivia's mind. Come and join the multitude."

I tried to hide my instinctive shudder. "I've got to tell people that Jupiter is Olivia. They're bound to come and talk to you after that. When they do, it's in your best interests to keep quiet about the fact that telepaths talk to each other."

"I don't see why that's in my best interests."

"Because I don't believe you're doing this to cure Olivia. You're fighting a mob of others for control of what used to be Olivia's mind. You know you can't hold them off much longer. There's very little of Olivia herself left now. You're hoping that resetting Olivia's mind while you're the dominant personality will wipe out all your competitors and leave you in sole control."

Jupiter's guarded expression confirmed that I was right.

"If that does happen," I said, "then you'll want every advantage you can get, including the ability to consult other telepaths."

"Agreed," said Jupiter. "Now let me tell you about the man who threatened my career, and how I taught him a lesson he'll never remember. In fact, he didn't remember anything at all after I reset his mind to…"

I tapped my dataview to end the call.

CHAPTER TWENTY-EIGHT

I put down my dataview and buried my face in my hands. If anyone asked my opinion, I would have to argue in favour of Olivia being reset, because she was too big a danger to the Hive to be left as she was. Her doctors would have tried every other possible treatment already, so the only remaining alternative was death, and the Hive would never waste a telepath like that.

Jupiter hoped that the reset would leave her in control of Olivia's mind. That was a huge gamble to take. Or perhaps it wasn't. Jupiter's original was an expert in reset psychology. Did she know of a similar case where a dominant intruding personality had survived the reset, or even had that happen with one of her own cases?

If Jupiter survived the reset, would that mean the remains of Olivia didn't, or would the two of them be left fighting for dominance? If that was the case, then I could understand Jupiter being confident of winning.

I sighed and lifted my head. There was no point in wasting time speculating when I knew so little about mental resets and the link between memories and personality. I needed to make a second call before Lucas got worried and came looking for me.

I picked up my dataview again, and issued another invitation to my conference call with the same one-word message as before. "Alone?"

Again the response was quicker than I expected. "Wait."

It seemed that Sapphire was awake late after Soren's death,

but someone was with her. It was over five minutes before the second response came. "Yes."

I took a deep breath, tapped my dataview, and Sapphire appeared on the screen. The last time I'd seen her, she'd had a beautiful, masklike face. Now she was grieving, weary, and defeated.

"I must apologize for the extremely bad manners of my Beta Strike team. They should never have..."

"No," I interrupted her. "I didn't call you to ask for an apology. What happened wasn't your fault. It wasn't Soren's fault either. In fact, it wasn't even Mercury's fault. He'd been successfully treated, left his firebug career behind him, and was doing useful work in Salvaging Processes. He'd probably never have caused trouble again if Jupiter hadn't contacted him and fed him with fantasies about lighting the greatest fire of all."

I paused. "Jupiter is the reason that I'm calling you. I need to warn you that I've discovered her identity. Jupiter is Olivia. To be exact, Jupiter is one of the target personalities that have invaded Olivia's mind."

Sapphire's eyes widened, and she ran a hand through her long blonde hair. "Are you sure? Olivia reached the final stages of fragmentation years ago. I could believe her usurping personalities capable of anything, but there are so many of them that each can hold sway for only a few minutes at a time."

"I'm very sure," I said grimly. "I called Olivia and spoke to Jupiter myself. I think she's a relatively new arrival, and she's achieved dominance over the rest of the personalities. I don't know if it counts as bad manners or not, but I'm going to have to tell my Tactical team about this."

"I agree there is no other option," said Sapphire.

"I'll try not to give away the fact that telepaths talk to each other. I hope I've persuaded Jupiter to keep the secret too. She hopes to gain permanent control over Olivia's mind, so..." I shook my head. "I've got limited time now, so I'll explain that in another conversation. More urgently, I need your help to avoid becoming like Olivia. I'm suffering residual effects from my contact with target minds."

Sapphire's face took on that masklike quality I'd seen during our previous conversation. "Limited residual effects are normal after contact with a difficult target mind."

"These are getting worse. After the run where we found Fran's body, my Tactical team felt I was showing classic fragmentation symptoms. After the run chasing Mercury, I hit my Tactical Commander and screamed abuse at him."

I had to moisten my lips before I could continue. "Later on, I tried to apologize to Lucas, and he said he wasn't sure it was me that hit him. Only minutes ago, I was thinking through the best way to say something, and someone else spoke for me. Olivia said she could see more than one person looking out of my eyes, and she's right. Mercury is still inside my head!"

"Limited residual effects are normal," repeated Sapphire. "We refer to them as the echoes of target minds. Most of them fade away rapidly, but the more powerful ones can gain a longer-lasting foothold in your consciousness. You need to find a way to cleanse yourself of these more powerful echoes before they become a serious threat to your own personality. I wish I could help you do that, but I can't."

"You *must* be able to help me. You've been reading minds for twenty-five years, and you haven't been overwhelmed like Olivia. Keith has been reading minds for thirteen years, Mira for seventeen years, Morton for over four decades. How do you cleanse yourselves of the powerful echoes?"

"Keith's telepathy only operates intermittently," said Sapphire. "This appears to act as some sort of safety valve. Whenever his telepathy ceases to function, it releases the echo personalities from his mind. That means their effects may sometimes make him stressed and bad-tempered, even cause him to commit regrettable actions, but they never become a long-term threat to his own consciousness."

"What about the rest of you? Your telepathy isn't intermittent. You must have other methods."

"We do, but I'm not going to tell you about them."

I'd been keeping my voice quiet, in case anyone else was in the park and heard me, but now I lost control and cried out in desperation. "Why won't you help me? Do you want me to become like Olivia? Do you want me to be taken over by dozens of competing personalities? Do you want the Hive to have only four functioning telepaths instead of five?"

"No," said Sapphire sadly. "That's why I won't answer your questions. When Olivia started showing fragmentation symptoms, we tried to help her. Morton, Mira, and I all explained our methods of removing echoes to her. Claire was alive back then, and told Olivia her methods and those used by two previous telepaths as well. We should never have done that. It was a terrible mistake."

"What? Why?"

"Because we didn't know what we were doing. We each had a method that helped us rid ourselves of echoes, but we didn't understand why they worked for us until after we saw what happened to Olivia. Then, when it was far too late, we realized some key things. The way to cleanse your core identity of alien influences is by being yourself, as fiercely and strongly as you can. The method that works for one person can't possibly work for another, because everyone's core identity is different."

Sapphire sighed. "The rest of us watched as Olivia changed from a caring girl to the tormented shell of herself that you saw today, and knew it was partly our fault. If we hadn't tried to help Olivia, if we hadn't distracted her with our own methods of removing echoes, she might have discovered how to help herself before it was too late."

"Oh," I muttered the single monosyllable.

"The Hive tries to prevent telepaths talking to each other," said Sapphire. "Perhaps it's true that the Hive knows best in this matter. It may be a good thing if Jupiter gives away the secret of us talking to each other, and our communication channels are blocked."

As I opened my mouth to reply, my dataview screen went blank. Sapphire had ended the call.

I dropped my dataview and hurried along the path, eager to get away from the spot that had new bad memories to add to those of my final confrontation with Fran. When I reached the area with the picnic tables, I turned off the path, went across to the stream, and knelt beside it. I dipped my hands into the cool, clear water, scooping it up to bathe my sweaty, tear-stained face, and then slumped sideways into the thick grass.

I stared upwards at the lights of the moons in the ceiling. I wasn't alone in my head. Mercury was here with me. I could feel his presence, like a stubborn splinter stuck deep in my mind, and there would be others joining him soon.

I was in danger of becoming another Olivia, lost in fragmentation. Sapphire wouldn't help me. No, Sapphire genuinely *couldn't* help me. I had to find a way to help myself before it was too late.

CHAPTER TWENTY-NINE

When I woke up, I could tell from the breeze and the birdsong that I was still in the park, but I was lying on something soft rather than the ground. I opened my eyes, blinked at the brightness of the suns in the ceiling, and peered down to find someone had stolen the cushions from the couches in my apartment and brought them here.

I thought I knew who the thief was. I turned my head and saw I was right. Lucas was lying next to me on some more cushions.

He smiled at me. "Good morning. Would you like a cold breakfast now, or prefer to wait for something cooked?"

His words, his voice, and his body language were all aimed at making it seem perfectly normal for us to wake up in a park. The effect would have been more convincing if he'd made a joke about it.

I hadn't used my telepathic abilities since the chase after Mercury ended with me slapping Lucas. I reached out to his familiar mind now and found his multi-layered thoughts in tumult. He was pretending things were normal. He had to. He daren't add to the pressure on me by admitting he was worried, let alone that he was close to panic.

… difficult to assess how much is Amber's own reaction to the stress she's been under, and how much is due to fragmentation, but…

… my team telling me I'm not being objective about this.

How can I be objective? I'm a Tactical Commander, but I'm still a human being. I can't look at Amber and coldly...

... the parks help her, and going Outside helps her, but they aren't helping her enough. We have to find a better answer before the invading personality becomes so entrenched that...

I hastily pulled out of Lucas's thoughts, and found myself joining in his pretence that nothing was wrong. "I'm starving, so I'll eat now."

We both stood up. I stretched, yawned, reached for my dataview, and discovered it was missing.

"I think I left my dataview somewhere. My jacket as well."

"I found them when I was looking for you last night." Lucas waved an arm at the nearest picnic table. "They're over there with our breakfast."

I glanced at the table and saw my dataview and jacket were lying next to two covered dishes. "Thank you. I was lucky that it didn't rain last night."

Lucas laughed. "That wasn't luck. The park keeper turned off the regular night-time rain because you were in here."

"Oh. I must remember to thank her."

We went across to sit at the picnic table. Lucas lifted the covers off the plates, while I picked up my dataview to check the time. "It's eleven o'clock in the morning. Waste that!"

Lucas shrugged. "We both needed the sleep."

I reached eagerly for my plate, and crammed a pastry into my mouth. Lucas let me finish eating my breakfast before he spoke again.

"Would you be able to cope with us holding a team leader meeting today?"

"Yes. In fact, I'd like it scheduled for as soon as possible. There are some things I need to discuss urgently. Just allow me time to shower first."

Lucas hesitated as if he was considering asking a question, but then nodded his acceptance. "If that's what you want, then I'll notify the others."

He sent the messages, and then we called in at our apartment to shower and put on fresh clothes. When we arrived at meeting room 4, Megan, Adika, and Nicole were already there. I noticed that Nicole was sitting in an ordinary chair. Her health varied from day to day, and this was obviously one of the better days when she didn't need her powered chair.

Lucas and I sat down in the two remaining chairs, and Lucas immediately started talking. "I intended to use this meeting to review the events of yesterday, but Amber wishes to discuss something first."

He turned towards me, a concerned frown on his face. I told myself that I wouldn't really be lying to him or the others. Everything I said would be the exact truth. I was just rearranging the details of how I got my knowledge.

"The chase after Mercury descended into chaos."

"I totally agree," said Adika bitterly. "The way that Sapphire's Beta team eavesdropped on our..."

"That breach of protocol is being dealt with jointly by all Telepath Unit Tactical Commanders," interrupted Lucas. "I'm happy to discuss it with you later, but we need to let Amber speak now."

"The chase was chaos," I repeated. "I ended up with a jumble of Soren's thoughts, Mercury's thoughts, and Forge's thoughts all churning together in my head. I couldn't make much sense of any of it until I woke up this morning. That was when I remembered Mercury's thoughts as he fell from the ladder. He was thinking that he was dying, so he'd never light the greatest of fires now, and remembering a conversation he'd had with Jupiter."

Lucas leaned forward in his chair, his eyes studying me intently. I dodged his gaze and kept talking.

"Jupiter was standing in a bookette room. She was wearing a Carnival mask and cloak, so Mercury couldn't see her face or hair. They were discussing him lighting the greatest of fires, when someone else came into the room and spoke to Jupiter."

I paused. "Jupiter reacted by ending the call. As she did that, she pulled off her cloak and turned to face whoever had come into the room. Mercury only caught a split-second glimpse of Jupiter before his dataview screen went blank. She was younger than he'd expected, probably in her mid-twenties. She had shoulder-length, light-brown hair that was decorated with silver flowers, and she was wearing a long white dress."

Lucas was still studying me. Did he believe what I was saying? I moistened my lips and told the key lie.

"Mercury didn't see who it was that had come into the room, they were outside his view, but he did hear a voice say one word. Olivia."

"Olivia," repeated Adika. "Could that be Olivia the telepath? The description sounds credible."

Lucas finally turned away from me, and looked round the table at the others. "It's a possibility worth investigating. Olivia is highly unstable. She's read a lot of target minds herself, and could access Telepath Unit records on others, so she had all the information needed to recruit Mercury and Mars. She would have learned about Fran being fired from her Tactical Commander's thoughts."

Lucas shook his head. "I've been puzzled by two things about Jupiter. Firstly, how good she was at luring in her chosen recruits with their exact personal fantasies. Secondly, how she knew highly restricted information. Both those things would be explained if Jupiter was Olivia. She has been reading minds for eight years."

"But how can we establish whether Olivia is innocent or guilty?" asked Adika. "We'd normally ask Amber to read a suspect's thoughts, but she mustn't go anywhere near Olivia, let alone try to read her mind."

Lucas shrugged. "We'll have to let Olivia's Tactical Commander handle this."

Adika gave a snort of derision. "Olivia's Tactical Commander wouldn't just be investigating Olivia's innocence or guilt but his own competence. He's bound to say that she can't possibly be Jupiter."

"Lottery chooses Tactical Commanders who are willing to put aside their ego, question their own decisions, and admit to their mistakes," said Megan.

Adika snorted again. "This would be an extreme mistake."

"That's a valid point," said Lucas. "I'll have to find another solution. Now, it's clearly been stressful for Amber to describe Mercury's dying memory. Could the rest of you wait in the next room for a few minutes, so she can have a break before continuing this meeting?"

There was a scraping of chairs as Adika, Megan, and Nicole stood up and went outside. Lucas waited until the door was closed behind them before turning to me.

"Amber, I could tell you were lying about most of that story, but my impression is that you genuinely believe Olivia is Jupiter."

"I don't *believe* Olivia is Jupiter. I *know* that Olivia is Jupiter. I can't explain how I know that, but I'm absolutely certain it's a fact."

Lucas frowned. "The last time you hid things from me, you were protecting Forge. Are you protecting him again?"

"No."

"But you are protecting someone? An innocent party who is somehow caught up in this?"

I considered that. I wasn't sure if I was protecting myself, or if I was protecting the other telepaths, but I was definitely protecting someone.

"Yes, I am."

"If I promise to keep it a secret, can you explain the full truth to me?"

I shook my head. "That would put you in a very difficult position."

Lucas ran his hands through his hair. "So you know that Olivia is Jupiter. You can't tell me the details of how you know that, because it would cause problems for an innocent party and put me in a difficult position?"

I nodded eagerly. "That's right."

Lucas was silent for a moment. "I accept your judgement on this, but please don't read my mind for a while. I can't stop myself coming up with theories about what you're hiding from me. If you read those thoughts, then your body language will tell me if I'm right or not."

I wondered whether Lucas was just accepting my judgement,

or if he was also afraid to push me for the full truth in my current state. Either way, the important thing was that he believed my claim that Olivia was Jupiter.

Lucas drummed his fingers on the table. "Adika is right. If I accuse Olivia, then her Tactical Commander will say she can't possibly be guilty. He won't believe he's failed to notice something as drastic as Olivia organizing an attack on the Hive."

"So what do we do?"

"I'll have to ask one of the other Tactical Commanders to go in and investigate as an impartial third party. Penelope would be the best choice. Emotions are running very high in Sapphire's unit after Soren's death, so Penelope wants this case solved just as badly as we do. She'll insist on questioning Olivia herself. We just have to hope that questioning uncovers evidence of Olivia's guilt."

I thought back to my conversation with Jupiter. If she was still the dominant personality in Olivia's mind during Penelope's questioning, there'd be no problem proving her guilt. Jupiter would openly admit what she'd done, and use it as an argument in favour of resetting Olivia. The only questions Jupiter would refuse to answer were those about Mars and his mission.

"I'll get the others back in now," said Lucas.

He tapped at his dataview. I'd planned to discuss two issues at this meeting. Having dealt with the first, I felt a cowardly urge to leave the second until another day, but delaying would just make things worse.

Adika, Megan, and Nicole came back in and sat down. I noticed Megan looking anxiously at me. I tried to give her a reassuring smile, but it probably looked more like a grimace.

Lucas turned to Adika. "I'll be asking Penelope to investigate the possibility of Olivia being Jupiter."

Adika sat back in his chair, and gave a smile of satisfaction. "That's an excellent idea. We can depend on Penelope finding out the truth. She's terrifyingly thorough."

"I didn't realize that you knew Penelope," said Lucas.

"We both came out of Lottery with Mira. I was on the Strike team, and Penelope was on the Tactical team. Penelope was obsessed with ballroom dancing back then. She'd had to split up from her old partner before Lottery, and insisted on teaching me to dance so that I could replace him."

Megan stared at him. "You've never mentioned being in a relationship with Penelope."

Adika looked oddly embarrassed. "We were nothing more than ballroom dancing partners. We won several competitions before Penelope moved to be deputy Tactical team leader in Sapphire's unit."

I blinked, tried to picture Adika in a ballroom dancing competition, and failed.

"Anyway," said Adika hastily, "I think asking Penelope to investigate is an excellent plan."

"Good," said Lucas. "Was there anything else you wanted to discuss, Amber?"

I took a deep breath. "Yes, we have to discuss the fact I'm suffering from fragmentation. You all helped me through that business with Elden. Now I need you to help me through this."

CHAPTER THIRTY

There was a shocked silence before Lucas spoke. "We've all been doing everything we can think of to help. You must know that."

"You've all been doing everything you can, except openly discussing the problem with me. That's what I need you to do now."

"I came out of Lottery with Mira, so I was in her unit when she hit the fragmentation issue," said Adika. "Telepaths often behave a little erratically after contact with a target mind, but Mira started lashing out at people in a way that was completely out of character. It reached the point where our Tactical Commander ordered everyone to leave the unit."

"What do you mean?" asked Lucas. "Your Tactical Commander can't have thrown everyone out of the unit."

"Yes, he did," said Adika. "Well, virtually everyone. Our Tactical Commander said it was vital that Mira only had contact with the most familiar and supportive minds. The five or six people closest to her stayed in the unit, while the rest of us were put on indefinite leave."

Adika pulled a face. "All these years later, it's still painful remembering that time. We were all given alternative accommodation in a housing warren on Level 20. We were a Telepath Unit in exile, rejected as useless, worried sick about Mira, and expecting the unit to be disbanded at any moment. It was a huge relief when we were called home again and found

Mira was back to her old self. I never discovered what happened when I was away. Everyone was warned not to talk about it or ask questions."

"I can see the logic in protecting a telepath from contact with target minds, but not in sending away their own unit members," said Lucas. "It obviously worked in Mira's case though. Do you think that approach would help you, Amber?"

"No. All of my people, whether they're Strike team or cleaners, Tactical team or maintenance staff, do everything they possibly can to help our unit and to help me in particular. On a telepathic level, I can constantly sense their supportive minds surrounding me. I'd hate any of them to be sent away and left feeling rejected and useless."

I tried to find a way to repeat what Sapphire had said without giving away the fact I'd spoken to her. "I don't think learning how other telepaths dealt with this can help me. If that knowledge would be any use at all, then surely you'd all be imprinted with the full details of how every telepath resolved fragmentation problems."

"That's very true," said Lucas. "The fact our imprints contain nothing about how telepaths deal with echo personalities is highly significant."

Lucas had referred to echo personalities, so I could use that term myself now. "I think those details are excluded from your imprints because the method of removing echo personalities is different for every telepath. Some of the information that *is* included in your imprints might be helpful though."

I paused. "I've seen lots of disjointed thoughts in your minds about the development path for true telepaths. Can you explain that to me coherently, Lucas?"

"Of course," said Lucas.

"Stop!" said Megan.

Lucas gave her a weary look. "Megan, we've discussed the risks and benefits of explaining things to Amber several times now. Do we have to have the same argument yet again?"

"I'm not arguing about you explaining things freely to

Amber," said Megan. "I've talked to Buzz about this, she agrees with you, and I accept her authority in this area. I just feel that Buzz should be present for this discussion."

"You're right." Lucas made a call on his dataview. "Buzz, could you please join us in meeting room 4?"

"I've just finished a counselling session in meeting room 8," Buzz's voice answered him. "I'll be with you in one minute."

"Who…?" Lucas broke off his sentence. "She's gone. Does anyone know who Buzz is counselling?"

"She's counselling Eli," said Adika. "When he had major surgery on his leg, the doctors put in several plates to hold the bones together. He's just heard that he'll need a follow-up operation to take those plates out, and he's finding the idea of more surgery very stressful."

"I understand Eli needing counselling, but why is he getting it from Buzz? I thought we already had psychological help available for the Strike team."

"We do," said Adika, "but Buzz is far better than a standard psychologist. She has this unusual method of chatting away, discussing her own life as well as yours, but it somehow works. Everything seems much clearer after you've talked to her."

The rest of us stared at him. "You've been getting counselling from Buzz as well?" asked Lucas.

"Not formal counselling," said Adika. "I just had a conversation with her yesterday. I'd been puzzled about how I was reacting to something, and Buzz said four words that made everything clear. I was really impressed, and thought she might be able to help Eli as well."

The door opened and Buzz walked in. I noticed that she was wearing a casual tunic and leggings instead of her old top and skirt, but they were still in her favourite red. She pulled a chair across from the side of the room and sat down at the table.

Lucas frowned at her. "You've been recruited as Amber's counsellor at a time when she's in desperate need of support. I'm not sure it's a good idea for you to divert your efforts into counselling other people in the unit as well."

"I regard counselling Eli as just an extension of my work

counselling Amber." Buzz turned to me. "Am I right in thinking that Eli being distressed about something would worry you, Amber?"

"Yes. I know that people are never going to be happy all the time, but it bothers me when one of my unit is deeply upset about something. In the case of Strike team members, it makes it harder to do my job too. When I'm running high speed circuits, checking if any of them are hurt, it's easy to confuse emotional pain with physical pain."

Buzz faced Lucas again. "You see my point. Amber has a very close connection to the members of her Strike team. If I reduce Eli's distress, then I also reduce the strain on Amber."

Lucas gave a bemused shake of his head. "I suppose that's true, but your counselling of other unit members mustn't distract you from helping Amber."

"Amber's own counselling will be my first priority at all times," said Buzz.

"Accepted," said Lucas. "Now, we've called you into this meeting because Amber has been discussing her fragmentation problems with us. She's asked me to talk through the whole development path for true telepaths with her. Are you happy with me doing that?"

Buzz grinned. "I'm ecstatic. Amber wishes to know exactly what problems she's facing, which I regard as a positive reaction. Since I'm not imprinted with this information, the explanation will also be helpful to me. Please carry on."

"I'd better begin by admitting that the Hive's understanding of telepathy is limited," said Lucas. "Do you want me to run through the whole development path from the beginning, Amber?"

"Yes. I'd like to know how my own progress compares with that considered normal for a telepath."

"Well, we believe that a true telepath has their abilities at birth, but blocks them as a defence measure against the impact of the hundred million minds in the Hive. When Lottery discovers a true telepath, special techniques are used to lower their protective mental barriers. Once the telepath's abilities have been brought to the surface, they are sent to Hive Futura, our old seed

Hive. Since Hive Futura's population was reabsorbed into the main Hive long ago, it's a safely peaceful place for a telepath to go through their initial training stage."

Lucas paused. "The first critical point in a telepath's progress is returning to the main Hive. Telepath Units are located in as quiet an area of the Hive as possible, but some telepaths do have problems. Those generally occur immediately the telepath returns to the Hive, and are easily resolved by a further period of training at Hive Futura."

"I remember everyone was concerned about me returning to the main Hive," I said, "but I didn't have any difficulties."

"Once the telepath has successfully made the transition back to the main Hive, then they start training with the Strike team," Lucas continued. "That rarely causes any problems. The telepath is having contact with many more minds now, but these are familiar, safe minds, those of people loyally serving their Hive and determined to protect their telepath at all costs."

I nodded.

"The second critical point is when a Telepath Unit goes fully operational, and the telepath has their first contact with a genuine target mind in an emergency situation. They are encountering the mind of what you describe as a wild bee for the first time. The telepath is hit by highly disturbing actions, thoughts, and memories. There is always a strong reaction from the telepath afterwards, and in some cases it can be extreme."

I wrinkled my nose. "My first emergency run was... quite harrowing."

"Your reaction wasn't out of the range we consider normal," said Lucas, "but we were still very worried about you back then. It's easy to misjudge the extent of the trauma caused by a telepath's first emergency run."

"This was the critical point where York took his own life?"

"Yes." Lucas winced, and hurried on with his explanation. "Once a telepath has coped with their first few emergency runs, there's usually a relatively peaceful period. The telepath continues growing in skill and experience, and everything appears to be going perfectly."

He pulled a face. "However, those appearances are deceptive. The repeated contacts with target minds are a cumulative strain, the telepath begins to find it harder to throw off their influence, and starts suffering from fragmentation symptoms. This is the third critical point in a telepath's development, where the telepath battles to dissipate the lingering echo personalities of target minds. A telepath's abilities are first brought to the surface during Lottery, which is right after Carnival. The fragmentation issue usually hits straight after Halloween."

"This is supposed to happen straight after Halloween?" I asked. "But Halloween was a couple of months ago."

Lucas threw up both his hands in despair. "I know. We watched you nervously after Halloween, looking for signs of fragmentation, but there weren't any. After a month had gone by, we decided that you must have dealt with the problem with incredible ease. We were deeply relieved, so it was a horrible shock when you started showing fragmentation symptoms a few days ago."

Buzz raised a hand. "I don't know what's been happening to Amber since she came out of Lottery. Is there any reason why fragmentation would have started later for her than for other telepaths? Was it longer than usual before Amber's first emergency run, or has she had a less stressful time than average?"

"No," said Lucas. "Quite the opposite. Amber returned from Hive Futura ahead of schedule, we were pushed into dealing with our first emergency run before our unit was even officially operational, and Amber suffered immense stress over a particularly complicated and dangerous case. If anything, we were expecting her to be hit by fragmentation symptoms earlier than usual, so..."

He broke off his sentence, and slapped the palms of his hands on the table top. "Wait! That's the answer. It has to be. I was so busy panicking that I didn't see it, but..."

He smiled at Buzz. "You are gold. You are pure gold."

"What's the answer?" asked Adika.

Lucas turned to face me. "Amber, you did get hit by fragmentation symptoms earlier than usual. You've already found a way to deal with the lingering effects of reading target minds."

I frowned at him. "If that's true, why have I got Mercury stuck in my head?"

"Because you were hit by the fragmentation issue when we were on that camping trip Outside. You were in contact with the unsettling mind of Elden. A mind that was especially stressful for you to read because of your own personal history."

"But Amber didn't seem to have any problems after reading Elden," said Megan.

"No, she didn't," said Lucas. "I was surprised by that at the time, but I gratefully accepted it. If I'd stopped to think it through properly, I'd have realized Amber must have been affected and somehow found a way to deal with it."

He paused. "Amber, this happened when we were a long distance from the Hive, so it was totally quiet on a telepathic level. I think your mind used something about that quietness to cleanse itself of invading echo personalities."

"It did?"

"I'm sure it did," said Lucas, "and it worked beautifully, so beautifully that we didn't even notice it happening, but then we came back to the Hive. The strain of reading target minds started building up again, and your tactic to deal with it didn't work when you were surrounded by the thoughts of a hundred million people."

He shook his head. "You've just had several appallingly stressful runs, so naturally you're having problems. Being in the park helped you a little, taking you Outside helped more, but you were still too close to the noise of the Hive."

Lucas smiled. "If we take you well away from the Hive for a while, Amber, then your mind should be able to deal with your fragmentation."

"You're saying that we have to go camping again?" Adika grimaced. "It's winter, Lucas. It's freezing cold Outside."

Lucas laughed. "I'm saying that we need to take Amber well away from the Hive to somewhere totally quiet on the telepathic level, but we don't have to go camping to do that. We can just fly in an aircraft to Hive Futura."

Adika gave a sigh of relief. "How long do you think we need

to be away? If Amber is right, then we've identified Jupiter and should be able to stop her causing more trouble in future. We still have to deal with Mars though. If we can't do that ourselves, then we should hand the case to another unit."

"Going to Hive Futura will help us deal with Mars as well," said Lucas.

"Really?" asked Adika, in his most sarcastic voice. "You think that flying off to Hive Futura is the best way to deal with an attack that will happen right here?"

"Yes," said Lucas. "I have absolutely no idea who Mars is, or how to hunt him down, but I do know what he's planning to attack. I've been trying to work out how to stop him, and failing, but going to Hive Futura means we can use a whole new approach."

"Would you like to explain what you mean?" asked Adika.

Lucas gave him a deliberately maddening grin. "No, I wouldn't. Our primary reason for going to Hive Futura is to help Amber recover from her fragmentation problems. Apart from the people in this room, and the members of my Tactical team, I want everyone to believe that is our *only* reason for going there. Once Amber is recovered, I'll explain how this move will also help us deal with Mars."

Adika turned to me. "Amber, do you remember me saying it was perfectly normal behaviour to hit Lucas, and that I often wanted to hit him myself?"

"Yes."

"Well, I'd like to hit him right now." Adika shook his head. "When are we leaving for Hive Futura, Lucas?"

"Tomorrow morning."

Adika nodded. "And who is going on this trip?"

Lucas gave him the maddening grin again. "Everyone in the unit."

CHAPTER THIRTY-ONE

Lucas's announcement sent almost everyone in my unit into a frenzy of preparation work. Since Buzz and I were the fortunate exceptions who had little to do but get on an aircraft tomorrow morning, we spent the afternoon in the park.

I wasn't sure those lazy hours counted as a counselling session, because the words fragmentation and Futura were never mentioned. We didn't even talk about what was going on between Buzz and Forge. We just fed the birds, admired the flowers, and coaxed two tiny black and white monkeys into coming down from the trees to take pieces of fruit from our hands.

We finally went to sit by the stream, and I started telling Buzz a silly story about when I was thirteen. I'd been panicking because I was about to leave home and live on Teen Level, and my eight-year-old brother, Gregas, kept heartlessly asking my parents if he could have my old room. I'd got to the point when I caught him inside my room, measuring the length and width to prove it was a fraction larger than his own, when a dreadful thought occurred to me.

"Waste it!"

"Is something wrong?" asked Buzz.

"I've just remembered that the day after tomorrow is Gregas's fourteenth birthday. Gregas, Lucas, and I were supposed to be visiting my parents for a celebration meal. I'll have to warn my parents that Lucas and I won't be able to be there after all."

"Will it be difficult for you to explain why you can't be at the birthday celebrations?" asked Buzz.

"My family don't know I'm a telepath, but they're aware I run a Security Unit, so I can say something vague about problems with an enemy agent. Any mention of enemy agents makes Gregas happy. He loves the Hive entertainment channel thrillers about Hive England Defence teams chasing agents from other Hives."

Buzz laughed.

"I'd better go and call my parents right away, so they don't put in a lot of wasted effort. They aren't just expecting the two of us, but my bodyguards as well."

When I left the park, I found the unit corridors were full of people towing crates on luggage trolleys. I dodged my way through the chaos to the safety of the apartment I shared with Lucas.

I called my parents from the bookette room, where their holo images were so realistic that it felt like I was physically standing next to them. I was about to tell them some vague enemy agent story, when I remembered Rothan's parents and younger brother sitting in the Fire Casualty Centre waiting room. They'd known that Rothan did hazardous work connected with the security of the Hive, but they'd still had a terrible shock when he was critically injured.

I'd been limiting what I said to my parents, playing down the risks of my new life as much as possible, because I didn't want to frighten them. I had to rethink that approach now, and be more open about the dangers involved. If I didn't find a way to solve my fragmentation problems, if I became a poor broken thing like Olivia, then Lucas would have to explain that to my family.

I moistened my lips and carefully chose my words. "I'm sorry I haven't called you for a while. My unit is dealing with a very bad case involving a fire."

"The fire that was reported on Hive channel 1?" asked my mother.

"Yes."

My father frowned. "That fire was caused by an enemy agent then?"

"Yes," I repeated. I knew I could trust my parents to keep whatever secrets I revealed, but it was best to follow the same approach as the Hive did with the staff of specialist casualty centres, blaming enemy agents rather than admitting some of our own Hive citizens were involved. I didn't want my parents living in fear, wondering if one of their own neighbours might be a potential killer.

"Lucas and Rothan were caught in the fire," I said. "Lucas only suffered from mild smoke inhalation, and he's completely better now, but Rothan's lungs were badly damaged so he's still having treatment."

My mother gasped. "Rothan is the quiet, polite boy who likes blueberry crunch cakes. He is going to be all right, isn't he?"

I smiled. It was usually Adika, Rothan, and Eli who acted as my bodyguards when I visited my parents, and I could understand my mother thinking of Rothan as being the quiet one in comparison to Eli.

"Yes. Rothan's doctors say that he should make a full recovery and be back with us very soon. We're still chasing one of the enemy agents though, so Lucas and I won't be able to come to Gregas's birthday celebrations."

"Gregas has cancelled the birthday celebrations anyway," said my father. "He called a few minutes ago to say that he's having a party with his teen friends instead."

I laughed. "I'm not sure if I should be offended Gregas puts his friends ahead of his family, or just relieved that he has friends."

"Given how unhappy Gregas was when he first moved to Teen Level, I'm definitely relieved he has friends," said my mother.

My father spoke in heavily confidential tones. "We suspect there may be a particular friend that is a girl."

I shook my head. "I can't believe that Gregas has a girlfriend."

"Not a girlfriend as yet," said my mother. "Merely a friend that is a girl. We have to wait and see if it progresses further."

There must be about half a million girls of Gregas's age in the Hive. I made a noise to express my disbelief that any of them would agree to be the girlfriend of someone like Gregas.

I chatted with my parents a little longer before ending the call. I was on my way to the living room when I saw Lucas come in the front door. I raised my eyebrows at him.

"I thought you'd be busy for the rest of the day."

"I'll probably be busy for the rest of the day and most of the night as well," said Lucas, "but I need you to help me with something."

"Yes?"

"I don't want to put you under any pressure, but I've asked someone to come to our unit. She should arrive shortly. I just need you to do a brief check of her thoughts when I talk to her."

I gave him a startled look. "This person is female and you think she may be Mars? I'm sure from Mercury's thoughts that Mars is male."

"I have to allow for the possibility that Mars has persuaded someone to help him. I'm as certain as I possibly can be that our visitor has no connection with either Mars or Jupiter. We must be absolutely sure about it though, so I need you to confirm that her mind has none of the characteristics of a wild bee. Do you think you can cope with doing that?"

"I think so."

"Our conversation may include references to Mars's mission. Please do your best to ignore those. I have to put some plans in place to deal with Mars, but there's no need for you to worry about them yet."

I pulled a face and answered the words Lucas was avoiding saying. "I agree that I need to sort out my own problems before I start worrying about Mars."

Lucas led the way to the community room where I'd talked to Buzz. We sat down and Lucas checked his dataview. "Our visitor is on her way up in the lift."

A couple of minutes later, Adika opened the door and came in. He had an odd, awed expression on his face. "Your visitor is in the next room waiting for you, Lucas."

Lucas stood up. "Please stay here with Amber. She's going to do a quick check on our visitor's mind. In the unlikely event that she finds a problem, you should come and tell me at once."

"Finds a problem," Adika repeated. "You think there's a possibility that…?"

"I think it's a vanishingly small possibility, but I have to ask Amber to check. Making a mistake about this would be disastrous."

Lucas went out of the room. I closed my eyes, linked to his familiar mind, and saw the view through his eyes as he went into the room next door. A woman in a Hive Defence uniform was standing there.

I was quite small and slightly built, but I had to be at least a head taller than this woman. I wasn't sure of her age. I could see there were faint lines on her face, but they looked more like the lines of strain and illness than of age, and there was something youthful about the way her fair hair hung in a single, long plait down her back.

As Lucas started speaking to her, I moved from his mind to hers, and was shocked. I was used to the brilliance of Lucas's mind outshining that of others, but this woman's mind was as dazzling as his.

I hovered on its threshold, saw the level upon level of thoughts were the same as those of Lucas too, but then was hit by the differences. The levels of Lucas's mind glittered like a Carnival crowd, but those in this woman's head rang with strands of music. It took me a moment to adjust to that, and separate the thoughts from the rippling notes.

… interesting to meet Tactical Commander Lucas at last. He's not what I was expecting, more diffident and…

… obvious that he's deliberately delaying telling me the reason for this conversation. He must be aware…

There was a peculiar hiatus in the thought level I was reading, and then it suddenly flashed brighter.

… Is the man seriously getting his telepath to check my thoughts and make sure that I'm trustworthy?

All the thought levels in the woman's mind broke up in amusement. I heard what she was hearing – the sound of her own laughter. I saw what she was seeing – Lucas's disconcerted face.

The thought levels started moving again, focused down to less of them than before, and all concentrated on the same words. It was the telepathic equivalent of shouting at the top of her voice.

... Hello, Amber. I'm Melisande. I know that you're reading my mind. Please come and tell your Tactical Commander that I'm not a threat to the Hive.

I hesitated.

Don't worry, Amber. I'm not angry with you. If I was angry with anyone, it would be your Tactical Commander, but I'm not. At least, I won't be if he has a good reason for doing this.

I reluctantly opened my eyes and stood up. Adika looked at me in alarm. "There's a problem?"

"No. Melisande appears to be a loyal member of the Hive. She wants me to join her and Lucas."

I went out of the door, took a deep breath, and entered the next room. Melisande smiled at me.

"I don't believe that I'm a threat to the Hive, Amber, but I've heard of cases where people were not aware of their own actions. Therefore it's possible I'm a danger and don't know it. Please reassure your Tactical Commander and myself that I have a perfectly ordinary mind."

I glanced at Lucas, and saw him make a helpless gesture with his hands. I faced the woman again. "Umm, you certainly aren't a threat to the Hive. Your mind isn't ordinary though, it's stunning, and filled with musical notes."

"Really?" Melisande seemed intrigued. "My music has to be just a hobby now, but I sometimes pine for the career Lottery denied me."

Lucas must have noticed my puzzled face. "Amber, you remember me explaining the optimization phase of Lottery to you, how it matches people to work that will make them happy and fulfilled?"

"Yes."

"I also explained that Lottery discovers about one in a million people with an ability so crucial to the Hive that they never enter the optimization phase. As a telepath, you were one of those people. Melisande is also one of those people. She is Hive Gold Commander, with authority over both Hive Defence and Law Enforcement."

I had only the vaguest idea what that meant, but Melisande was clearly staggeringly important to the Hive.

"Do you ever pine for the career you'd have had if you weren't a telepath, Amber?" asked Melisande.

"I didn't discover I had any special talents when I was on Teen Level, so I'm not pining for anything in particular, but I sometimes wish I was an ordinary person with ordinary work."

"You've ended up with more responsibility and pressure than you expected or wanted," said Melisande. "We have a lot in common."

"Perhaps," I said doubtfully.

"I get regular status reports from the Hive Telepath Units. I know you are at a critical point in your telepathic development, Amber. I hope you will soon resolve your problems. Not just because telepaths are vitally needed protectors of our Hive, but because I like you."

"Thank you."

Melisande turned to face Lucas. "Tactical Commander, if you are satisfied I'm not a danger to the Hive, then perhaps you will explain to me exactly what is going on."

"My apologies that I needed to establish your innocence, Gold Commander," said Lucas. "Our unit's current case involves the recent Security Unit fire. We've established that a destructive echo personality has achieved dominance over the telepath, Olivia, and recruited several people to inflict serious damage on the Hive. The Security Unit fire was started by one of those recruits."

"You're sure about this?" demanded Melisande.

"Tactical Commander Penelope has spent this afternoon interviewing Olivia. The echo personality, calling itself Jupiter, has openly admitted recruiting three people. The first, a bitter ex-member of our unit, turned against her fellow conspirators and was murdered. The second, a firebug, fell to his death while attempting to escape capture. There is the remaining threat of an unknown third recruit, who is hiding his true identity behind the name Mars."

Lucas paused. "The echo personality, Jupiter, has access to all Olivia's knowledge. I believe Jupiter has ordered the third recruit to attack Operation Rainbow Cascade."

Melisande's face tensed. "Olivia has been a telepath for eight years. She could have read any amount of information about Operation Rainbow Cascade in people's minds during that time. We have to assume that Jupiter has passed all that information to Mars."

"The situation is even worse than that, Gold Commander. Jupiter appears worryingly confident that Mars will succeed in his mission. I believe Jupiter chose to recruit Mars because he plays a significant role in Operation Rainbow Cascade."

Melisande nodded. "Hence your need to check that I myself am not associated with Mars. I assume Tactical Commander Penelope has tried all possible methods of getting more information from Jupiter."

"Jupiter still wants Mars's mission to succeed, so won't voluntarily give us information about him. Olivia herself is too deeply lost in fragmentation to help us, and we obviously can't get another true telepath to read her mind. Tactical Commander Penelope asked a borderline telepath to try to get an insight from Olivia, but that failed."

"What about drugs and psychological techniques?" asked Melisande.

Lucas sighed. "Tactical Commander Penelope has tried both, but they're useless. All that happens is that Jupiter temporarily withdraws, allowing another echo personality to take control of Olivia. Those echo personalities seem to have access to Olivia's memories, but know nothing about Jupiter's actions."

"If my understanding of fragmentation is correct, then this Jupiter personality is merely an echo of a real mind that was once read by Olivia. Could you learn something useful by finding that real person?"

"We have already found that person, or at least who that person was. Jupiter spoke freely about how her original was an expert in reset psychology, and even told us an unnecessarily gruesome story about taking revenge on someone by resetting their mind back to the status of a newborn baby."

Lucas paused. "There is only one such case on record, it was dealt with by Olivia's unit a few months ago, and ended in the death of the reset psychologist. We're therefore left with no clue to which of the many tens of thousands of people involved in Operation Rainbow Cascade is Mars."

"It's impractical to get telepaths to read so many minds that are scattered across the length of the Hive," said Melisande. "You settled for getting Amber to read my mind, since my role as Gold Commander includes co-ordinating Operation Rainbow Cascade. I therefore assume you have a plan to stop Mars, it is essential he does not learn of it, and you are about to give me the details."

"Yes, Gold Commander. I'm confident Mars isn't in our unit, and none of our people are supplying him with information, because Amber would have noticed any aberrant mind. I just needed to have your mind checked before I handed you full details of both our investigation and our plan to deal with Mars."

Lucas took a data cube from his pocket and handed it to Melisande. "I'm hoping we'll be able to use the first plan, which involves Amber helping us, but I've included two alternative plans as well."

I couldn't resist reading Lucas's thoughts at this point. The first of his alternative plans was to hand the case to another unit.

... had to include my honest assessment that Sapphire is the only other telepath with the mental and physical capabilities to handle this. The problem is that her unit has been hit hard by the deaths of Soren and his daughter. If they took on this case, we could have Sapphire's entire Strike team running wild during the chase, desperate for revenge rather than protecting the Hive. After what Penelope confided in me, I wouldn't be surprised if Sapphire ran wild herself. The death of one of her lovers is bound to...

... could argue that we're keen for revenge too, but there's the key difference that Rothan is alive and recovering. If...

... will be clear to Melisande that my second alternative,

sending out Strike teams without the support of a telepath, is total desperation. We must know Mars's moves before he makes them, or...

I pulled out of Lucas's head. Now that Mercury was dead, there was no reason for fire to feature in our case. I'd been reassuring myself that if I needed time to recover from my fragmentation, I had the option to hand the case to Sapphire. Her Beta Strike team was bound to be in utter disarray after Soren's death, but she could use her Alpha Strike team to hunt Mars.

Now that I knew Sapphire and Soren had been lovers, I had to agree with Lucas's assessment of the situation. Handing our case to Sapphire could mean the chase after Mars degenerated into the same sort of wild hunt for vengeance that led to Soren's death.

I was in a weirdly similar situation to that of Lucas when he was having his crisis of confidence. If I handed this case to Sapphire, and people died as a result, then those deaths would be my fault, while Lucas's desperation alternative of sending out Strike teams without a telepath's support was unthinkable.

I couldn't hand this case to another telepath, and I couldn't let my Strike team go out to risk their lives without my protection. This trip to Hive Futura must help me recover from my fragmentation, because I had to hunt down Mars myself, and I couldn't do that when Mercury was inside my own mind and working against me.

CHAPTER THIRTY-TWO

The next morning, we set off for Hive Futura. When Lucas said that everyone in the unit would be going with us, he really meant it. I picked up from his thoughts that this was partly because of his plan to deal with Mars, but mostly because of my reaction to Adika's story about Mira's unit members being sent away.

Lucas felt that I needed to be a long distance from the Hive mind to cleanse myself of the invading echo personalities, but the presence of the supportive minds of my unit members would help me, and he was desperate to give me every possible help.

There were only a very few exceptions being left behind. Emili wanted to keep visiting Rothan at the Fire Casualty Centre. The park staff had to stay to care for the park. Two of the Liaison team remained to coordinate our communications with the main Hive.

Everyone else, even including the maintenance and cleaning staff, made the journey to the nearest aircraft hangar. That was on Industry 1, the same level as our unit, but nearly half the zone away. We rode along an express belt, in a lengthy line of nervously chattering groups, everyone heavily burdened with bags or backpacks except me. The precious telepath only had to carry her padded jacket.

I had an embarrassing moment of realization. I'd grown so accustomed to people doing jobs for me, that I hadn't thought of packing a bag myself. I wondered if Hannah would have done that, or if I'd arrive in Hive Futura to discover I didn't even have a change of clothes.

No, of course that would never happen. Hannah was too conscientious. Megan was too efficient. My entire unit watched over me with paranoid care. If I fell asleep in the park, I'd wake up the next morning to find the park keeper had turned off the rain. Somewhere among the bags on this express belt, or already waiting at the aircraft hangar, was an entire wardrobe of my clothes.

"Why are you frowning?" asked Lucas. "I hope you aren't worrying about Operation Rainbow Cascade."

"No. It's obvious that Mars will try to destroy something crucial to the Hive, and we have to stop him, but I've got too many other worries to want more details at the moment. I'm actually far more curious about Melisande. Her mind is very like yours, high-speed and multi-levelled. If these Gold Commander positions are so essential to the Hive, why didn't Lottery assign you to one of them?"

Lucas looked startled by my question. "Because the Hive only has one Gold Commander position, and I'm psychologically incapable of filling it. Melisande was born with health conditions that meant she wasn't expected to live beyond her seventh birthday. She spent her childhood having a series of operations, fighting for her life every day, with the result that she is immeasurably tougher mentally than I am."

He paused. "I might conceivably be in the situation where two different groups of people are in danger, and I have to give the order to the Strike team to save one group and leave the other to die. I hope that never happens, I'd find it terribly difficult, but it's nothing compared to the choices Melisande could face. If the Hive ever suffered devastating damage, if it was necessary to abandon one zone of people to die in order for the rest to survive, the Gold Commander would have to give the order to sacrifice ten million lives. I couldn't do that, but Melisande could and would. She knows everything there is to know about paying the price for survival."

"Oh." Next time I caught myself wishing that I hadn't been born a telepath, and could have the ordinary peaceful existence I'd always expected, I would have to think about Melisande and remember that my life was easy in comparison to hers.

Lucas studied my face. "There's something troubling you about Melisande. If you have any reason to doubt her trustworthiness, you must tell me right away."

I flushed. "It's not that Melisande isn't trustworthy. It's just... Well, when I saw her mind, I couldn't help thinking that she would be a far better girlfriend for you than I am."

Lucas's eyes widened and his voice rose in disbelief. "You're feeling threatened by Melisande?" He shook his head. "You've got this situation backwards. It shouldn't be you that's feeling threatened by Melisande, but me. She's attracted to women not men, and she's clearly intrigued by your telepathy. When she said that she liked you, Amber, she was making the statement that she'd be interested in a relationship if you were."

"What? Oh." I blinked. "I didn't go deep enough into her mind to hit any sexual imagery. Well, if I was attracted to women, and if I wasn't already in a relationship, then I'd be interested in Melisande too. Neither of those things are true though."

Lucas smiled. "I'm relieved to hear it."

I went back to thinking about the other people in my unit. Megan, Adika, Lucas, and Hannah all knew Hive Futura. They'd been there with me when I had my initial training as a telepath. The Alpha Strike team hadn't been to Hive Futura, but they had been in an aircraft with me before, and I was sure the Beta Strike team could cope with this trip as well. I was worried how the rest of my people were feeling though. They'd never seen an aircraft before, but now they were about to step into one, and fly through the nightmare terrors of Outside to long abandoned Hive Futura.

I closed my eyes and reached out with the telepathic sense that gave me such a different view of the world. There was the bright glow of Lucas's mind next to me. I couldn't resist taking a moment to admire the brilliance of it, and was instantly drawn in by the bewildering number of thought levels. The highest levels of Lucas's mind were usually pure analysis, free from emotions, but now they burned with fear for me.

I have to be right that going to Hive Futura will help Amber, because I've no idea what else to...

I hastily moved to lower levels, and was startled to see

images of Olivia. Lucas hadn't visited her himself, but he'd watched recordings of all Penelope's conversations with her.

... the Jupiter personality wasn't just openly admitting guilt, but offering details to prove it, as evidence in support of the argument that Olivia should be reset. Jupiter was very careful not to give us any information that could lead us to Mars though. An echo personality with this strength of mind is unprecedented, so...

Next came several levels that were checking through the preparations for this trip.

... can count on Megan to have thought of all the...

... enough power cells to...

... would just take one missing connection lead to mess up the...

... plenty of time to get things sent after us if...

Below that, fear and anxiety ran wild again. I left Lucas's mind and touched the clarity of Adika's thoughts. He was torn between amusement and irritation that Lucas still hadn't told him what he thought Mars was planning or how he intended to deal with it.

... agree that we mustn't pile more pressure on Amber, but I...

... his meeting with his Tactical team went on for...

... Buzz is right. I can't talk to Megan yet. We're all too on edge about Amber's condition at the moment. Me, Megan, Lucas, everyone. Once Amber has done whatever telepaths do to clean their minds of the lingering slime they pick up from their targets, I can discuss future plans with Megan, and then...

The lower levels of Adika's thoughts suddenly filled with a fantasy image of Megan that made me urgently leave his head. I hovered in the dark void between minds, thinking through what I'd just seen. Adika had reacted so calmly to the news of Megan's planned baby, that I'd assumed he'd accepted their relationship was over, but I'd been wrong. I hoped he wasn't going to try to change Megan's mind, because she was unshakeably determined to have her dead husband's child, and any argument would just cause yet more trouble between them.

Adika had said that he'd talked some things through with

Buzz. I was reassuring myself with the thought that she'd have warned him against doing anything unreasonable, when I remembered Buzz had a history of trapping attractive young men in lifts with her.

My imagination conjured up a surreal image of Adika trapping Megan in a lift, and I moved on to a cluster of minds further back on the express belt. These were the Liaison team, tightly grouped around Nicole, their thoughts flashing bright with emotion.

Either the Alpha or Beta Strike team would go out with me on every emergency or check run. Sometimes a member of the Tactical team went along with us on a check run to talk us through the background details of the situation. No Liaison member ever joined us on a run though. They did their support work from the safety of our unit.

This time was different. This time they weren't watching others go out to defend the Hive. This time they were going too. Lucas had told them they were needed to support their telepath through a crisis, and hinted that the Hive had some great need of their help too. They didn't know why that meant them going to Hive Futura, or what they would be required to do when they got there, but whatever it was they were fiercely determined to do it.

Further back still were the members of my unit who weren't on operational teams. The people who worked in our medical area, did maintenance work, ordered supplies, and carried out the thousand and one jobs needed to keep our unit running smoothly.

I touched the thoughts of one of the maintenance workers. She was thinking about all the times the unit speaker system had started its distinctive warbling at night, and how she'd wake up, lie in her sleep field, and listen to the words that followed. All the times it had happened during the day, and she'd paused in her work to watch the people running in response to the calm, computerized voice.

"Unit emergency alert. Unit emergency alert. We have an incident in progress. Operational teams to stations. Strike team to lift 2."

Sometimes it was the Alpha Strike team going out with

Amber, sometimes the turn of the Beta Strike team. Either way, she could only wait until another voice spoke over the unit speaker system. This one would be a human voice, usually Lucas, but occasionally Megan or Nicole. Whoever it was, she'd hold her breath as they started talking, waiting to see if they would say the words she wanted to hear, the words that all those waiting in the unit wanted to hear.

"Amber and her team are back in lift 2 and on their way up. Everyone is fine."

She'd relax again after that, listen to the unit gossip about what had happened on the run, and be happy again until the next time the warbling came. She'd never thought that the day would come when the unit speaker system would call people to the lifts, and she'd be one of those responding. Today was that day. Today she wasn't waiting helplessly in the unit. Today she was heading out with Amber and both the Strike teams. Yes, she was near the back of the line, and carrying her toolbox not a gun, but it still felt good.

I moved on to another random mind. This one was a technician, his hand adjusting the crystal unit in his ear, trying to get the unfamiliar thing in a comfortable position. His mind was troubled with thoughts of Outside, and memories of the Halloween tales he'd heard during his childhood. Lucas had given everyone a talk the previous evening. He'd promised them that they'd get into the aircraft when they were inside the Hive, and get out of the aircraft inside Hive Futura. They wouldn't be Outside at any point. The technician hung on to that thought. He could cope with anything else, but not being Outside with the hunter of souls and his demonic pack.

I drifted across more groups of minds. They were ordinary members of the Hive, not selected to go into danger like the Strike team, but they were all filled with a mix of valour, fear, and determination. They'd been offered the chance to stay in the unit if they couldn't face going to Hive Futura, but none of them had taken it. I was incredibly proud of them.

I opened my eyes, and discovered Lucas was smiling at me. "Is everyone all right?" he asked.

He'd obviously noticed I had my eyes closed, and worked out what I was doing. "Yes. They're being amazingly brave about this. I didn't know."

"Know what?"

"That when I'm out on a run with the Strike team, you make an announcement over the unit speaker system when we're coming home."

He laughed. "Of course you didn't know that. Everyone else in the unit has been through the suspense of waiting for our people to come back from a run, even Adika has let Rothan and the Alpha team go out on an occasional simple check run without him, but you're out there every single time."

"I've never thought of that before."

A couple of minutes later, Adika gave the order to jump belt. I saw large signs announcing this was a restricted Hive Defence area. Adika led the way through open doors into the chill air of the cavernous aircraft hangar.

I paused as I saw what was ahead of us. Piles of crates, in colours varying from reassuring green to worrying black and red stripes. Beyond them, a row of seven massive aircraft waited to take us to Hive Futura.

CHAPTER THIRTY-THREE

I turned to Lucas. "I know there are over a hundred people in the unit, but do we really need seven aircraft?"

"We're not just taking people, but a lot of equipment as well."

The Alpha and Beta Strike teams were already leaping into action, seemingly competing to see which team could load heaps of crates into the aircraft cargo bays fastest. Megan and several of her Admin team started organizing the rest of the unit members into groups.

"The aircraft are designated as Aerial one to Aerial seven," said Lucas.

"Let me make a wild guess," I said. "We'll be travelling in Aerial one."

"Yes, we'll be in Aerial one with Adika and the Alpha Strike team. I'm sure the Beta Strike team will complain about being relegated to Aerial two, but they were recruited and went into training several months after the Alpha team, so they'll have to accept taking second place for a while yet."

Lucas led the way over to the centre aircraft, up a narrow flight of steps, and in through the door. I chose a window seat and watched the busy activity outside. I saw Nicole was manoeuvring her powered chair cautiously up a ramp to another aircraft door, with the Liaison team following her.

A thought occurred to me and I turned to Lucas. "I hope the other aircraft have their windows covered. The Alpha and Beta

Strike teams should be able to cope with the view of Outside, but it would terrify the rest of the unit."

He smiled. "Aerial three through seven have their windows covered."

"Good."

A sudden burst of heavy footsteps and chattering voices came from behind me. The Alpha Strike team were boarding the aircraft, and Eli's voice rose above the others.

"It's not surprising that the Beta greenies shifted more crates than we did. There are twenty of them on the Beta team, and only eighteen of us. They had Forge helping them as well, while Rothan is still in the Fire Casualty Centre."

The Strike team members found their seats and sat down. I looked through the window again, and saw the doors of the other aircraft were closing, and the steps were being shifted to the side of the hangar.

Lucas's dataview chimed. "We're ready to leave."

The hangar doors opened. There was a faint vibration as our aircraft's engines started, and then it moved Outside and up a slope to a flat area surrounded by trees. The sound of the engines abruptly increased, and we lifted up into the air.

I looked out of the window beside me, and saw the trees were growing smaller and smaller. I'd conquered my terror of the Outside and the Truesun, but I still suffered from my old fear of heights. I knew it was impossible to fall out of a reinforced glass window, but still instinctively tensed.

"All right?" Lucas held out a hand towards me.

"Yes." I held his hand gratefully. "Weirdly, I'm only nervous when we're taking off. Once we're high in the air, everything below us looks so tiny that it seems unreal."

I turned back to the window. It was a bright but cloudy day. Our aircraft was hovering above an untidy expanse of pine trees, but over to my left was an area of grassland that looked far neater, and had some paths crossing it. That had to be one of the Outside country parks.

The Hive promoted the myth of Outside being a nightmare place, where the Truesun blinded you during the day, and demons hunted you at night. I understood why the Hive did that. It wanted its citizens to think of it as the only safe place in the world, so they'd never consider invoking their right under Hive Treaty to move to a different Hive.

It seemed inconsistent that the Hive would also provide free access to Outside parks, but it wasn't. A small minority of people had a psychological need for more space and contact with nature than they could get in the Hive's parks and beaches. The Hive dealt with that in the same way as it dealt with all the varied strengths and weaknesses of its citizens, by accepting their innate differences and channelling them into something that benefited the Hive.

Those who needed access to Outside were allowed it so long as they kept quiet about their shameful activities, and they provided a useful workforce for necessary jobs Outside the Hive.

I studied the country park for a moment, trying to see if any people were walking through it, but then something in the sky caught my attention. One of the other aircraft was flying on that side of us. A second appeared, and a third. I turned to look at the windows on the opposite side of our aircraft, and saw the other three aircraft were flying beside us on that side. I was reminded of the way the Strike team clustered around me during an emergency run.

"Lucas, are the other aircraft positioning themselves to protect us?" I asked.

He peered out of the window. "Yes, they're going into a defensive formation around us."

I frowned. "Why are they doing that? No other Hive would dare to breach Joint Hive Treaty by sending aircraft into our territory."

Lucas smiled. "Our pilots are from Hive Defence. It makes sense that they're paranoid about attacks by other Hives."

I sighed. Yes, Lottery would select Hive Defence staff with an innate distrust of other Hives, and their imprints would contain information that encouraged their suspicions.

The note of the engines changed, and we started moving faster, the other aircraft holding the defensive formation on either side of us. I heard an excited cry from somewhere behind me.

"High up!"

There was a burst of laughter from the rest of the Alpha team. I laughed myself, but instantly sobered up again. Lucas's theory was that my mind had dealt with target echoes before on our long camping trip. He thought that once I was free from the tumult of a hundred million thoughts, my mind would cleanse itself of Mercury's echo. I fervently hoped that was true.

Right now, the clamour of the Hive mind was still close beneath us. I stared out of the window at the ground below. The Hive was originally built with most of its levels underground, and the rest sticking up above the surrounding countryside, but later it was covered with spare soil and rocks. We were currently flying over the flat, conifer-covered area above the Hive, but would soon reach...

Yes, I could see it now, the steep slope in the ground that meant we'd reached the edge of the Hive. Beyond it, a river weaved its way between some low hills.

I closed my eyes on that view, and looked at the world with my telepathic sense instead. The great roar of a hundred million people's minds was behind me. Ahead and on both sides of me, was only a gentle rustling sound, made up of the thoughts of animals and birds.

On the telepathic level, things were much quieter now. Had my mind already driven out the invading influence of Mercury? No, I could still feel his alien presence in the corner of my mind.

I told myself that I shouldn't expect this to work so soon. The Hive was still too close, too noisy, too distracting. I waited until it was further away, checked for Mercury again, and found him still with me. I waited, checked, waited longer, and checked yet again. My unwelcome passenger was still there.

I was getting tense now. That probably wasn't helping. The colour, shape, texture of Lucas's mind was radiating anxiety from next to me, and that definitely wasn't helping. Minute after minute passed by, and the Hive grew more distant and faint until I couldn't sense it at all, but Mercury was still in my head when I heard the sound of the aircraft engines change.

I opened my eyes, looked out of the window again, and saw

our aircraft was slowing and losing height. I'd been unconscious from sedatives when I flew to Hive Futura after Lottery. When I flew back to the main Hive, I was conscious but terrified of the Truesun, so all the aircraft windows had been covered.

Now I had my first view of Hive Futura from the air. Like the main Hive, it had been buried in soil, so it was a vast, flat-topped hill sticking up above the surrounding countryside. The pine trees covering it were like those at the main Hive too, but there was one difference that surprised me.

"Lucas, why is Hive Futura square rather than oblong?"

"The main Hive was originally built as one square zone, but was later extended on the southern side, gradually adding the extra nine zones we have today. Hive Futura was built as one square zone too, with the idea it would be extended in future as well, but that never happened. The main Hive population dropped and Hive Futura's population was reabsorbed. Hive Futura has been abandoned since then, but basic maintenance is carried out in case it's needed again."

Our aircraft circled above Hive Futura, lost more height, and landed in an open clearing. I could see a slope leading down to what had to be an aircraft hangar, but its double doors were closed.

"How do we get inside?" I asked.

"Our pilot will transmit the remote activation code for the hangar doors."

Lucas had barely said the words when the hangar doors slid open. Our aircraft moved on down the slope, and through the doors. The aircraft hangar here looked virtually identical to the one we'd left back at the main Hive. The vibration of our aircraft engines stopped, and the other aircraft arrived and took up positions next to us.

Adika opened our aircraft door, peered out, and beckoned to the Alpha Strike team. "The hangar doors have closed again. We can jump down and help the aircraft pilots put the steps in place for the others. After that, you've got all the fun of unloading those crates."

"If we have another crate shifting competition," asked Eli hopefully, "will you join in on our side?"

Adika gave him a pitying smile. "I would love to help you heave crates, Eli. Unfortunately, a Strike team leader has to treat the Alpha and Beta Strike teams with complete impartiality, so I'll just have to stand and watch the rest of you work."

He jumped out of the open doorway before Eli could reply, and the Alpha Strike team followed him.

Lucas turned to face me. "The Strike team may make jumping look easy, but it's a long way down to the ground. We'd better wait for the steps to be put in place."

I hesitated, wondering how to break the news to him that Mercury was still firmly entrenched in my mind.

"There's no need to worry, Amber," said Lucas. "I'm sure that your mind knows how to deal with fragmentation, but your fear of heights makes travelling in an aircraft a stressful experience."

Lucas knew that Mercury was still with me. Well, of course he knew that. He was an expert at reading faces, and mine must be screaming my disappointment.

Lucas smiled at me. "We can't expect anything to happen until you've recovered from the trip. Everyone needs to get unpacked and settled in here, so I suggest that we forget about the whole thing for today, and plan to go out for a nice relaxing walk with the Strike team tomorrow morning."

He paused. "There's no need to worry," he repeated. "We've got plenty of time to sort this out."

I did my best to smile back at him, but it probably wasn't very convincing. Lucas said we had plenty of time, but we didn't. The attack on the Hive was only a few days away.

CHAPTER THIRTY-FOUR

The aircraft hangar at Hive Futura was bitterly cold, so everyone pulled on their padded jackets before starting work. Naturally I didn't have anything to do, so I just sat on a crate at the edge of the hangar, watching a scene of purposeful activity.

Megan was pointing out exactly where the Strike team members should put specific coloured crates. I saw Eli dump a black and red striped crate next to several matching ones, and exchange graphic looks with Dhiren. I wasn't an expert in body language like Lucas, but it was clear those crates were extremely heavy.

Hannah was unpacking kitchen unit food packs from green crates. The Liaison team were piling bags and backpacks on luggage trolleys. Lucas, the Tactical team, and several maintenance workers were unloading mysterious equipment from crates and connecting it together.

"Excuse me," Dhiren's voice spoke from next to me.

I turned my head to look at him.

"I'm afraid we need your crate of power cells," he continued apologetically.

I stood up, watched Dhiren carry my seat away, and decided I was useless here. I knew which apartment Lucas and I would be using. It was the same one that Lucas had been given on our last visit to Hive Futura, and was only two cors to the east. I might as well go and be useless there instead.

The direction sign by the great hangar doors told me that

way was north. I was about to turn to face east when I noticed there was a small door under the sign, half hidden behind one of the aircraft. Presumably that was to allow people to go Outside without opening the main doors.

The quietness here at Hive Futura was supposed to help me banish Mercury's echo, but it was just making me increasingly aware of him lurking on the fringes of my mind. If I focused my attention on him, he'd scuttle away like an insect hiding from the light, only to reappear elsewhere a moment later.

I glanced at Lucas, and saw he was fully occupied talking to our unit electrical maintenance specialist. I walked across to the small door, and scowled as I saw it had a complex lock.

Adika came hurrying up. "Where are you going, Amber?"

"I just wanted to have a look Outside." I gave him a pleading smile. "Can you unlock the door for me?"

"I'm not sure it's a good idea for you to go Outside."

"What if I order you to let me go out there?"

Adika folded his arms. "As telepath, you are the head of our unit. Should you give me a direct order, I have no choice but to obey it, unless it endangers your safety. I'm not sure whether this would endanger your safety or not, so I'd have to check with Lucas."

I groaned. "If you tell Lucas I'm going Outside, he'll want to come with me, and that will ruin the whole point."

"I'm not sure I understand what the point of this is anyway," said Adika, "unless you just want to sneak Outside to annoy Lucas. I admit that I'd have some sympathy for that as a reason. Lucas mentioned that we'll be doing training exercises while we're at Hive Futura, but he won't tell me any details about them. I'm sure the rest of his Tactical team know what he's planning, but they aren't talking either. Can you read their minds, find out what's going on, and explain it to me?"

"You know that I don't tell anyone the things I see in other people's minds. At least, I try not to, though it's sometimes difficult remembering exactly who knows which things about what person."

I nodded at the locked door. "The point of going Outside

without Lucas is that he's brought us here to solve my fragmentation issues. His theory is that my mind knows what to do, and just needs the quiet of being away from the Hive mind to be able to do it, but he's scared to death that he's wrong and it won't work."

Adika frowned. "I thought Lucas was certain that bringing you here would work."

"He's doing his best to project total confidence. He's probably fooled everyone else here with his act, but I'm a telepath and can see his true feelings. Lucas is terrified that he'll lose me to fragmentation."

I tugged my hair with both hands. "I need my mind to do something, but I've no idea what. I'm sure I need to relax for this to work, but how can I relax when I know that failure won't just be disastrous for me, Lucas, and my unit, but everyone in my Hive as well? Lucas's fear is piling extra pressure on me, so I'll have a better chance of doing this if I go Outside without him."

Adika sighed. "If you're only planning to stand by the door, not go hiking across the countryside, then a couple of bodyguards should be enough to ensure your safety. You stay hidden behind this aircraft, Amber. I'll be right back."

I watched Adika walk off, and took out my dataview. It turned on normally, but when I tried to check my personal mail, I saw an unnerving message in large red letters. "You are not connected to the Hive."

What? I held my dataview upside down and shook it. The message was still there. I didn't understand what was wrong. The last time I was in Hive Futura, I'd been able to call my parents using a secure link to the main Hive. Hadn't we got a secure link set up yet? Was that what the huddle of the Tactical team and the maintenance workers were doing now?

Adika arrived back, with Eli and Forge following him. I thrust my dataview into my pocket, and waited eagerly while Adika undid the lock on the door and opened it.

"Waste that!" he said.

I stared out through the door at a magical sight. There were feathery white crystals drifting down from the cloudy sky. Every branch of the surrounding pine trees had an etching of white to brighten the sombre dark green, and a thin white blanket of the stuff covered the ground.

"What is it?" I demanded. "What's happening?"

"I think it's just started snowing," said Adika, in a grim voice. "Forge and I visited Rothan at the Fire Casualty Centre yesterday evening. We told him about our trip to Hive Futura, and he warned us that we might have problems with snow. Apparently it can be so cold at this time of the year that the rain freezes into white crystals called snowflakes."

"It's beautiful," I said, glorying in the spectacle.

"It's... extremely inconvenient," said Adika, in the voice of someone who was tempted to use far stronger language. "Aircraft can cope with snow, but nobody is going Outside on foot in this."

"It can't be that dangerous if it's just frozen rain," I said. "Surely that's just like the ice we have in drinks."

Adika was unrelentingly doom laden. "Rothan warned me that snowdrifts can get very deep, and if it's snowing too hard then the bad visibility means people can get lost and freeze to death."

I held my hand out of the door, palm upwards, and watched with fascination as a white crystal landed on it and melted into a drop of water.

"Snow is also..."

Adika let his sentence trail off, because I'd run out into the snow, and was looking up at the sky in wonder. "Everywhere is white and silver," I shouted back at the others. "Outside is celebrating Carnival!"

Adika groaned, walked out from the doorway, and took my arm. "You need to go straight back inside now, Amber."

"No. This is where I need to be. This is *exactly* where I need to be." I shook off his hand, and walked a few steps further into the magical land of white crystals. I could feel Mercury shifting uneasily in the back of my mind. He liked the safety of the Hive and I was standing in the terrifying Outside. He adored warmth and this was a place of cold. He loved fire and here was only ice.

Adika's voice came from behind me. "I should never have

agreed to bring Amber out here. Forge, you'd better go and get Lucas."

I ignored the distraction, reaching out with my hands to the falling snowflakes, reaching out with my thoughts to the Carnival landscape around me. Mercury was desperately clinging to my mind. I could feel his talons digging into me, and his voice screaming defiance, but I dropped to my knees and thrust my bare hands into the bitter cold of fallen snow.

"Lucas, what do we do?" asked Adika, from behind me.

"Leave Amber alone," Lucas's voice answered him. "We came here so she could deal with her echoes, and she's doing it now."

Mercury was strong, but in this place, and at this time, I was much stronger. Our surroundings were both physically and mentally hostile to him. A land of snow, where the minds of my people were united in support of me.

My telepathic view showed me the moment Mercury lost his grip on me. His ghostly figure drifted out into the falling snowflakes, fell apart into a dozen fragments, and then vanished completely. Of course he would vanish once he left me. Mercury had no reality of his own, so he couldn't exist outside my mind.

Other, much fainter, ghostly figures left me now, and fell apart in turn. I felt a surge of power, and my mind expanded to take in the world around me. The familiar thoughts of my unit members. Some strangers who had to be our aircraft pilots. The countless minds of birds and animals. I was sensing all the levels of thought, down to the subconscious and beyond it.

There, in the depths of the mind that I'd never reached before, I found something I hadn't known existed.

"Amber, has Mercury left you?" asked Lucas.

"He's gone," I said. "They've all gone. I can't believe that I didn't realize this before."

"What didn't you realize?"

I stood up and turned to smile at Lucas. "The Hive mind is composed of the thoughts of a hundred million people, but it's just a small and very noisy part of something much bigger that includes the minds of all the animals, birds, and every tiny living creature. Call it the universal mind. Down beyond the deepest unconscious levels of the mind, we're all part of it. You. Me. Our unit. Everyone."

Lucas snapped his fingers. "You sometimes get a mental itch. A warning that someone's in trouble. I've never understood how you do that. Could it come from this unconscious connection?"

"Probably."

Sapphire had said that the way to cleanse your core identity of alien influences was by being yourself, as fiercely and strongly as you could. The method that worked for one telepath couldn't possibly work for another, because everyone's core identity was different, and my ability to delve down to the subconscious levels of the mind made me especially different. That was usually a liability, entangling me in the emotional needs of others, but in the quietness away from the crowded Hive, where the universal mind was dominated by the supportive thoughts of my unit staff, it was my greatest strength.

I laughed, stretched out my arms, and pirouetted, dancing in the snow. Lucas laughed as well, took out his dataview, and tapped it. Now I was dancing to music.

The bewilderment on Adika's face changed to something wistful. I touched his mind and saw images of when he went ballroom dancing with Penelope. They'd never actually been in a relationship, but he'd been hoping things would progress in that direction. Penelope's promotion to deputy Tactical team leader in Sapphire's unit had separated them and ended that hope. They'd both decided their careers were more important than their personal lives.

Adika had given up Penelope and ballroom dancing for his career and his duty to the Hive. He'd given up a lot of other things over the years as well. Now he'd finally achieved his goal of being a Strike team leader, he'd found himself having strange thoughts. Brooding on those past decisions with something that was closer to nostalgia than regret. There was his fascination for Megan too.

Megan was exactly the type of woman to attract me, a polished beauty with good legs, but the way she kept changing her mind about me was maddening. I didn't know why I was still bothering with her until Buzz said those four words. "You both want children." Everything suddenly made sense. Yes, I wanted children, a family, all the things that...

Adika hadn't known what he wanted until Buzz told him. I hadn't known it either. Things were often clearer to an onlooker, but I shared the full confusing maelstrom of someone's hopes and fears, while Buzz just got a brief revealing insight into their central driving emotion.

I reached out my hand towards Adika, and copied the steps of the partner in his mind. He hesitated, and then joined me in the dance. I wasn't good enough to do the steps properly, but Adika adjusted for my mistakes. The music built to its climax, and he lifted me effortlessly above his head for the last dramatic pose. I was startled by the sound of clapping from Lucas, Eli, and Forge.

"High up!" said Eli.

Adika gave an embarrassed cough, and lowered me to the ground. I ran across to Lucas, and he hugged me close to him.

"It's so beautiful out here," I said.

"It's extremely beautiful," said Lucas, "but you're shaking from the cold. We should go back into the aircraft hangar before you freeze."

"Can we go out again later?"

"Definitely," said Lucas. "You can go Outside every day while we're here. Once we're back at the main Hive, we'll set up a schedule for further regular trips Outside, to make sure that you never suffer fragmentation problems again."

I reluctantly let Lucas lead me back into the aircraft hangar. Adika, Forge, and Eli followed us inside, and locked the door behind them before hurrying off to rejoin those unloading crates from aircraft.

"I'll send a message to Gold Commander Melisande to tell her the good news that you've dealt with the echo of Mercury," said Lucas.

I watched him working on his dataview. "You can send messages to the Hive? When I tried to check my mail, my dataview said something about not being connected to the Hive."

Lucas looked up at me. "We've set up a security block to ensure that nobody accidentally gives away what we're really doing here. You should have been authorized to bypass the block, but it must have been overlooked. I can do that now."

I shook my head. "There's no need. I talked to my parents before we came, so I haven't got any urgent calls to make."

Lucas looked down at his dataview again. "Gold Commander Melisande is delighted to hear that you've dealt with your fragmentation issues. She hopes to congratulate you in person when you return to the Hive."

I frowned. "Perhaps you should mention to Gold Commander Melisande that I'm in a committed relationship with you."

"I've already done that, and she wished us every happiness. I don't think there are any double meanings in the congratulations comment. At least, I hope there aren't."

I'd thought that Lucas had got over his old insecurity about his relationship with me, but I caught a hint of it in his voice now. "You didn't mind me dancing with Adika earlier?"

Lucas smiled. "You care deeply for your Strike team, Amber. You rush to help them whenever they have a problem, but I know that your feelings for them don't lessen your feelings for me."

He studied my face. "You look very tired after dealing with your echoes, Amber. Do you want to go to our apartment and rest? I can tell everyone that you've dealt with your fragmentation issues, and then come and join you."

"No," I said. "However tired I am, I should be the one to tell my people that news."

CHAPTER THIRTY-FIVE

I stood by the wall of the aircraft hangar, and everyone pulled empty crates into rows and sat facing me. I felt an odd, bone-aching weariness, as if my battle with Mercury had been a physical one rather than purely mental, but I forced myself to ignore that and started speaking.

"You all came to Hive Futura to help me with my fragmentation problems. Many of you don't understand what fragmentation is, or how it can tear a telepath apart. You just knew I was in trouble, and that you coming here could help me."

I paused. "That was enough to make you get into an aircraft and fly here. I can't find the words to say how amazing I think that is, and how amazing I think you all are. You came here to help me solve my problems, and you've succeeded."

There was an excited babble from my audience. "You've dealt with your echoes, Amber?" asked Gideon eagerly.

"Yes." I repeated the words that Sapphire had said to me. "Becoming a telepath was hard. Being a telepath is even harder, and I'm sure there'll be other problems ahead, but having you with me, being surrounded by your mental support, has helped me deal with this one."

I felt the wave of emotion coming from my listeners as they absorbed that. Elation, delight, but overwhelmingly a sense of pure relief. These people had been aware that something was harming their telepath, threatening the existence of our unit. The fact most of them hadn't understood what the problem was had made it even more frightening.

There was a strangely quiet moment, as if people's feelings were too strong to put into words, and then Hannah spoke.

"Does that mean we're going home now?" she asked. "Should I start repacking all those crates of food?"

The straightforwardly practical question broke the tension, and the crowd burst out laughing.

I waited for the noise to die down. "No, we won't be going back yet. We came here for two reasons. The first was to help me with my fragmentation. The second was to deal with a threat to the Hive."

"Can we finally get some details on Lucas's plan?" demanded Adika.

"Yes. No." I hesitated. "I'm not sure."

I'd been blocking out my weariness, but now it was flooding back, overwhelming me so it was hard to think. I threw a glance of appeal at Lucas, and he stood up and came to whisper in my ear.

"Do you need to go and rest now, or should I give a briefing on the situation with Mars?"

"I think I just need to sit down."

Lucas took my arm and guided me over to sit on a crate.

I felt foolish. "I don't know why I'm so tired."

Lucas smiled. "Extreme mental exertion can be physically tiring. It's one of the reasons telepaths need rest after an emergency run."

He went to stand facing the audience "As Amber just said, our second reason for coming here was to deal with a threat to the Hive. For security reasons, I couldn't give a general briefing on this subject until we were actually here at Hive Futura."

"Hurry up and explain what's happening," said Adika impatiently.

Lucas laughed. "Some of you will know far more about the events in our current case than others. To summarize the situation, the telepath Olivia has been suffering from severe fragmentation for years. An especially malevolent echo personality, calling itself Jupiter, has taken control of her."

Lucas used his dataview to display an image of Olivia's head, fringed in red, on the hangar wall. Below her appeared a row of three other heads. The first was Fran. The second was Martin, the firebug who I couldn't help still thinking of as Mercury. The third was an anonymous black silhouette.

"Jupiter used Olivia's telepathic abilities and knowledge to recruit three people to make a joint attack on the Hive. Fran, an ex-member of this unit with a deep grievance against us, was given a mission to ambush and stab Amber. Martin, a skilled firebug, was given a mission to light a great fire. The third recruit has his identity hidden behind a false name, Mars. All we know about his mission is that it had to be timed to happen five days from now."

Lucas paused. "Olivia's activities have been restricted, and Fran and Martin are dead, so now we just have to deal with Mars."

The images of Olivia, Fran, and Martin vanished from the wall, leaving only the black silhouette representing Mars.

"Most of you won't be aware that the year before the last Lottery was a disastrous one for the Hive, with three especially drastic incidents happening. The first incident was a telepath being stabbed. Fortunately, the injury was only slight."

"A telepath was stabbed?" Adika interrupted in a sharp voice. "Who? What happened?"

Lucas shook his head at him. "I'll discuss that with you later. The second incident was a vast fire in Burgundy Zone. The third incident was a target killing himself by entering the Blue Zone power complex and jumping into the central core of its power supply nexus. The resulting damage left the whole of Blue Zone without power for two days."

Lucas glanced round his audience. "I think you'll all agree there's a suspicious similarity between the first two of these events and the missions that Jupiter gave Venus and Mercury."

"You mean that Jupiter was trying to recreate all those three events in a single day?" asked Adika. "You think Mars is going to kill himself by jumping into the central core of power supply nexus 7?"

"I believe Jupiter was trying to recreate all those three events in a single day," said Lucas. "However, there were to be significant changes. Venus was to stab a different telepath. Mercury was to light a great fire, but it would rage through Purple Zone, not Burgundy. I think Mars will attempt to damage a power supply nexus, but we can't assume it will be the one in Blue Zone, and he won't necessarily use the method of jumping into the central core."

Lucas tapped at his dataview. The black silhouette of Mars was replaced by the standard oblong image of the Hive, showing the ten coloured zones running from Burgundy at the north end to Violet at the south.

"Each zone of the Hive has its own dedicated power complex containing the crucial power supply nexus. Mars therefore has a choice of ten potential targets. We know the timing of the planned attack, so in theory we could mount a guard on each complex. The problem is that even if we ignored every other emergency in the Hive, and committed all five of our telepaths and their Strike teams to standing guard on a power complex, that would leave five zones with their complex guarded only by conventional means."

"Your Tactical team can't predict which zone will be targeted?" asked Adika.

"We can't make predictions with a high enough level of certainty considering what is at stake," said Lucas. "There are one hundred million people in this Hive. That's ten million people in each zone. The power outage in Blue Zone last year caused many accidents that resulted in serious injuries and even deaths. I won't burden you with the knowledge of the exact numbers."

I pulled a face. One of my own friends on Teen Level had been badly injured during that power outage. I wasn't surprised to hear that others had died.

"If Mars succeeds in damaging a power supply nexus," said Lucas, "then we can expect the consequences to be at least as bad as the previous time, and probably far worse. In last year's incident, power supply nexus 7 suffered extensive damage, but the people in Power Services worked to exhaustion point and managed to repair it within two days. Any greater damage would mean the nexus was impossible to repair. Building a totally new nexus would take months, so we'd have to evacuate everyone from that zone of the Hive."

Lucas winced. "Just imagine how difficult that evacuation would be with no working belt system and only small, hand-held emergency lanterns for light. Ten million terrified people trying to walk long distances through pitch-dark corridors to another zone of the Hive."

"Some of us don't need to imagine it," said Forge grimly. "Amber and I were in Blue Zone during the power outage."

"Me too," said Rafael.

Several other people joined in with comments. Lucas waited for the noise to die down before speaking again.

"We don't know which power supply nexus will be targeted by Mars. We don't know who Mars is, and a huge number of maintenance workers have access to key power systems. We can't get telepaths to read all their minds."

Lucas looked round at his audience. "Mars could have a very high position in the Hive. We must make absolutely sure that he doesn't learn of our plan. Everyone in Law Enforcement, even the Tactical Commanders of the other Telepath Units, believes our unit has only moved to Hive Futura in an attempt to solve Amber's fragmentation symptoms. Gold Commander Melisande is the sole person who knows it is also part of our plan to deal with Mars."

He paused. "With so much at stake, we can't afford anyone accidentally saying something that gives away the truth. Therefore your communications with friends and family back at the main Hive will need to be limited to recorded messages, so they can be checked by the Tactical team before they are sent."

"Wait!" said Adika urgently. "I've just realized that if Mars is targeting a power supply nexus, then the timing of this attack is…"

Lucas held up a hand to stop him. "Yes, I know. I'm just getting to that."

He turned to his audience again. "The timing of this attack is deeply significant. You all know the Hive has bulkhead doors at each zone boundary. You all know those bulkhead doors can be closed to seal off a zone in the case of a catastrophic disaster. You all know there is a test closure of those bulkhead doors for one hour every three months. What most of you *won't* know is that the three-monthly closure of the bulkhead doors is actually not a test at all, but a safety precaution while essential power supply maintenance is taking place across the Hive. This power supply maintenance is known as Operation Rainbow Cascade."

I was startled to hear Forge's voice speak, its tone filled with alarm. "You think that Mars is going to attack a power supply nexus during Operation Rainbow Cascade?"

"Yes," said Lucas.

"Waste that!"

Forge's words were echoed by other voices. It seemed that information on Operation Rainbow Cascade was included in the imprints of Tactical team members, and also those of the Strike team who'd been imprinted for Strike team leader. I didn't bother reading any of their minds to find out what it was, because Lucas was obviously about to explain it.

"The power for a zone is supplied by a single fuel rod in the central core of its power supply nexus," continued Lucas. "Every three months, the depleted fuel rods are replaced with fresh ones during Operation Rainbow Cascade. Since a specific problem during a fuel rod changeover could result in a massive explosion, the bulkhead doors are closed as a damage containment measure."

I frowned. "When I was reading Mercury's mind, I saw the detail that Mars expects to die carrying out his mission. You think that Mars may not just be attempting to damage a nexus, but cause this sort of massive explosion?"

"Exactly," said Lucas. "Operation Rainbow Cascade is coordinated by the Hive Gold Commander. It begins at ten minutes before midnight, when the belt system slows to minimum speed across the Hive, and the bulkhead crossing points are blocked off on every level. At midnight, all the bulkhead doors close. At five minutes past midnight, the fuel rod is changed in Burgundy Zone. Five minutes later, the rod is changed in Red Zone. The cascade continues across the Hive until the rod has been changed in Violet Zone, then the bulkhead doors are reopened, and the belt system returns to its usual operating speed."

"Can I ask a silly question?" I asked.

"You are a telepath, Amber," said Lucas solemnly. "It's impossible for you to ask a silly question, because any question you ask is automatically classed as highly discerning."

"It would be a lot faster to change all the rods at once. They're changed in turn so if something went wrong then only one zone of the Hive would be left without power at a time?"

"That's right," said Lucas. "The fuel rod replacement process seems relatively simple. The central core of a power supply nexus has two fuel rod containers. The fresh rod is inserted into the empty container and then activated by using its unique security code. The nexus links are switched from the depleted rod to the fresh one, and the depleted rod is deactivated, removed from the central core, and sent to be recharged."

He paused. "There are only two major problems that can happen during the fuel rod replacement process. One is that the new rod is faulty. The nexus has a buffering system, which can supply power to that zone of the Hive for about ten minutes. The nexus links have to be switched back to the old rod within that time or that zone of the Hive loses power."

"But surely the zone can't keep running on its depleted fuel rod for the three months until the next changeover," said Megan.

"No, it can't," said Lucas. "In that case, the Gold Commander would allow the cascade across the Hive to continue while the zone with the faulty rod removes it and gets a reserve one from storage. Once cascade ended, the opening of the bulkhead doors would be delayed while that zone is given the activation code for their reserve fuel rod and goes through the changeover process again."

Megan nodded.

"The other possible problem with changing the fuel rod is

that the nexus links connect to the new rod but fail to disconnect from the old one," said Lucas. "There are safety systems designed to prevent that happening, but if it did then the nexus would be supplied with double the normal amount of power. The problem has to be corrected before the buffering system overloads, or there's a huge explosion. Hence this situation is termed a deadly embrace."

"And Mars is going to try to make a deadly embrace happen," said Adika. "We can't delay Operation Rainbow Cascade – the existing fuel rods would run out of power within a few days – so I hope we've got a plan to stop Mars."

Lucas nodded. "We do. We'll allow Operation Rainbow Cascade to run on schedule, but set things up so it's impossible for Mars to cause an explosion."

"How will you manage that?" demanded Adika.

Lucas smiled. "It takes two fully functioning fuel rods to blow up a power supply nexus, and no zone is going to have access to more than one of them until after we've caught Mars."

I was totally confused. "But the zones can't change fuel rods unless they've got two of them."

"They will have two fuel rods," said Lucas, "but not two fully functioning ones. Gold Commander Melisande is arranging for every zone in the Hive to be given a new fuel rod that's faulty. To be exact, she's sending them the fuel rods that are normally used at our sea farm. These can only supply a tiny amount of power in comparison with a normal zone fuel rod."

He paused. "Operation Rainbow Cascade will start as usual. The new fuel rod will be put in place in Burgundy Zone. When they attempt to switch the nexus links to the new fuel rod, the power will immediately fail. Burgundy Zone will then switch back the links to the old fuel rod, and report the faulty fuel rod to Gold Commander Melisande. She will allow the cascade to continue, while crucially not announcing the failure to the other zones, since Mars must not be alarmed by anything unusual happening."

Lucas paused. "Each zone in turn will report a faulty fuel rod, until the one where Mars has set up a deadly embrace. In that zone, the power supply nexus will be connected to both the old and new fuel rods. The power won't fail, it will actually increase slightly, but should remain within the range that can be handled by the buffering system. Workers in that zone will believe they have successfully changed fuel rods, and report success to the Gold Commander. They'll only discover there's a problem when they attempt to remove the depleted fuel rod and find it's still connected."

"Yes, but Mars will realize he's failed to blow up the nexus," said Adika. "He could find another way to damage it."

"We have to assume that Mars will try to work out an alternative method of destroying the nexus," said Lucas. "He'll have been fully briefed about the five telepaths and their Strike teams by Jupiter. Even if Mars suspects his sabotage has been detected, and the alarm raised, he'll know that only one of those five telepaths will be able to point him out as the guilty party."

Lucas laughed. "Mars will believe he has plenty of time to come up with a new plan and carry it out before a telepath can reach him. Jupiter will have told him that Telepath Units are located at the top of the Hive, in a quiet area far away from the hubbub of minds surrounding the power complex. If Mars has chosen to target a zone with a Telepath Unit, then the telepath and their Strike team will have to travel at slow belt speed across half the zone to reach the power complex. If he's chosen to target a zone without a Telepath Unit, then there'll be the additional delay of getting through a sealed zone bulkhead."

"I don't see why you're laughing at this, Lucas," said Adika. "Would you mind explaining the joke?"

"The joke is that when Operation Rainbow Cascade starts, our entire unit will be aboard our aircraft and holding position directly above the Hive. As soon as Gold Commander Melisande gets a report of a successful fuel rod changeover from a zone, she'll relay that to us. We will then land in that zone's aircraft hangar, only a few cors away from the power complex. We'll set up a mobile Liaison and Tactical operations centre in the hangar, and Amber and the Strike team will head out to hunt Mars."

Adika laughed. "I like that idea."

"While we're chasing Mars, the plan is that Operation Rainbow Cascade will continue until all the other zones have reported faulty fuel rods. They'll all get their reserve fuel rods from storage, but Gold Commander Melisande will wait until we've caught Mars before she gives out the unique security codes to activate them."

He shrugged. "Operation Rainbow Cascade will then be rerun from the beginning, allowing all zones to change to functioning new fuel rods, before the Hive bulkhead doors are finally reopened."

Lucas looked around the watching unit members. "Every single one of you will have a part to play in saving the Hive from a devastating explosion. We'll be holding our first training exercise tomorrow morning. We're bound to discover that we've forgotten some things, or need duplicates of key equipment, so we'll be sending an aircraft back to the Hive every morning to collect supplies. If any of you feel you can't cope with this, then you can go back to the Hive in that aircraft, but I hope you'll stay because you're all needed."

He paused. "One last thing. All of you will have seen the Light and Dark pageants held before the festivals of Carnival and Halloween. You will have watched the light angel fighting to defend the Hive from the forces of darkness. Five days from now, we'll be flying out to defend our Hive from being plunged into darkness, and Gold Commander Melisande has given us a codename to be used in this operation. We will be known as Light Angel."

CHAPTER THIRTY-SIX

I woke with the comforting warmth of Lucas's arms holding me close to him. I lay still for a while, too blissfully content to move, before hunger made me open my eyes. I was confused to find we were lying on the carpeted floor of a strange room, but then I remembered we were in Hive Futura.

I studied Lucas's sleeping face. He'd had a strained look around his eyes since the Security Unit fire, and he'd been so busy arranging this trip that I wasn't sure he'd slept at all the previous night, but he finally looked relaxed and peaceful.

I automatically drifted from studying his face into studying his mind. Down near the subconscious, multiple thought levels were still working away, checking and rechecking his plan to deal with Mars. Lucas could never stop analyzing problems, even when deeply asleep.

Most of his mind was filled with amorphous imagery though. I watched in fascination as one level suddenly flared to life, engulfing neighbouring ones with the clarity of its pictures and its rushing torrent of emotions. Lucas was dreaming. He was reliving watching me dancing with Adika, reliving the way we'd danced in this apartment last night, reliving the way we'd kissed on the couch and…

Lucas's dream was shattered by the sound of his dataview playing a wake-up alarm. The higher levels of Lucas's mind abruptly shifted to full consciousness, his eyes opened, and he smiled at me.

"We've been sleeping in some odd places lately. In tents, in parks, and on carpets. Have you developed a phobia of sleep fields, Amber?"

I laughed. "If you think through what happened last night, you'll remember that ending up on the carpet was your idea."

"Oh yes." Lucas blushed. "I was so relieved about you getting rid of your echoes, that I got a little carried away."

I gave him a smug look. "You have to admit that I was right."

"The telepath is always right," said Lucas. "Right about what exactly?"

"On our first visit to Hive Futura, you had this same apartment, and we spent a lot of time together in this room. Remember how I tried to talk you into having a relationship with me, and you turned me down."

"I didn't want to turn you down. We'd known each other for less than two weeks, but your telepathy accelerated everything so it felt like two years. You understood and accepted me in a way nobody else ever had. Not my work colleagues, not the friends I'd had on Teen Level, and certainly not the parents who'd cut their ties with me as soon as they could. I was just afraid of what would happen when we arrived at the unit and you met the host of attractive young men on your Strike team."

"I know." I gave him the smug look again. "I told you back then that meeting my Strike team wouldn't change my feelings for you, and I was right."

I saw Lucas's thoughts accelerate. "That's why you told Megan you wanted us to have this apartment rather than the larger one you had back then?"

"Yes. I know this will sound ridiculous, but being here now... Well, it's as if it puts something right that once went wrong. This is how we should have been back then."

"It's not ridiculous, it's..." Lucas's words were drowned out by his dataview playing the same wake-up alarm again, but even louder. He groaned. "I'd better go and shower. I hope our maintenance people have managed to solve the problem with the hot water."

Investigation showed the water temperature had improved

from yesterday's breathtakingly cold to bearably tepid. By the time we'd showered, dressed, and were finishing breakfast, someone was outside the apartment, repeatedly pressing the door chime.

"That has to be Adika," said Lucas. "Have you remembered to wear your body armour under your clothes?"

"Yes. I've got my ear crystal and gun as well."

"Have you got your wristset light?"

"I'll be right back." I dashed off, rummaged through my bags, found one of my collection of wristset lights, put it on, and returned to find Adika lecturing Lucas.

"You can't be serious about using our cleaning staff as guards," he said.

Lucas grinned at him. "I see you've carefully read the detailed planning document that I sent to everyone."

"Yes, and most of it makes sense. I love the devious approach of giving all the zones faulty replacement fuel rods to remove the risk of an explosion, but your idea of using our unit cleaning staff as guards is ridiculous."

Lucas picked up our jackets from where they were lying on a chair, and passed mine to me. "We need some guards to stop curious bystanders disrupting our mobile operations centre. It's not worth tying up several of the Strike team on such a simple job."

"If anyone does try to interfere with our mobile operations centre, then cleaning staff won't have the courage to argue with them," said Adika.

Lucas led the way to the apartment door and opened it. "You're underestimating the courage of our cleaning staff. Every day, I'm awed by the bravery of Hannah as she comes to do battle with the mess in our apartment."

We arrived at the end of the corridor, and found a large crowd gathered in an open area. Lucas checked the time on his dataview. "One minute to go. Is everyone here, Megan?"

"I haven't seen Buzz or Forge yet."

"They're late?" Adika somehow managed to make the simple question into a threat of intense suffering for Forge, and, if he could get away with it, Buzz as well.

Megan glanced round the crowd. "Ah, Buzz and Forge are over by that structural pillar, so everyone's present."

"We can head to the hangar now then," said Lucas.

"Telepath Unit is moving," shouted Eli's exuberant voice.

Everyone laughed, and Adika led the way towards the aircraft hangar. Lucas leaned across to whisper in my ear.

"Amber, the seven aircraft pilots are with us. Can you check their minds, and make sure they're all dependable?"

I took Lucas's arm, letting him guide my steps as I swapped from using my eyes to viewing things with my telepathic sense. There was a long line of glowing minds, Lucas's mind flaring brighter than the rest. I had an odd thought. What did my own mind look like? There were no mirrors in the telepathic world to show me my reflection.

I thrust away that irrelevant distraction, skimmed past the familiar minds of unit members, and hit a group of six strangers. No, I corrected myself, there were actually seven strangers, but they were packed closely together. I noticed that four members of the Alpha team were in front of them, and four more behind them, in what seemed suspiciously like a pre-arranged formation.

I checked one of the nearest Alpha team minds. Yes, Dhiren was tensely watching every move the pilots made. Adika's instructions had been clear. Any stranger was a potential danger to the precious telepath. Even strangers who were Hive Defence pilots must be closely watched until declared safe by Amber.

I went back to the minds of the pilots. Three of them were virtually indistinguishable. All young men, excited to be part of this operation, and mildly irritated at the Strike team members constantly following them around. There was one woman who'd come out of the last Lottery, two older women, and an older man whose thoughts were tinged with darkness.

I frowned, went deeper into the older man's mind, and was hit by his pent up emotions. Being here, learning about our mission, had rekindled an intensely personal distress. He would do anything he could to help stop Mars. Anything at all.

I opened my eyes and whispered to Lucas. "All the pilots are perfectly loyal members of the Hive."

"Is there any particular one we should entrust with the job of ferrying supplies from the main Hive?"

"One of the men is older than the others. His husband was in Blue Zone during the power outage, and was badly injured in an accident, so he knows only too well what's at stake here. There is absolutely no risk of him betraying our secrets."

Lucas nodded. We'd arrived at the aircraft hangar entrance now. When we went inside, we found the place was still freezing cold. Everyone stopped to put on their jackets, and then Lucas stood on a crate and waved at people to gather round.

"Can you all hear me through your ear crystals as well as me shouting at you? If not, then check your ear crystal is set to receive both command channel and your group channel. Ask a member of the Liaison staff for help if necessary, because you'll need your ear crystals working during the training exercises."

He paused. "I hope you've all read the detailed plan I sent out. If not the whole thing, then at least the section covering your own part in it."

I was guiltily aware that I hadn't read the detailed plan. However, I had read Lucas's mind when he was thinking about the detailed plan. I hoped that would work just as well.

"Hive Futura has an identical power complex to the ones back at the main Hive," said Lucas. "This morning, Amber, Adika, and the Alpha Strike team will be familiarizing themselves with the layout of that power complex. I'll be going with them, our unit Electrical Maintenance Specialist, Sakshi, will act as our guide, and Forge will be coming along to play target with the Alpha team chasing after him. Everyone else will be practising setting up the mobile Liaison and Tactical operations centre in the aircraft hangar, with the Beta Strike team helping carry things."

There was a loud chorus of groans from the Beta Strike team.

Lucas waited for them to settle down before speaking again. "This afternoon, the Alpha and Beta Strike teams will trade places, so the Beta Strike team can learn their way around the power complex."

This time the Beta Strike team cheered.

"Everyone on guard duty should report to Megan immediately, so she can order the right size of hasty uniform for them."

"High up!" The wild yell came from the back of the crowd. I couldn't see who'd shouted that, but I thought it sounded like Hannah.

"Pilot Ralston will soon be flying one of the aircraft to the main Hive to collect additional supplies," Lucas continued. "If you discover you need any extra equipment, then you should inform Megan. We haven't had anyone ask to return to the Hive yet. Again, Megan should be informed of any such requests."

He paused. "That's all for now. Gideon is in charge while I'm away, so refer all your problems to him."

"Thank you so much, Lucas," said Gideon. "Can I point out that I'm seventy and supposed to have a reduced workload?"

"Why are you suddenly talking about reduced workloads, Gideon?" asked Hallie. "It's normally impossible to get you to leave the Tactical office."

"The Tactical office is warm," said Gideon. "This aircraft hangar is so cold that it's making my bones ache."

Lucas grinned at him. "I promise you won't have to suffer for long, Gideon. I'll be back in an hour, and then you can spend the rest of the day in your nice warm apartment."

Lucas jumped down from his crate, and beckoned a slim girl in a maintenance uniform over to join him. Adika and Forge led the Alpha Strike team out of the aircraft hangar, with Lucas, Sakshi, and me swept along somewhere near the middle of the group.

We stopped outside the door, and everyone turned to look expectantly at Sakshi. She seemed unnerved to be the centre of attention, running her hands through her long black hair before speaking.

"Yes. Um. I should explain that I'm not an expert on power complexes. I wouldn't normally be expected to work in one. My imprint only includes enough basic information on them to allow me to provide help in emergency situations."

"Don't worry about that," said Lucas, in an encouraging

voice. "I'm sure that the rest of us will be struggling to understand even the basic information. Perhaps you could start by explaining where the power complex is located."

"Yes. A power complex contains the crucial power supply nexus and its ancillary support areas. The precise position of the complex varies from one zone to another, but they are always right at the top of the Hive, and close to their zone's aircraft hangar to ease the problems of transporting the heavy fuel rods."

Sakshi was getting more confident about addressing her audience now. "A newly charged fuel rod is flown in by a specially adapted freight aircraft, and then transported on a customized trolley to a storage area in the power complex. After a fuel rod has been changed, the depleted rod is taken back to the aircraft hangar, and flown off to the Geothermal Energy Hub for recharging."

She pointed at the floor. "You see there's a green line running along the floor here. That marks the green route, with a reinforced floor capable of taking the weight of a fuel rod. Whatever zone of the main Hive you're in, the fastest way to get from the aircraft hangar to the power complex is to follow the green route."

Sakshi headed off, following the green line along the corridor, with the rest of us behind her. We walked two or three cors before we reached some security doors. Sakshi entered a code, and they opened to let us through.

"We're now entering the power complex," she said.

"Our theory is that Mars will try to set up a deadly embrace," said Lucas. "Would he need to be inside the power complex to do that?"

Sakshi nodded. "You'd have to override the safety systems to set up a deadly embrace, and manually intervene to stop the automatic alarms sounding. I'd expect Mars would need to be inside the power complex to do that, and probably inside the power supply nexus itself."

"The fact Mars expects to die in his own explosion seems to confirm that," said Lucas.

Sakshi led us the length of another corridor, before pausing to gesture at a door labelled in giant red letters. "RESTRICTED ACCESS."

"That's the fuel rod storage area. Before we go any further, I need to remind you of the general maintenance rule that anything coloured red is dangerous. Since most of Hive Futura is empty at the moment, the fuel rod in this nexus is one of the low power ones, but touching the nexus core could still kill you."

She started walking again, still following the green line on the floor. "The power supply nexus is roughly cylindrical in shape, with the top end on Industry 1, and the base down on Industry 10."

I blinked. I'd had a vague idea that a power supply nexus would be big, but I hadn't expected it to extend down ten whole levels.

"Since the aircraft hangars are on Industry 1," Sakshi added, "we're going to arrive at the top of the power supply nexus."

We walked on for another cor or two. Adika was ahead of me, blocking my view, so I didn't realize we'd reached the power supply nexus until he stepped sideways. I found I was standing on some sort of wide balcony, with a low wall in front of me, and looking out at a vast red object.

"There are identical circular galleries on each level of the nexus," said Sakshi. "We're on the highest of them, which is called gallery 1. If you look over the parapet, you can see the other nine galleries below us."

I peered cautiously over the wall, saw a dizzying drop below me, and took a hasty step backwards. I'd been afraid of heights ever since I was six years old, and the chase after Mercury seemed to have increased my fear. Not because any residual echoes of Mercury's personality were left in my mind, but because I had the ghastly memory of him and Soren falling to their deaths.

"We'll walk round the full circle of the gallery," said Sakshi, "so you can see the radiants sticking out from the nexus core. There are fifteen radiants on each gallery, each linked to a workstation. Make sure that you don't touch any of their controls. They adjust the power going to different levels of Hive Futura."

We followed Sakshi round the circular gallery. The radiants were equally spaced around the nexus core, and looked vaguely like black pipes sticking out of the giant, red central cylinder. Each of them had its own workstation, with a technical display and an incomprehensible mass of controls. We finally arrived back at our starting point.

"If this was a power supply nexus in a zone of the main Hive," said Sakshi, "there would be people on the workstations adjusting the power flows in response to fluctuating power demands from the different levels. It's not necessary to do that sort of manual intervention here at Hive Futura though."

"How many people are we talking about?" I asked.

"A normal shift would have two hundred people in the power complex, with thirty of them here in the nexus. The galleries are linked by internal staircases to the north, south, east, and west of the power supply nexus. These allow workers to move rapidly between galleries to deal with any problems."

Sakshi paused. "During the fuel rod changeover, there'll be a lot more people on duty though, especially here in the nexus. Swapping the nexus connections from the old fuel rod to the new one triggers a wave of power surges, so you need a member of staff at every workstation to deal with them as fast as possible. That means all three regular shifts will be present at once, as well as many additional reserve staff."

I frowned. If there would be fifteen people on each of the ten galleries of a power supply nexus during the fuel rod changeover, then the telepathic view of this place would be a blurred mass of a hundred and fifty minds crammed closely together.

"We'll now climb the north internal staircase to reach the power control centre," said Sakshi. "That's even higher than Industry 1, jutting upwards into the Hive's outer structural shield."

She headed for a narrow, spiralling staircase. I was horrified to see it stuck out over the edge of the gallery. Even worse, its steps and sides were made of a sort of metal grille, so anyone using it would be able to see through them to the nine level drop below. My head started to swim just looking at it.

I opened my mouth to confess that I couldn't face climbing

that staircase, but everyone on the operational teams of my unit knew I was afraid of heights. Multiple voices were already speaking, asking variations of the same question.

"Is there another way to get to the power control centre?"

Sakshi looked startled by the mass questioning. "Yes. Each gallery of the power supply nexus has exits to the north, south, east, and west. Those all lead to corridors with access to external conventional staircases. The internal staircases in the power supply nexus itself are much more exciting though. I've only known about them from my imprint before, so it's thrilling to see the real thing."

I glanced at the staircase again and shuddered. Sakshi might think of it as exciting, but I felt that petrifying was a better description.

"We'll take the boring, conventional staircase," said Lucas firmly.

Sakshi sighed, but led the way back into the corridor where we'd arrived, turned left, and started climbing a gloriously solid staircase. "There are external lifts as well, but the lift system is out of action here at Hive Futura."

"We're sticking to using staircases, both here and when we arrive back at the main Hive," said Lucas. "It would be a huge mistake to set foot in a lift when someone is trying to sabotage the power supply."

"Can I ask something?" asked Forge.

"Go ahead," said Lucas.

"I understand the need for multiple internal staircases, but why are there so many exits to corridors and sets of external staircases as well?"

"I'll explain that when we're in the power control centre," said Sakshi.

We reached the top of the staircase, turned down a corridor, and walked on to another circular gallery. We were above the red central cylinder here, so there weren't any radiants, but some technical displays were set into the wall.

There was a point where part of the gallery extended into the empty space above the central core, rather like a diving board sticking out over a swimming pool. Sakshi went across to it, sat in a luxuriously cushioned chair, and gave an excited giggle.

"The Power Controller supervises the whole power supply nexus from here. There's a clear view of all the people on the workstations below, and they can look up and see the Power Controller too."

I didn't want to try looking down at those galleries again myself. I linked to Sakshi's mind, so I could see the view from her eyes, and react to it with her emotions. She was thrilled to be sitting in the Power Controller's chair, seeing the ranks of galleries below her, imagining them filled with people hurrying to obey her every command.

There was a moment of pure self-indulgence, where she fantasized about saving the Hive from a great power surge, and then she forced herself to continue with her explanation. "You can see down into the nexus core itself from here. That would be much more spectacular if the fuel rod was a full power one."

Sakshi paused to study the menacing glow at the top of the red central cylinder, and wistfully think how blindingly bright it would be with a full power fuel rod. "As you can see, the power control centre has access to the four internal staircases and four exits, the same as each gallery. You'll notice a bulky metal object over the far side, which is the hoist system used to manoeuvre fuel rods into place in the central core."

She turned to look at Forge. "You asked the reason for having so many exits and external staircases. That's because the floor and walls surrounding the entire power supply nexus form a reinforced containment vessel. Should the nexus power buffering system reach critical overload, the emergency siren sounds, and workers have less than a minute to leave before blast doors close to block off all the exits."

Sakshi pointed upwards. "The only area that isn't reinforced is the ceiling. In the event of a power supply nexus exploding, the design is intended to channel the force of the blast upwards. That should mean it blows a hole in the roof of the Hive rather than ripping through inhabited areas. The design has never been tested in practice though."

"And our aim is to prevent it being tested now," said Lucas. "Thank you for the guided tour, Sakshi. I think everyone's got the idea of the layout, so you and I can go back to the aircraft hangar and leave them to carry on with their training exercises."

I felt Sakshi's reluctance as she got up from the Power Controller's chair. She and Lucas headed out of one of the exits, and I pulled back into my own head.

"Alpha team, you can go down to gallery 10 and wait for the order to chase your target," said Adika. "I'll stay here with Amber."

"Do you want me to read Forge's mind during this, and say what he's planning to do?" I asked.

Adika shook his head. "You and I will just be watching this training run. Its purpose isn't really to catch Forge, just to get everyone used to moving around the power supply nexus, and I want to see how the Alpha team manage without any instructions from us."

"Does that mean we can choose our own leader for this?" asked Eli.

"It does." Adika went to stand next to the Power Controller's chair. "Everyone set your ear crystals to listen only now, so Forge doesn't overhear your plans."

I wasn't sure whether that order included me or not, but I adjusted my ear crystal anyway. There was a mass clattering of feet as men hurried down the internal staircases. Adika gestured at the Power Controller's chair and I went shakily forward to sit in it. I avoided looking down at the sheer drop in front of me, and studied the display screens set into the wide arms of the chair. They were blank, probably disabled in some way.

"We're ready on gallery 10," Eli called up to us.

"Forge, you can position yourself wherever you like and use whatever methods you want to evade capture," said Adika. "At least, you can use any methods that don't damage the power supply nexus."

Forge didn't move.

Adika raised an eyebrow at him. "You're not exactly hard to find here, Forge. Don't you want to position yourself somewhere else?"

"I'm happy where I am," said Forge.

"If that's what you want, then Alpha team can start chasing their target."

There was more clattering from below. The Alpha Strike team members were climbing back up the spiralling staircases.

"The idea is that you try to evade capture, Forge," said Adika pointedly.

"I know." Forge stayed where he was until the first of his pursuers reached the top of the staircases, then gave them a mocking wave, vaulted over the parapet, and vanished downwards.

CHAPTER THIRTY-SEVEN

I panicked, instinctively linked to Forge's mind, and found him casually swinging down from the girders of one gallery to the next. He paused when he reached gallery 7, and laughed when he saw the frustrated faces of the Alpha team members looking down at him.

"Forge, the idea is that you try to evade capture, not plummet to your death," Adika's voice shouted from above.

"I'm not going to fall," Forge called back. "This place is like a colossal children's climbing frame."

... and here they come, chasing down the staircases after me. Which leaves me a whole quarter of the gallery where I can just...

I, Forge, was climbing up again now. The galleries were a mass of girders and support beams, each of them offering a selection of possible handholds. I joyously swung from one to the next, pulling my weight effortlessly upwards, and gave a teasing salute to Eli as I passed by him. He made a rude gesture at me in return.

I was on gallery 2 now, then gallery 1, and then heaving myself back over the parapet of the power control centre. I saw Amber in front of me, sitting in the Power Controller's chair. Her eyes were closed which meant she was reading someone's thoughts. Probably mine.

I was Forge looking at Amber. I was Amber reading Forge's thoughts. I was Forge thinking of Amber reading his thoughts.

There was an instant of entangled confusion before I had the sense to move from Forge's mind to Adika's mind.

Adika was leaning over the parapet, watching the Alpha Strike team running back up the internal staircases. This time they stopped when they reached gallery 2. Most of them spread out around the circular gallery, while four continued upwards, one heading up each staircase.

Adika turned to Forge, and saw him throw a brief glance at the number of men standing ready to grab him if he tried climbing down past them, before laughing and sprinting off through an exit. A couple of minutes later, he reappeared on gallery 10, waving up at the Alpha team.

Adika was simultaneously amused by Forge's tactics and disapproving of the Alpha team's response. They should have remembered the exits and external staircases.

Matias was standing on gallery 1, next to one of the spiralling, internal staircases. He grabbed the pole at the centre of its spiral, and started sliding down it. Adika had been wondering who'd be first to work out that you could slide down those poles. He found it interesting that it was Matias.

The rest of the Strike team saw what Matias was doing, and copied him. Forge looked up at the eighteen men sliding down poles towards him, and vanished through the nearest exit. The Alpha team braked to a halt, and started running up the staircases again to gallery 1. Adika was thinking that if he was Forge he'd wait for them to get back up to gallery 1 and...

The thought ended in a hiatus as Adika laughed. Forge was back on gallery 10 again.

I was aware of a nagging feeling of guilt. I frowned, pulled back into my own head, and sat there with my eyes still closed. We'd come here so everyone could learn to move around a power supply nexus, and that included me. In theory, I wouldn't need to enter a nexus during the chase after Mars, I'd be stationed somewhere outside it with my bodyguards, but unexpected things could happen during emergency runs.

I couldn't climb those nightmare spiralling staircases, but I'd successfully walked the circuit of gallery 1. I should be able to adjust to looking at the view from this chair through my own eyes, instead of sheltering behind the emotions of others.

I took a tight grip on the arms of my chair, told myself it was impossible for me to fall, opened my eyes, and looked cautiously over the parapet. The Alpha team were on gallery 1, only a level below me. I focused on them rather than the sheer drop down to gallery 10.

"Waste this!" said Eli. "We'll all go back to gallery 10 again, and repeat the herding upwards manoeuvre, but covering both the internal and external staircases."

I shuddered as I watched the Alpha team sliding down the poles of the staircases. Forge saw them coming, and vanished out of an exit like before, but this time he reappeared on gallery 1.

"Having fun, Forge?" Adika called down to him.

"Great fun." Forge stood watching as the Alpha team moved up towards him, and then stopped on gallery 2 like before. Four of them hurried off through the exits, four positioned themselves on staircases, while the other ten spread out round the gallery to block any attempt to climb down past them. As the four on staircases started moving upwards, Forge climbed a staircase into the power control centre.

"Excuse me," he said, as he sprinted past Adika to an exit.

Three minutes later, Forge was back on gallery 10. Eli looked down at him, an outraged expression on his face.

"How did you get there?" he yelled. "We had a man blocking each of the external staircases."

"I got into the vent system, and climbed down a ladder in that," Forge called back.

"Amusing though it is to watch this," said Adika, "I think we'll stop now."

"We can't stop now," said Eli. "We only need one more try to catch Forge."

Adika laughed. "I think you could keep chasing Forge all day, and still not catch him. Everyone, come up to the power control centre now."

He waited until everyone was gathered in the power control centre before speaking again. "I think we've established that it's virtually impossible to trap Forge in a power supply nexus."

Eli nodded. "Forge has the advantage of being a climbing specialist. Mars should be much easier to catch."

"If it turns out that Mars works in a power supply nexus, then he'll be so used to the staircases and poles that effectively he'll be a climbing specialist too," said Adika drily.

"We'll be able to shoot Mars though," said Dhiren. "We can't shoot Forge."

Eli grinned. "Now you mention it, shooting Forge is a tempting idea."

Forge laughed, but Adika remained grimly serious. "If Mars is inside the power supply nexus, we won't be able to shoot at him. We can't risk firing guns in an area packed with people and essential equipment. What will make the real difference is we'll have Amber telling us what Mars is going to do before he does it."

He paused. "Now, our genuine target is attempting to sabotage the power supply nexus, so there's an obvious risk of the power going out during the chase. I hope that everyone remembered their wristset lights."

Adika looked at me. I pointed proudly at the light attached to my wrist.

"Forge, we'll give you a moment to choose your position before I turn the lights out," said Adika.

Forge headed down one of the staircases.

"You're going to make us chase Forge in the dark?" asked Eli, in a wounded voice. "That's unfair tactics."

"I hate to break this news to you, Eli," said Adika, "but we can't expect our targets to use fair tactics all the time."

"I know that," said Eli, "but if we can't catch Forge with the lights on then we definitely can't catch him in the dark. I give up."

"Eli has decided to give up playing leader," said Matias promptly, "so I'll organize the next chase."

"I didn't mean I was giving up as leader," said Eli.

"It's too late to change your mind now," said Matias. "You've tried, you've failed, and now it's my turn to do the planning. When the lights go out, we'll all slide down the poles to gallery 10, and I'll explain our tactics."

"But..."

Kaden patted Eli on the head. "Hush, Eli. It's time to give Matias a chance."

Adika went across to one of the controls, and adjusted it. The lights went out, and there was an instant of total darkness before the narrow beams of wristset lights started appearing. I belatedly remembered to turn mine on as well.

I heard the sound of moving feet, and then Adika and I were alone again. "Matias taking charge was an interesting development," said Adika. "He was one of my candidates for the deputy team leader posts, but he's been rather subdued since I chose to promote Rothan and Forge."

Adika peered over the gallery wall. "It's awfully quiet down there, and judging from the lights nobody is moving around."

I made a rapid check of Matias's thoughts. "Forge hasn't turned his wristset light on. He's hiding somewhere in the power supply nexus, so Matias has got the whole Alpha team staying still and listening for any movement that gives away Forge's position."

"An interesting approach," said Adika thoughtfully.

I frowned. "You surely aren't thinking of replacing Rothan? He's supposed to be making a full recovery."

"Of course I'm not thinking of replacing Rothan, but the last few days have made it clear that I need to choose a fourth in command. Someone to act as a temporary replacement when either Rothan or Forge is injured."

Adika hesitated before continuing. "Lucas's priority, everyone's priority, had to be helping you recover from your fragmentation issues, Amber. Now that you've achieved that, I've had a chat with Megan."

I pictured Megan's reaction to him trying to talk her out of her baby plans, winced, and checked Adika's mind to see how bad the damage was. I was stunned.

"You're getting married!"

"Yes." Adika smiled, the levels of his mind overflowing with self-satisfaction. "Megan feels we shouldn't get married until after she's had Dean's child, but she's agreed to announce our engagement right away."

... respect Hiveism's idea that Dean's spirit will have returned to the Hive, but Megan's plan makes more sense to me. A legacy of a living, breathing son or daughter, possibly both if Megan has twins, is...

... might have met Dean once or twice, can't honestly remember, but he was Strike team too, my fallen brother in arms, so...

... and then our own children. And if something went wrong before then, if a bad run took me the way one took Dean, it's reassuring to know that Megan would do the same for me as...

I pulled out of Adika's thoughts, and back into my own mind. A minute ago, I'd been stunned to discover that Adika and Megan were going to get married. Now I couldn't understand why I hadn't expected this to happen. I'd known that Megan had been worried there'd be a gap in her life and that of her baby where Dean should have been. Adika would fill that gap, and as for Adika's feelings... They'd been summed up perfectly by the words I'd just seen in his head.

"My congratulations," I said. "I wish you every happiness."

"Thank you," said Adika.

We watched the wristset lights below us. What had been a terrifying drop was now just blackness with scattered dots of light. Sometimes those dots were still. Sometimes there was a slow, purposeful, mass movement. Sometimes a single light would rush from one spot to another.

"I wanted to give Matias a chance to prove his leadership ability," said Adika eventually, "but we really need to get back to the hangar and..."

A cry of triumph came from below, followed by the sounds of a struggle, and the wristset lights all converged on one spot. "We got him!" said Matias's voice.

"They *finally* got me," Forge's voice echoed him in mockery.

Adika turned the lights on again, and adjusted his ear crystal before speaking. "Everyone, meet up on gallery 1, and then we'll head back to the aircraft hangar."

Adika and I went down the conventional external staircase,

and walked into gallery 1. "How did Forge manage to hide for so long without someone stepping on him?" asked Adika.

"Forge was clinging to the underneath of gallery 5 the whole time," said Eli. "He isn't a human being. He's a spider."

"I wasn't clinging on to anything," said Forge. "I was lying across two of the support beams. You'd have spotted me within the first two minutes if you'd thought to shine your wristset lights up as well as down."

We walked back to the aircraft hangar, and found clusters of people working on equipment, while others stood watching with an air of resigned boredom. I went over to where Lucas was sitting on an empty crate.

"How is the mobile operations centre progressing?"

"I'm torn between using the words abysmal and disastrous," said Lucas. "We haven't managed to get either the Liaison or the Tactical areas working yet. We can't depend on the standard power supply when we're chasing Mars, so we have to adapt everything to run from power cells."

He shrugged. "The aircraft has returned from the main Hive with some vital missing parts, so things should go much better this afternoon. I've discovered one major oversight on my part."

"What oversight?"

"When we arrive at the main Hive, we'll have to set up the mobile operations centre in the aircraft hangar for speed and security. Therefore we're rehearsing setting it up in the aircraft hangar here. The problem is that most of the unit staff are petrified of Outside, so we have to evacuate them into the corridors before we can open the hangar doors to let our aircraft in or out."

"Will that be an issue during the actual chase after Mars?"

"Hopefully not," said Lucas. "When we arrive at the main Hive, we'll close the hangar doors as soon as our aircraft are inside, and we shouldn't need to reopen them again until after we've caught Mars. I suppose we could take some screens with us, so we can block the view of the hangar doors if necessary."

I shook my head. "I don't think a few screens would be enough to reassure people who've grown up with a deeply ingrained fear of the hunter of souls and his demonic pack."

"True. Even my own Tactical team couldn't face staying in the hangar when the doors were open. Intellectually, they know the horror stories about Outside are just myths, but they're up against a lifetime of social conditioning." Lucas sighed. "How did the Alpha Strike team do in training?"

"Not very well, but that's because they were chasing Forge around what he described as a colossal children's climbing frame."

Lucas laughed. "I thought Forge would make them work hard in there."

I moved on to the subject that was worrying me. "Sakshi said there'll be someone at every workstation in the power supply nexus, dealing with power surges during the fuel rod changeover. That's a hundred and fifty minds on the galleries, and several more in the power control centre as well."

"Yes," said Lucas. "I hadn't realized so many additional staff would be in the power supply nexus during Operation Rainbow Cascade."

"Finding Mars's mind should be relatively easy, I'm expecting it to be quite distinctive, but describing his location to the Strike team will be incredibly hard."

I pulled a pained face. "When I look with the telepathic view, the galleries and staircases are invisible. I'll just be seeing a mass of minds sprawled across ten levels of the Hive, and making rough estimates of where Mars is. The view from his eyes won't give me any clues, because all those galleries and workstations look the same. I can't count on being able to give the Strike team a description of Mars, or even a name, because people rarely think about those things."

"I've been considering this point too," said Lucas. "We won't be able to evacuate the staff from the power supply nexus, because uncontrolled power surges would cause immense amounts of damage. Even if you manage to give the Strike team enough information for them to locate Mars, they'll be charging into a three-dimensional maze that's packed with innocent bystanders."

He shrugged. "Whether those people react by getting in the

way and demanding explanations, or by running in panic, there's a risk of Mars escaping in the confusion. We need to take instant control of the situation, and I've thought of one way to do that, but I know exactly how hard it would be for you."

I frowned. "What's your idea?"

"We dress up Buzz as a nosy and send her into the power control centre."

I gulped. I'd been worried that my fear of heights could be a problem during the chase after Mars. It had never occurred to me that my difficulties with nosies would be an issue.

"Obviously, we'd let you read Mars's mind first, and get all the information you can," said Lucas. "Buzz would then enter the power control centre, and stand by the Power Controller's chair. Everyone in the power supply nexus would be able to see her there. Buzz could distract them while the Strike team got into position, and then make them stay in their seats while Mars is arrested."

He paused. "This approach would help us take control of the situation, but I know how hard it is for you to work near nosies. It could be impossible for you to keep reading the target's mind."

I pictured a power supply nexus packed with people, all reacting to the arrival of a nosy, and winced. "It would be a struggle to read anyone, even my own Strike team members. Not everyone reacts badly to a nosy, but there'd be a hundred and fifty people in the nexus. There's a danger they wouldn't react as individuals but as a crowd, so the emotions of anger and loathing start multiplying."

"Yes, with crowds you can get mass emotional contagion, where the emotions of all the individual members start synchronizing," said Lucas. "We can't risk that happening, so I'll have to think of another way to…"

I lifted a hand to stop him. "There isn't another way that could work as well. The sight of a nosy has an instant impact on everyone. People would immediately accept Buzz's authority, and believe whatever she told them. Everyone except Mars, because he knows the nosies are fakes. He'd still be distracted though, so…"

I broke off. "I'm going to have to think about your plan for a while, and decide if I can cope with it. Can we talk about something else now?"

Lucas nodded.

"There's some surprising news from Adika," I said. "He and Megan are engaged, and will be getting married after she's had the baby."

Lucas's mind flared brighter as his thought levels went into high-speed analysis mode. I'd been stunned by this news, and only understood why it was happening after reading Adika's mind. Lucas worked it out for himself in thirty seconds. "Hopefully that will solve their relationship problems."

"Adika certainly seems very happy at the moment."

"I'd better go and congratulate him."

We went across to where Adika and Forge were standing with the Alpha Strike team.

"Amber told me that you and Megan are planning to get married," said Lucas. "My congratulations."

"Thank you." Adika glanced at where Megan was working, and smiled before turning to me. "Amber, will you want to come along to watch the Beta team training session this afternoon, or would you prefer to rest?"

"I'll come along," I said. "I need more practice running circuits on their minds."

"We shouldn't be wasting training time on the Beta team greenies," grumbled Tobias. "If the Alpha team carry on training this afternoon, we'll learn how to catch Forge much faster."

"Really?" Forge glared at Tobias. "You were struggling to catch me, and now you want to use your failure as an excuse to steal my team's training time? Being recruited earlier gives you a huge advantage over the Beta team, so you smugly call them greenies, but..."

Adika frowned and opened his mouth to intervene, but another voice cut in first. "I'm in total agreement with Forge on this. I've only been away for a few days. If the Alpha team have already fallen apart to the extent that they need to steal the Beta team's training time, then I'll disown the lot of you."

We all turned to face the new arrival. Rothan stepped forward to hug Forge, and then smiled round at the rest of us. "Have you missed me?"

"Of course we've missed you," I said, "but what are you doing here?"

"You sent an aircraft back to the main Hive to collect vital items you'd left behind. I felt those vital items included Emili and me."

"You know that Amber means you should be back at the main Hive having medical treatment," said Adika. "You were critically ill only days ago."

Rothan shrugged. "The genetically tailored replacement cell treatment has fixed the damage to my lungs, and the Fire Casualty Centre has discharged me. I'll need daily follow-up checks for infection over the next month, but I can have those from our own medical staff."

"Won't you need some time to get fit again?" asked Eli.

Rothan laughed. "I haven't been out of action long enough to get unfit."

Adika patted Rothan on the shoulder. "In that case, we're glad to have you back with us."

There was a babble of conversation, but I just stood there watching in silence. I was remembering Rothan's younger brother sitting in the waiting room at the Fire Casualty Centre. The boy had been thinking how cowardly he was in comparison to Rothan, and now I was feeling exactly the same way. Rothan had been trapped by fire, choking from smoke, but calmly kept lifting others to safety before escaping himself. My difficulties with nosies seemed trivial in comparison.

If Rothan could put his horrific experiences in the fire behind him, and come to help us catch Mars, then I should be able to cope with Lucas's plan to take control of the situation in the nexus. After all, the crowd of people there would be reacting to the nosy as a terrifying inhuman creature, but I would know it was just Buzz dressed up in a grey mask and clothes. That would surely make things easier.

CHAPTER THIRTY-EIGHT

When we flew back towards the main Hive, there were a multitude of stars shining in the night sky. I stared out of the aircraft window at them, wondering if some of those stars were the other worlds that orbited the Truesun. Was I looking at Mercury, Venus, Mars, or Jupiter right now?

I glanced round Aerial one. The Alpha Strike team all had electrical items wedged uncomfortably on their laps. There was no conversation at all, not even a joke from Eli to break the tense silence.

We'd rehearsed the plane disembarkation and setting up of the mobile operations centre dozens of times in the last few days. Our best time was four and a half minutes, but one lost or broken item of equipment could add another ten minutes to that.

Gold Commander Melisande's voice spoke from my ear crystal. "Light Angel, what is your status?"

"Light Angel is airborne and should be above the Hive in eleven minutes," said Lucas.

"Light Angel, I'm talking to you on a private communications channel so no one else can hear us," said Melisande. "At this moment, even my own team are unaware of the expected threat and your planned intervention. I'm assuming that you still wish me to keep them in ignorance."

"Yes," said Lucas. "Mars may just be a maintenance worker with access to key power systems, but we have to allow for the possibility of him being highly placed in either Power Services or Gold Command."

"It is now twenty minutes to midnight," said Melisande. "Operation Rainbow Cascade is entering the final ten minute countdown. We'll need you in position over Burgundy Zone aircraft hangar in twenty-five minutes."

"We'll be there."

Lucas's voice sounded perfectly calm, but I checked the top levels of his thoughts and found them in turmoil.

... logic says that Mars must be going to sabotage Operation Rainbow Cascade. I'll be the laughing stock of Law Enforcement if logic is wrong and...

... worried about asking Amber to do this, especially when Buzz is playing the part of the nosy. Amber's already been through too much in...

... taking this approach, but how could our telepaths have checked the minds of everyone involved? It's not just the people from all three work shifts, but the host of extra temporary staff in each power complex, and...

Words vanished and were replaced by a sequence of rapidly changing images. Hasties cordoning off all the bulkhead crossing points. People in maintenance uniforms checking that every bulkhead door on every level had sealed, and the shutters had come down across all air vents and crawl ways. Power workers crammed into the galleries of a power supply nexus.

Overwhelmed by the images, I pulled out of Lucas's mind, and looked at the screen of the dataview he was holding instead. There was the usual oblong diagram of the Hive, with a group of flashing dots approaching it that marked our aircraft's location.

"Five minute countdown," said Melisande.

I was expecting silence for another few minutes, but our pilot's voice spoke in an urgent tone. "Lucas, I've got Hive Defence calling me. They're querying why our formation doesn't have flight clearance and is off-course for our home zone aircraft hangar. I'm going to have to tell them something or they'll launch fighter aircraft."

"Tell them to call Hive Gold Command channel 9," said Melisande. "I'll deal with it."

A minute later, our pilot spoke again. "We've now been sent blanket authorization for flight manoeuvres connected with a Hive Gold Command emergency defence operation."

Another long silence. "Five seconds to Operation Rainbow Cascade," said Melisande. "Four, three, two, one. We're initiating belt system slowdown and cordoning off the bulkhead crossing points. Where are you, Light Angel?"

"We've just reached the Hive," said Lucas. "On approach to Burgundy Zone aircraft hangar now."

After the quietness of Hive Futura, I was keenly aware of the thunder of the Hive Mind close to me. A hundred million thoughts. A hundred million people depending on us to keep them safe. I rubbed my sweaty hands on the fabric of the clothes I was wearing. I could do this. We could do this.

"I have confirmation of belt system slowdown and bulkhead crossing points blocked from all zones," said Melisande. "Ordering bulkhead doors to close in ten seconds."

"Light Angel is now holding position above Burgundy Zone aircraft hangar," said Lucas. "Ready to transmit remote activation code for the hangar doors."

"Bulkhead doors are closing now," said Melisande.

There was a very long pause. Maintenance people would be calling in confirmation that the bulkhead doors had closed, but that process was only scheduled to take five minutes. We seemed to have been waiting far longer than that.

"Clearing Burgundy Zone to initiate fuel rod changeover," said Melisande.

We all waited tensely. Lucas had his finger poised over his dataview, ready to send the signal to open the Burgundy Zone aircraft hangar doors.

"Light Angel, Burgundy Zone reports a faulty fuel rod," said Melisande.

"Light Angel acknowledging," said Lucas. "Moving to position over Red Zone aircraft hangar."

I heard the note of the aircraft engines grow louder as we started moving, and then quieten again.

"Light Angel is now holding position above Red Zone aircraft hangar," said Lucas.

"Clearing Red Zone to initiate fuel rod changeover," said Melisande.

Red Zone reported a faulty fuel rod, so did Orange Zone and Yellow Zone, but then we were holding position over Green Zone aircraft hangar and the calmness of Melisande's voice changed to urgency.

"Green Zone reports successful fuel rod changeover."

"Light Angel is landing." Lucas's forefinger stabbed at his dataview, and I saw a light appear below us as the Green Zone hangar doors slid open in response to our signal.

"I'm allowing the cascade to continue as planned," said Melisande. "Clearing Turquoise Zone to initiate fuel rod changeover now."

There was a lurch as our aircraft swooped downwards and into the hangar. A couple of bewildered people in Hive Defence uniforms started running towards us, only to back away rapidly as they saw more aircraft were following us in.

I heard the voice of our pilot magnified to deafening levels by a loudspeaker. "Stand clear! Hive Gold Command emergency defence operation in progress. Call Hive Gold Command channel 9 for confirmation."

Our aircraft came to a halt. Adika opened the door, and hit the button to deploy the emergency evacuation chute. The Alpha team started leaping out of the door in turn, clutching electrical equipment protectively to their chests as they slid downwards.

Lucas turned to me. "You're sure you can do this, Amber?"

"Yes."

He gave me one swift kiss, stood up, and we went to follow the Alpha team down the evacuation chute. By the time we'd reached the ground, Aerial two had parked neatly next to our aircraft, but I noticed something odd about the lighting. I looked up at the ceiling, and saw the hangar lights were flashing erratically.

"What's happening?" I asked.

"Power surges," said Lucas. "The power supply nexus has two fuel rods in deadly embrace, so there are bound to be power surges, but the new fuel rod is only low power. The problems can't possibly be this bad, unless..."

He ran his fingers through his hair. "Mars must be doing this. He'll be wondering why the power isn't overloading the nexus buffering system yet. Everyone else in the nexus will be trying to minimize the power surges, but Mars is working against them. He's concentrating the excess power in areas near the nexus, in the hope that it will trigger an explosion."

"Does that mean Mars is definitely in the power supply nexus itself?" I asked.

Lucas nodded. "From what Sakshi has told me, Mars couldn't do this from anywhere else."

The door of Aerial two was open now, and the Beta Strike team were sliding down their evacuation chute. Aerial three and four had parked too, but nobody would leave those aircraft until the hangar doors were safely closed.

I glanced over my shoulder, and saw that Aerial five and six were inside the hangar and moving into position, while Aerial seven was still coming in through the hangar doors. As I faced Lucas again, the hangar lights flashed blindingly bright before everywhere was plunged into darkness.

"Waste it!" said Lucas. "The hangar power circuit has overloaded."

The hangar area wasn't completely dark. There was some light coming from the uncovered windows of Aerial one and two, and more scattered lights started appearing as Strike team members switched on their wristset lights. I belatedly remembered to turn my own light on as well.

Lucas tapped the crystal unit in his ear. "We'll need the emergency lanterns set up and..."

His words were drowned out by a hideous rending sound of metal against metal. I turned and saw the dark shape of Aerial seven skid violently sideways and then crash onto one side. I was still trying to work out what had happened when Lucas started snapping out orders over the crystal comms.

"Alpha Strike team, grab the hangar fire extinguishers and get them to Aerial seven. The power failure must have sent the hangar doors into emergency closure mode. They caught Aerial seven's tail section, and tipped it over. Spray the aircraft with foam as a precaution and then get everyone out. Beta Strike team, move to Aerial five and help the medical staff disembark. We may have casualties, so your priority is setting up their medical area."

Figures ran past me, their wristset lights glowing. Two emergency lanterns suddenly flashed on next to Aerial seven, and I saw Adika wielding a massive fire extinguisher. I was trying to remember who'd been travelling in Aerial seven, but my brain was numb with shock.

"Emili, can you hear me?" asked Lucas. "What's your status in there?"

There was no response, but the mention of Emili had started my brain working again. Lucas's Tactical team members were in the last aircraft, along with Buzz, because they wouldn't be needed until the mobile operations centre was ready.

I closed my eyes, and reached out with my thoughts towards the toppled aircraft. I was trained to skip at speed between the minds of my Strike team members. I wasn't familiar enough with the minds of the Tactical team to do that, but I could work my way systematically through the minds in Aerial seven, checking for people who were injured. The lights were still on inside the aircraft, so I was hit by a succession of views of sprawling bodies and scattered possessions.

"Everyone's dazed," I said. "There's someone with what feels like a fractured wrist. A man with a probable broken rib. A woman with an injury to the leg that seems to be severe muscle damage rather than a break. A semi-conscious man with a cut leg." I paused. "You need to get to that man fast. He's losing too much blood."

There was a crackle from my ear crystal, and Emili's voice gasped out words. "Who has the cut leg, Amber?"

"I don't know," I wailed. "I don't know your minds well enough to..."

"Is he at the near end of the aircraft to us or further away?" asked Lucas.

"He's the furthest person away from us. On his own."

"He's right at the back of the aircraft, Emili," said Lucas.

"It's Kareem!" Emili yelled the name at deafening volume. "We need to get a tourniquet on Kareem's leg!"

"We've managed to force the door open and I'm inside," said Adika. "Emili's reached Kareem. Is anyone else in immediate danger, Amber?"

"Everyone else seems to just have bruises." I was horribly aware that I wouldn't know if anyone was dead, but I didn't say that aloud. If I'd thought to count the number of minds as I checked them, then I'd know if everyone was all right. It was too late to do that now, because the familiar minds of Alpha team members were joining those in the aircraft.

I drifted randomly between minds for the next minute or two. Adika was checking the bloodstained tourniquet on Kareem's leg. Rothan was reaching out a hand to touch Emili's cheek. Eli was lifting Gideon up through the door that had been at the side of the aircraft but was now in the ceiling.

Finally satisfied that everyone was alive, I pulled back into my own head and opened my eyes. I was startled to see the hangar lights were coming back on. No, they weren't back on at full power, so this must be some emergency lighting system.

I looked round and saw figures in Hive Defence uniforms were working on a control panel on the nearest wall. Several more were standing near Aerial seven and holding fire extinguishers. However confused they were by our arrival, these people knew how to deal with crashing aircraft and power failures.

"Everyone is out of Aerial seven, and casualties are in medical hands," said Adika.

Melisande's voice instantly spoke as if she'd been waiting to hear that news. "Tactical Commander Lucas, will your unit be able to continue to apprehend Mars?"

"I believe so, Gold Commander." Lucas took a deep breath. "We have to go back to our original arrival plan now, everyone.

We must set up our mobile operations centre and get to Mars before he causes more accidents with his power surges."

The frantic activity of the last few minutes changed to our well-rehearsed arrival sequence. I checked the thoughts of a random maintenance worker as he left Aerial three, sharing his fear as he saw the toppled Aerial seven, and the heroic effort he made to concentrate on helping set up the mobile operations centre.

"Megan, are you in the medical area?" asked Lucas, on the crystal comms.

"Yes."

"Status report on the casualties, please?"

"Jasmine is operating on Kareem to stop the bleeding. He'll be fine, and all the other injuries are straightforward."

I heard Lucas sigh in relief.

"I'm afraid that Buzz has a badly damaged hamstring though," added Megan. "We're still assessing the injury, and deciding whether to operate or use alternative treatments."

Buzz joined in the conversation, her voice strained as if she was in pain. "I can't walk at the moment, Lucas, but I could still do the nosy act in a powered chair."

"No, you can't," said Lucas. "We need our nosy to be positioned next to the Power Controller, where everyone in the nexus can see them. You wouldn't be able to get to the power control centre without using a lift, and I'm not sending anyone into a lift during these power surges. We'll have to get one of the Strike team to play the part of the nosy."

"There's the minor flaw that the Strike team are all large, muscled men, and won't fit into my nosy outfit," said Buzz. "Couldn't someone carry me and my chair up to...?"

"No!" Megan interrupted her. "I can't allow you to leave our medical area in your current condition."

Emili's voice spoke over the comms. "Lucas, Kareem is obviously out of action, and Hallie is being treated for a broken wrist, but the rest of our team are heading to the mobile operations centre now. I'm staying here to change into Buzz's outfit so I can play the part of the nosy."

"Nobody is playing the part of the nosy," said Lucas. "If neither Buzz nor the Strike team can do it, then we'll abandon the idea."

"We must have someone playing the nosy, Lucas," said Emili. "If we don't take control of the situation in the power supply nexus, then people will be frightened by the Strike team charging in to chase Mars. If there's a panic, and people start crowding onto those spiral staircases to get away, there'll be deaths from falls or being crushed."

Lucas groaned.

"I can do this," said Emili.

Her words sounded determined, but there was a tremble in her voice that worried me. Emili had had a dreadful time when Rothan was injured, and now she'd just escaped from a wrecked aircraft. She was in no state to be playing the part of a nosy on an emergency run. She didn't need to do it anyway, because there was a far better solution.

"No, I'll play the nosy," I said. "Buzz's outfit will fit me at least as well as Emili."

My words were followed by a stunned silence. Lucas was still standing next to me. He took the crystal unit from his ear, and gestured at me. I took my ear crystal out too.

"It will be impossibly hard for you trying to work near a nosy, Amber," he said. "You can't make things more difficult by playing the part yourself."

I shrugged. "Whether I'm near the nosy, or playing the nosy myself, I'll still be hit by the massed emotions of the people in the nexus."

Lucas frowned as he thought that over.

"The plan was that I'd give the Strike team all the information I could before we sent in our nosy," I continued arguing my case. "We knew I'd probably be unable to work after that. This way I can at least do something useful."

Lucas groaned again. "If you insist, then you can wear the nosy outfit. We'll assess the situation in the power supply nexus before making the final decision on whether to send you in or not."

I put my ear crystal back in, and headed for the medical area before Lucas could change his mind. I found Buzz lying on a wheeled trolley, her face twisted with pain. The grey nosy mask and matching outfit were lying on the floor next to her.

"You can't play the nosy, Amber," she said. "You've got too strong a phobia of them."

I picked up the grey outfit and started pulling it on over my clothes. "I used to be terrified of the Truesun. I faced that and I can face this."

"You're absolutely sure?"

"Yes."

Buzz grabbed the sides of the trolley, took a deep breath, and pulled herself up into a sitting position. "In that case, you'll need me to help with the mask."

I sat on the floor so she could fit the mask over my head, seal it into place at the back, and adjust my neckline. "The acoustic distortion control is on the right side of your neck," she said. "Are you comfortable?"

"Is anyone ever comfortable wearing these things?" I heard my words come out in an unrecognizably weird, throbbing voice. The acoustic distortion system in the mask was working beautifully.

"Not really. Good luck."

I could see the Strike team members were already gathering by the aircraft hangar exit. As I walked towards them, I caught sight of my reflection in the glass of one of the aircraft windows, and stopped to stare at it.

The shape of the grey mask made my head look as if it bulged in strange places. Special filters turned what you could see of my eyes to a peculiar purple colour. Even the grey clothes had added layers of gauze that were weighted to make them shift in odd directions as I moved. The whole effect was that of something alien and frightening.

This was the image that had terrified me in childhood and all through Teen Level. I had become my own nightmare.

CHAPTER THIRTY-NINE

Adika's heavily muscled arms swept me off my feet, and the Alpha and Beta Strike teams converged on us. Normally my Strike teams dressed in ordinary clothes over their mesh body armour so we could move unobtrusively around the Hive. Today most of them were a menacing sight in grey, heavy-duty combat armour. Adika, Eli, Matias, and Kaden wore blue hasty uniforms because they would be playing the role of the hasty guards in my nosy squad. Forge and Rothan had the red and black uniforms of those working for Power Services.

"Alpha Strike team is moving," said Adika.

"Beta Strike team is moving," said Forge.

Lucas's voice spoke in my ear crystal. "Tactical ready."

"Liaison ready," said Nicole. "Tracking status green for both Strike teams."

"We are green," I said, and shuddered as I heard my words come out in the distorted voice of a nosy.

My combined Strike teams swept out of the aircraft hangar to an open area where the lights were on at full brightness. They ran on at full speed for three cors, and reached the security doors that guarded the way to the Green Zone power complex. Rothan entered a code, and the doors opened.

"We're entering the power complex," said Adika.

"Sakshi, can you hear me?" asked Lucas.

"Yes, I'm with Liaison."

"Mars has been causing power surges on Industry 1. Does that tell us anything about his location in the power complex?"

"He must be in the power supply nexus itself, at the workstation controlling the power for Industry 1. The workstations controlling Industry 1 through 15 are normally on gallery 1."

"Strike team, stay on your current level," said Lucas. "Follow the green route for two more corridors, and then wait while Amber searches for Mars's mind and confirms he's on gallery 1."

I was carried by a door marked "RESTRICTED ACCESS", which would be the fuel rod storage area, and then we stopped. I closed my eyes, reached out past the tense thoughts of the Strike team, encountered scattered groups of minds in nearby offices, and then found what I was looking for. A tightly knit blur of thought that had to be the people in the power supply nexus.

Mars should be near the top of the nexus on gallery 1, so I started with the minds there, moving rapidly between them until something caught my attention.

... normal to have power surges after changing the fuel rod, but they should have stabilized by now. We can't remove the depleted fuel rod until...

A red warning was flaring on the display screen by my right hand. Industry 1. Again! Waste it, what's wrong with the operator at workstation 1. She's already blown the power on...

"Workstation 1, why aren't you dumping that excess power?" I snapped the words in frustration. "If you can't distribute it properly yourself, then just dump it across Industry 2 to 4 and let their operators handle it."

I was clearly in the mind of the Power Controller. An equally frustrated voice answered him. "Sir, I've been ordering power dumps but my controls aren't responding."

I turned to my deputy. "Get down there and take over that workstation yourself."

"Yes, sir!" She sprinted for the nearest staircase.

I disentangled myself from the Power Controller's mind and spoke myself. "There's something odd."

I shuddered again at the sound of the nosy voice. "Lucas, I'm going to have to turn off the acoustic distortion system on this mask. It's too distracting. Remind me to turn it back on when I need it."

"I will. What have you found that's odd?"

I adjusted the distortion control on the right of my neck, and spoke in my normal voice. "We're sure that Mars is male. The person at the workstation controlling the power on Industry 1 is female. She's saying that she's been ordering power dumps but her controls aren't responding."

"That sounds like someone's controlling her workstation remotely," said Sakshi. "It's possible to use one workstation in the nexus to control another, but only a Power Controller would know how to do it."

"I've already read the mind of the Power Controller," I said. "He doesn't understand what's happening."

"His deputy might be imprinted as a Power Controller as well," said Lucas.

"His deputy is female." I groaned. "I'll have to work my way through everyone in the nexus."

I skimmed lightly across minds that were jammed side-by-side and one on top of another. They were all worried about the power surges, so I was afraid I'd miss Mars among all the other stressed thoughts, but then I found him. A mind that burned bright with anger and violence.

"Target acquired," I said. "Mars is on a gallery near the middle of the nexus. Probably somewhere between gallery 4 and gallery 7. He can't work out what's gone wrong with his plan. The nexus core should have exploded by now. It was supposed to rip the heart out of Green Zone, the same way that Lottery ripped the heart out of his life."

"What's Mars planning to do next?" asked Lucas.

"He's been overriding power dumps, concentrating all the power surges on Industry 1, but that hasn't even sent the power buffering system into the danger zone. Mars has given up hope of using the power surges to cause an explosion, and is trying to work out another way to destroy the nexus. One option would be to…"

I broke off my sentence. "No, I can't make sense of that thought train at all. It's just a jumble of incomprehensible technical terms. Whatever Mars's idea is, it involves leaving his workstation, and he knows that's impossible during these power surges. The Power Controller would notice the unmanned workstation at once and order him back. Mars is going to wait until the power surges stop and the Power Controller orders the removal of the depleted fuel rod. A lot of people will be moving around the nexus during that procedure."

"The power surges will diminish now that Mars isn't deliberately encouraging them," said Lucas, "but they won't stop while the original full power fuel rod is in a deadly embrace with a low power fuel rod. We've got time to assess the situation properly before going for the strike. Why does Mars feel Lottery ripped the heart out of his life?"

I went deeper into Mars's mind. Down near the subconscious, emotions seethed. He was brooding on the injustice that had changed him from being a defender of the nexus to being its destroyer.

"Mars cheated in the Lottery tests. No," I corrected myself, "it wasn't Mars that cheated. His uncle was involved in his testing process. How could that have happened? I thought Lottery candidates were allocated to centres a long distance from their home area to avoid relatives or friends being involved in their assessment."

"They are," said Lucas. "Most people come out of Lottery and are assigned to work in their home zone, but the uncle must have been needed to fill a vacancy in a distant zone. By random chance, he ended up assessing his own nephew. The uncle should have reported the conflict of interest."

"Well, the uncle didn't." My voice was filled with Mars's bitterness. "He adjusted several of Mars's scores upwards."

There was a groan from Lucas. "Changing even a single test result would be enough to derail the Lottery assessment process."

"Mars came out of Lottery as a Level 4 Power Controller. He started work as a member of a Power Control team, expecting to gain experience, be promoted to deputy, and later become a

Power Controller himself. Mars loved his work in the power supply nexus, but he kept making errors of judgement."

I paused. "Mars tried harder, did everything he could, but then he made an error that sent a huge power surge through a hydroponics unit. Several people were injured, and the unit was severely damaged."

Lucas sighed. "There'd be a thorough investigation after that."

"Yes." My bitterness turned to mourning. "The tampering with Mars's test scores was discovered. His level changed from 4 to 37, but the truly terrible thing was being taken away from the work he loved. He was used to the thrill of being part of the power heart that drives the Hive, but he was made to do tedious chores like changing faulty light units instead."

I was angry again now. "He complained about the unfairness, he'd known nothing about the cheating, but nobody would help him. They admitted that basic, repetitive work was wrong for him, but said his possible assignments were limited by his imprint."

"We have an identity for Mars," said Nicole. "Gareth 2508-0717-241. He's one of the temporary staff called in to assist during the fuel rod changeover. We can't tell you which workstation he's on, because people are continually moved around to allow the regular workers to deal with the more serious power surges. We're sending you Gareth's full records now, Lucas."

"Find the most recent image of Gareth that you can, and send it to everyone's dataviews," said Lucas.

I was still caught up in past events, alternating between seeing them from Gareth's viewpoint, and seeing them from my own. "Surely they could have retested Gareth. Removed his old imprint and given him a more suitable one."

"He'd had his old imprint for over two years before the problem was discovered," said Lucas. "Removing it at that point would have removed many of his personal memories as well."

"He'd have been willing to take that risk," I said.

"Gah." Lucas made a pained noise. "I've seen the changes

that Gareth's uncle made to his Lottery scores. They weren't just adjusted to make him look more talented, but to hide some unstable personality traits. Removing Gareth's imprint was ruled out as an option because it might have caused a mental breakdown. He was given a treatment plan instead, which included occasional temporary work that was more suited to his nature."

"Yes," I said. "Gareth's treatment plan included helping out in the Green Zone power supply nexus where he'd once worked, but that was only during the three-monthly fuel rod changeover, and he was only allowed to do the very simplest tasks."

"Gareth's monthly assessment records show he was making gradual progress," said Lucas. "In time, he'd probably have become content with his new life, but Jupiter intervened to encourage his anger and frustration. Does Gareth have any weapons on him, Amber?"

"He's got nothing but the uniform he's wearing."

"Are there any heavy or sharp objects in reach?"

"No."

Lucas was silent for a moment. "Do you still want to try playing the nosy, Amber? The Strike team know what Gareth looks like, so it may not be necessary."

"What Emili said was right. If the Strike team charge in and start chasing Mars without warning, then there'll be panic and people will get hurt."

Lucas made the pained noise again. "Accepted. Our nosy squad should position themselves ready to enter the power control centre. Forge, move to one of the entrances to gallery 3. Rothan, move to gallery 8. The rest of the Alpha team cover the entrances to galleries 6 through 9. Beta team cover entrances to galleries 2 through 5."

He paused. "Nobody shows themselves until I say so. Gareth reacted to a threat from Fran by lashing out and killing her. If he feels in danger, he will kill again, and he has over one hundred and fifty potential victims in the nexus. I know that I don't need to say this, but Gareth must not get anywhere near Amber."

"He won't," said Adika grimly.

"Move to the external staircase and then split up to go to

your individual positions," said Lucas. "Amber, turn your mask's acoustic distortion system back on now. You should be familiar with the scripts I worked out with Buzz. We'll be roughly following the second one. Jupiter will have told Gareth that the nosies are fakes, not genuine telepaths at all. Encourage him to think that's true, and you're just bluffing."

I adjusted my distortion control. "Understood," I said, in the throbbing tones of a nosy.

Buzz's voice spoke from my ear crystal. "I'm listening in, Amber. If you seem unsure what to say, I'll suggest possible lines, but you can always stand in silence for a while. That's a standard nosy tactic, intended to give the impression they're reading someone's mind."

Adika carried me up the stairs to our position outside the power control centre, and then put me on my own feet. He, Eli, Matias, and Kaden went into a protective formation around me, the four hasties guarding the grey-masked nosy.

"Nosy squad ready," said Adika.

"Alpha team in position," said Rothan. "I'm ready outside gallery 8."

"Beta team in position," said Forge. "I'm outside gallery 3."

"Nosy squad can enter the power control centre," said Lucas. "If Amber becomes distressed at any point, then get her out of there immediately."

Our formation walked into the power control centre. A man was staring at a display on the wall, heard our footsteps on the metal floor, and casually turned his head to look at us. His eyes widened in horror.

"Nosy." He hissed in disgust.

Another man heard him, turned towards us, and repeated his word. "Nosy."

"Nosy. Nosy. Nosy." The warning was echoed down the galleries of the power supply nexus. I felt the power workers responding with emotions of alarm and fear.

The Power Controller swung his chair round to face me. "I'm Power Controller Sajjad. What are you doing here? I can't have my staff distracted in the middle of a delicate operation."

I didn't reply, just walked across to stand next to him. I risked a single glance down at the galleries, and saw a host of upturned faces looking at me. Some were filled with revulsion while others were simply startled. I heard the inevitable chanting start, softly at first but getting rapidly louder.

"Two twos are four. Two threes are six. Two fours are eight."

As the chanting increased in volume, the level of emotion around me increased as well. Loathing. Anger. Disgust. I felt an instinctive urge to join in the chanting myself, but fought against it.

"Stop that noise right now!" yelled the Power Controller. "Focus on your work."

"Rothan, Forge, make your entry while everyone's distracted," said Lucas. "You're pretending to be two of the temporary staff, so act as if you're perfectly at home in the nexus."

The chanting had stopped but raw emotions were still beating at me. I fought to keep my link to Gareth's mind. He was startled by my arrival, but reassured himself that the nosies were all fakes. Jupiter had told him how Law Enforcement used the bluff of the nosy squads to deter people from committing crimes. She'd even explained how nosies were sent to arrest people known to be guilty to build up the myth that they were really telepaths.

Gareth hadn't been sure whether to believe her or not at first, but then he'd tested it for himself, deliberately standing near a nosy squad and thinking of all the destruction he could cause in a power supply nexus. There'd been no reaction at all. He'd done that a dozen times since then so it became a private game. He'd stand among a crowd, pretending to be frightened but secretly laughing inside. Feeling comfortably superior to both the nosies who couldn't read minds, and the gullible fools who believed they could.

"Forge, go down the internal stairs to gallery 4 now," said Lucas. "Rothan, go up to gallery 7. Circle around the gallery as if you've been told to head for a specific workstation. Tell us whether you see Gareth or not."

"What are you doing here?" repeated Sajjad.

I finally turned to look at him. "Someone here is guilty. Someone here is planning to attack their ex-partner."

The tide of fear and loathing was still spreading through the crowded nexus, still building in magnitude. Lucas had called this process mass emotional contagion. It wasn't affecting Gareth though. In fact, he was relaxing. He didn't care if there was any truth in my accusation or not. It was nothing to do with him.

"I admit that's a serious issue," said Sajjad, "but it can surely wait until my people have finished their work."

"This cannot wait," I said. "Your people should continue working as normal while we are here."

"That's easier said than done," said Sajjad. "The presence of one of you... telepaths is disturbing."

"There is no reason for loyal members of the Hive to be disturbed by my presence." I hesitated, unsure what to say next. I had hostile waves of emotion pounding at me, I was fighting to hold my link to Gareth's mind, and I couldn't remember my script.

"We are here to protect the innocent," Buzz's voice prompted me. "Only the guilty have anything to fear."

"Gareth's not here." Forge's voice whispered from my ear crystal.

"Nor here," said Rothan.

I looked down at the galleries again, and repeated Buzz's words. "We are here to protect the innocent. Only the guilty have anything to fear."

"Forge, check gallery 5," said Lucas. "Rothan, check gallery 6. Amber, keep bluffing. We need you to hold Gareth's attention just a little longer."

"Only the guilty have anything to fear," I repeated desperately.

"I can sense that the guilty person is very close to me," prompted Buzz.

I repeated her words and felt something strange happen. The massed pressure of hostility suddenly eased. The people working further down the nexus were reacting to what I'd said with relief.

The nosy wasn't here for them, didn't care about them, and wouldn't bother reading their minds.

Being near a nosy, sensing the crowd's reactions, was horribly difficult for me. I'd assumed that playing the part of the nosy myself would be even harder. I'd been both right and wrong about that. I wasn't being randomly hit by the emotions of the crowd, they were actively directing their anger and disgust at me, but there was the extra factor that the crowd responded to my words. I had some control over this.

The people further down the nexus were relieved, but those close to me were even more frightened than before. Sajjad started babbling nervous sentences. "It's not me that you want. I'm very happily married. Well, reasonably happily married. Every couple has their..."

"Not you." I turned to look at the nearest power worker, and was shocked when she began screaming.

"Get that thing away from me! I can feel it poking around inside my head!"

This woman was obviously as scared of nosies as I'd been as a teen. Possibly even more scared. I was supposed to hold everyone's attention while Forge and Rothan sneaked round the power supply nexus, but Gareth's thoughts told me the screaming had taken the distraction too far.

... are all torn between watching their workstations and listening to that fool having hysterics. Now's my chance!

He reached out a hand to stroke his workstation in a farewell caress, and then started walking towards the nearest staircase.

"Gareth's moving," I shouted. "He's going to take the easiest option to damage the nexus. He'll climb the stairs to the power control centre and jump into the core."

My voice echoed round the power supply nexus, with the acoustic distortion adding a throbbing urgency to my words. Power supply workers were as protective of their precious nexus as my Strike team were of me. The assault of hostile emotions abruptly ceased as they reacted to my warning. I was no longer an unwelcome intruder here. Their nexus was in danger, and I was an ally helping them protect it.

Gareth had got halfway to the staircase, but had stopped, stunned by my words. Jupiter had been wrong after all. The nosies really were telepaths and this one was reading his mind!

"Strike time!" snapped Lucas's voice in my ear crystal.

I saw the view from Gareth's eyes, as menacing figures in grey, heavy-duty combat armour rushed into the nexus. All the power workers were on their feet by now, and looking around in alarm. Gareth pushed his way past two of them, but saw an armoured figure was already blocking the nearest staircase.

"I can see Gareth on gallery 6," said Rothan's voice. "He's on the far side from me."

"I see him too," said Forge. "Do I climb down to Gareth's level?"

"Forge, position yourself on the gallery directly above Gareth," said Lucas. "Amber, we need those power workers sitting down at their stations again."

"My guards will deal with the threat to the nexus!" I shouted. "Return to your workstations and continue performing your duties for the Hive."

People were obeying my order, going back to their workstations. Gareth turned, hoping to get to another staircase, but there were armoured figures everywhere, inexorably closing in on him. I saw the desperation in his mind, and the abrupt change of plan.

"Gareth knows he can't reach the power control centre and jump into the core," I called out. "He's going to kill himself jumping off the gallery instead."

"Forge, grab him when he tries to jump!" ordered Lucas.

"I'm not in position yet," gasped Forge's breathless voice.

Gareth was heading for the gallery wall. I shouted again to try to delay him. "Gareth, you don't need to do this. You can still choose life instead of death."

The thought in his head answered me. He'd made his choice when Jupiter first contacted him. He'd made it when he killed Fran. He'd made it when he rigged the power systems to create a deadly embrace. There was no point in his existence without the nexus.

Gareth was about to vault over the gallery wall, when he saw

Forge swing down from above to block his way forward. There were power workers standing at the workstations on either side of him, and armoured figures advancing from behind. For a second, he believed he was trapped, but then he thought of a way out.

The thought was instantly followed by the action, so I had no time to shout a warning. Gareth hurled his whole weight against the young man standing next to him, seizing his shoulders and shoving him bodily over the gallery wall.

There was a wild yell of terror from the man as he fell. Forge swung sideways to pull him back to safety, and that left Gareth the clear route he needed. In one swift movement, he pulled himself onto the gallery wall and dived downwards. I was startled that his last thoughts weren't of anger but of love.

I love you and I know you love me too. There is no point in my life without you. I planned that we would die together, but I die in your arms instead.

Gareth welcomed the sight of the floor rushing towards him. Caught in his emotions, I felt the eagerness to die in the loving embrace of the power supply nexus too, but Lucas's voice was shouting in my ear.

"Amber, get back in your own mind now!"

I pulled myself free before Gareth hit the ground. I was myself again, but Gareth's last thoughts were still echoing in my head. I found myself repeating them aloud.

"Gareth loved the power supply nexus, and believed it loved him too. There was no point in his life without it. He wanted them both to die together, but he has died in its arms instead."

I'd forgotten where my physical body was, and the part I was supposed to be playing. I was horrified to hear my words come out in weirdly distorted, grieving tones. I realized that every power worker in the nexus was staring at me in disbelief. Waste it, had I wrecked everything?

"Gareth loved the power supply nexus," repeated Sajjad, in a stunned voice. "You're talking about the man who worked here until he caused a serious accident. You said he was planning to attack an ex-partner. The power supply nexus was that ex-partner?"

What I'd said about an attack on an ex-partner had just been a random, pre-prepared story intended to create a distraction while Forge and Rothan located Gareth's position in the power supply nexus. Fiction had collided with reality though, and what Sajjad had said was perfectly true.

"Yes," I said.

"Now I understand why you couldn't wait until later to intervene." Sajjad gave me a look of awe.

I used the standard nosy lines again. "We protect the Hive. We protect the loyal members of the Hive."

"Well, it wasn't planned to happen this way," said Lucas's calm voice in my ear, "but this has turned into the greatest nosy publicity exercise of all time. Everyone who witnessed it is going to be utterly convinced that nosies are genuine telepaths."

He paused. "Has someone checked that Gareth was killed in that fall? If he's still alive, then he'll need urgent medical attention."

"He's very, very dead," said the voice of one of the Beta team.

"Forge, does the man you caught have any injuries?"

"No, he's just badly shaken," said Forge.

"In that case, our medical team should come and collect Gareth's body," said Lucas. "Gold Commander, what is the status of Operation Rainbow Cascade?"

"Other zones have been continuing to report new fuel rod failures," said Melisande. "I intend to let the sequence complete, sort out the deadly embrace situation in Green Zone, and then rerun Operation Rainbow Cascade using the fully functional reserve fuel rods from storage."

"Since this has turned into a nosy publicity exercise, I suggest that Amber tells Power Controller Sajjad about the deadly embrace now," said Lucas. "If she's suitably cryptic about the issue of the faulty fuel rod, then it should create some interesting new myths about the mysterious powers of nosies."

"A good plan, Tactical Commander," said Melisande. "I shall give no explanation of the faulty fuel rods at all, and let rumours run wild across the Hive."

Sajjad was looking expectantly at me. I wasn't sure if I'd missed him asking a question or not. It didn't matter if I had. Nosies often stood in silence without speaking.

"Power Controller Sajjad, check your systems," I said. "Your power supply nexus has a deadly embrace."

"What?" He shook his head. "That's impossible. We're still waiting for the power surges to die down, so we haven't removed the old fuel rod yet, but we can't have a deadly embrace. If two fuel rods were connected to the nexus at once, then the power would have already overloaded the buffering system."

"We protect the Hive," I said. "We protect the loyal members of the Hive. Power Controller Sajjad, check your systems."

He gave me a bewildered look that turned to panic, ran to one of the wall displays, and started tapping at it. The calm green lights on it suddenly changed to flaring red. A second later, Sajjad's magnified voice rang out across the power supply nexus.

"We are in deadly embrace. Gareth must have sabotaged the links, so the old fuel rod hasn't disconnected from the nexus. The nosy has somehow made the new fuel rod fail, so we haven't had an overload yet, but we need to get that new fuel rod disconnected fast. Commence back out sequence now, while I report to the Gold Commander."

There was frantic activity around the nexus. A couple of minutes later, I heard a musical laugh from Melisande. "I've just had a somewhat hysterical Power Controller talking to me about a nosy and a deadly embrace. I told him that something mysterious had been happening throughout the entire cascade sequence, with every new fuel rod failing in turn."

She paused. "I'm not sure if the man thinks Amber made every new fuel rod fail by herself, or if he thinks this was a mass intervention by nosies across the Hive, but he's sure that the nosies prevented a great disaster."

"Time for everyone to head back to the aircraft hangar," said Lucas.

I turned and left the power control centre, with my hasty squad following me. When we stopped outside gallery 1 to wait for the others, I closed my eyes and searched for Forge's mind. I was worried how he'd feel about failing to save Gareth, but I found his thoughts untroubled by guilt.

Forge had been faced with a simple choice. He could either

prevent Gareth from jumping or save the man he'd thrown from the gallery. His own certainty about the right decision had been reinforced by the rule imprinted on his mind. If you ever had to choose between saving a destructive target and an innocent bystander, then you saved the faithful citizen of the Hive.

I left Forge's mind, and let my thoughts reach out across the power supply nexus for one last time. The minds there were filled with a mixture of awe and fear. Lucas was right. This had turned into the greatest nosy publicity exercise of all time.

Gareth had made his choice between life and death. Forge had had to choose which man to save. Now I had to make a decision too. I could walk away knowing that I'd made the lies about the nosies stronger than ever, or I could go back into the power supply nexus, take off my mask, and shatter the myths forever by telling the people there the truth.

I didn't like the way the Hive lied to its citizens, making them believe that the patrolling nosies in their disturbing masks were telepaths, using that sham to deter everyone from committing crimes. I felt those lies were morally wrong, but right now I was deeply aware what could happen if people learned the truth about nosies.

Mercury had learnt the truth. He'd started a fire that led to eight deaths including his own, and he'd intended it to be far worse. Everyone in that Security Unit was supposed to die. Rothan was supposed to die. Lucas was supposed to die.

Mars had learnt the truth. He'd killed Fran and tried to blow up a power supply nexus. I'd no idea how many people would have died or been injured in the explosion, and how many more in accidents caused by the following power failure. There'd have been a host of incidents like the one where the hangar doors closed on Aerial seven, injuring Buzz, Kareem, and Hallie. The death toll could have been tens of thousands.

The Hive was home to a hundred million people, all packed closely together and hugely vulnerable to attack. I had ethical doubts about the nosy myth, and the grey-masked figures had been the focus of my personal childhood nightmares, but the system worked. It saved lives.

I opened my eyes, the Strike team gathered around me, and we headed back to the aircraft hangar. For a telepath like me, who felt the emotions of others as if they were her own, lives would always be more important than ethics, especially when they were the lives of people I loved.

CHAPTER FORTY

Six days later, there was a vote on whether Olivia should be reset. Melisande, a few other Gold Command staff, the Telepath Unit Tactical Commanders, and all the other telepaths were included in that vote.

I hated the idea of tampering with someone's memory and identity, but I'd experienced what it was like to have Mercury entrenched in my mind. I could imagine how Olivia had suffered as more and more invading echoes moved into her head.

So I'd voted in favour of the reset, because it seemed the only hope for the unhappy, tortured remains of Olivia. Lucas voted in favour as well. It was a secret ballot, so I didn't know how the other telepaths had voted. None of them contacted me about it, and I felt it was too soon for me to try contacting Sapphire again.

The majority voted in favour of the reset, so it was carried out that evening. Lucas and I spent the crucial few hours watching a random set of bookettes, but I couldn't focus on any of the storylines. My mind was too busy picturing Olivia lying unconscious on a table, while an expert worked on the delicate process of unravelling eight years of her memory chain.

The good would go along with the bad. Moments of tears and laughter, despair and hope, would all be wiped away. I realized I'd only been thinking of how a reset would affect Olivia, and not about the people who'd loved her.

Olivia was losing all her memories since before Lottery. There'd be friends she'd made since then. There might be someone who cared about her the way Lucas cared about me. What were those people thinking this evening, knowing that all knowledge of them was being erased from her mind? I should have thought about that earlier, but if I had, then would it have changed my vote? Olivia's friends, and the possible lover, would surely want what was best for her.

The message finally came that the process was complete. Olivia would be allowed to wake up naturally. It would take time to establish two significant facts. Whether her personality was that of the old Olivia, or Jupiter, or someone entirely new. How her telepathic abilities had been affected by the reset.

Lucas and I went to bed, and I slept surprisingly well, but I had another ordeal to face when I woke up. Fran's memorial service was being held in a park on Level 20. I felt I should attend. I couldn't have avoided firing Fran, and I wasn't responsible for the decisions she'd made after leaving us, but my actions had set her on the path that led to her death.

Lucas and Buzz chose to come along to support me. Buzz was still using a powered chair after her leg injury, and Forge said he'd accompany her to help if she had any problems. Nicole and Megan decided to join us as well. Nicole said it was her duty to represent the Liaison team, while Megan gave no explanation at all.

I expected Adika to insist on me taking at least four bodyguards with me. I was startled when he announced he was coming himself, and bringing the entire Alpha Strike team as well. I suggested that was excessive protection, but Adika, worried by memories of our last trip to Level 20, remained adamant.

So it was a large deputation that arrived in the memorial area of the park. We found it totally deserted. For a moment, I wondered if we'd come to the wrong place, but I couldn't believe Lucas or Nicole would make such a basic mistake. Besides, there was a black podium at the centre of the grassy circle, and the flowers in the surrounding borders were all white, so this had to be the memorial area.

A minute later, two people arrived and stood at a slight distance from us. One of them was Richar, the man who'd been friendly with Fran. The other was Mika, the incident coordinator for the Security Unit fire. I noticed Mika put her hand on Richar's arm, with the nervous air of someone unused to making physical displays of affection. Richar looked down at her hand as if startled, but significantly didn't move away.

It seemed as if the Security Unit fire might have had one positive result in bringing these two together. I wondered if I should go over and say something to them. I'd never been to a memorial service before, so I didn't know the correct behaviour.

I'd just decided that I should leave talking to them until after the service, when a woman in a white robe arrived. She placed a large, silver-lidded cup on a special stand in front of the podium. I looked at it uneasily. That cup would contain Fran's ashes.

The woman went to stand at the podium. "We are gathered here for the memorial service for Fran 2489-1276-993. Records show that no petition has been lodged regarding the nature of this service. As a Law Enforcement Ministrant, I am permitted to authorize such petitions myself provided they are not of a nature disrespectful to the Hive. Does anyone wish to present a petition now?"

She looked round hopefully. I had no idea what she was talking about. I cheated by briefly reading her mind.

... no petition, no information, no contact from anyone at all. I like to make every service as comforting and fulfilling as possible for friends and family, but it's hard to do that with no information about their religious preferences or...

... decent number of attendees at least. I was afraid that no petition meant...

... the large group has to be from the Telepath Unit where Fran worked. The records show the telepath fired Fran, so she won't be here herself. Pity. I'd have been interested to see...

... just have to do the standard service, with a few added details from her work record, unless...

"Does anyone wish to speak during the service and share their special memories of Fran?"

The Ministrant looked round at us again. I hastily stared down at the grass. I felt my memories of Fran were highly unsuitable for a memorial service.

The Ministrant sighed. "In that case, I shall honour Fran with the standard Hiveist service."

She paused before speaking in a deeper, more solemn voice. "From the Hive we come."

I'd never been to a Hiveist service. Megan and several of the Alpha Strike team obviously had because they instantly responded. "To the Hive we will return."

Megan's voice sounded oddly shaky. I glanced across at her, and was shocked to see she was crying. I hadn't realized that she'd felt that level of affection for Fran. No, I was sure she hadn't felt that level of affection for Fran. What was going on here?

The mere thought of the question was enough to link me to Megan's thoughts. She was crying because she was remembering her husband's memorial service, and because her medical treatment yesterday had implanted her with the embryos of his twin children. She was moving on to begin a new life with Adika, but her husband would be part of that life too.

The tears were happy not sad, so I left Megan's mind. The Ministrant was talking about Fran's life now, listing the positions she'd held and the many years of work she'd done for the Hive. I tried to think positive thoughts about Fran, but I kept remembering moments of petty spite, like the time I'd been praising Hannah and Fran had interrupted to scold her.

Eli had seemed worryingly subdued on our way here, so I checked his thoughts next. I found he was brooding over his last counselling session with Buzz. They'd discussed the follow-up operation on his leg, and decided it would help if he talked to his surgeon. If Eli knew exactly why the operation was needed, what would be done, and how long it would take him to recover, then he'd feel more in control.

The problem was that Eli hadn't just developed a fear of surgery, but a fear of surgeons as well. The obvious solution would be for me to talk to his surgeon myself, and ask the questions that were troubling Eli.

I moved on to Forge's mind next, worried that the memorial service would be an unpleasant reminder of Gareth's death. I found Forge wasn't thinking of Gareth or Fran. Like Eli, his thoughts were centred on Buzz. Forge's only previous relationship had been with Shanna on Teen Level, and she'd made it clear from the start that she demanded regular public displays of affection and commitment from him. Buzz wasn't laying down any rules at all. It occurred to him that Shanna and Buzz were total opposites, both in appearance and character.

The Ministrant had stepped down from the podium, and was looking expectantly round the group from our unit. "Who wishes to release Fran's spirit so she can return to the Hive?"

I pulled back into my own head, but avoided meeting her gaze. Nobody else moved or spoke. The Ministrant turned to look at Richar and Mika.

"No!" Richar said the word in an explosive tone of rejection. "After the things she did, Fran's spirit should not be allowed to return to the Hive. Cast her ashes Outside, so the hunter of souls can take her to join his demonic pack."

Shocked by Richar's words, I instinctively checked his thoughts. He'd been told that Fran had conspired with the people who'd burnt the Security Unit, seriously injured him, and killed several of his colleagues. He was angry about that, but it was his bitterness over the birthday present that had brought him here today. He'd been stunned when Fran had handed it to him. No one had remembered his birthday in decades. The thought of a present, however trivial, had meant a huge amount to him, but Fran had just been manipulating him.

Let Fran's spirit know that I answer betrayal with betrayal.

Mika had drawn her hand away from Richar's arm, and was looking disgusted by such behaviour at a memorial service. Richar flushed, turned, and strode away. Fran's bitterness against me had led to her death. Richar's bitterness against Fran had just destroyed his fledgling relationship with Mika.

I understood Richar's feelings. I understood Mika's feelings. The problem with reading the deeper levels of people's minds, was that I sometimes understood and sympathized too much. The embarrassment on the Ministrant's face sucked me into reading her thoughts.

... the time when two men started fighting over who should

release a woman's spirit, the person who slipped off the podium and dropped the cup, but never anything as disastrous as...

I moved forward to pick up the cup, and was rewarded by the wave of relief in the Ministrant's mind. I saw the image in her thoughts of what to do, stepped onto the podium, opened the lid of the cup, and held it above my head.

The Ministrant slipped her hand into the pocket of her robe, took out a small sphere, and pressed its button. I felt a sudden gust of wind from overhead that sent the ashes blowing across the park. When the park breeze went back to normal, I lowered the cup, handed it back to the Ministrant, and returned to my place at the front of my unit.

The Ministrant scattered the last of the ashes among the flowerbeds, and turned to face us. "Fran's spirit has returned to the Hive, as we all will return in time."

She hesitated a second, before turning and walking away. I got the impression that she'd normally wait in case anyone wanted to speak to her, but she felt that it was safer to let this ceremony end as fast as possible.

"You didn't have to release Fran's spirit," said Lucas.

I shrugged. "If I hadn't, then the Ministrant would have had to do it herself, and that would have been even more painfully embarrassing for everyone."

Lucas took his dataview from his pocket and tapped it. "The preliminary report on Olivia has arrived."

"Yes?"

"They don't want to stress her too much, so they've just done basic tests. The brain activity is similar but not totally identical to Olivia's brain activity test during Lottery. The other tests suggest that Olivia is now only a borderline telepath."

Lucas sighed. "That's an unfortunate result for the Hive. We know there's a genetic factor involved in people becoming borderline telepaths. We hadn't understood what makes someone move beyond that and develop into a true telepath, but now it seems as if individual personality could be important."

If Olivia was now only a borderline telepath, that was an

unfortunate result for the Hive, but I felt it might be the best result for her. I pictured her as almost but not quite the same person as the girl who'd gone into Lottery, free to live without being troubled by the echoes of target minds.

Lucas's dataview gave an urgent chime. He stared at the screen and frowned. "Morton and his Beta Strike team are on an emergency run, and their target's taken refuge deep inside the wave machinery on Level 67 beach. Morton can't go clambering around in there, so his Tactical Commander is calling for emergency handover to another telepath."

"Tell them we'll take it," I said.

"You're sure? I know the funeral was difficult for you."

The life of a telepath involved dealing with an endless series of cases. Most were simple, some complex, while a few hit us with the totally unexpected. Fran's case had been one of those. It had pushed both Lucas and me to the limit, but it was over now.

"I'm sure," I said. "I want to forget about Fran, and move on to something new."

"In that case…" Lucas tapped his ear crystal. "Emili, are you there?"

"Of course," Emili's voice answered.

"Morton's unit is calling for an emergency handover at Level 67 beach," said Lucas. "We're taking it. Amber, Adika, and the Alpha Strike team are fully equipped so they can go straight to the beach. Forge had better go with them, because a climbing specialist could be helpful inside the wave machinery. The rest of us will head back to the unit."

Adika picked me up and started running towards the nearest park exit. We were flanked by Rothan and Forge, and the Alpha Strike team chased after us. Our route went past the park event area. A crowd was gathering around the circular event stage, and I saw their heads turning to look at us.

On any other level of the Hive, people would have been confused by the sight of us, but we were on Law Enforcement Level 20. The people here knew the secrets of the Hive. They knew that the nosies were fakes, they knew about Telepath Units, and they knew exactly what they were seeing now. This was a telepath and her Strike team in full flight, heading out to respond to a Hive emergency.

A man pointed at us and shouted. "They're Light Angel!"

Rumours had been going round Law Enforcement about an attempt to sabotage a power supply nexus, and an entire Telepath Unit flying in from the horrors of Outside to prevent disaster. I heard an odd rhythmic sound, and realized the crowd had started clapping.

I adjusted my ear crystal, and the camera extension unfolded at the right side of my face. "Emili, are you receiving the images and sound from my camera?"

"Yes."

"Send them out to the whole unit," I said. "The crowd is applauding what we did to defend the Hive, and that applause isn't just for me and the Strike team. It's for every single one of us."

The sound of clapping grew louder as we went by the crowd. The rest of the Hive didn't know what we did to protect them, they must never know what we did, but the people in Law Enforcement knew it and we were their heroes.

Message From Janet Edwards

Thank you for reading *Defender*. This is the second full length book in the Hive Mind series, and I have several further books planned. There is also a prequel novella, *Perilous*, which is set a year before Amber went through Lottery, and gives some extra background to the characters and events in the series.

You may also be interested in my books set in the very different Portal Future universe, where humanity portals between hundreds of different colony worlds scattered across space. These books include the Earth Girl trilogy, the Exodus series, and related stories.

Please visit my website, www.janetedwards.com, to see the current list of my books. You can also make sure you don't miss future books by signing up to get an email alert when there's a new release.

I'd like to thank Andrew Angel for Beta reading *Defender*. Any remaining problems are entirely my fault.

Best wishes from Janet Edwards

Printed in Poland
by Amazon Fulfillment
Poland Sp. z o.o., Wrocław